Dust to Dust: Book Two of The Irish Rogues

Katie Ashley

Song Lyrics

You've fought the fight.
    You bear the scars.
    You've done your time

Let me in the walls.
    You've built around
    We can light a match
    And burn them down
    Let me hold your hand and dance around and around the flames
    In front of us.
    Dust to Dust.
    ——The Civil Wars

Acknowledgements

Thanks eternally to my content/developmental editors, **Kim Bias** & **Flor Meurinne,** for making Poison and Wine & Dust to Dust the best they could be. Your love and support of my writing means so much.

To **JR Ward** for her Black Dagger Brotherhood series—without my obsessive reread of this adored series, especially Lover Awakened, I would've never gotten the idea for a mafia series and a scarred, tortured hero...even though he's not a vampire like Zsadist, lol. Z will always be my favorite brother, and I owe him a lot for breathing life into some plot bunnies!

To my daughter, **Olivia,** who is my biggest cheerleader and greatest supporter even though she's far too young to have ever read my books! Thank you for giving so freely of your time and allowing Mommy to hunker down with her laptop to write the books with the "no-no words".

Most of all, I thank you, **dear reader,** for embracing this new series. It's been a hard journey through writer's block and auto-immune related brain fog. It feels so good to be back to writing.

Trigger Warnings

Sexually Explicit Scenes
Knife play
Language
Violence
Torture
Kidnapping
Attempted SA (Not by MMC)
Mention of Rape
Forced Sedation/Drugging
Parental Death(Flashback)
Death of a Friend

Prologue: Quinn

B elfast
Two years ago

I fucking hated parties.

All the people. All the noise. All the fake smiles and false bravado.

Considering I was a young, wealthy bachelor, one might assume I relished social activities. The free-flowing alcohol, the beautiful new women to seduce, the business connections to make.

But that wasn't me.

It never had been. Given the choice, I'd take a good whiskey in a quiet room any day. Or even better, a hike along the bogs in the wilds of the countryside.

Anything to be alone.

I especially hated tonight's party. I fucking loathed the guest of honor. That statement would be surprising to most since we were celebrating my father. Most children don't encounter their first bully until they enter school. But for my brothers and myself, we had from the moment we were born.

At our estate, hundreds of guests gathered to celebrate my tormentor. To the outside, Hugh Kavanaugh was a gregarious man who wined and dined the rich, but also had a heart for the less fortunate. A larger than life presence who commanded the respect of those around him.

He appeared as a loving husband who doted on my mother with diamonds, fancy cars, and a beach house. At the same time, he stepped out on her every time a slut in a short skirt walked by. She was a prisoner outfitted in designer clothes. To leave him was out of the question. The first time she tried he threatened she'd never see her sons again. Since hers was the purest of maternal love, she endured hell to be with her children.

Some might boast he was a devoted father to his five sons and only daughter. That his success enabled us to attend the finest schools, wear the fanciest of labels, and vacation in exotic locations. But for every accolade we received, we wore a physical or emotional bruise because of it.

No one on the outside would ever believe the monster he truly was. Only those in his clan or those who saw him behind closed doors ever saw the mask slip. Only then was his true psychotic nature revealed.

Satisfied with my role as a wallflower, I surveyed the crowd around me. Most of the guests I knew from growing up here in Belfast. Bored with the Irish underworld and with his ego swelling, my father had set his sights on bringing our business to Boston eight years ago. I'd been just eighteen when I'd said goodbye to the only world I'd ever known, including my mother and youngest siblings who weren't allowed to come.

As usual, my younger brother, Dare, surrounded himself with a bevy of beauties. God only knew which he would be taking to his bed for the night. Knowing him, it wouldn't be just one.

Across from him with a gang of his friends, Kellan longingly eyed Dare's circle of women. Like me, Kellan was quieter than our outgoing brothers. Unlike me, Kellan had the truest heart and purest soul.

My youngest brother, Eamon, hung around the food tables, stuffing his face while eyeing our mother to see if she was distracted enough for him to sneak champagne or whiskey. With a chuckle, I shook my head at him. Considering he was thirteen, I could only imagine he'd be puking his guts out most of the night if he managed any alcohol.

At the massive grand piano in the corner, my beautiful sister Maeve, provided the musical entertainment for the moment. Her stiff posture wasn't just about elegantly performing the concerto. Maeve detested performing in front of crowds. She and I were alike in our dislike of large groups of people.

If anyone looked closely past the makeup artist's work, they would see the red welt my father had left on her cheek. My jaw clenched at the sight while my fingers tightened around my glass.

Before the party had started, our family had congregated in the sitting room overlooking the front lawn. Maeve had barely made it over the threshold before my father informed her she would be playing at the party.

As she wrung her hands, tears had spilled down her porcelain cheeks. "No, Da, I can't play in front of all those people. Please don't ask that of me."

It was the worst way to appeal to him. He hated tears and shows of emotion, even from women. Maeve would've been better off telling him to go fuck himself.

But she was too pure and kind to ever do that.

So, his palm had cracked against her cheek.

At her cry of pain, the room exploded around me. As I launched myself at my father, my whiskey glass crashed on the floor. Grabbing him by the lapels of his suit, I shoved him against the wall. When one of my father's bodyguards made a move to restrain me, Callum drew his gun, causing my mother and Maeve to scream.

"Take one more step, and I'll blow your brains out," Callum growled.

At the same time, Dare and Kellan moved to shield Mam and Maeve. I narrowed my eyes on my father. Since we'd spent the last eight years away in Boston, Maeve had been spared the brunt of my father's psychopathic nature.

"As long as I draw breath, you will never lay one finger on her again." When he remained sneering at me, my forearm slid under his jaw. "Did you hear me?"

"You've got a hell of a lot of cheek to put your hands on me like this."

"As the head enforcer, I'm exactly what you taught me to be, aren't I?"

"And I'm the head of your fucking family!"

Callum spit at my father's feet. "You're nothing more than a fucking coward when you hit your own daughter."

"I don't give a shite what you think."

At that moment, we were interrupted by the butler announcing the first guest had arrived. Reluctantly, I pulled my hands off of him. "*Mallacht Dé ort,*" I spat before stalking off. I did hope for God's curse on him. He was a scourge on our family for sure.

Hours later the bastard who had sired us now stood in the center of the room, basking in the adulation from the crowd. His chest puffed out when anyone complimented Maeve's piano playing. "The angel told me she wanted nothing more than to play for my birthday. Who could possibly tell her no?"

"Fucking cunt," I muttered into my whiskey.

"I'll second that," Callum said as he sidled up next to me. "Nice work earlier."

"Thank you. I only wish I could've saved Mae the sting."

"Aye. I agree." Callum's usually blue eyes darkened to black as he stared at our father. "I'm going to end him one of these days."

"Sooner than later, I hope."

We fell into silence then. After all, what else can there be said after voicing a shared desire for patricide? Instead, we surveyed the crowd and sipped our whiskey.

With a sardonic twist of his lips, Callum asked, "Enjoying yourself?"

"Immensely."

He grinned. "Aye. I'd rather fuck Father Leahy's sister again than be here tonight."

A laugh burst from my lips at the reference to Callum's previous night's escapades. "Was she really that bad?"

Callum's eyes bulged. "Besides the fact she tied me up and beat the shite out of me with a riding crop, she wanted to take me up the arse. Like she actually had the strap-on thing in her drawer."

"Maybe you should've tried it. I've never been one to say no to a tongue or a finger in mine," I teased.

"Cop on to yourself, arsehole."

I laughed at his remark of taking it too far. "What do you bet Dare has?"

Callum snorted. "Aye. Or at least a vibrator."

"Who would've guessed a priest would have such a kinky sister?" I mused.

"Not me for damn sure."

As I once again surveyed the crowd, my gaze honed in on the man talking to my father. He appeared to be close to mine and

Callum's age. It wasn't the first time tonight that I'd noticed him with my father.

Nodding my whiskey at the two of them, I asked, "Whose that fecker sniffing around Da?"

Callum's expression darkened. "You've been in Boston too long if you don't remember him. That's Oisinn O'Toole."

"The arsehole who used to torture animals in the neighborhood and get the shite beat out of him by the older kids?"

With a snort, Callum replied, "Aye, that's the one."

"Why the feck is Da giving that ejit any attention?"

"Since we've been gone, that ejit, as you rightfully call him, has somehow made a name for himself and his branch of the O'Toole family. They've edged out the Walsh's and the Doyle's to be the most powerful family in the city."

"Jaysus. Who would've thought?"

Glaring at Oisnn, Callum grumbled, "Not me."

"What's he wanting with Da?"

He winced. "He's been pressuring him for an alliance with our family."

"Guess that means your cock is on the block for marriage." With a smirk, I added, "If I remember correctly, he's got three *very* unattractive sisters."

"Fuck you," Callum muttered around the rim of his glass.

"Come on, boyo. You're almost thirty, and you've already dodged two marriage contracts. The noose is tightening."

"It's not the marriage I'm opposed to. It's the choices."

Growing up, we feared the impending shadowy chains of arranged marriages. It was just the way things were done in our world. After all, we were the products of an arranged marriage. My mam's family, the Byrne's, ran Drogheda as well as parts of Dublin, so their union had united a large chunk of Ireland.

At that moment Dare and our cousin, Rian, ambled over to us. As the only child of my Uncle Seamus, Rian was raised just like my brother. "What are you two cunts gossiping on about?" Dare questioned with a grin.

"Oisnn O'Toole."

Disgust filled his face. "I hadn't thought of that fucker in years."

"You better get used to him since he's going to be Callum's brother-in-law," I mused.

"Bite your fucking tongue," Callum snarled.

Rian shook his head. "I heard Da say that Uncle Hugh told him Oisnn wants Maeve."

While I growled, Callum spat, "Not on his fucking life."

"But Maeve's barely seventeen," Dare remarked.

Disgust shadowed Rian's face. "He said he's willing to wait until she's of age for the marriage."

"She's still just a kid," I protested.

With a nod, Rian said, "That's what my da said. He couldn't believe Uncle Hugh was even entertaining the idea."

"Over my dead body will I ever allow Maeve to be given to that bastard," Callum said.

"Aye. And mine as well," I added.

As Dare and Rian nodded in agreement, Callum stiffened beside me. "What the fuck is *she* doing here?" he questioned.

Expecting to see one of my father's many mistresses, my gaze followed Callum's across the crowded room. At the sight of the tall brunette, I sucked in a harsh breath. "Fuck me," I muttered.

This woman didn't belong to my father. At one time, she had been mine.

Or at least I thought she had.

Maura had been the love of my life. Even though her father was only a soldier in our clan, I'd asked my father if he would broker a marriage for us. To my surprise, he gave his permission.

Then when I proposed, Maura cut me deeper than any man ever had.

At the sight of me on my knees with a glittering diamond, she'd recoiled in horror. She explained the months we'd spent together was just a fling–a very lucrative one for her considering the trips I'd taken her on and presents I'd bestowed. Moreover, she loathed this world and never wanted to be tied down to a man from the clan.

Tonight it appeared her aversion to clan men had wavered since she was on the arm of one of my father's wealthier soldiers. When her gaze found mine, her lip curled in disgust before she ushered her new man far away from us.

Pain seared through me, causing my chest to tighten. I hated that after all these months, she still managed to cut me.

"She's got fucking cheek to show her face here," Rian sneered.

"Someone should warn Colin off that conniving cunt," Dare added.

Unable to bear being in the same room, least of all house as her, I shoved my whiskey glass into Callum's chest. "I'm out of here."

After he clasped the glass, he shook his head. "Sorry, mate."

"If Da asks after me, tell him to go fuck himself," I grunted.

Callum's lips quirked up. "That would be my pleasure."

As I started out of the room, someone fell in step beside me. When I glanced over, Rian grinned. "Thought you might need some company."

"I'd rather be alone."

Rian clapped a hand on my shoulder. "I'm well aware that you'd rather slink away to lick your wounds alone–"

"I'm not fucking slinking."

He laughed. "Come on. Let me buy you a pint at the pub."

Since we were kids, Rian and I had been close. Sometimes I felt closer to him than I did Callum or Dare. Whenever the two of them teamed up against me, Rian always had my back. I wasn't surprised that tonight it was him trying to cheer me up.

"Fine," I replied, as we made our way down the hallway to the back door.

Once we got outside, I sucked in a harsh breath of the cool night air. After power walking down the backstairs, our feet crunched on the gravel.

Jaysus, what a mess of a night.

At Rian's playful nudge, I turned to look at him. "If it makes you feel any better, Colin's got the smallest lad I've ever seen."

A laugh burst from my lips. "Do I even want to ask how you know he's got a tiny cock?"

Rian grinned back at me. "How quickly you forget we were the same age in school." With a wrinkle of his nose, he replied, "I had to see the wee schlong in the showers after rugby practice."

I snorted. "It must've been traumatizing for you to remember all these years later."

"He tried hiding it. Especially when I was around since we both know how well-endowed the Kavanaugh men are."

"Get on with ya," I replied.

As we started for the garage, Rian skidded to a stop before a shiny sports car. After letting out a low whistle, he said, "Get a load of that Aston Martin."

"It's Da's."

A snort escaped his lips. "Since when would a dryshite like Uncle Hugh buy a car like that?"

I laughed. "He didn't. It was a gift. They just delivered it this afternoon."

"Ah, that makes more sense." After sliding his hand down the shiny, red hood, he waggled his brows. "Where's the key?"

I groaned. "Not bloody likely."

"Why not?"

I crossed my arms over my chest. "Because I'm too fucking old to be stealing my Da's car."

"Don't look at it as stealing—it's just *borrowing*."

"You know Da won't look at it like that. Especially since he hasn't even had the chance to drive it himself yet."

Rian's eyes lit up. "You mean, we could break her in?"

Holding up my hands, I countered, "There's no *we*. I want no part in this."

"Stop being a dryshite for one second and do something spontaneous."

His words sent a jolt through me. They were so much like Maura's when we were together. Maybe I did need to get my head out of my arse and start living more.

With a roll of my eyes, I said, "Fine. I'll get the key."

Rian clapped his hands together. "Now you're talking."

I walked around the car and over to the garage. "Evening, Vance," I said to the guard on duty.

"Evening."

"Where's the key to the car they delivered today?"

His salt and pepper brows popped wide. "The Aston Martin?"

"That one."

"You sure you're wanting to take that one, boyo?"

I flashed him a shark-like smile. "Aye. I'm in the mood to piss my Da off."

He snorted before eyeing the box that held the keys to all the estate cars. After taking out a shiny one, he replied, "It goes without saying not to feck up the car, but watch yourself with the key. It's two thousand pounds to replace it."

"Jaysus," I muttered as I took the key from him. I then shot him a sheepish look. "If anyone asks, you didn't see me take these."

He chuckled. "Yes, sir."

As I started back to the car, Rian leaned back against the hood. "Why don't you drive to the pub, and then I'll drive your pissed self home?"

"That sounds like a plan."

The next thing I knew Rian had snatched the key from my hand. Laughing, he replied, "You're too gullible, mate."

"If any Kavanaugh is breaking her in, it'll be *me*," I protested.

"Fat fecking chance!"

Before I could snatch the key back, Rian sprinted over to the driver's side with me close on his heels. Cackling, he flung the door open and slid across the seat.

As he fumbled to put the key in the ignition, I jerked one of his hands off the steering wheel. "I've got fifty pounds on you, you langer! Don't make me drag you out of there and beat your arse."

Rian threw his head back and laughed at my comment. "You'd really kick my arse before letting me drive this car?" At my nod, he sighed. "All right. I concede."

"Glad to talk some sense into you."

He started to get out, but then gave me a cheeky wink. "Sucker."

"You asshole!" I protested with a laugh.

Grinning, Rian brought his other leg into the car. "Bitch seat is waiting," he mused as he slid the key in the ignition.

And then came a deafening roar.

Before I could pinpoint its origin, heat consumed the right side of my body. It singed my clothes along with my exposed skin. As a scream of pain tore from my lips, a force sucked me backwards and propelled me into the air, twisting my body around like I was a weightless rag doll. I slammed against something hard that sent a crackling through my joints.

The world around me silenced as my eyes fought to focus. Blinking repeatedly, I stared up at the blurry onyx sky. When at last I could see through the fog, I turned my head toward the car.

A fireball raged where it had once been.

"RIAN!" I screamed, but the words only came out as a croak. When I tried pulling myself to my feet, my legs gave out, sending me sprawling back onto the ground. Digging my elbows into the grass, I began army crawling to the car.

Men started pouring in the area. Their arms gesticulated wildly while their mouths opened wide in shouts and screams that I couldn't hear. All I could make out was a high pitched whine like that of a gnat. Ignoring the chaos, I continued crawling to the car. Rian was my brother. I had to save him.

The closer I got to the car, the more intense the heat became. One side of my face felt like wax melting down a candle. Narrowing my eyes, I tried focusing on the car. The door had been blown off in the blast. Engulfed in flames, Rian's body lay half in and half out of the car. The smell of burnt flesh entered my nose, causing my stomach to lurch.

I reached a hand out to him, but then my entire body was snatched up and away by strong arms. "No! Rian!" I groaned.

When I peered up to the face of who had me, Callum stared down at me with tears streaming down his cheeks. For a moment, my gaze only focused on the moisture streaking down his agonized face. When was the last time I'd seen him cry?

His mouth moved as his chest heaved with sobs, but I could still only hear a ringing in my ears. Someone barreled into Callum, sending us reeling. When I tore my gaze from him, my chest clenched as my Uncle Seamus sank to his knees in front of the car. Even though I couldn't hear his tormented screams, they wracked my body like lashes from a whip.

Rian was dead.

And it was all my fault.

Chapter One: Isla

"This is fucking torture!"

As I spun upside down on the pole, I eyed my younger sister's red, scrunched face. With a glare at the offending floor to ceiling metal before her, she crossed her arms over her chest in a huff. I bit down on my lip to keep from laughing. Brooke always had a dramatic flair when things irritated her.

After pulling myself upright and sliding down onto my feet, I walked over to her. Placing a hand on her shoulder, I gave her my best reassuring smile. "No one said you have to master it the first time. I certainly didn't."

She blew an errant strand of blonde hair out of her face. "You know I suck at shit like this."

"Says the girl with a college volleyball scholarship," I tossed back.

Wrinkling her nose, she countered, "It's not the same thing."

"Pole dancing is about athleticism. Unlike me, *you* don't have a non-athletic bone in your body."

"But you're the dancer."

Considering I'd toddled out onto the stage for my first recital at two, she was right about that. I'd taken every dance class known to man from classical ballet to tap and jazz to hip hop. In elementary school, I'd transitioned into competitive dance. Thankfully, my experience was a lot less traumatic than what you saw on an old episode of *Dance Moms*.

I'd stopped competing when I entered MIT. I now parlayed my former dance background to teach dance classes at a local studio. I'd been chosen to be the lead instructor for the studio's new pole dance classes. Even though it worked well with my course schedule, it didn't pay enough for tuition and books.

"It's not that I can't get the hang of it." Brooke's hand came to cup her breasts. "The pole bangs the hell out of these."

I glanced down at my own chest that was stretching the limits of my latest sports bra. "I have to agree that Triple D's aren't entirely pole friendly."

"Try having engorged ones filled with milk," Brooke lamented with a wince.

As if on cue, an agitated shriek came from the carrier in the corner. I held up my hand. "I've got him."

She snorted. "Good luck considering you don't have what he wants."

With a laugh, I hustled across the black and white checkered studio floor. By the time I reached him, my nephew's howls had ratcheted up a few decibels. "Easy, Little Man," I cooed as I unbuckled him from his carrier.

Like Brooke had anticipated, Henry rooted around on me for a few seconds before realizing I was not his milk bearer. His tiny brows scrunched up while hiccupped snorts of rage erupted from him. "I'm so sorry, Little Man. I'll get you to mommy."

Thankfully, Brooke met us in the center of the studio floor. As I eased Henry into her waiting arms, the familiar pang of disbelief rocketed through me. A year ago I would've never fathomed my eighteen-year-old sister becoming a mother.

As a four-year varsity letterman and A/B student, Brooke didn't fit the stereotypical teen pregnancy statistic. The only factor you might consider was absent parents. But that wasn't our parents fault. They didn't choose to leave us two years ago in a car accident after helping pack up my dorm for the summer.

At the thought of my parents smiling faces, memories of that fateful day assaulted my mind.

My father clutching his chest—his face flushing crimson.

My mom screaming his name as she unbuckled her seatbelt to try to take the wheel.

The car careening across two lanes.

My trembling fingers dialing 911 before the phone was knocked out of my hand by the sharp descent of the SUV going over the embankment.

The squealing sound of steel being wrenched and crushed against a stout oak tree.

The crack of my head against the passenger window.

The horn continuing to blare long after the SUV had come to a stop.

The metallic smell of blood that seeped through the SUV.

My father's widowmaker heart attack set off the chain of events that took my mother's life along with his. If she hadn't unbuckled her seatbelt to try to steer the car, the medical examiner felt she would've survived.

Like I did.

Instead, we lowered two caskets into the ground of the Episcopal church where my father had been a minister. Whoever coined the phrase life can change on a dime wasn't kidding. I went from a carefree twenty-one-year-old to a burdened executor of an estate. I also became a surrogate mother to Brooke who was almost seventeen. Besides some of our aunts, uncles, and cousins, we were all each other had left.

At the ache in my chest, I turned from Brooke to go to the mini-fridge in the corner. After grabbing two bottled waters, I made my way over to the couch where Brooke was nursing Henry. His dark eyes, that he had inherited from my father, tracked my movement. I swept my fingers through the dark silky strands of his hair—the very same color as my mother's.

He was a tiny piece of their immortality. A living symbol that the life of one we love is never lost. It was the reason Brooke had bequeathed him with the name Henry to honor our father. I only wished my dad could be here for Henry to take the slack for his deadbeat asshole of a sperm donor.

When my phone beeped, I grabbed it off the desk. One glance at the message and my stomach plummeted to my knees.

This is Paula at Alainn. I'm confirming your audition tomorrow at two.

After sucking in a ragged breath, I texted back, "Yes! I'll see you tomorrow."

With trembling fingers, I put my phone back down on the desk and stepped away. As I started back over to Brooke, anxiety trailed up and down my spine. Absently, my fingernails scraped along the label on the water bottle as a battle waged in my mind.

Stop stalling and ask.
It's just a little favor.
Oh, you know it's so much more than that.
It could change everything between the two of you.
Even if you don't ask her, everything is going to change once she knows about your audition.

As the battle raged on, my index finger continued scratching over the crinkly paper.

"Isla?" Brooke questioned.

I glanced up from the bottle. "Huh?"

Her brows furrowed. "Is there something wrong?"

A nervous laugh trilled from my lips. "What makes you say that?"

"You've been obsessively stroking that water bottle for like a minute."

Busted. My finger froze before I hustled over to the table to drop off my distraction. With my back turned, I could still feel Brooke's gaze on me. Forcing a smile to my face, I whirled around.

"Isn't it weird how types of water taste different? Like water is water. The taste should be universal. Well, unless it's like the difference between cold and hot. Not to mention ice water and tap water."

Brooke quirked her brows at me as she adjusted her nursing bra. "You're nervous."

"Am I?"

"You always ramble like crazy when you are."

A ragged sigh rumbled through me. "I need to ask a favor."

"You got all worked up for that?"

"Maybe."

With a laugh, Brooke replied, "I'll do it."

I cocked my brows at her. "But you don't even know what it is."

She grinned. "As much as you help with Henry, I'd have to be a selfish bitch not to do a favor for you."

Flopping down beside her on the couch, I protested, "Anything to do with Little Man is a pleasure."

After shifting Henry to her shoulder to burp him, Brooke asked, "What is it that you need?"

"I need my hair and makeup done. Like really glam it up."

While she was sporty, Brooke had always been addicted to following trending makeup and hair styles. She was going to college to get a business degree to run her own salon one day.

"Of course." Furrowing her brows at me, she asked, "But why do you need to be glam for a Tuesday afternoon?"

Although I knew the time would come where I had to tell Brooke my intentions, I still wasn't ready. Shrugging my shoulder apathetically, I replied, "Just an audition."

"What kind of audition?"

"Dance," I answered truthfully.

Brooke narrowed her dark eyes on me. "What aren't you telling me?"

Unable to look at her, I rose off the couch. As I wrung my hands, I fought to find the words. "I haven't told you where the audition is because I know you're not going to like it."

"Spit it out, Isla."

"Tomorrow I have an audition at *Alainn*."

Brooke's eyes bulged. "*Alainn*? But that's a..."

"I'm aware of what it is."

"Please tell me it's for a waitressing job." When I didn't respond, Brooke gasped. "Isla you can't audition for a stripper!"

"They're called dancers there."

"Fuck the semantics, Isla! You're talking about flashing your tits and grinding on strange men's dicks."

Although I shuddered at both her words and the thought of actually doing it, a mirthless laugh escaped my lips. "I'm aware of what the job entails." Drawing my shoulders back, I countered, "And *Alainn* isn't a seedy club. They have millionaires and billionaires as clients. It's *very* competitive to get a job there. I'm lucky I even got an audition."

Brooke furiously shook her head. "It's still a *strip* club."

Rubbing my temples, I replied, "Once again, I'm aware of what it is."

"While I'm sure you can dance the g-string off any girl there and work the pole like no other, aren't you worried about being around men in that capacity?"

With a roll of my eyes, I countered, "You act like I've been trapped in a convent. I've been with men before."

"The two guys you've dated and screwed are *not* the type of men at *Alainn*."

"I've been with three guys," I corrected.

Brooke furrowed her blonde brows. "Wait, who was the third?"

"Victor." When she stared blankly at me, I replied, "That guy from the dance competition."

She rolled her eyes. "Fine. Two epically vanilla guys along with a random one-night stand. I'm sure all three of their ideas of kinkiness were probably doggy style."

I blushed at her summation. Brooke was right that I wasn't exactly sexually adventurous. I'd lost my virginity at eighteen to my high school boyfriend of two years. Although he was in the Top 5 of our graduating class, he couldn't find my clit to save his life. The same could've been said of my long-term lab partner in college as well as Victor.

The sad fact remained I was 0-3 when it came to orgasming with a guy.

Holding up my hands in surrender, I countered, "I didn't see anywhere on the application where I needed to list my sexual partners or my safe and hard limits."

"You're seriously telling me you're not going to lose your shit the minute some random man runs his hands all over your tits while he grinds into your pussy?"

With a shriek of horror, I motioned to Henry. "Don't talk like that in front of him!"

Brooke snorted. "There's Exhibit A of you being a prude."

"I am not," I argued. "And for your information, the men aren't allowed to touch us. We can touch them during a dance, but they will be forcibly removed if they get handsy."

"There's still the dick factor."

"I can handle it."

Motioning around the studio, Brooke asked, "You've got a good gig here. Why would you want to leave?"

"The pay is abysmal when it comes to grad school tuition."

"Becoming a stripper will fuck with your future," Brooke stated.

This time I didn't bother arguing about her cussing in front of

Henry. Instead, I exhaled a shaky breath. "This is me we're talking about. The scientist in me would never embark on anything without testing many theories."

And that was the truth.

Dance might've been my hobby, but science was my passion. Growing up, I'd been the nerdy girl always reading or doing STEM activities. In high school, I earned the nickname Bernadette from the character in *The Big Bang Theory*. Since she was a smart scientist who was blonde with big boobs, I suppose it wasn't too much of an insult.

My parents had always supported my future in the sciences. The day I'd gotten my acceptance from MIT we'd gone out to dinner to celebrate. My scholarship would ensure I wouldn't be a financial burden to parents or myself through loans.

"I can dance under a fake name, wear a wig to disguise my identity, and only use this studio on my job history," I explained.

Although she should've been satisfied with my plan, Brooke's eyes shuttered. "Why are you doing this?" she questioned in an agonized whisper.

"It's complicated."

Her eyes flew open to glare at me. "I know I don't have your mega brain, but I think I can comprehend if you explain it."

"Like I said, I need the money for school."

"But your scholarship—"

"Became invalidated after I took that semester off after the accident."

Brooke gasped. "You never told me that."

"Since you'd just broken up with Brad after finding out you were pregnant, I didn't want to worry you."

"Dammit, Isla, I don't want you keeping secrets from me."

"I was only trying to protect you."

"I don't want to be protected—I want to be there for you like you have for me."

A sad smile curved on my lips. "You know I couldn't make it without you."

"Then shoot straight with me. How bad is it?"

I exhaled a ragged breath. "As you know, Mom and Dad did well, but they weren't exactly financially secure."

While my dad was a minister, my mom was an insurance adjuster. Five years ago, however, her health had deteriorated with a diagnosis of Rheumatoid Arthritis. She wasn't considered sick enough for disability, so when she was forced to quit work, it ate into what savings they had.

"But they had life insurance," Brooke protested.

I nodded. "It paid off the remainder of the mortgage, so we'll always have this house. It also left us both small savings." With a sigh, I said, "The reason I'm auditioning for *Alainn* is because graduate school is expensive, and I've long since run out of my savings."

"Then take mine."

"Absolutely not! That's for you." I jerked my chin at Henry who she bounced on her knee. "Not to mention him."

"You can pay me back when you're making the big bucks as a molecular biologist."

With a laugh, I replied, "That could take years."

"I trust you."

I shook my head. "It's not happening."

Brooke glared at me. "You'd rather take your clothes off than take my money?"

"You're my baby sister. I could never take anything from you." With a smile, I reached over to take Henry from her. "Except maybe him."

As I snuggled Henry close to me, his tiny lips quirked up. "Your Auntie Isla would do anything for you and your mommy." When I glanced at Brooke, tears shone in her eyes. Reaching for her hand, I said, "Like Mom always said, we're putting the cart before the horse. Just because I got an audition, it doesn't mean I'll get the job."

"You will," she lamented.

"How can you say that?"

After swiping the tears from her eyes, she replied, "Besides being a phenomenal dancer and amazing at the pole, you're exactly what their clients want."

"A busty scientist whose idea of a good time is curling up with a medical journal and a mug of Earl Grey tea?" I teasingly asked.

Brooke snorted. "You're the Madonna Whore."

My eyes bulged. "Excuse me?"

With an exasperated huff, Brooke said, "Yet another reason why I can't believe you're considering stripping." When I maturely stuck my tongue out at her, she replied, "Let's put it this way: you're their lady in the streets and their freak in the sheets."

Warmth flooded my cheeks at the allusion. "I don't know about that."

Worry once again creased Brooke's brows. Since we both shared a wild stubborn streak in our DNA, she knew it was useless to argue once I'd made up my mind. Reaching over she took my hand in hers. "Just promise me if you ever feel uncomfortable or unsafe, that you'll quit, and we'll find a way to pay for your tuition together."

As I stared into her eyes, I wanted nothing more than to be able to say yes. But I knew that regardless of whatever feelings the job might unearth, I couldn't let it get to me. My goal wasn't just to pay my tuition. It was to ensure that Brooke made it through school, and that Henry received the most love and care possible.

After forcing a smile to my face, the lie rolled easily off my tongue. "I promise."

Chapter Two: Quinn

"This is fucking torture!"

A dark chuckle rumbled through my chest as I eyed the man strung up before me. "That's because it is." My fist connected with his jaw again, sending a spray of blood and saliva misting through the air. At his groan, I snatched some of his blood and sweat stained hair and jerked his head up to meet his gaze. "It's what happens when a loyal clan member such as yourself decides to double cross us on a shipment."

"But I–"

I threw a harsh uppercut to his jaw. As I flexed my tingling fingers, Conrad had the audacity to snivel. Nothing pissed me off more than a man who couldn't take his punishment. Or in this case, his torture. "This shit will keep going until you give me a name."

He shook his head wildly back and forth. "I swear I don't know."

I tsked at him. "Now that's not what I wanted to hear, Conrad."

This time my fist connected with the doughy flesh of his upper abdomen. At the crack of his ribs, he squealed before a sob tore through his chest. The noises of agony fed the beast within me.

The depraved monster who fed on suffering.

Sometimes I pondered if the monster within me was a product of nature vs. nurture. Was my DNA tainted with a bloodthirst that could only be quelled through murder and violence? Or was it because of the way I'd been raised.

In the end, it seemed to be a mixture of both.

Conrad apprised me through his swelling eyes. When I grabbed the knife off the table, he started jerking wildly against the chains. "Help, help!" he shrieked.

A cruel smirk curved on my lips. "Don't waste your breath. We're in a soundproof room."

My words, coupled with the gleam of the knife, caused a wet spot to bloom in the front of his pants. With a disgusted grunt, I said, "Did you have to go and piss yourself?"

When I flicked the blade under his chin, a shudder rolled through his body. "Tell me. Which part of the body will you miss the least, and I'll start there?"

"Kolosov!" he howled.

And there it was–the breaking point. Every man had one. For some, it came sooner than others. Some like Conrad needed more physical persuasion while others you break simply with threats to those they loved.

"Are you ever going to entertain business proposals from Bratva scum again?"

"Never," he swore.

"I want to believe you, Conrad. I really do."

He began blubbering, his salty tears mixing with the blood on his face. "Please, I swear."

I jerked my knife from his chin. "This is your warning. You fuck with us again, and I'll be taking pieces out of not only you, but your family."

Conrad sobbed so hard he could only nod his head. I flashed him a shark-like smile before clapping him harshly on the back. "Have a good day."

After I exited the door, I turned to the two soldiers waiting outside. "Leave him strung up for another hour. Then send him on his way."

"Yes, sir," they murmured in unison.

With my hands and clothes covered in blood, I needed to clean-up before any unsuspecting person could see me. After nodding to the men, I headed down the hallway to the bathroom.

From the outside the Beacon Hill penthouse where my brothers and I resided appeared just as the others in the neighborhood. However, I could vouch that none of their spacious basements possessed a windowless, sound-proofed torture room, nor did they contain a medical room that could've doubled for any ER trauma bay.

While I'm sure most included a bathroom or two, I could pretty much bet their showers didn't resemble ours with its numerous jets that sent high pressure water to rinse away blood and bodily fluids.

After stripping naked, I stepped into the stall and let the water beat against my body. I had exactly half an hour before I was expected at *Alainn*, which meant beautiful in Irish. It was the gentlemen's club my three brothers and I owned. Every Thursday at noon, we met to go over the weekly financials.

Although our darkened souls resided in Boston's underworld, we kept a legitimate front through our business holdings, which included commercial real estate as well our newly opened nightclub, *Bandia*.

Once I finished with the shower, I grabbed a towel and wrapped it around my waist.

When I glanced in the mirror, the familiar disgust filled me at my reflection. My gaze trailed the puckered scars that ran down the side of my face. Time had faded them from the angry red welts they'd first been.

It had been two long years since the car bomb that had been rigged for my father had almost killed me. Instead of a physical death, I'd experienced an emotional one since life as I knew it had irrevocably changed.

I would never look at life the same since no one would look at me the same. When you'd spent twenty-seven years being what the world considered conventionally handsome, it came as a great shock when you no longer were. While I'd never really been vain, I had enjoyed the attention.

And then it was gone.

At 6'5, I'd always been an imposing motherfucker. But I'd never really experienced true fear and outright revulsion in another's eyes until I had my scars.

The greatest agony hadn't come in my physical deformity. It had been losing Rian. While time might've faded my scars, they did little to ease the ache in my chest at his memory. The only comfort I took in his death came from the medical examiner who ruled he had been killed instantly. The thoughts of him burning alive while I couldn't save him was too much to bear.

At the same time, it didn't truly lessen my grief or anyone else's. Some nights I woke to the anguished wails of my uncle Seamus as he crouched beside the burning car. I'd been told he'd done the same thing at Rian's funeral. His grief was so intense that Callum and Dare had been forced to carry him up the church aisle.

Other nights I'd wake to the haunted face of my aunt Elena. She remained sedated for the first year of Rian's loss. He was her only child–the miracle baby she and Seamus never thought they could have. And then on the anniversary of his death, she took one of Seamus's pistols and shot herself.

I didn't get to pay my last respects at the funeral. I remained heavily medicated in the burn unit of the ICU. I stayed there for a tortuous month of therapy. Doctors tried telling me I was lucky. That with numerous reconstructive surgeries I could almost be as I was before.

I told them to fuck off.

I was done with the antiseptic smell of hospitals. The uncertainty of treatments. And the narcotics were starting to take hold of me.

And then there were other nights when I woke to fiery torment burning along my left side. The doctors called it "phantom pain", and it was only in my mind. I didn't know how anything in my mind could be just as painful as what I'd experienced in the moment. But it was a special kind of agony.

Somedays I didn't know why I kept putting one foot in front of the other. But then I would look at my brothers. I gleaned strength from them, and in turn I gave them strength.

There wasn't anything in the world I wouldn't do for them. It was the reason why I was about to drag myself downtown to crunch numbers, which was something I fucking loathed.

After slipping on a fresh suit, I didn't give my reflection a final glance. Instead, I flicked off the light and left.

Even though it was barely noon, *Alainn* had a teeming lunch crowd, most of which were made up of businessmen. If it had been Dare or Callum, they would've made their way through the main room, exchanging pleasantries with some of the big spenders. But the thought of that made my skin crawl.

Instead, I took the back stairs up to our office. Since we were all co-owners, it possessed one desk, but it included a large mahogany table like you'd see in a boardroom. When I slipped inside, I wasn't surprised to already find Kellan sitting at the table.

With his head buried in his laptop, he didn't look up. "Hey."

"Hey yourself," I replied as I walked over to the drink cart. "Where's Dare?" I asked, as I poured myself a whiskey.

"Getting blown in the bathroom," Kellan replied nonchalantly as if Dare were merely on the phone.

As if to corroborate Kellan's story, a low groan came from the expansive private bath followed by a guttural, "Fuck yes!"

I snorted. "It doesn't bother you?"

Kellan glanced up. "I've learned to tune him out."

"Aye, I know what you mean," I chuckled. After throwing back a sip of whiskey, I asked, "What about Callum?"

"He was interviewing warehouse supervisors."

"Again?"

With a nod, Kellan replied, "Men like Sean are hard to find."

Six months ago one of our warehouses by the docks was firebombed. We lost Sean, who was one of our best supervisors as well as our close friend.

The bathroom door opened, and Dare appeared with a leggy brunette. A broad smile lit up his face. "Afternoon, brother."

"Afternoon," I muttered dryly.

After smacking the brunette's ass, he replied, "See you later, Crystal."

"Christie," she corrected.

"Right, right."

While I snorted at Christie flouncing out of the room in a huff, Kellan shook his head. "You're a pig."

He grinned. "Come on. I was pretty close."

With a roll of his eyes, Kellan stared back at his laptop. A ding echoed on all our phones. I glanced down at mine. "Callum's on his way up."

As Kellan closed his laptop, Dare and I took a seat at the table. After Kellan passed us each a copy of the monthly report, Dare cocked his brows. "Looks like between here and *Bandia*, I'll be able to open my casino sooner than later."

Studying the numbers, I replied, "Looks like it."

Callum swept through the door then. "How's it looking, boys?" he asked.

Kellan grinned while shoving a red folder at him "Grand as always."

As Callum quickly perused the folder's documents, he replied, "I'm glad to hear it."

"It wouldn't kill you to say thanks, would it?" Kellan teasingly questioned.

While I couldn't help rolling my eyes at his cheek, Dare countered, "Get fucked, boyo. You're not even old enough to have a drink here. It's Quinn and I that keep this place afloat."

With a scowl, Kellan countered, "I will be of age in three months."

After ruffling Kellan's hair, I countered, "Then keep yer trap shut until then."

Callum pointed at me. "Speaking of running this place. I've got an audition for you."

As Boston's finest gentlemen's club with millionaires and billionaires for clients, we were barraged with applications from dancers. With all the area colleges, we received the high-end coeds who had years of rigorous dance training under their belts. But it wasn't just dance ability that made a stripper, nor was it their pole aptitude. It came down to whether they could make every man feel desired and special.

When we'd first started the club, Callum had decided that I would be the ringer. The maker or breaker when it came to hiring. If they could successfully give me a lap dance without pissing themselves in fear, then they were hired.

It wasn't about my physical appearance at the time either. The club came before the bombing. No, it was about the fact that I possessed an aura that drove fear into women. I guess it went with being the family's enforcer.

But in the last year, it started grating on my nerves. I was tired of having beautiful young women balk at riding my dick. I'd never admit it to my brothers, but it was starting to give me a fucking complex.

I couldn't fight the growl that reverberated through my chest. "I'm not a fucking plaything you can trot out when it serves your purpose."

Callum snorted. "As if anyone could ever think of you like that."

"I'm serious, Callum."

"I know. But I need your services."

At my continued hesitation, Dare clapped me on the back. "You're the only man I know who begrudges a lap dance from a fine as hell woman."

"Fuck you," I muttered.

"Quinn's not the only one who would," Callum remarked.

Dare's brows rose questioningly. "Who else?"

He eased back in his chair with a smile. "Me."

Since Callum had married Caterina, he hadn't partaken in any lap dances. He was completely true to his wife, which still shocked the hell out of me. None of us, except for Kellan, had ever truly fancied monogamy.

When his phone buzzed, Callum grimaced at it. "Speak of the devil?" Dare questioned with a grin.

"Yeah, she had a doctor's appointment earlier."

Scowling at him, I countered, "Shouldn't you ask the wee lass how it went?"

"She already let me know everything was fine."

When I continued scowling at him, Callum sighed. "Look, she's asking to come see me at the office. There's no way in hell I can tell her where I'm at."

Dare's brows popped. "Sister Sassy doesn't know we own this club?"

Rolling his eyes at him, Callum replied, "Caterina would lose her mind if she knew about this place. In her book, I already have enough vices on my plate. There would be nothing of my dark soul left to salvage if she found out."

While Dare chuckled, I tsked at him. "You're just digging your grave deeper for when she does find out."

"I believe you have a dancer waiting to ride your dick." He wagged his eyebrows at me. "Her pole dance was to some shite Taylor Swift song."

My growl echoed through the room. "I'll pay you back for this, fucker."

Callum grinned as he rose out of his chair. "I look forward to it."

Chapter Three: Isla

As I eyed my reflection in the mirror, I tried hiding my disgust at the voluptuous bombshell that stared back at me. Brooke had gone above and beyond when it came to making me flawless for my audition. She worked tirelessly until my blonde hair cascaded in loose waves down to my butt.

Then she started on my makeup. She'd given me fluffy eyelashes and glittering eyelids with purple eyeshadow that matched my sequined purple bustier and g-string set.

Frowning, I surveyed my bright red lips. "Are you sure the lipstick isn't a bit too much?"

Brooke shook her head. "The stage lights will wash you out. You want your lips to show up above all else. You want them thinking of your lips around their dick."

"Ugh, seriously?"

With a roll of her eyes, Brooke replied, "And there's yet another reason why I can't believe you think you're going to be a stripper."

"*Dancer*."

"Semantics."

"Just because I don't want to think about random dudes' dicks doesn't mean I can't be a stripper."

Rolling her eyes, Brooke replied, "Seriously? The whole job is thinking about dudes and their dicks."

"Whatever. Can I get dressed now?"

"One sec." Brooke then spritzed a setting spray on my makeup. "Now you're good."

I pulled on a wrap dress over my sparkling undies. When I was done, I slipped on a pair of what I liked to call my power heels. When you're barely 5'3, you need all the help you can get.

When I hurried out of the bathroom, Brooke was waiting with a bag that contained my stripper heels, a replacement bustier and g-string for the audition in case something broke or ripped, and my makeup bag for touch-ups.

Without a word, we both nodded and then started out into the hallway. Brooke's best friend, Jennie, was taking care of Henry while we were gone. She bounced him in her arms outside my room.

"What do you think of your auntie Isla?" I cooed. His eyes widened before his lip quivered. "Oh no. It's just me, sweet pea."

An indignant howl erupted from him. "Great. I just traumatized him with my slutty look."

"Yes, I'm sure this will be the day he talks about in therapy instead of his jackass of an absentee father," Brooke teased.

I laughed. "Smartass."

We then pounded down the stairs. As we hurried into the kitchen, I grabbed the keys. Holding them out to Brooke, I asked, "Can you drive?"

"Sure."

As we headed out of the kitchen and into the garage, I said, "When we get there, you can just wait for me in the car."

"Screw that. I'm coming in with you."

I rolled my eyes as I opened the passenger side door. "There's no way in hell they're going to let you come in. You aren't twenty-one."

A wicked gleam flashed in Brooke's eyes as she dug her wallet out of her purse. "But my ID says that I am."

With a shriek of horror, I snatched the card out of her hand. "Where did you get this?"

Shrugging, she replied, "A friend of a friend."

After eyeing the front and the back, I said, "This is a really good quality one."

Brooke nudged me playfully. "And how would you know, *Saint Isla?*"

I snorted. "I might be slightly angelic, but I'm sure as hell not a saint."

"You disappoint me. I never imagined a sister of mine would have a fake ID."

"What if I told you I got it to be able to get into high-tech labs, rather than for alcohol?"

Brooke threw her head back with a laugh. "Now *that* sounds like you."

"Whatever." With a flick of my wrist, I handed her back the ID. "Come on. Let's go."

After she shoved her ID back in her wallet, Brooke walked around the front of my car. When she got in and cranked up, I willed the rising bile in my throat not to spew all over the dashboard.

To get my mind off of the audition, I started playing with the radio–pinging between True Crime and *The Life Scientific* podcasts. By the time we arrived in front of *Alainn*, I fought to keep from having a panic attack.

After Brooke flicked on the blinker to head into the parking garage, she turned to look at me. "Just say the word, and we'll *Thelma and Louise* it out of here."

A laugh burst from me. It certainly lightened my mood. "No. I'm doing this."

"You look like you're about to piss your pants."

"Maybe they'll have a Golden Shower kink."

It was Brooke's turn to burst out laughing. "Now you're talking like a stripper."

"*Dancer*."

She gave me a genuine smile. "Semantics."

My expression grew serious. "I'm doing this, B. I'm doing it so that one day I'll be Dr. Vaughn and debt free from student loans. Not to mention, you'll be a college graduate, and Henry will be well-adjusted and happy."

Although tears sparkled in Brooke's eyes, she replied, "And it will all be from you flashing your tits and dry humping."

Once again, I laughed. "Damn straight."

"Then let's do this."

After we parked, we crossed the street and arrived in front of the club. When we got to the front door, a beefy bouncer eyed us with disinterest. "Um, hi, I'm Isla Vaughn, and I have an audition."

Turning his head, he spoke into the radio on his shoulder. "Paula, you have an audition here."

"Send her in," crackled the reply.

When Brooke started to follow me, he stopped her. "I need to see your ID."

While my heart started beating out of my chest, Brooke appeared cool as a cucumber. "Sure. Just one sec."

As she dug into her purse, I pinched my lips shut. The last thing I needed right now was to let my nerves cause me to verbally vomit. With complete self-assurance, Brooke handed him her ID.

I sucked in a breath as the bouncer studied it curiously. He glanced between it and Brooke. "Fine. You can go in."

She flashed him a sugary-sweet smile. "Thanks."

Grabbing her arm, I dragged her behind me into the club. When we swept through the entrance and into the main room, we both gasped. Part of the allure of *Alainn* was anonymity, so there weren't any pictures of the interior online.

I'd had an image in my mind of what I imagined it looked like, which was based on club scenes from movies. I couldn't possibly have envisioned the crystal chandeliers, white linen table cloths, and high-end furniture.Men in expensive tailored suits passed us, blinding us with their shiny Rolex's.

"Holy shit, this place *is* posh," Brooke remarked.

"It sure is."

"Isla?" a voice behind me questioned.

I whirled around to see an attractive woman in her mid-forties staring expectantly at me. Nodding, I replied, "Yes, I'm Isla."

She extended her hand. "I'm Paula. We spoke on the phone."

"It's nice to meet you."

"Likewise." Her gaze flicked to Brooke. "And you are?"

Just as I was about to answer my sister, Brooke flashed her a megawatt smile, "Her stylist."

A nervous laugh bubbled from my lips. "She's my sister."

Paula smiled. "I can see the resemblance. Your stylist/sister will need to stay at the bar. We can't have non-employees in the back with our dancers."

Brooke nodded. "Sounds good." As she started for the bar, she shot me an intense look. "You've got this."

"Thanks," I whispered.

With Brooke heading over to the bar, Paula motioned me to follow her. We weaved in and out of the crowd. I tried not to flinch at each pair of breasts that were practically thrust in my face.

Instead, I drew my shoulders back and strode behind Paula like half-naked women were just another Tuesday occurrence.

When we entered the Employee Only entrance, I fought to keep the surprise off my face at how high-brow the dressing room was with the same marble floors as in the main room. I felt like I was stumbling around a mansion rather than a strip club.

Paula unlocked the first door on the right side of a long hallway of rooms. When we stepped inside a small stage with a pole sat in the middle of the room along with expensive looking leather couches.

"So, here's what is going to happen. First, you'll work the pole and do your dance for me. For the second part, one of the owners will do the private dance part of your audition."

Inwardly I groaned at the mention of the private dance. It was the bane of my existence and what I feared would screw up my chances. Forcing a smile to my face, I replied, "Sounds good."

"Great. You can step into the bathroom over there to get ready. Then when you come out, we'll start."

Unable to speak, I merely nodded. On shaky legs, I made my way over to the bathroom. I didn't know why the marble tile floors and counters surprised me.

After stripping out of my dress, I didn't bother glancing at my reflection. Instead, I just turned out the light and left the bathroom.

It was do or die time.

Chapter Four: Quinn

As I entered the private room, I inwardly groaned. Callum hadn't been giving me shite about Taylor Swift. *Lover* jolted through my brain as a petite blonde twirled on the pole. "Fucking coeds," I muttered under my breath as I made my way over to Paula, our chameleon who handled PR as well auditions and wrangling of the dancers.

Even though I'd known her for two years, she remained visibly uncomfortable in my presence. Although she fought it, I always saw the change in her pulse and breathing when we were alone.

But today she appeared more at ease. Her smile seemed almost genuine. Jerking her chin to the stage, she said, "If she survives the lap dance, she's going to be a star."

With a grunt, I replied, "What makes her so special?"

"Besides being fucking aerobatic on the pole? She's got everything to drive the men wild. A real wide-eyed innocence coupled with off-the-charts sex appeal."

After three years, I couldn't help being a little skeptical. "We'll see."

"Isla?" Paula questioned.

The girl quickly dismounted the pole. The moment I saw her face a jolt thundered through me. Of all the hundreds and hundreds of women I'd encountered in my twenty-nine years, she was the most beautiful one I'd ever seen. So beautiful, she stole my breath.

With her blonde hair and blue eyes, she had an ethereal quality to her. She could've been the Irish goddess and fairy queen Cliodna–the most beautiful woman in the world according to our folklore.

For the first time since the accident, I found myself truly desiring a woman not just in the bedroom. In the past two years, I'd taken numerous women to my bed. Some became regulars and some were non-repeaters. I'd never wanted to pursue anything with them other than sex. They were a means to scratch an itch I had.

But Isla was different.

It wasn't about her beauty. She appeared approachable. Not to mention she was the epitome of a girl you took home to your mother, which was ironic considering she was about to take her clothes off for me. Her tiny stature brought out the protector in me.

As her wide-eyed gaze trailed from my chest up to my face, her throat bobbed. My skin shrunk over my bones at her appraisal. I waited for the obligatory flash of terror or disgust to fill her eyes that I'd seen so many times over the last two years. The forced smile. The feigned appreciation to be in my presence.

To my surprise, she blurted, "You're a long drink of water, aren't you?"

While Paula turned a laugh into a cough, I furrowed my brows at Isla. "Excuse me?"

"You're so *big*." The minute the words left her mouth a red flush entered her cheeks. "I mean, you're really tall."

"Aye, I am."

A giggle escaped her perfect red lips. "Of course anyone who stands next to me is tall. I'm so vertically challenged."

Furrowing my brows, I flicked my gaze to Paula. Amusement danced in her green eyes. "Isla, this is Quinn Kavanaugh."

She thrust out of her hand. Surprise flooded her face when I didn't offer her mine. A shaky smile curved on her face. "It's nice to meet you, Mr. Kavanaugh."

When I nodded at her, Paula said, "Isla is in graduate school at MIT. She also grew up in Southborough."

"Fascinating," I grumbled. Ignoring Isla's surprised gasp, I motioned to the leather couch. "Let's get on with it."

Paula patted Isla on the shoulder. "Good luck."

"Thanks," Isla murmured.

Once we were alone, I shed my suit jacket, and threw it on the back of the couch. After flopping down on the cushions, I widened my legs in the usual stance. When I glanced up, Isla stood frozen.

"All right. Lose the top and let's get on with this."

"I-I can't," she murmured.

I cursed myself for not making a bet with Callum on how far in the dance she'd actually get. I shouldn't have been surprised that she wouldn't even get on my lap. She probably couldn't bring herself to sully her pure body with the likes of me.

Anger flooded me at her judgment. I'm sure if it had been Dare or Callum she would've happily crawled up into their laps.

With a growl, I shot out of my seat. "Thanks for not only wasting my time, but yours."

Just as I started past her, she grabbed my hand, her fingertips sliding along the patch of scars. The touch of her skin sent electricity pricking from my fingertips all the way up my arm, causing me to shudder. Normally whenever someone touched me I felt nothing but a volatile mixture of shame and anger.

But not with Isla.

Unable to process the emotions swirling within me, I flung her hand away. Glowering down at her, I snarled, "Don't touch me!"

After cowering back, an apologetic look appeared on her face. "I'm sorry. It's just that I needed to get your attention."

I shook my head at her. "We're done here."

"Please. Just let me have another chance. I'm nervous, that's all."

"Ms. Vaughn, there's a reason we have practice runs at private dancing under the guise of auditions. There's also a reason why I'm used to make or break girls. Regardless of how good you are at the pole or at dancing, it comes down to whether or not you can get a guy off. You balked at even trying, so you failed."

When she winced, the slightest sliver of regret filled me. Normally, I didn't give two shits if I hurt the dancers' feelings. But I didn't like that I had insulted her. I sure as hell didn't like that I cared about hurting her.

"I know that. But once I get through my first one, I know I can do it. I'm a very fast learner when it comes to mastering concepts."

The former regret I'd felt vanished to be replaced by irritation. "I've heard that excuse a thousand fucking times."

"Please, I really need this job."

"Just like I've heard that one as many times as well."

"It's the truth. I lost my grad school scholarship."

Sneering, I replied, "Partying too much at the frat house?"

She winced. "No, I lost my parents two years ago in a car accident."

You're a real fucking bastard, you know that? But I didn't give in to my feelings of regret. Instead, I cranked up my cruelty. Anything to get rid of her and what she awakened within me.

"We all have trauma, Ms. Vaughn."

"I know. I swear I'm not asking for any favors. I mean, I *am* asking a favor for a second chance. It's not just about me. I'm in charge of my younger sister now. Well, since she's turned eighteen, I guess she's in charge of herself, but trust me, she desperately needs a motherly figure, even though she's a mother herself."

As I blinked at her, Isla sucked in a breath and then just kept running her fucking mouth. "Although she was the perfect student and athlete, her grief at my parents' death led her to accidentally procreate with the most worthless jackass of a sperm donor. He wants nothing to do with the child, nor does he help financially. I've tried to get Brooke to take him to court, but she won't. Don't get me wrong, her son, Henry, is the most amazing four-month-old in the world. But being a teen mom isn't what I would want for my baby sister, you know? And then–"

"Do you ever just shut the fuck up?" I demanded.

With crimson dotting her cheeks, she tucked her head to her chest. "I'm sorry. I'm the worst rambler when I get nervous. Like I seriously can't make it stop. I used to get in so much trouble in school because of it. I would be nervous about a test, and then all the sudden I would be popping off–"

When she met my exasperated gaze, she pinched her lips shut. "I'm done."

I waited for a few moments to see if she was telling the truth. When she didn't respond, I said, "It's only out of morbid curiosity that I've not thrown you out. Although I don't want you going on another verbal rampage, I would like to know how the hell do you expect to be a dancer if you can't perform a lap dance?"

She shook her head wildly back and forth. "No, it's not that I *can't*. It's just..." She nibbled on her lip. "I don't know how."

I crossed my arms over my chest. "Excuse me?"

"I swear, I prepared for this. I watched a ton of Youtube videos, so I know the basics of how to do it. But I'm having some sort of a block."

"I'm sure even if I don't ask, you're going to tell me why you have a block."

Her head bobbed enthusiastically. "You see, I don't have a lot of experience with men. I've only dated two guys, and they're what my sister swears are totally vanilla. I've never even had an orgasm. I mean, with a *guy*. Obviously I've given them to myself."

Although I shouldn't have, I couldn't help asking, "Not even when they went down on you?"

"Nope. Not even then."

"What kind of pussies have you been dating that can't get you off?"

Isla's eyes bulged comically wide when she finally realized her admission. "Oh God, did I really just tell you I'd never had an orgasm with a guy?"

"Aye, you did."

With a shriek, her hands came over her face. After a few seconds of shaking her head back and forth, she removed her hands and gave me a tight smile. "Can we just forget I said that?"

"I can try," I mused.

"Good. Anyway, what I meant to say, before I got horribly off course, is I'm not sure how to properly perform a lap dance to your liking."

"I see."

"You could teach me," she suggested in a soft voice.

I eyed her curiously. Had my own hang ups about my appearance caused me to have preconceived notions about her? Or was she just playing the innocence card to try and convince me to give her another try.

"To be clear, your earlier aversion to performing wasn't about you being scared of me and my scars?"

Isla frowned. "Why would I be scared of those?"

I cocked my head at her. "They seriously don't intimidate you?"

She shook her head. "It's not like you can help them, right?"

"No," I mumbled.

"Are they terribly painful?" When she reached out to touch one on my face, I jumped back before smacking her hand away. Her blue eyes widened in horror. "I'm so sorry. I don't know what came over me."

As I tried to stop my erratic breathing, I glared at Isla. "What the fuck is your problem?"

"Nothing. I swear." When I remained glowering, she added, "Although there's absolutely no excuse, I'm a molecular biologist. Well, I mean, that's what my undergrad is in. I've studied hypertrophic scars. Actually, it was more about the treatments like laser or cryotherapy."

"My scars...interest you?"

She nodded. "If I had to wager, I'd say they were from burning. Am I right?"

Although I should've been intrigued by her ability to guess, it also slightly unnerved me that she was able to know me so well. "I'm not one of the guinea pigs in a lab for you to poke and prod, Ms. Vaughn."

Before I could answer, she rushed on, "It's not just about science. My grandfather had shrapnel scars on his chest and stomach from Vietnam." Her expression grew sad. "Years and years later they would still ache."

I opened my mouth to bite back that I didn't give a shit about her grandfather's fucking scars. But then I quickly closed it.

And then the realization rocketed through me.

There was a woman standing in front of me who wasn't repulsed by my scars. While there was empathy, she hadn't pitied me. She wanted to understand my pain.

It was both freeing and frightening.

Tilting her head at me, Isla questioned, "So will you teach me?"

If I allowed myself to teach her, I would be breaking not only my rules, but the club's. My lap dance was the test to make or break a dancer. Within the parameters of those rules, Isla had obviously failed and should be shown the door.

By teaching her, I'd be allowing Isla to cheat. In a way, I'd be choosing her over my brothers. Well, at least over their business model.

Who the fuck was I kidding? A man like me didn't concern himself with morality. What would it hurt to give Isla a leg up? I could assure her silence to the other girls about her audition. No one would be the wiser.

"Please," Isla implored.

"Fine," I grunted.

Her blue eyes popped wide. "Really?"

"Yes."

"Oh, I can never thank you enough!"

"Can you at least shut up and listen?"

"Mm, hmm," she replied with a cheeky little smile.

God, this woman. She was like staring down the barrel of a gun and not flinching or moving. She would be the fucking death of me.

Without another word to Isla, I took my place on the sofa. After once again assuming the position, I said, "The first thing you're going to do is touch me."

Her gaze dropped to my crotch. "There?"

To both of our surprise, a laugh tore from my lips. "No. You never touch a cock. Well, at least not with your hands."

"Oh, um, okay."

"You're not going for the obvious right out of the bat. You want to tease the desire from them. You want them aching for you."

When Isla licked her lips, I fought the urge to groan. "I can do that," she murmured.

"The way you're going to set them on fire is with your hands on their body."

She frowned. "Do I start at the top and work my way down?"

With an exasperated sigh, I demanded, "You've ridden a guy, right?" At her squeak, I replied, "Where is the focus of your hands when you're fucking?"

"Uh, his shoulders and chest."

"Right. Start with the chest."

As she bent over me, the sweet smell of her shampoo filled my nose. It had a hint of vanilla. Isla tentatively placed her hands on my chest. At the gentle swirl of her palms on my pecs, I growled and smacked my hands over hers. "Harder."

She licked her lips. "Okay."

I slid her hands down my chest and over my abdomen. When we got closer to my cock, she tensed. "We're not touching that, remember?"

"Right," she murmured.

After bypassing my crotch, I slid her hands down my thighs and then back up to my hips. "Yes, like that."

"How long do I do it?"

"You want them rising to the occasion before you ever get on their lap."

Her cheeks warmed again. "I see."

"But you're not staying on the thighs the whole time. Go back to the chest and even up the neck. Then you're going to withdraw your touch to tease them even more."

She frowned as she took her hands from me. "What do I do now?"

"You dance to tease me. You move your body like you want to fuck me."

To my surprise, Isla didn't protest that she didn't know what to do. She had a dancer's heart. Slowly, her hips began to sway.

Her hands traveled over her body.

Her eyes closed in exaggerated bliss.

Her mouth opened for her tongue to lick along her lips.

As I stared at her, heat began to stir below my waist. At the sight of her arms going around her back to undo her top, my breath hitched. When the glittery material fell free from her breasts, my mouth ran dry as my cock slammed against my zipper.

She opened her eyes to pin with a stare. With a shy smile, she flung her top to the floor. "You didn't tell me to, but I thought it was the right time."

"Good instincts."

And fucking mouth-watering tits. They sat high and heavy. The kind you knew were natural. My hands itched at my sides to touch them. I wanted to squeeze them before teasing the nipples into hardened points with my fingertips. Then I would take the aching peaks deep into my mouth.

It was then Isla's gaze dropped to my lap and now tented pants. "Oh," she murmured.

"That's what you do to me."

"But I haven't done anything yet."

"You don't have to, Little Dove. Just the sight of you makes me ache."

She swept a piece of hair behind her ear and then peeked at me through her eyelashes. "I do?"

"Don't *ever* second guess your beauty and sex appeal again. You keep your head high like the fucking goddess you are.

Isla's chin turned up. "What do I do now?" she questioned, her voice lower and more seductive.

"Turn around to where your back is facing me." Always obedient, Isla did as I asked. It was a hell of a fucking turn-on. I got even harder imagining commanding her in the bedroom.

"Place your hands on my knees, and then slide your ass slowly down my chest and onto my lap."

At the sight of her full, round ass cheeks inches from my mouth, a long groan erupted from my lips. Isla's descent froze before she threw a look at me over her shoulder. "Are you all right?"

I chuckled. "You better get used to that noise. Men are going to be making it all the time around you."

"Oh," she murmured before ducking her head.

"Don't shy away from your power, Isla. You're the one who controls this. You control my pleasure and theirs. Don't ever forget who is in charge."

At her nod, I then said, "Now start rolling your hips on my dick. Imagine you're riding me reverse cowgirl."

I had to give it to her–the girl could work a cock. The dancing ability she possessed gave her an effortless swivel of her hips. "You can bounce on me, too."

At her practically twerking, I couldn't fight the groan that escaped my lips. "Do you like that Quinn?" she questioned breathlessly.

Although I fucking loved the sound of my name on her lips, I couldn't help but ask, "Who said you could call me by my first name?"

Ever obedient, Isla replied, "I'm sorry. Do you like that, *Mr. Kavanaugh.*" When I didn't reply, she threw a tentative look over her shoulder. "Do you like that, *sir?*"

"Fuck me," I muttered. Although it was pure sin hearing her call me sir, there was something within me that wanted to hear my name from her lips. It made it far more intimate. Sir was a name reserved strictly for sex while my given name gave us a connection beyond the act we were currently engaged in.

"Quinn is what you should call me."

She nodded. "What is it you'd have me do now, Quinn…sir."

A dark chuckle rumbled through me. "Oh, so you're a cheeky lass, huh?"

"I just want to please you," she argued.

"It pleases me when you do as I tell you to, and I told you to call me Quinn."

"But I know you liked me calling you sir," she argued.

"Aye, you're right. I do like it. I like it too much."

As she gazed longingly at me over her shoulder, I shook my head. "Enough." Sliding my hands around her waist, I lifted her to her feet. "It's time to switch things up. Men are visual. Although they'll enjoy seeing your ass, they'll want your tits in their face."

Instead of needing further direction, Isla rose off my lap to do a slinky turn to where she was facing me. As she swiveled her hips and curved her body, she lifted one of her legs. She pointed her toes as she slid her foot over one of my thighs. As she straddled me, she stared down at me with lust glittering in her blue eyes.

Instead of directing her, I allowed her to take the reins. Her hands came to my hair. As she jerked her fingers through the strands, her luscious tits brushed against my cheeks. She inched tediously back down on my dick, cupping my face in her hands before running her hands down to my shoulder. Lifting her hips, she began to ride me just as she would if my cock was buried deep in her walls.

When we locked eyes, every molecule in my body detonated, causing me to shudder. In that instant, I knew nothing would ever be the same for me. The connection between us was undeniable. From the mystified look in her eyes, I knew she was experiencing it too.

When I thrust my hips into her center, Isla sucked in a harsh breath, her fingertips painfully gripped my shoulders. It felt as if she was holding on to me for dear life. As I thrust into her center again, she whimpered.

"That's it, Little Dove. Tell me how much you want me."

With a shake of her head, she protested, "I shouldn't like this."

"Yes, you should."

She licked her lips. "But only with you."

I nodded. "But only with me."

Although we were both gasping and panting from the intense pleasure between us, I wanted more.

I *needed* more.

To get what we both needed, I had to cross a line I'd never crossed with a dancer before. After sucking in a ragged breath, I rasped, "I want to touch you."

Chapter Five: Isla

"I want to touch you."

The deep timbre of his voice shot straight to my core. Although it was so very, very wrong, I wanted him to touch me, too. I ached for it.

I'd never wanted a man so much that I'd just met. Or that I knew so little about. It was like I entered the club and checked all my usual inhibitions at the door.

Despite how much I wanted his touch, I found myself asking, "Are you supposed to? I mean, are the men supposed to?"

"Never," he growled. "No man is to *ever* touch you."

Feeling brave, I countered, "You're a man. What about you?"

To my surprise, Quinn appeared repentant. "I shouldn't."

"But you want to."

"With every breath within me," he rasped.

A shudder rippled through me at his words and the intensity of his stare. No man had ever had such a reaction to me. Quinn appeared as a man dying of thirst in a desert of my making.

"You can touch me," I whispered.

Anguish replaced the desire in his expression. "I'm not worthy."

His reply took me by surprise. "If this is about your scars, they don't bother me. In fact, I kinda like them."

Quinn's brows popped wide. "Do you, Little Dove?"

"I do. They give you character."

"While that's an interesting way to describe them, I wasn't talking about my appearance."

God, I was such an idiot. Embarrassment flushed my cheeks. "Oh, I'm sorry. It's just I--"

"I'm talking about the man within me. He's not worthy."

"Why?" I whispered.

"He's a bad man."

I stared into Quinn's blue eyes. Although he had a menacing exterior, the same wasn't reflected in his eyes. There was a softness to them. But they were also ringed with pain. I knew that look. I'd seen it in my own eyes many times over the last two years.

"I don't believe you."

The softness in his eyes turned dark. "You're very naive, Little Dove."

"Maybe. But I also see more than you think. Or that you allow."

"And what do you see?"

"A man who has erected so many walls around him to hide from the world. But I see through the tiny cracks and fissures to the goodness within."

He stared at me, unblinking and unmoving. Time crawled by. At that moment, it felt like we were the only two people in the world.

"There's goodness in you, Quinn. But don't worry. I won't tell anyone."

With a growl, he grabbed me by the back of the neck and jerked my face to his. I gasped just as his mouth slammed down on mine. Quinn thrust his tongue into my mouth, tangling with my own.

The kiss was fiery and desperate. It felt like our very life and existence depended on the breath and closeness we gained from each other. Quinn's teeth grazed my bottom lip before biting down, causing me to moan and him to grunt with pleasure.

I'd never been kissed like this in my life. I hadn't even dreamed it could be like this. It was the kind of kiss you watched in the movies, but you never thought you'd get to experience in real life, least of all in a strip club with your potential future boss.

He wasn't just kissing me–he was possessing me.

My hands came to encircle Quinn's neck, drawing him closer to me. With the scarred skin on his neck, I took care to be as gentle as I could. Something deep within me said that even if I was to scrape my nails along the flesh, he wouldn't hurt me.

Although he could've snapped me in two like a twig, I couldn't help feeling safe next to him. Everything about him was overwhelming from his imposing figure to his ability to render me breathless from just a kiss.

Feeling lightheaded, I finally jerked away. As my chest rose and fell in harsh pants, my gaze locked with Quinn's hooded, hungry one. My finger traced his full bottom lip. When his tongue snaked out to lick it, white-hot heat flooded my core.

"Are you going to lie to both me and yourself and say that we shouldn't have done that?" he rasped. When I shook my head slowly from side to side, he asked, "Then what is it you want to say, Little Dove?"

"No one is to kiss me but you," I ordered.

A beautiful smile lit up his face. It seemed so out of character for him. My heartbeat thrummed wildly in my chest at the sight of it. More than anything, it was the fact I was the one receiving it.

"That's right. No one but me."

Reaching for his hands on either side of his hips, I brought them to my waist. With my eyes still on his, I slid them up my ribcage before bringing them to my breasts. "Touch me."

Quinn gave a curt nod of his head before his warm hands cupped my breasts. When he squeezed them, we both moaned. As he tweaked my nipples, I continued rubbing myself against him. The more I felt of him over his pants, I knew he had to be huge. Just the thought of having him deep inside me sent hot, sticky desire streaking down my thighs.

"I want to taste you."

"Please."

His nostrils flared. "That word on your lips will be my undoing."

With one hand on my waist and another at the base of my neck, he tipped me back. His lips licked and bit down the column of my throat. I shivered as he slid his tongue along my breastbone. When his mouth closed over one of my nipples, it instantly peaked under the warm suction of his mouth. My breath came in needy pants.

The pleasure grew between my legs. My thighs began to tremble from the intensity. Biting my lip, I tried to mute my cries of pleasure.

Quinn's massive hands gripped my hips. He rolled them harder against the thrust of his own hips. The added friction of my thong rubbing against my clit was my undoing. With a cry, I threw my head back as an orgasm charged through me.

Through the fog of intense pleasure, Quinn's voice called to me. "That's it, Little Dove. Come for me."

Long after the first burst of gratified emotion, my walls continued to clench. Quinn's hips began a frenzied churn against my core. Locking eyes with him, I watched as his body tensed and then a long groan erupted from his lips.

"Oh fuck, Isla," he murmured as his body jerked.

I clung to him as he rode out his orgasm. Whatever connection I felt we had before seemed to intensify in our shared pleasure. When he was finally spent, he leaned forward to place a tender kiss on my lips.

At that moment, the door burst open so hard it banged on the hinges, causing me to scream. Although I tried criss crossing my arms in front of my breasts, Quinn pulled me behind him, shielding me from view. As I peered over his shoulder, a young man stood before us, a stricken look on his face.

"Get the fuck out of here, Kellan!" Quinn commanded.

Kellan shook his head. "Callum needs us." He then glanced between me and Quinn before shooting him a desperate look. "It's important."

"Jaysus," Quinn muttered. He tossed a glance at me over his shoulder before replying, "I'll be right there."

Kellan quickly turned on his heels and hurried from the room. "I have to go," Quinn gritted out.

Not knowing what to say, I mumbled, "It's okay."

After Quinn got off the couch, I pulled my knees to my chest and wrapped my arms around them. At the sight of him grabbing a box of tissues, I ducked my head in mortification. I'd somehow stumbled out of passionate fantasy into the harsh light of reality.

How had I allowed myself to make my potential my boss come? Even worse, how had he made me come?

With what little I knew about lap dances, the fact Quinn had come meant I'd done my job. However, none of my knowledge mentioned anything about it happening to me. Or that he would *want* to do it to me.

I kept my head down through the rustling of his pants and then the crinkling sound of a ball of tissues hitting the trash. It took everything within me to keep my mouth shut and not let my nervous ramblings trickle out of me. There were so many unanswered questions.

Besides what we shared sexually, there had been a definite connection between us. I never would've allowed what happened between us if there hadn't been. There was no way he could've kissed me the way that he did if he hadn't felt something for me as well.

Unable to hold it in any longer, I rose off the couch and started for him. But he quickly sidestepped me and went for the door. With his hand on the doorknob, Quinn turned back to me. "I'll tell Paula to get you on the schedule."

And then he was gone.

In a stupor, I stood in the middle of the room, bare-chested and with my cum still coating my thighs.

I'd gotten the job.

I'd had my first male-induced orgasm.

It had been a hell of a day.

At the knock on the door, I frantically snatched my top off the floor. "Yes?"

Paula peeked her head in. After eyeing me curiously, a smile twitched at the corner of her lips. "I hear congratulations are in order."

I bobbed my head. "Yes, Mr. Kavanaugh told me."

"You can start tomorrow night."

My mouth gaped open. "So soon?"

She laughed. "We don't have a training program here, so there's no reason not to get you in the rotation."

"Right. Sure. I can totally be here tomorrow."

"You can do your audition dance for the first week, and then we'll talk about switching things up."

I nodded. "Sounds good."

"Great. You can get dressed now."

"Thanks."

As I started over to my bag, Paula said, "I think you'll want to do that in the dressing room."

"Oh, okay."

She gave me a knowing smile. "We don't have any mirrors in here, and you'll want to fix your makeup."

And with that, she left me to my mortification.

"Oh my God!" I cried at my reflection in the dressing room mirror.

To my horror, my lipstick was a smeared mess, not to mention my mussed hair. Paula probably thought from the looks of me that Quinn had fucked my brains out. Embarrassment filled me that she probably thought that's why he'd given me the job.

When I made my way out into the main room of the club, I hightailed it over to the bar where I'd left Brooke. To my utter horror, a beer sat in front of her while a twenty-something looking guy chatted her up.

Or knowing Brooke, it was the other way around.

"Time to go," I said as I walked up.

While Brooke nodded, the guy reached out for her hand. "Do you really have to go?"

At Brooke's plastered-on smile, I realized she hadn't truly been interested in him and was just passing time. "Yeah, I do. It was nice talking to you, and thanks for the beer."

"Can I get your number?"

Brooke opened her mouth, but I interrupted her by saying, "Maybe in two years when she's actually twenty-one and is using a real ID, not a fake one."

With a snort, Brooke hopped off the stool and let me drag her off. "I can't believe you were talking to him."

She rolled her eyes. "Seriously? You took forever, and I was bored out of my mind. What else was I supposed to do?"

"Try not getting hit on by older men?"

"Whatever. He was harmless. So, how did it go?"

"I got the job."

She grinned. "I knew you had it when you started walking over. You were all glowy."

Her words caused me to stumble. "Are you okay?" Brooke asked.

"Um, yeah, totally fine." When she shot me a look, a nervous giggle burst from my lips. "Actually, I'm not okay. I mean, I'm good, but there's a reason why I'm good. And at the same time, a little confused."

"Isla, what the hell are you talking about?"

"I wasn't glowy because of getting the job. It was something else."

"They told you they'd never seen a better pole dancer before?"

"No, that's not it at all."

"Then what?"

"So, one of the owners gave me my lapdance audition. At first, I was like, 'I can't do this' and then he was all 'I'll teach you how'. And then—" My cheeks flushed at the memory while wetness pooled between my thighs.

"And what?" Brooke prompted.

As we stepped into the sunshine, I leaned into her ear and whispered, "He made me come."

Brooke's eyes popped comically wide. "He what?"

Glancing around us, I replied, "You heard me."

She slowly shook her head back and forth. "I'm just trying to understand how that happened with your *boss* of all men."

"Trust me. I'm just as clueless as you are."

"Was he hot?"

"Incredibly."

"Really? That's awesome. I mean, it was good to have a hottie to get you through your first time. It's not like all the dicks you have to ride will be attached to hot men."

Wrinkling my nose, I replied, "Thanks a lot."

"So what did he look like?"

"You might've seen him. He had to rush out at the end because of some emergency, so he might've come by the bar on the way out."

Her eyes widened. "Oh my God, I totally saw that commotion with all these men running around. First, there was drama with some woman screaming at this man, and then she ran out and he was hot on her heels. Then a few minutes passed and two other men were running past us."

"I bet one of them was Quinn."

"The guy with the strawberry blonde hair? Oh my God, Isla, he's so hot!"

I shook my head. "No, he had dark hair and was impossibly tall and built."

Brooke gasped as her hand flew to her mouth. "The scary as hell guy with the scars?"

"He's not scary," I huffed indignantly.

"Are you insane? Even Wesley was like, holy shit that was one of the owners who is quote, 'scary as hell'."

With a roll of my eyes, I countered, "He wasn't scary to me."

Brooke continued staring incredulously at me. "Is this the moment where you admit your deep dark secret of having crushes on serial killers?"

"Quinn is not a serial killer."

"He looks the part."

I scowled at her. "Maybe to you he does, but to me, he's hot."

"Regardless of his looks, the man has serious talent to make you come."

"I would agree."

"So how did he do it?"

"It's hard to describe. It was the most erotic thing I've ever experienced."

"Obviously since you've never come before."

Nudging her playfully, I replied, "Shut up." As we started for the car, I couldn't help the dreamy sigh that escaped my lips. "It was everything—his voice, his hands—"

"Wait, I thought they weren't supposed to be able to touch you?"

"They're not. Only him."

"So what, he fingerbanged you?"

I shook my head. "No, it wasn't like that. He didn't even have his hands on my breasts or my...you know."

Brooke rolled her eyes. "You're going to be a stripper, Isla. You need to say the word."

Jerking my shoulders back, I replied, "Fine. My *pussy*."

With a grin, Brooke raised her hand to high five me. "Good job."

Once I did, I said, "See, I'm not a total prude."

"Apparently not if you were able to get off without him touching you. Like did he look you in your eyes and compel you to do it?"

Giggling, I replied, "No. It was like the most intense dry-humping I've ever had. I don't know. Something about the friction coupled with the power of him just sent me over the edge."

"That's hot," Brooke remarked.

"It was."

"What happens now?"

"What do you mean?"

"Duh, do you go back for seconds?"

"He's my boss."

"Is there something in your contract that says you can't date him, least of all fuck him?"

"There was nothing in the NDA that I signed."

"Then you have free reign for more orgasms."

I drew my bottom lip between my teeth. Did I want more with Quinn? My body definitely wanted more physically with him. I couldn't imagine he would object if I broached the subject. But I couldn't see that happening. Despite Victor and our one-night-stand, I wasn't a girl who did sex without feelings.

And for the life of me I couldn't imagine dating Quinn. How could I possibly tell people where and how we met? It didn't seem like a good start if I had to lie about the very basic aspect of our relationship.

With a resigned sigh, I replied, "I don't know. The moral side of me thinks it's maybe not a good idea to be screwing my boss."

Unlocking the car doors, Brooke countered, "Since you're going to be a stripper, I think it's okay not to listen to your moral side."

"You bitch!" I teasingly shrieked.

She held her hands up. "Sorry. Just calling it like it is."

"It's more complicated than just screwing my boss."

"Why?"

After staring down at the ground, I replied, "Because I felt something when I kissed him."

"You felt his giant dick beneath you."

I snapped my gaze up to scowl at her. "I'm being serious."

Brooke's amusement faded. "You mean, you felt a real connection?"

I nodded. "Nothing seedy like a hookup." I swallowed hard. "Like a relationship."

"Did he say anything?"

"That's the worst part. After we got interrupted, he said he had to go and then reached for a box of tissues."

Brooke wrinkled her nose. "Ew. Really?"

"Unfortunately."

"That's grim."

"I thought as much." With a shrug, I replied, "Maybe he regretted getting carried away in the moment and didn't know what to say or do."

With a roll of her eyes, Brooke replied, "I doubt he was putting that much thought into it after just getting his rocks off."

A laugh bubbled from my lips. "Stop it."

Brooke grinned. "Come on. Forget about the scary boss man. Let's go pick up Henry, and grab a celebratory lunch to honor your new journey in stripperhood!"

"Sounds good."

Chapter Six: Quinn

As I swept through the employee entrance of *Alainn*, a wave of emotions hit me. The last time I'd come through the doors I'd been racing out to rescue Caterina. When Kellan had burst into the room and interrupted Isla's and my post orgasm haze, I would've never imagined it would be because Caterina had been kidnapped by her father and former fiancé.

Five days had passed since then. But in some ways, it felt like an eternity.

It was the first time I'd ever entered as the majority owner of the club. After Caterina's reaction to Callum owning a stake in a gentlemen's club, he had promised her to give it up. Instead of dividing it between Dare, Kellan, and me, he'd given his entire stake to me. When I'd questioned why, he'd replied, "You earned it for all the auditions."

My first order of business was to head to the bar. If I was even going to get through tonight, I was going to need a strong whiskey. I waved over Conleth, the bartender.

At the sight of me, a broad smile stretched across his face. "Good to have you back, boss."

"Thanks. Give me my usual."

With a nod, he grabbed the whiskey. As he poured the tumbler he asked, "How's Mrs. Kavanaugh?"

I smiled at the reference to her. Besides my mother and my sister, there wasn't another woman I cared about as much as I did Caterina. She was more than just my sister-in-law—she had become my sister.

"Like a complete and total badass, she's making a full recovery." That's all I could think of to describe how physically and emotionally strong Caterina was. After surviving a kidnapping by her bastard father and psycho ex-fiance, she had endured a traumatic beating that thankfully didn't result in the loss of her early pregnancy.

Thanks to help from her brothers we had located her quickly and stormed in to rescue her. When Callum found her unconscious, he had scooped her up and rushed her to a waiting ambulance. The rest of us were left to take care of Caterina's father's men.

Once that threat had been neutralized, the only two men left standing were Alessio, Caterina's father, and Carmine Lucero—the man she had once been promised to in an arranged marriage.

Callum had given us strict instructions that Alessio would be dealt with by Caterina's brothers. Besides kidnapping their sister and allowing a man to beat her to try to force a miscarriage, Raphael, Leandro, and Gianni Neretti had a lifetime of trauma related to their father much like my brothers and I did.

Instead, we'd turned our attention to Carmine. All the worry and fear for Caterina bled out through our fists. At that time, we didn't know if she and the baby would live. So, we had inflicted as much pain and suffering as we could.

It had been quite cathartic.

Of course, we refrained from finishing him off. That honor belonged to Callum. As for Alessio, we had tied him up and forced him to watch Carmine's beating. Just as we were finishing up with Carmine, Caterina's brothers arrived from New York.

Two years ago, I stood to the side as I watched Callum raise a gun to the head of our father. Because of the unexpected coup that had unfolded between us and our father, we didn't have the time to inflict the torture he deserved.

Instead, it had fallen to Callum as the first son and future leader to pull the trigger.

For the Neretti brothers, they didn't have a time limit, so they were able to pay back the sins of the father before they snuffed out his life. Dare, Kellan, and I were gone by then. Although we'd gotten word that Caterina would recover and that their daughter was as strong as her mother, we still wanted to go to the hospital to be there for Callum.

"Is she still in the hospital?"

With a shake of my head, I replied, "As soon as she woke up, Callum insisted on bringing her home. He has round-the-clock nurses taking care of her, which is completely pissing Caterina off."

Conleth laughed. "I'd say the ol' boyo has met his match."

"Aye. He has and then some," I mused before throwing back my whiskey.

As Conleth reached to refill my glass, I asked, "How have things been around here?"

"The new dancer is making quite a name for herself."

At the mention of Isla, my cock twitched in my pants. In the past five days, each and every moment I wasn't focused on eradicating the impending Bratva threat, my mind had been on the petite blonde.

The taste of her eager mouth.

The smell of her arousal in my nose.

The feel of her breasts in my hands.

The wild abandon on her face when she came.

Despite all the sexual reminders, there were also the ones of her kindness. Her acceptance of my scars. Her nervous rambling coupled with the conviction of her character.

I couldn't remember any woman having as much affect on me. In the short amount of time we were together, Isla made me desire something I hadn't in years.

A relationship.

But I'm sure I'd managed to fuck that up considering the way I'd left things between us. I'd acted like an utter and complete bastard to her. There had been so many things I wanted to say to her at that moment, but instead, I'd only shut down.

It was like my mind had short-circuited the moment Kellan appeared to demand I come with him. I couldn't process anything in that moment except the fear of whatever had led Callum to seek our help. I went straight into enforcer mode, and there was no place for any feelings for Isla.

As Conleth refilled my whiskey, he brought me out of my thoughts. Trying not to sound like Isla was anything more than a dancer, I replied, "She's a new piece of ass. Of course, she's popular," I said.

"I'd wager she stays popular for quite awhile."

The whiskey burned harsher down my throat. "What makes you say that?"

When a lascivious grin stretched across his face, I fought the urge to knock it off his face. "With her innocence coupled with those tits and that ass, she's going to be raking in the dough for the club."

"Good for us," I muttered around the mouth of my glass.

"Speak of the devil," Conleth mused. When he jerked his chin at the stage, I swiveled on the stool to focus on the stage.

With a techno version of *Material Girl* playing, Isla swayed her hips on the stage. Her pink corset and thong were encrusted with diamonds. Pink elbow length gloves covered her arms while a long pink wig flowed down to her ass. Although it looked good on her, I missed her blonde waves.

"She's pretty in pink, eh?" Conleth chuckled.

"She sure is fuck is," I replied before I could think better of it.

Answering Isla's siren song, I grabbed my glass of whiskey and rose off the stool to get closer to the stage. Once I found an empty table, I eased down into a chair.

As if she felt my eyes on her, Isla met my gaze as she spun upside down. A smile flickered on her lips before she turned her focus back on her dance. She made the intense aerobatics look effortless.

While her legs kept her balance, her torso came free from the pole. Bringing her arms around her back, she undid her top. At the sight of her bare breasts, my cock slammed against my zipper, causing me to shift in my seat.

Jesus, what was happening to me? In the two years we'd owned *Alainn*, I'd never gotten hard from simply seeing a dancer's breasts. If anything, I'd gotten desensitized to them.

At the sound of someone beside me, I pulled the table closer, trying to hide my erection. "What the hell are you doing out in the crowd?" Dare asked as he plopped down beside me.

Reluctantly, I tore my eyes off of Isla. "Just having a drink."

He frowned. "You never have a drink out here."

With a shrug, I replied, "You know, I'm not such an OCD hardass that I don't mix things up sometimes."

Dare snorted. "Whatever."

As Isla slunk down the stage towards us, Dare's disinterested stare focused on Isla. He did a double take before shaking his head. "Feck me, she's a bleedin' vision," he murmured.

I shifted in my chair. This time it wasn't my cock making me uncomfortable but instead it was Dare's hungry appraisal of Isla. While many of the other men wore the same expression, it didn't get to me as much as it did with Dare.

"She's the new dancer you auditioned the day Caterina was kidnapped?"

"Aye."

Dare ran his tongue over his lips. "She's seriously exquisite."

Although I gritted my teeth at his remark, I replied, "She's very talented."

Tearing his gaze from the stage, Dare wagged his brows at me. "Is she now? I guess that means her audition went very well."

"You know if it hadn't, she wouldn't be up there." As I watched Isla effortlessly spin, I said, "She came in here working the pole better than most of the girls who have been here for years."

"Fuck that. I want to know about her working *your* pole during the audition."

I snorted. "You're a sick shite, you know that?"

He grinned. "Come on, man. Anyone with a half working cock would be creaming their pants to have her grinding on them."

My mind rocketed back to that day. How I'd come so fucking hard in my pants for Isla. I couldn't imagine how intense it would've been to actually be inside her.

Dare's eyes bulged. "I knew it!"

"What?"

"She made you come. That's never fucking happened before, has it?" When I didn't reply, he grinned at me. "I can't blame you, mate. Mm, as soon as she comes off that stage, I'm taking her for a private dance."

"Not bloody likely," I snapped.

"Excuse me?"

I cut my eyes over to Dare's incredulous face. "I said it's not happening."

"Why the fuck not?" Dare demanded.

There wasn't any reason I could give him that didn't involve me outing my feelings for Isla. Once I did that, I knew he and Callum would ride my ass constantly about it. Whatever there was between us, it was too precious to have it tainted by my brothers.

"Because you and I both know you don't shit where you eat."

"It's never stopped us before."

Dammit. He had me there. In the past, we'd all sampled from the feast of women the club provided.

"Well, it's going to stop with Isla. She's getting along well with the other girls. If one of the owners seeks her out, it'll cause contention with the others."

Dare busted out laughing. "Seriously, Mate? *That's* the best excuse you could come up with?"

With a shrug, I replied, "I'm just stating facts. You know how the girls can be. Isla's already the most sought after girl, which is only going to spark jealousy."

"Cut the bullshit."

"I'm not."

Clapping me on the back, Dare shot me a serious look. "Quinn, you know it's more than okay for you to use her whenever your dick gets hard."

With a growl, I shoved him, causing his eyes to pop wide. "Don't talk about her like that. Isla is so much more than a wet hole for my cock."

A smirk curved on his lips. "Just as I thought. You want more than to fuck her."

"I do not."

"Yes, you do."

"Feck off."

"With all seriousness brother, there's nothing wrong with you dating her."

I grunted. "I'm the last thing that wee lass needs."

Dare playfully rolled his eyes. "Yeah, just what every girl hates: a rich, handsome man who is obsessed with her," he teased

"You and I both know that I come with seen and unseen baggage that negates all that."

While I expected sympathy, if not pity, to reflect in Dare's eyes, I wasn't prepared for the growl of frustration. "Don't fucking run yourself down in my presence, boyo."

With a mirthless laugh, I replied, "It's my physical and emotional trauma, and I'll deal with it how I please."

Dare shook his head. "Not if it means refusing to see things for what they are."

"And what is that exactly?"

"That despite what you went through in the bombing you are still a very eligible bachelor who that lass would be very lucky to land."

As I stared into his intense blue eyes, I appreciated his comment more than he could ever imagine. Unable to express that in words, I merely nodded at him. "While all that might be true, let's not forget for one minute that you and I both have our cocks on the block for arranged marriages. Last time I checked, Isla's family isn't someone we need an alliance with."

Dare's lip curled in disgust. "Neither of us has to take part in that bullshit."

"Protecting the family through strong alliances isn't bullshit," I growled.

"There are other ways to do it that don't involve a marriage."

"You sure didn't voice that when it was Callum's cock for the taking."

"Our position was completely different then, not to mention Callum is the oldest."

Shaking my head, I replied, "With Bratva breathing down our necks, we need to align ourselves now more than ever."

When we'd murdered Catererina's ex fiance, Carmine, it had kicked open a hornet's nest with Bratva. Carmine had just married his seventeen-year-old daughter off to the son of the Pahkan in Jersey. When Mikita Komarov realized he'd given his first born son to a fucked alliance, he had taken his anger out of us as well as Caterina's brothers.

"Then let Callum put Kellan and Eamon on the market in our place. Hell, Seamus is only forty-six. He'd make a good alliance when it's all said and done, not to mention it would do him good to have a wife and family after Elena and Rian's deaths."

"They're fourth and fifth sons. They aren't as attractive a match as we are as the second and third sons. As for Seamus, you know he's voiced wanting to find a widow to take care of him."

Dare sighed. "Don't you think you're getting your knickers in a twist for no reason? I mean, has Callum or Seamus even broached the subject of a marriage for you?"

"No." At Dare's knowing look, I argued, "But they've been busy."

"Regardless of whether you're about to be married off, you can still have a little fun with her."

I shook my head. "Isla isn't the type just to fuck around with. She's the kind of girl you settle down with."

"Is she now?" Dare mused.

"Aye. Because of that, I'm prepared to make it known that she doesn't ride anybody in the clan's dick." I gave him a knowing look. "My brothers included."

He had the audacity to wink at me. "Like I would ever make a play for her knowing how you feel."

"I appreciate that."

A wicked gleam burned in his eyes. "That's not to say I won't be thinking of her the next time I wank off."

I shoved him so hard he fell out of his chair. "Bastard," I muttered under my breath as he chuckled on the floor.

Once Isla's dance was over and I'd left Dare laughing at my expense, I made my way back to my office. As I walked over to my desk, my thoughts weren't about the growing Bratva threat or making my way through the mountain of business receipts.

Tonight I had a singular focus.

And it was all on Isla.

Watching her work the pole had worked me up. The image of her swaying hips, bouncing tits, and jiggling ass made my cock rock hard. Because I'd had a wee taste, she was beyond just a fantasy now.

She was an all-out obsession.

But one I couldn't act on.

After flopping down into my chair, I opened my laptop. Once I entered the security program, I eyed the many screens before me. Each gave a birds eye view in each of the private rooms.

I slid my finger across the tracking pad to the room where a pink wig stood out among all the others. When her voluptuous body came into focus, my erection clawed to be free. But I ignored it for a moment.

Instead, I remained captivated by the woman in front of me. Through the speakers came a sultry R&B beat. I couldn't help being surprised it wasn't another Taylor Swift song.

She motioned for a middle-aged man in a business suit to have a seat on the couch. After shedding his jacket, he obliged. Once he got comfortable, Isla went into her dance. She'd been right about being a fast learner. She integrated all the moves I'd shown her.

As I watched her hips sway in front of her client, I made quick work of undoing my belt and unbuttoning my pants. Lifting my hips, I pushed my slacks and underwear down over my thighs.

With precum leaking from the tip of my cock, it bucked against my stomach. After bringing my hand to my mouth, I spit into my palm. As Isla's top hit the ground, I tugged my fist up my erection, mixing my saliva with the precum. The sensation caused me to hiss.

When Isla straddled the guy, I remembered how her warm thighs had pillowed mine. The way her white-hot core had scorched against my dick through my pants. She rolled her hips just as I'd taught her the other day. From the pleasure etched across the guy's face and his moans and grunts, he was enjoying her abilities.

At that moment, I couldn't help being jealous of the bastard. I wanted it to be my cock she was riding. Of course, I had something he didn't have. I knew what her silky skin felt like under my fingertips. The weight of her luscious tits in my hands. The taste of her tongue and lips.

My hips rose and fell in time with hers as I pumped my hand harder and harder. My fingers were a shitty substitute for Isla's thong-clad pussy. "Oh fuck!" the guy shouted as his hips surged forward. His fingers gripped the expensive leather as he rode out his orgasm.

As Isla rose from his lap and turned to the camera, I focused on her tits. A cry barked from my lips as I imagined shooting my cum on them, marking her as mine and only mine.

But when I came back to myself, I realized I could never act on my fantasy. She wasn't mine to take. Nothing good would come to her by getting involved with me.

Chapter Seven: Isla

As I made my way to the bar to settle up on tips, I couldn't believe I'd been dancing at *Alainn* for a week. The past seven days had flown in a flurry of sequins and beading, dollar bills, and very appreciative male attention.

In all honesty, I actually enjoyed it. I got to do something I loved–dancing–while making extremely good money. I'd gotten over being topless after the second day, and thankfully, we weren't asked to take off our g-strings.

The only thing I didn't enjoy was the private dances. It went without saying that Quinn had spoiled me for the act. Regardless of how handsome or sexy the man was, it did nothing for me.

I worked hard to mask the repulsion I felt as their erections pressed into my ass or my core–especially when they didn't bother hiding their wedding bands. Just as Quinn had assured me, no one was allowed to touch me. The one time a client had grabbed my breast one of the bouncers quickly appeared from the doorway to remind him if he wanted to continue coming to the club, he'd keep his hands to himself.

Despite what we had experienced together, Quinn had barely said more than hello to me since he'd returned to the club. While he might not have said anything to me, he'd watched my set from start to finish. The intensity of his gaze on me was unnerving. I tried reasoning with myself he was probably just making sure he'd made the right choice to hire me.

I couldn't help being curious about him. Everyone from the dancers to the bouncers seemed to shy away from him. On his first night back at the club, I walked up to him after my set to say hello. Conleth's mouth dropped obscenely wide like he couldn't believed I'd dared to approach Quinn, least of all give him a pleasant greeting.

After Quinn returned my hello with a tight smile, Conleth fumbled with the whiskey bottle he was pouring. I don't know what was more shocking: that I, a lowly dancer, had braved the beast to say hello, or the fact Quinn had returned the greeting.

Tonight as I worked on my makeup in the dressing room, I decided to try to dig up a little gossip about him with the two girls who had been the nicest to me, Mabry and Lenora. They'd both been dancing at *Alainn* for two years. Mabry was a finance major at Boston College while Lenora was a psych major at UMASS Boston.

"So, it's good seeing Quinn back at the club," I remarked in my most casual voice.

Lenora snorted. "Excuse me? Did you just call Mr. Kavanaugh by his first name?"

I winced. "Oh, um, are we not supposed to?"

She slid a tube of red lipstick across her lips. "You won't if you know what's good for you."

Embarrassment tinged my cheeks. "My bad."

Mabry smiled at me in the mirror. "It's fine, Isla. You're still learning the ins and outs of the job." As she fluffed her dark hair, she said, "As for Mr. Kavanaugh, I'm glad he's back, too."

Lenora made a face. "Seriously?"

With a nod, Mabry replied, "Whenever he isn't here, clients always try to get more handsy. Just knowing he's in the building or his brothers makes me feel so much safer."

"His brothers run just as tight a ship, and I'll take them over him any day."

Nibbling my lip, I wondered what it was about Quinn, uh, Mr. Kavanaugh that made her have such a strong reaction. "Has he been an asshole to you?"

"Isn't he to everyone?" Lenora replied.

A nervous laugh tumbled from my lips. "Well, yeah, but I mean has he done something to make you so angry?"

Lenora shook her head. "No. It's not like that."

"Then what is it?" I prompted.

She sighed. "I hate the whole beast attitude that he conveys that makes everyone, including myself, cower in fear."

Mabry nudged Lenora playfully. "That's because you hate alpha men, and Mr. Kavanaugh is the King of Alphas."

Wrinkling her nose, Lenora replied, "True. Very true."

Since I still hadn't learned much, I asked, "Was he on vacation this week?"

"His sister-in-law was kidnapped," Mabry replied, which caused Lenora to hiss her name.

The glittery eyeshadow palette in my hand fell to the floor. "Excuse me?"

Mabry bent over to grab the palette. As she handed it to me, she replied, "Yeah, it happened the day of your audition."

At her words, my mind went back to Kellan interrupting us. "That's horrible!"

"Thankfully, they found her quickly, and she's recovering now," Mabry said.

"I can't even begin to imagine how life-altering it would be to be kidnapped."

"From what I hear, she was used to it," Lenora quipped.

"What?" I questioned to which Mabry quickly replied, "Nothing."

After shooting Lenora a look in the mirror, Mabry said, "Mrs. Kavanaugh is recovering at home now."

"So, Mr. Kavanaugh has been absent helping his brother with her recovery?" I questioned as I slid the pink eyeshadow over one of my lids.

Lenora snickered beside me. "What?"

With a grin, Mabry draped her arm over my shoulder. Her dark eyes danced with amusement. "Sometimes I forget how fresh and naive you are."

Jerking my chin up, I replied, "Then be a good Mother Hen and educate me, so I can stop feeling like such an outsider."

She scoffed. "Girl, I'm not old enough to be your mother."

"My auntie?"

Lenora laughed. "You better watch it before you get your ass kicked, Newbie."

I widened my eyes. "But I was only joking. I swear, I wouldn't dare insult you."

Mabry playfully smacked Lenora. "She's just teasing. While I'd prefer being your slightly older sister, I'll take auntie."

At my exhale of relief, Lenora said, "Go on and educate the girl, Sis."

"Why can't you?" Mabry countered.

"Oh no. I wouldn't touch that with a ten-foot pole."

A shiver ghosted down my spine. "Okay, you can stop teasing me because you're seriously starting to scare me."

The amusement on Mabry's face faded. After glancing over her shoulder to scan the dressing room, she whispered, "This knowledge is powerful. Where there is power, there is danger."

"You mean, it's dangerous for you just to talk about this?" When she nodded, fear overcame me. Shaking my head, I replied, "Then I don't want to know."

"It's probably better than you don't," Lenora replied.

I was grateful I'd already finished lining my eyes since my fingers were trembling. When Mabry's hand came to my shoulder, I jumped. After I jerked my gaze to hers, she gave me a reassuring smile. "Just keep your head down, do your job, and you won't have any problems."

"I will."

At that moment, Paula stuck her head in the dressing room. "Isla, you're up."

Although I remained physically and emotionally shaky from the conversation, I plastered a smile to my face. "Coming."

To say I was slightly on edge after talking with Mabry and Lenora would be an understatement. While I'd set out to get answers about Quinn, I'd ended up with even more questions. Some that I didn't think I wanted answers to.

But I managed to set aside my fears about Quinn and do my job. After my set, I stayed busy right up until closing with private dances. With each dick I rode, I focused on reworking the labs I'd done last quarter. Anything to not think about the man in front of me or Quinn.

Once all the clients had left for the night, I made my way to the bar to close out. At the sight of me, the bartender, Sarah's, eyes lit up. "Hey Isla, while I close you out, could you run this liquor invoice up to the boss's office?"

At the prospect of seeing Quinn, I swallowed hard. "Um, why me?"

Sarah grinned. "Because you're the only one he doesn't growl or grunt around."

"He doesn't?"

She popped her brows at me. "You haven't noticed?"

"Not really. I mean, I haven't been here that long."

"Conleth said the boss actually *smiled* at you last night."

"Yes, but—"

"That's pretty much unheard of, which means you're the best person to take this to him."

Since I didn't think there was any way I was getting out of it, I reached out to take the invoice. "I'll be right back."

On shaky legs, I spun away from the bar and went over to the elevator. As I stepped inside, I couldn't fight the anxiety building in my chest. When we reached the second floor, the ding caused me to jump out of my skin. "Get a grip, Isla."

Pushing myself forward, I started down the long hallway, my heels clicking along the floor. When I reached the office, I froze with my fist in the air. I don't know how long I stayed like that before I finally knocked on the door.

Shifting on my heels, I nibbled on my lip as I waited for a response. When no one came, I decided to knock harder.

Still nothing.

"Um, Mr. Kavanaugh?" I called, my voice echoing through the silent hallway.

When I tried the doorknob, I found it unlocked. Easing it open, I peeked inside, praying I didn't find Quinn screwing some dancer.

The room was darkened with just the desk lamps emitting shadowy light. "Mr. Kavanaugh?" I called.

Once again, I didn't receive an answer. Sarah hadn't specified that I had to deliver it directly into his hands. Surely, I could leave it on his desk without a problem.

Easing through the crack I'd made in the door, I hightailed it as quickly as I could over to his desk. After dropping it in the center, I spun around to make a run for it. That's when I heard a long, guttural groan.

I gasped before my hand flew to my mouth. Slowly, I turned my attention to the private bathroom. Light seeped out from the bottom of the door.

Since I wasn't sure if it was a sex groan or one of pain, I decided it was best to get the hell out of there. When I started to the door, my heel slid in something wet on the floor. A shriek escaped my lips as my arms and legs flailed as I tried not to fall.

Just as I'd righted myself, the bathroom door flung open. Quinn lunged out, training a gun on me.

Once again, a shriek escaped my lips as my hands flew up to shield me. "Please, it's just me, Isla."

Quinn immediately jerked the gun down to his side. "What the fuck are you doing?"

"S-Sarah asked me t-to bring up an invoice." Jerking my thumb over my shoulder, I added, "When no one came to the door, I just put it on your desk."

Quinn's cold eyes continued to apprise me. "Get the fuck out of here."

"Yes, sir."

Before I turned to go, my gaze traveled down his body. To my surprise, his white shirt was untucked and unbuttoned. Both dark and bright red blood stained one side. It was then that I realized what I had slid on.

Blood.

"Oh my God, you're hurt!" Before I could think better of it, I rushed over to him.

When my hand came up to touch his side, he smacked it away. "I said, get the fuck out of here!"

I shook my head before repeating, "You're hurt."

"No shit," he snarled.

"Let me call an ambulance."

A sinister chuckle erupted from him. "You're so naïve, aren't you, Little Dove?"

Furrowing my brows, I asked, "What do you mean?"

Quinn drew in a deep breath, which caused him to wince. "An ambulance brings police sniffing around, and that's the last thing I need."

"I'm sure you need stitches."

"I do."

"Then why are you still standing here and not going to a hospital?" I demanded.

He cocked his head at me. "For the same fucking reason I won't call an ambulance."

"Did you hit your head as well? Because you're not making any sense."

Amusement danced in Quinn's eyes. "No, I don't have a head injury."

"Then let me drive you to the hospital." When he still continued smirking at me, I added, "Please."

The mirth faded from his eyes. "You would do that?"

As I bobbed my head, I reached for his hand. With a futile tug, I pleaded, "Come with me."

Seconds inched by as Quinn stared at me. His gaze dropped to where our hands were joined before he brought his eyes back to my face. Finally, he closed the gap between us.

As he towered over me, electricity crackled between us, and I couldn't help taking a step back. "Do you want to help me because I'm your boss, or because I made you come?" he asked.

Jerking my hand from his, I sucked in a disbelieving breath at his words. The room seemed to spin with his emotional whiplash. "How can you be talking about *that* at a time like this?"

"Answer my question."

"I would help you because I care about people in need, and you're obviously in need."

"I'm always in need when you're around," he replied in a gravelly voice.

When I dared to look up into his eyes, heat surged between my legs at the desire in his. "Are you in need too?"

"You're hurt," I protested.

A smirk curved on his lips. "I'd have to be dying not to want to meet your needs."

"Considering all the blood you've lost, it's possible you could be," I argued.

"The bullet only grazed me."

I swayed on my knees, which caused Quinn to reach out to steady me. "A bullet?" I questioned in a pained whisper.

"Yes. Since it's not the first time it's happened, I know I'm not knocking at death's door." When I stared at him wide-eyed and open-mouthed, he said, "I've popped a Percocet for the pain along with some Motrin for the inflammation. I've called our family doctor to come in to stitch me up. I had planned to clean the wound while I waited for him, but then someone interrupted me."

Slowly, I nodded my head as I processed his words. I'd never seen a gunshot wound, nor did I know anyone who had ever been shot. Growing up, I'd been sheltered from the harsher realities of the world and living in the city.

"But how did you get shot? Did someone try to mug you on the street? I know this is a good area, but no offense, you probably brought it on yourself by the way you look."

Quinn's blue eyes narrowed. "Excuse me?"

"To a thief, you look like a flashy guy with your expensive suits and your watch. You're the perfect target. I bet you drive an expensive car as well, don't you?"

Quinn's blood-stained hand came to cup my chin. "You are the purest of souls, Isla Vaughn."

"Why do you say that?"

"Because despite what I told you the other night, you still refuse to believe that *I'm* the bad man. That whatever happened to me tonight was my fault because of who *I* am."

Scrunching my brows, I asked, "Why would I think that?"

"I guess you haven't been here long enough for the rumors to make it to your innocent ears."

The conversation with Mabry and Lenora flashed before my eyes. "I might have heard some things," I whispered.

He cocked his head at me. "About me and my family?"

Nodding, I replied, "Your sister-in-law was kidnapped."

Quinn's blue eyes darkened. "Aye, she was. She would've been raped and a miscarriage forced on her if we hadn't rescued her."

As my stomach rolled, my hand flew to my mouth. "Oh God."

Leaning back against the bathroom door, he prompted, "What else did *they* say?"

"They said–" I swallowed hard. "They said that it was dangerous to know more, so I told them I didn't want to know."

"They're correct, and you're smart."

"But..."

"But what, Little Dove?"

"I don't think you're dangerous," I murmured.

"You're so naive."

The synapses in my brain shorted out as all the possibilities of who and what Quinn was ran through my mind. "Do you do bad things to women?"

"Never," he spat.

A relieved breath whooshed from my lips. "Do you do bad things to men?"

"Aye."

With my chest clenching, I could only croak, "But why?"

"It's who I am and what I do."

Shaking my head, I replied, "I don't believe you."

"You yourself said I'm an asshole."

Warmth rushed to my cheeks. "I shouldn't have said that."

"You were only being honest."

"Even if I think you're an asshole, I don't think you're capable of hurting people."

"Do you know what it means to belong to an Irish clan?"

My stomach recoiled. "Like you dress up in bedsheets and hate on anyone who isn't white?"

Quinn stared at me before a laugh burst from his lips. "Jaysus, Mary, and Joseph, I'm not talking about the bleedin' KKK."

"Thank God," I murmured.

"In Ireland, a clan is like a gang. Here in America the closest comparison is the mafia."

My hand flew to my mouth as I realized what Lenora and Mabry had been referencing. "You're in the mafia?" I whispered.

"You don't have to whisper. The club is swept every day to make sure the Feds or our enemies haven't placed any bugs."

Oh God. How could this be possible? I was working in a club owned by the Irish mafia.

"You're in the mafia," I said, this time as a statement and not a question."

"Aye, my family is head of an Irish clan that includes not just Boston, but Belfast as well. My older brother, Callum, is the leader, and I'm the enforcer."

"I need to sit down." After Quinn motioned to the couch, I flopped down on the cool leather. "My boss is in the mafia."

A wicked grin flashed on his face. "The only man to ever make you come is in the mafia."

With that summation, I rose onto shaky legs and started across the floor. "Where are you going?" Quinn demanded.

I motioned to the liquor cart. "I need a drink."

Chapter Eight: Quinn

With amusement, I watched Isla shakily pour a tumbler of whiskey. I would've wagered a hundred bucks that she'd never had a sip in her life. When she threw back a determined gulp, I held my breath.

Her eyes bulged before the amber liquid spewed from her lips. "Oh God."

I snorted. "Not your taste?"

"It's horrible."

"Why am I not surprised, Little Dove?"

With a curious look, Isla pursed her lips at me. "Why do you keep calling me that?"

"Doves are birds of peace and innocence. Those are qualities you possess."

She rolled her eyes. "I'd hardly call me dancing in a gentleman's club innocent."

"Compared to someone in my world, you are innocent."

"I guess." She tilted her head at me. "I suppose I could say you're corrupting me."

A growl came from low in my chest as the monster thought of all the ways I could corrupt her beautiful body. I knew I had to get away from her.

When Isla's blue eyes widened, I said, "Stay here. I need to get cleaned up."

"I can help you."

I snorted. "You got squeamish at me just saying the word bullet."

"I can handle it." At my continued disbelief, she countered, "I'm a scientist, remember? I'm used to handling all kinds of gross things."

When I opened my mouth to tell her okay, I quickly shut it. If she was to help me, she'd have to see me without my shirt.

Without my shirt, she'd see the rest of my scars.

I couldn't let that happen. It was one thing to see them on my face and neck, it was another to see them down my side. Regardless of her initial interest in them, I couldn't bear to see revulsion reflected in her eyes.

I'd rather take another fucking bullet.

"It's okay. I can do it myself."

She playfully rolled her eyes. "Quit being so stubborn and let me do it."

When she took a step towards me, I stepped back. Throwing up my hands, I snapped, "What is it with you? I said I don't need your fucking help."

Isla's blonde brows furrowed. "I'm sorry." After gnawing on her lip, she said, "I'll just go."

As she started for the door, I grabbed her arm. "Don't go."

"But you—"

"I was being an asshole."

She shook her head. "I shouldn't have pressured you."

"Stop arguing and start helping me."

With a huff, she replied, "Fine."

As Isla followed me into the bathroom, I inwardly groaned at the bright lights that were about to highlight my scars. I would've given anything to turn them off. To save more than her from having to see them.

With a grimace, I eased the shirt off my shoulders and down my arms. At Isla's gasp, I froze. When I dared to look at her, she wasn't staring at my scars. Instead, her gaze was on my still gaping wound. "T-That looks h-horrible."

I quirked my brows at her. "What happened to being a scientist?"

Crimson dotted her cheeks. "It's a lot different seeing things in the lab."

"Does that mean you're not going to help me clean my wound?"

"Maybe if you can distract me."

"Shouldn't you be the one doing that to me?" I countered.

Her shaky hand reached for the gauze and alcohol that I had put out on the counter. "Yes. But in this case, I'm going to be selfish."

My chuckle was short-lived when she gently swiped the gauze across the wound. I sucked in a harsh breath. With gritted teeth, I said, "The first time I saw you I thought you could be the Irish goddess and faerie queen, Cliodna."

"Why?"

"Because in our folklore, she was considered to be the most beautiful woman in the world."

Isla's hand froze. She jerked her focus from my wound to my eyes. "You think I'm beautiful?" she questioned softly.

I shook my head. "No. I think you're the most beautiful woman in the world."

Her cheeks reddened. "Thank you, but I think you're exaggerating."

"I can assure you I'm not. Every man at this club thinks the same thing I do."

A nervous giggle fluttered from her lips. "Stop. You're embarrassing me."

"Don't tell me you're not used to men complimenting you."

She shrugged. "Sometimes."

"Then you must've been around more boys than men. Of course, I suppose that should've been evident with your lack of orgasms."

"Quinn!" she admonished.

A laugh barked from me at her outrage. "It's the truth."

"Can we please change the subject? I'm more than just my looks, you know."

"Oh yes, I'm well aware of that."

She smiled shyly. "What else was special about that Irish goddess besides her beauty?"

"Cliodna possessed three magical birds. It's said their song was so sweet they could send the wounded and sick into a peaceful sleep."

"Avian anesthesia," she mused.

With a laugh, I replied, "That's right." I stared into her eyes. "Cliodna's birds are another reason why I call you dove."

Isla didn't respond. Instead, she worked at cleaning the dried blood on my abdomen. When my muscles involuntarily clenched under her fingers, I sucked in a breath. Her gaze shot to mine. "Did I hurt you?"

"It depends on your definition of hurt."

Her brows furrowed in confusion. "Sorry. I'll be easier."

"But I like it rough."

At her gasp of realization, I leaned in, my blood-stained hands cupped her alabaster cheeks. When I stared into her eyes, desire shined back at me. Dipping my head, my lips brushed against hers.

At her tiny moan, I deepened the kiss, my tongue licking at the seam of her mouth.

A shudder went through me at the taste.

So sweet.

So pure.

So addicting.

At the buzzing in my pants pocket, she jerked away from me. "Fuck," I grunted, as I fished my phone out. "What?" I demanded.

Silence echoed on the line. After a few seconds, a throat cleared. "I'm terribly sorry to bother you, Mr. Kavanaugh. Is Isla with you?"

"She is."

"Oh, okay. I just wanted to make sure. She hadn't returned from delivering the receipts to you, and I need to cash her out."

"I'll send her back down shortly."

"Yes, sir."

When I hung up, I stared into Isla's expectant blue eyes. "As usual, my reputation precedes me."

"What do you mean?"

"Sarah just called to check on you."

"Seriously? Why would she be worried?"

"Because you were with me." I waggled my brows. "The monster."

"The *asshole*," she corrected with a teasing smile.

A deep chuckle rumbled through my chest. "Right."

At that moment, my office door whipped open, and Shane stepped inside with one of the doctors on our payroll. "I'd like to go a whole week without having to patch up someone from your clan," Dr. Feeny remarked with his usual sour expression.

"Mine isn't as bad as what Callum just put you through."

Isla glanced between me and Dr. Feeny. "Well, I better go and cash out."

"Thank you for bringing those files and helping clean me up," I said.

"You're welcome. Please get some rest and take care of yourself."

"I'll try."

Smiling, she replied, "You better."

For a moment, I thought she might give me a kiss goodbye. Instead, she hurried past Shane and Dr. Feeny and out the door. When I saw their questioning expressions, I rolled my eyes. "Don't fucking ask."

Chapter Nine: Quinn

"Come on, Quinn, say yes," Caterina pleaded.

As I stared across my desk at my very persuasive sister-in-law, I shook my head with a chuckle. "Now I know why Callum never stands a chance when it comes to you."

A smirk curved across her lips. "What can I say? It's a gift that I can charm each and every one of the Kavanaugh men."

Dare snorted in the chair next to her. "Aye, you sure as hell do, especially since Quinn and I don't reap the same benefits as Callum."

Caterina shrieked in horror at his innuendo before playfully smacking his arm. "Dare, I can't believe you said that."

He grinned at her. "After eight months of being blessed with my presence, it's an honor that I can still shock you."

"Since I like your handsome face as it is, I'll refrain from telling Callum of your remark," she huffed.

I barked a laugh. "Watch out, boyo. She's going to snitch on you."

Dare held his hands up. "You're the one denying Callum's pregnant wife her heart's desire."

After rolling my eyes at Dare, I focused on Caterina. "Is my eejit brother correct about this mission you want to do?"

When she bobbed her dark head eagerly, I groaned. "Speaking of Callum, how can he possibly be on board with this? Especially when you made him give up his stake in *Alainn*."

"Because he sees it as a way for me to make peace with darker aspects of this family. Considering my background, it gives me a way to merge my past and present," she replied.

I flicked my gaze over to Dare who shrugged. With our line of work, it was hard to shock us, but when Caterina had appeared at my office door with a proposition involving the club, I was fucking floored.

Since her marriage to Callum, Caterina had insisted on continuing some aspects of her former life as a novice nun. In between nursing school and the social duties of being Callum's wife, she served others. Some days it was in the soup kitchen at our church and others it was the women's shelter.

But her proposed idea was a doozy. After coming across a post on social media, she learned about some clubs having House Mothers. It was a term given to a woman who not only cooked every night for the dancers, but she also counseled and encouraged them.

We currently employed two women who helped with the music, costumes, and makeup. They cued the girls on stage and set up their private dances. Caterina wanted no part in that, so it wasn't like we would have to lay off anyone.

She argued that since all of our dancers were college coeds or girls seeking a better life, they needed a female to have their back.

She also knew that most weren't getting proper nutrition, and as a ridiculously good cook, she wanted to use her talents in that area.

Although it sounded like a win/win for both Caterina and my brothers, I still wasn't completely sold on the idea. When I opened my mouth to voice that, Shane poked his head in the door. "Excuse me, Sir."

"I believe I said I was not to be interrupted," I blared.

"I know that, sir, but there's someone here who is insisting on delivering something to you."

When Dare palmed his gun, Caterina sucked in a harsh breath as her hand went to her abdomen. "Don't worry. If it was a serious threat, Shane would've neutralized it," I reassured her.

Although she appeared relieved, she continued rubbing her barely there baby bump. I turned my attention back to Shane. "Take the package and–"

"I'm sorry, sir, but she insists she deliver it herself."

"Ooh, it's a *she*," Dare remarked.

"Then take the package from her and tell her to fuck off."

The corners of Shane's lips quirked. "She said if you tried to refuse her, I was to tell you her name."

Caterina clapped her hands with glee. "Why didn't you tell us you were seeing someone?"

"Because I'm not."

"You're lying," she scoffed.

"I swear on the saints I'm not seeing anyone. Least of all some demanding woman bearing a package."

Caterina's gaze swept over to Shane. "What's the woman's name?"

"Isla," he replied with a shit-eating grin.

Fuck me.

Of all the times she had to show up, it would have to be now. As I glared at Shane, I grumbled, "Fine. Send her in."

I refused to look at Dare or Caterina who were practically on the edge of their seats. Regardless of what I said or did, I knew they were going to harass the hell out of me.

When the door swung open to reveal Isla, my cock jumped in my pants simultaneously as my heart raced in my chest. She stood in the doorway with a hesitant smile on her face. Although I'd seen her in nothing but a g-string, the red sweater dress and black knee-boots she was wearing seriously tempted me.

I gripped the arms of my chair to stop me from running to her side and dragging her into my arms.

Her gaze bounced cautiously around the room. "Oh, you really are in a meeting. I thought he was just shooting me a line, so I would go away." She jerked a thumb at the door. "I'll just come back."

"No!" I bellowed a little more forcefully than I meant to. While Dare turned a laugh into a cough, Caterina ducked her head. Meanwhile, Isla shifted on her legs like she might bolt at any moment.

With a flick of my wrist, I beckoned her. "Please come in."

As Isla hurried to my desk, she said, "Since I was off last night, I wanted to check on how you were doing. Some of the girls said you were back. I figured that meant you were doing better, but I really wanted to see for myself."

Trying to keep the mask up in front of Dare and Caterina, I coldly replied, "I'm fine."

I felt like the biggest bastard in the world when her smile faded with my tone. Staring down at the plastic container in her hands, she said, "Right. Well, um, since my dad was an Episcopal priest, my mom was always making this soup and bread to take to sick or healing parishioners. Because you're Irish, I thought you might enjoy some."

Before she could hand it to me, Dare asked, "What kind is it?"

"Irish Colcannon," she half whispered.

My eyebrows shot up in surprise while Dare's jaw unhinged. "Seriously?"

A nervous laugh bubbled from her lips. "Um, yeah. I didn't even know it really had a name until I went into my mom's recipe box. We always just joked it was 'the sick soup'."

When Dare started for Isla, I shot out of my chair. "Keep your hands to yourself!"

While Isla jumped, Dare merely grinned. "Easy, mate. I was just going for the soup."

Warily, I watched him take the container from Isla. After peeling back the lid, he inhaled deeply. A groan of pleasure came from his lips. "Fuck me. This smells just like Mam's!"

"Really?" I questioned.

"It sure as hell does."

Dare grinned at Isla. "Do you have a little Irish in you, Ms. Vaughn?"

She nodded. "My mother's great-grandparents came over from Cork."

When a teasing glint flashed in Dare's eyes, I anticipated his coming cheek by starting around the desk. Before I could reach him, he purred, "You know, if you cook as good as my mam, it'd be my pleasure for you to have a *large* amount of Irish in you."

At Isla's gasp and Caterina's groan, I shoved Dare. *Hard*. "Watch your mouth, or you'll be eating that soup through a straw," I snarled. Of course, that just made him laugh harder.

I then snatched the soup from him. When the smell invaded my nostrils, it was my turn to moan. "It does smell just like Mam's."

Caterina smiled at Isla. "Would you mind giving me the recipe? Considering how these two are salivating, I can only imagine my husband would like it as well."

Isla returned Catrina's smile. "I would be happy to."

Motioning between the two of them, I said, "Isla, this is my sister-in-law, Caterina. She's married to my oldest brother, Callum."

Recognition flooded Isla's face hearing Caterina's name. "It's nice meeting you."

"Likewise," Caterina replied. Tilting her head, Caterina apprised Isla. "Could I bother you with another favor?"

With a shrug, Isla replied, "I suppose so."

"You're the perfect person to weigh in on my idea for the club." Caterina cut her gaze over to mine. "Isn't she?"

Before I could answer, Isla said, "I'm not sure how well I can answer considering I've only been here for a week."

"You're a woman and a dancer–the exact market I'm targeting."

Shifting on her feet, Isla nibbled her bottom lip. "Okay."

Caterina's dark eyes lit up. "Please have a seat," she instructed, motioning to the chair next to her. While she eased down on the leather, I didn't return to my chair. Instead, I leaned back against the desk across from Isla.

"Just give me your honest thoughts about this," Caterina said. After Isla nodded, Caterina informed her of her plan. During certain parts, Isla's head would bob and a few times she smiled.

Once Caterina finished, she stared expectantly at Isla. After clearing her throat, Isla said, "I think it's a great idea."

Caterina beamed. "You do? You're not just saying that?"

Shaking her head, Isla replied, "No. I really do. But you really shouldn't just poll me. Why don't you come talk to the other girls?"

"I would love that. Maybe they could give their input on what they would like to see the mission be."

"I'm sure they would."

Caterina tilted her head at me. "Of course, I don't want to get their hopes up if we don't have permission."

With a snort, I replied, "Did you honestly think I was going to say no to you?"

She grinned. "I didn't want to come across too cocky."

"As long as your husband won't give me shit, you're welcome to start your mission."

"He won't. We've already discussed it."

"In or out of the bedroom?" Dare teased.

While Isla gasped, Caterina merely smacked Dare's arm playfully. "I think instead of Owen, you can accompany me to mass this week."

With a wink, Dare replied, "Not happening, Sister Sassy."

Caterina turned her attention to Isla. "Would you go with me to talk to the girls?"

"Sure. I'd be happy to."

"See you later, gentleman," Caterina said.

After she fell in step behind Caterina, Isla threw a glance at me over her shoulder. "I hope you enjoy the soup."

"I'm sure I will. Thank you for bringing it to me."

"You're welcome." After wiggling goodbye with her fingers at me, Isla followed Caterina out of my office door.

As I stared down at the soup, I realized I was in so much fucking trouble.

Chapter Ten: Isla

As Caterina and I entered the elevator, I fought to keep my nerves in check. The last thing I'd ever expected was for her to ask my opinion of her idea, least of all for her to ask for my help. Considering she was my boss's sister-in-law, I wanted her to like me.

Oh who was I kidding? She was the sister-in-law of the man I was confused about having growing feelings for. That fact made me pinch my lips together so I wouldn't ramble and make a fool out of myself.

As the door closed, she turned to me with a smile. "Quinn is quite a man, isn't he?"

"Um, well, I haven't known him long, but yes, he is."

"I'm sure at first, he can come across as standoffish."

"A little," I lied.

"Mostly like a brute."

An anxious laugh tumbled from my lips. "He's more like a beast. At least that's what some of the girls call him. I like to think of him like the Beast in *Beauty and the Beast*. You know, he's all grumpy and wants to be alone, but when it really comes down to it, he can be very kind and considerate."

Oh no. My nerves had overtaken me and run away with my tongue. With wide-eyed horror, I stared at Caterina. When she burst out laughing, I didn't know if that was a good or bad thing.

The elevator doors popped open, and I reluctantly followed Caterina into the hallway. "How have I never seen it before? He is *totally* the Beast."

Shaking my head, I argued, "No, no. I shouldn't have said that."

She waved a hand at me. "I called him a brute."

"But you're his family. I'm just a dancer who works at his club, and I insulted my boss."

"Oh I'd wager you're a lot more to him than that."

When my boots froze to the hardwood floors, Caterina continued walking on ahead. After realizing I was no longer at her side, she whirled around. "Isla?"

I shook my head to try and shake me out of my stupor. "Um, sorry. You just shocked me."

"Because I stated the obvious?"

"No, I don't think that it is."

She tilted her head at me. "Are you usually in the habit of bringing your bosses homemade soup?"

I chewed my lip. "Well, no. But at the same time, I haven't ever had a boss get shot."

Caterina grinned. "I'd wager you hadn't."

"I really just wanted to do something nice for him."

"Because you like him, don't you?"

At my embarrassingly high-pitched giggle, I inwardly groaned. I barely knew Caterina. How could I possibly tell her how I truly felt? I could barely admit my feelings to myself, least of all a stranger.

"He's my boss. Of course, I'm going to say I like him," I diplomatically replied.

With an exasperated look, Caterina argued, "That's not what I meant."

"I know."

"From what I saw back there, he has it bad for you."

My eyes bulged. "No, he doesn't."

"Oh honey, trust me, I know the Kavanaugh Caveman look when I see it."

"Caveman look?"

She grinned. "Whenever my husband gets all possessive over me, I tell him he's a caveman. I'd never seen it in any of his brothers until today."

I furrowed my brows at her. "I just thought that was his usual beast side."

"Oh, it was much more than that. He made it very evident to Dare that you were *his*."

A nervous laugh bubbled from my lips. "But he hasn't said anything like that to me."

"Just because he may not be able to vocalize his feelings, I have eyes, and I can tell how he's feeling." With a grin, she said, "Just like I'd say, you have feelings for him, too."

I shifted uncomfortably in my boots. I'd never expected Caterina to put me through an inquisition about what I may or may not be feeling for Quinn. Considering how confused I was about what was going on between us, I couldn't possibly answer her.

"Obviously, I have some feelings for him since I took the time to make him soup." When Caterina opened her mouth to argue, I rambled on. "And yes, he's ridiculously handsome and sexy. Any woman with a pair of eyes would think that. Even though he can be beastly, he really does have a caring and compassionate side."

"I'm glad you can see that," Caterina said softly.

"Then there's also the fact he's pretty much a sex god considering he gave me my first male induced orgasm, and we weren't even having sex."

After my admission, I clamped my hand over my mouth. At Caterina's wide mouth and eyes, I whispered, "Oh God. I can't believe I just told you that."

When I shook my head, she grabbed my hands and pulled them from my face. "You can't just lower a bomb like that and then clam up!"

I furiously shook my head while heat rushed to my cheeks. "I was trying to say and do all the right things for you to like me since you're Quinn's sister-in-law."

She grinned. "I think that means you really like him if you want me to like you."

"Fine. You're right. I like him." With a shake of my head, I replied, "But now I've said the worst possible thing."

"How is a handsome man making you come bad?" she teased.

"Because it makes me sound like a...ho." And then the realization hit me of what Caterina had actually said. My mouth dropped open. "Did you seriously just ask me what was bad about Quinn making me come? I thought I'd heard from the other dancers that you were a nun."

With a laugh, Caterina asked, "Are you judging me?"

Horror filled me with offending her. "No, no, no! I keep saying the wrong things. The last thing I would ever want to do was judge you."

Caterina patted my arm. "It's okay, Isla. It's my fault for making you nervous and putting you on edge about Quinn."

"I think I was just surprised that you would say something like that. You know, with you being holy and all."

With a chuckle, Caterina argued, "I was only a novice, and the operative word is *was*. I'm certainly not abstaining anymore," Caterina argued.

"Well, I'm the fallen priest's daughter who let her boss get her off during her audition."

Wide-eyed, Caterina asked, *"That's* when it happened?"

With a shriek, I once again covered my face. "Could this get any worse?"

At the feel of Caterina's hand on my arm, I peeked through my fingers. "Come with me."

"Okay," I whispered.

After Caterina poked her head into an empty room, she ushered me inside. "I wasn't a novice because I was pious–I did it to escape an arranged marriage my father was planning."

I frowned. "There's seriously still arranged marriages?" At Caterina's nod, I replied, "But this is the modern age."

"The mafia world is still very old-school. It doesn't matter if you're Italian or Bratva or Irish, like Quinn."

"I had no idea the mafia was stuck in the dark ages."

"But they aren't always bad. My marriage to Callum was arranged."

"It was?" I gasped.

She nodded. "Despite only knowing him three days before we were married, it was the best thing that could ever happen to me."

An uneasy feeling crept along my spine. "Will Quinn have an arranged marriage?"

Caterina's smile faded. "It's a possibility."

"Oh," I murmured, as disappointment filled me. It shouldn't have bothered me so much. It wasn't like Quinn and I were in a relationship that I'd just found out couldn't go anywhere. He was just the man I'd thought I'd discovered a connection with only to have it severed before it really even started.

But it still stung.

"Isla–" Caterina began.

I shook my head. "It's okay. I get it. Quinn's an honorable guy, so of course, he would do what his family asked of him."

"There are other ways Quinn can serve his family besides an arranged marriage. It doesn't mean there can't be anything between the two of you."

Caterina's words did little to ease the ache in my chest. "Seriously. It's okay."

She took my hands in hers. "There's no one in the world who deserves happiness more than Quinn. If you're harboring even the smallest feelings for him, I'll do whatever I can within my power to see the two of you together."

Hope surged in my chest. "You'd really do that?"

"I will."

"But why? I mean, you don't know me. I could be a serial killer or something."

The corners of Caterina's lips quirked up. "That fear really doesn't work on me considering the family I grew up in and who I'm married to."

My mouth gaped open. "You know, I'm not really a serial killer, right? I'm just a nerdy grad student who needed money for school and to take care of my family," I protested.

"Of course, I do, Isla."

"Phew, I'm glad to hear that."

Taking my hand in hers, she said, "The reason I'm able to see you is because of two halves of my past. Being in the mafia world and being a novice means I can see through people. I might not know you well, but what I know of you so far is good. There's also the fact that Quinn doesn't open himself up to anyone, especially to those outside the family. If he's reacting to you, that tells me a lot."

With my mind swirling with out-of-control emotions, there was one question I feared to ask, but knew that I should. "My feelings aside: do I want to have him react to me?"

It had been the question that had plagued my mind since our first encounter. Quinn wasn't the safe or easy choice. He wasn't the lab partner whose greatest worry was what job he would land post grad school.

From what little I knew of him, he was a man with physical and emotional baggage.

From his own lips, Quinn had admitted he hurt men. He belonged to an underworld I knew little about, and what I did was completely frightening.

Despite my feelings, I had to be honest with myself if he was someone I should allow to pursue me. It wasn't just me and my safety I had to consider. It was Brooke and Henry's as well.

As I stared intently into Caterina's dark eyes, I held my breath for her answer. "Are you worried because of the world Quinn belongs to?" At my nod, she replied, "Then I would say better the devil you know than the devil you don't."

I blinked at her. "That's your answer?"

She laughed. "Well, I wanted you to at least think about it for a minute before I explained myself."

"My head is spinning too much for any deep-seated words of wisdom. Just give it to me straight."

Caterina nibbled on her lip. "Considering the way I grew up, it's hard for me to answer in a way that relates to you, not to mention I wasn't really given a choice with Callum."

Groaning, I rubbed my temples. "Please, just give me a yes or no."

"If I were in your shoes, I would see Quinn for what he truly is: a man who loves with his entire body and soul. A protector who would risk everything to keep you safe. A man who places you as his sun where his entire world revolves around you."

"That was a lot better than just a simple yes."

"You're welcome." With a wink, she added, "I also need to add if he's anything like his brother, a very dedicated and giving lover."

I laughed. "I can handle that for sure."

Caterina tilted her head at me. "Besides the hot sex, do you feel better about the rest?"

"I do," I replied.

And it was the truth. Like she said, Quinn was the devil I knew. With other men, the skeletons remained in the closet to be discovered. Deep down, I knew Quinn would never do anything to hurt me.

What remained was only the small fear of what his world might do to me.

Chapter Eleven: Quinn

As I watched Caterina and Isla walk to the elevator, an odd feeling fluttered in my chest. It was something akin to happiness or maybe even pride that the two of them seemed to be getting along so well. Besides my mam and sister, Caterina was the most important woman in my life. Her opinion mattered to me as much as my brothers did.

"Once again, Caterina got her way," Dare mused behind me.

Laughing, I turned to face him. "Are you surprised?"

He shook his head. "Nope. We were doomed from the moment we snatched her from that convent."

"I suppose that's our punishment."

"God help us when the wain gets here. She'll have us wrapped around her wee little finger as much as her mother does."

"Aye. I imagine she will." I smiled at the thought of our future niece.

Jerking his chin at the bowl, Dare asked, "Any chance of me getting some of that?"

"None."

"Come on, Quinn. She made a lot."

"And I have a big appetite."

Dare grinned. "Aye for Isla's pussy."

"Watch yourself," I grunted at him as I went back to my chair.

Dare leaned in across the desk. "It appears she has an appetite for your monster cock."

"She does not."

"She *cooked* for you."

"You heard her. She was raised to do shit like that."

Dare rolled his eyes. "The wee lass was worried about you. Women don't spend their days off making soup for a man they don't care about regardless of how they were raised."

"As I told you before, it's not happening."

Crossing his hands over his chest, Dare countered, "You can keep telling yourself that, but you might not have a choice."

"There's always a choice, and unlike you, I have tight control of my cock and my emotions."

"Yeah, your emotions. But what about Isla's?"

I furrowed my brows at him. "What about them?"

He grinned. "Just like Caterina, maybe Isla always gets what she wants, and she clearly wants you."

To my utter surprise, Dare's words sent unease creeping along my spine. Was he right? Did Isla want me as much as I wanted her? Sure, we'd shared a kiss the other night, but that didn't mean she wanted anything more from me than sex.

Or did it?

If she pursued me, there wasn't a chance in hell I could say no. I might be able to face down the worst of enemies, but the thoughts of her sent dread through my chest. Frowning, I shifted in my chair.

When I finally met Dare's gaze, he winked at me. "Enjoy your soup."

Chapter Twelve: Isla

After talking one one-on-one with each of the girls on shift, Caterina got an unanimous vote. She left with a beaming smile and a promise to start as soon as possible. I'd just seen her out when it was time for me to take the stage.

Once I began my dance, I stared into the crowd, searching for Quinn. Two nights ago, he'd sat next to the stage and watched me. I found myself hoping he would do it again. Having his eyes on me set me on fire.

Just as I hooked my leg on the pole, a towering shadow caught my attention at the bar. Before I started spinning, I peered into the dark to lock eyes with Quinn. He stood with his arms crossed, leaning against the bar.

Closing my eyes, I let my mind drift back to our night together. The way his lips had felt against my skin. His hands on my breasts. The feel of his cock between my legs.

It had all felt so very, very good.

After opening my eyes, I sought out Quinn again. When he shifted on his feet, I swore I could make out a bulge in his pants. The thought of him wanting me caused slickness to coat my thong. Rubbing my center against the pole didn't help my growing desire. Instead, it just made me hornier. It was a poor substitute for Quinn's dick.

I needed relief from the ache between my thighs. I needed to come. Without Quinn to do it, I would have to take matters into my own hands.

Instead of coming off the stage into the crowd, I went back behind the curtain. "What are you doing?" Paula asked.

"Oh, um, I-I just need to go to the bathroom."

"Okay. When you're done, go straight to room five. I've got a dance lined up for you."

With a nod, I continued onto the dancer's bathroom, the fire continuing to burn between my legs. After I slipped inside, I quickly locked the door. My stripper heels clicked along the marble-tiled floor. With my breath coming in harsh pants, I slumped down on the green velvet settee in the corner.

As I widened my legs, I momentarily paused. "What the hell?" I murmured. Was I actually going to do this? Masturbating in a semi-public place was completely darkside for my usual vanilla self. But then Quinn's predatory gaze flashed before my mind, fanning the flames between my thighs.

Fuck yes, I was doing this.

Without another thought, I stuck my hand inside my thong. Closing my eyes, I went back to my night with Quinn. At the feel of my fingers against my center, I moaned. After stroking the moisture against my lips, I pinched my clit.

When I plunged two fingers deep inside me, I bit down on my lip to silence my moan. As I lifted my hips, I imagined straddling Quinn. The way his hard cock had felt between my legs. I wondered what it would feel like to have his fingers inside me. Or even better to feel his dick pumping inside me.

I wanted it all. His fingers in my pussy. His cock in my mouth. His cum down my throat.

With a cry, my walls clamped on my fingers. Throwing my head back, my hips kept pumping as I rode out the powerful orgasm. One of the best I'd ever had without a vibrator.

But the incredible high was short-lived. As I came back to myself, mortification rained down on me. Had I actually just made myself come in a bathroom while fantasizing about Quinn? What kind of freak did that?

I jerked my hand out of my thong with disgust before hurrying over to the sink to clean myself up. After wetting a paper towel, I washed the still-tingling flesh between my legs. As I started soaping up my hands, I stared at my reflection. "Get a grip, Isla. And not on yourself or Quinn's dick," I muttered.

After tossing the paper towel in the trash, I hurried out of the bathroom. I arrived at the private rooms to find Paula waiting for me. "Everything okay?"

As a matter of fact, no. My mild-mannered self just masturbated in the bathroom to my Irish mafia boss. Plastering a smile on my face, I replied, "Stomach troubles."

Inwardly, I groaned. Not only had I lied, but I picked something gross to do it with. Worst of all was Paula's sympathetic look. "Why don't you take a break after this one?"

I waved my hand dismissively. "No, no. I'm fine."

"Okay. He's waiting inside."

Chapter Thirteen: Quinn

With the taste of Isla's soup still radiating on my tongue, I wanted a taste of her. Since I couldn't have one physically in the flesh, I had to resort to fantasy. The one way to achieve that was through watching her dance.

When I took my usual spot at the edge of the bar, Conleth noted my presence with a jerk of his chin. I'm sure he'd been running his mouth with Sarah about how all the sudden I was interested in watching the dancers perform.

Well a certain dancer.

As Isla came out onto the stage, the leering whistles and cheers rang through the room. My fists clenched at my sides as I had to fight the urge to inflict pain on any man who lusted after her.

As her hips swiveled and swayed, Isla's gaze bounced around the room. It felt like she was searching for me. When her gaze finally locked with mine, she stared intently at me.

There was something different about tonight's performance. A longing had entered her expression. She bit down on her lip more and arched her center harder into the pole. Her hands seemed to linger longer on her breasts–the nipples pebbling under her touch.

Fuck me, was she turned on?

And was thinking of me turning her on?

My cock throbbed in my slacks at the very thought. There would be no getting out of jerking off in my office. Just the thought of Isla's hands or mouth on my dick made me moan.

When Isla finished her performance, she didn't come off the stage like she usually did. Instead, she slipped behind the curtain. I fought the urge to barge backstage and hunt her down.

But I couldn't do that with my fucking pants tented. Instead, I drew my jacket as best I could over me and ducked out to the elevator. As soon as the doors closed, I threw my head back against the wall and cupped my aching cock.

Isla was going to be the death of me.

A little after one, I rubbed my blurring eyes and decided to finally call it a day. Normally I didn't come to the club every night.

Dare and I usually alternated, but he was busy trying to get his casino going.

Of course, the club held a new allure for me.

When I came out of the elevator, that allure stood at the end of the hallway. To one ear, Isla cradled her phone, and the other she had her finger in to curb the noise from the club.

"Isla?"

She whirled around at the sound of her name. "Oh, hi."

"Is something wrong?"

"I'm just on hold with roadside assistance."

"What's wrong with your car?"

"Dead battery. They were supposed to be here an hour ago, but no one has shown up and no one is answering."

"Hang up."

Her blue eyes popped wide. "Excuse me?"

"I'll take you home."

She shook her head. "It isn't necessary."

"Yes, it is." I jerked my chin at her. "Hang up."

"It's too much of an imposition. I can just get an Uber," she protested.

With a grunt of frustration, I closed the gap between us. Then I eased her phone out of her grip. "*I will drive you home, Isla.* While we're en route, I will have our personal mechanic fix your battery. Then I will have it delivered to your house."

"But Southborough is thirty minutes away."

"It doesn't matter if it was five hours away. I'm taking you home."

"You're awfully stubborn," she remarked.

I laughed. "I could say the same for you."

She grinned. "Whatever."

After I took her bag from her, I said, "Come on."

Without another word of protest, Isla fell in step with me. As we walked by the bar to the back exit, Conleth's eyes bore into me. "Goodnight, boss," he called.

"Night," I grumbled.

As we started down the employee hallway, Isla tilted her head up at me. "Do you have to be so grumpy to everyone?"

"I'm not."

"Uh, yeah, you are." She jerked her thumb behind her. "Like back there. You sounded like it pained you to have to even acknowledge Conleth."

I shrugged as we exited the back door. "I'm just acting like myself." Pinning her with a stare, I added, "You know, a beast."

Her eyes widened. "Did Caterina tell you I said that?"

A laugh rolled through me as I nodded for Shane to open the SUV door. "I was talking about the other dancers. When did you call me a beast?"

Isla hesitated before she hopped inside the back. When I joined her on the bench seat, she finally replied, "I only said you were like the beast in the Disney movie."

"I'm not that hairy."

Her brows shot up in surprise. "Was that an attempt at humor?"

"I have my moments."

She grinned. "You're really hard to figure out."

"Not really. I'm pretty much what you see is what you get."

"That's not entirely true."

"How so?"

"You've only been kind to me."

"Are you sure about that?"

She grimaced. "You're right. You were a real asshole at the start of my audition, not to mention the night you were shot when I tried to help you. And then after we..."

Crimson dotted her cheeks.

"After what, Isla?" I teased.

She ducked her head. "You know."

"When we came?"

"Yes," she whispered as she stared at Shane behind the wheel.

"Don't worry about him. He's paid not to listen."

"I still don't want him to hear!"

Wagging my finger at her, I countered, "Don't change the subject. What would you have me say?"

She bit down on her pillowy bottom lip. "I don't know."

"I think you do."

"Fine. Here's what you could've said." Lowering her voice to mimic me, she said, "'Thanks for sharing that with me, Isla' or 'I'm having a hard time putting what I'm feeling into words right now, but that was truly intense'." She licked her lips. "At the very least, you could've said *something* instead of grabbing a box of kleenex and leaving me feeling used."

Fuck. I'd been a complete and total beast to her. Making her feel used was the last thing in the world I would ever want to do. At the same time, I didn't know why I was surprised. I'd been so cut off from feeling anything in the last two years but anger, resentment, and agony. What softness did I have to give a fragile little dove like her?

Reaching between us, I took her hand in mine. "I never meant to make you feel used or confused."

"It's okay."

I shook my head. "No, it's not. You are everything beautiful and bright in the world. You deserve only the same in return."

Her lips turned down in a pout. "You know now that I think about it, you haven't been very friendly to me since I started working. You haven't even asked me how I'm settling in or if people are treating me well."

Smirking at her, I replied, "Isla, how are you settling in, and are people treating you well?"

"There you go attempting humor again," she huffed.

"Like I said, I have my moments. Now answer my questions."

"Do you really want to know?"

I nodded. "Yeah, I do."

She shrugged. "I think I'm settling in pretty well. Everyone has been really nice to help me."

"That's good to hear. I'd hate to have to take care of anyone who wasn't treating you kindly."

Her eyes popped wide. "You wouldn't."

I flashed her a shark-like smile. "Maybe."

"Please, don't."

"As long as no one is being mean, I won't."

"It's more about jealousy than anything."

"Who?"

"A few girls who have been kinda bitchy about all the private dances I'm doing."

At that moment, any anger I felt about her being mistreated evaporated. In its place came the green monster of jealousy. "You're pretty popular with the clients, aren't you?"

"So far. I think it's just because I'm the new shiny thing."

I knew it was far more than that. While some men like to sample the fresh faces, they would return to the ones they enjoyed. For Isla to continue to be popular, she possessed something to keep them coming back for more.

Staring at her in the dim light, I asked, "Tell me, Isla. Do you enjoy doing private dances?" When she slowly shook her head back and forth, I cocked my brows at her. "Why not?"

"I could say I don't enjoy the leering looks or the feel of strange men beneath me."

"But that's not the reason?"

She shook her head. "They're not you."

My heartbeat broke into a wild gallop at her words. "Do you wish it was me in the private dances?"

"Yes."

"I wish I was there with you, too."

Her intense gaze dropped to my stare at my lips. "What do you want, Isla?" I questioned.

She jerked her eyes back to mine. "Nothing."

"You're a terrible liar."

She grimaced. "I want you to kiss me."

"I shouldn't."

"Why not?"

"Because I'm a bad man who will only corrupt you."

Leaning over me, Isla brought her face close to mine. "Just shut up and kiss me, Quinn," she commanded.

How could I not oblige her? Cupping her cheeks, I brought my lips to hers. God, they were heaven.

Warm.

Tender.

Silky.

Within seconds, Isla was sliding her tongue against my lips. When I opened my mouth and tangled my tongue with hers, she moaned. She tasted like the perfection she was. Although other men got to fantasize about her mouth, she was mine and only mine.

Time slowed to a crawl as I devoured her mouth. I couldn't keep my hands from roaming over her body. I cupped and squeezed her breasts through her top. When I started to slide my hand under her skirt, Isla's lips popped off of mine as she pulled away, panting to catch her breath.

"I want you," I rasped.

"I want you, too." She shook her head. "But not like this."

"You want a four poster bed and silk sheets?" I suggested.

She giggled. "It doesn't have to be that posh."

"I'll give you the world if it means I can bury myself inside you."

Her expression grew serious. As her hands came to cup my cheeks, she replied, "I don't need all of that. Just you."

"Do you need me, Little Dove?"

"I do. Do you want to know how much?"

"Aye."

With a cheeky little grin, she said, "I have a confession to make."

"I think you mistake me for a priest."

"I'm serious," she pouted.

"Fine. What is your confession?"

"Do you know what I did after my set tonight?"

"Make me insanely jealous by riding other men's dicks?"

She smacked me playfully on the chest. "No, that's not it."

"Then what?"

She dropped her head to whisper in my ear. "I made myself come in the bathroom."

A jolt shuddered through me at her words. I was right about her being aroused during her performance. "Did you get so turned on you had to touch yourself?" I questioned in a pained whisper. It was almost too much thinking of her fingering herself.

She bobbed her head. "I was thinking of you."

"Oh fuck," I grunted. "You're going to be the death of me, woman."

Isla giggled. "I could say the same about you. I've never, ever touched myself in a public place before."

"See, I am corrupting you," I replied.

With a seductive lick of her lips, Isla said, "But it's so good."

Groaning, I threw my head back against the headrest. "You've got to stop."

"Why?"

"If you don't, I'm going to jerk up your skirt and fuck you right here in front of Shane."

Isla squeaked in horror before pushing herself away from me. "I'm not ready for that." With a shake of her head, she added, "What I mean is I'll never be ready to have someone watch us...you know."

I laughed. "Considering you can't bring yourself to say it, I'm not shocked."

"Have you?"

"Once or twice."

"Did you like it?"

"While it can be hot, I'm glad to hear you say you're not down for it."

"Why?"

"I already have to share you enough with the men at the club, and I'm a selfish bastard."

"Good. I don't want to share you with any other women either."

As I stared into Isla's beautiful face, I still couldn't believe she possibly wanted me. Out of all the men she came into contact with at the club, she picked me. It was overwhelming.

And so far, I'd predominantly treated her like a plaything. I had to make amends. She deserved to be treated like the queen she was.

"I'm sorry I've been a beast to you," I said in a hushed whisper. I didn't need Shane hearing me be vulnerable in front of a woman. It wasn't what was expected of men like me.

Isla blinked at me. "What did you say?"

"I said I'm sorry I've been a beast." I once again spoke in a low voice.

She cupped her ear. "I still didn't hear you."

"Isla," I growled at her cheekiness.

With a grin, she replied, "Yes, Quinn?"

"Why are you giving me shit?"

"Maybe because you don't mind letting Shane hear you try to fuck me, but you can't let him hear you apologize?" She shook her head at me. "That doesn't fly with me."

"It's complicated," I gritted out.

"Then uncomplicate it."

In a low voice, I replied, "He works underneath me. He has to be able to respect me and see me as a leader."

"And apologizing to me is somehow going to undermine that?"

"Aye, it will."

Her expression clouded over. "Then this needs to stop before it goes any further. I plan on dating you, not your men or your lifestyle."

"It's unavoidable."

She crossed her arms over her chest. "It's archaic and misogynistic."

Iritiation rippled through me. Why couldn't she understand? Although she fought tooth and nail against the life, Caterina understood. "It's the bleedin' way it's done, and I'm not going against tradition," I bit out.

Ignoring me, she stared straight ahead. Of course, it would be at that moment we pulled into her driveway. She grabbed her purse and slung the strap over her neck. "Thank you for the ride home."

When I didn't make a move to get out, she huffed and tried the other door. After finding it locked, she threw a look at me over her shoulder. "Open the door."

The last thing on earth I wanted to do was let her go. Especially not when she was spitting mad at me. I knew if we allowed things to continue between us, it wouldn't be the last time. I didn't know how to be soft and tender with a woman. Sure, I could with Maeve and my mam, but this was different.

Isla was different.

"Let me out!" she shrieked as her hand frantically worked the door handle.

Shane wouldn't do it. Not until he got the nod from me that it was okay. Instead, I shook my head.

"Isla, look at me."

"I just want to go."

"Look at me," I commanded.

With a huff, she whirled around to pin with a heated stare. "What?"

In a booming voice, I said, "I'm sorry I've been a beast to you. I'm sorry I made you feel used the first night we were together."

There was no denying she heard me and that Shane did as well. "You are?" she questioned softly.

"Aye. And I'll work my arse off from now on out to treat you like the queen you are."

Isla stared intently at me. The corners of her lips quirked. "Good. I'm glad to hear it." She then jerked her chin at the door. "Let me out."

This time I nodded at Shane.

"Goodnight, Quinn," Isla said before she slipped out the door.

"Sweet dreams, Little Dove."

With a mischievous grin, she replied, "I think I'll go for a beauty and the beast fantasy."

"You're a cruel woman, you know that?"

She giggled before slamming the door. As she ran up the front walk and onto the porch, I caught Shane's gaze in the rear view mirror. He had the nerve to grin at me.

"If you fucking tell anyone, especially my brothers about what you heard tonight, I'll fucking castrate you."

He chuckled. "Aye, boss. My lips are sealed." Once Isla was inside the house, he put the SUV in reverse. "Can I just say one thing?"

"If it's to give me any shite about what was seen or heard tonight, I'd keep your bleedin' lips shut if you know what's good for you."

"I just wanted to say that she's good for you. I like who you are with her."

"And what am I like with her? A pussy?"

"Happy."

Although I should've told him to mind his own fucking business, I didn't. Instead, I merely grumbled, "Whatever."

Inwardly, I couldn't help smiling.

Chapter Fourteen: Isla

I couldn't sleep after my make-out session in the backseat of Quinn's SUV. Instead, I tossed and turned for hours as my mind whirled with out of control thoughts. It wasn't just the kissing and touching that replayed like a movie reel in my head and sent a tingling between my thighs.

It was more about the things he had said to me, and the feelings he had admitted.

His words echoed through my mind just as strongly as if he were with me and saying them again. I couldn't remember the last time a man had occupied my thoughts so completely. I'm not sure if one ever had.

It was obsessive.

When I finally did fall asleep, it felt like a mere second when my alarm went off. It was only a few days until classes convened for the fall. I had to head to campus and meet with my graduate advisor. I knew if I was going to make it through the day, I would need a few shots of espresso.

After a quick shower, I threw on a t-shirt and a pair of jeans. Since Henry hadn't woken up yet, I knew Brooke was still asleep. With Henry's birth, I'd insisted she take our parents' old room since it was the largest. Thankfully, that meant it was at the end of the hallway, and I didn't have to be too quiet. I still carefully tiptoed down the creaky hardwoods to the staircase.

Once I got downstairs, I grabbed my purse and headed out into the garage. When I tapped the opener, the door began to rise. Just as Quinn had promised, my car sat in the driveway. When I opened the car door, I was surprised that the key fob was in the front seat. I guess Quinn wasn't used to worrying about anyone stealing his vehicle. Of course, things like that didn't happen much around here like they did in the city.

When I grabbed the key fob, I noticed it felt lighter. I realized that my house key was missing. "What the hell?" I muttered.

At that moment, my phone rang. I furrowed my brows at the unknown number. Hesitantly I answered it. "Hello?"

"Good morning," a velvety deep voice said.

I sucked in a breath. It was Quinn. "Good morning to you, too."

"I wanted to let you know that I have your house key."

"Okay, do you have ESP or something?"

He chuckled. "No."

"Then it's more than a little spooky that you just called me at the precise moment I was wondering where my key was."

"Niall just told me that you'd gone to your car. I figured if you hadn't had time to miss it yet, I would let you know."

Furrowing my brows, I demanded, "Who the hell is Niall?"

"One of the men who works for me."

"And just how does Niall know what I'm doing?"

"Do you see the black Escalade down the street?"

Craning my neck, I peered out the car window. Two houses down at the Carmichael's was a black SUV, which I imagined was the Escalade he was speaking of. "Yes, I see it."

"Then wave to Niall."

"I'm not waving to some man who is stalking me."

"He's not stalking you."

"Then why is he watching me while creeping at my neighbor's house?"

"Because I asked him too."

"Seriously, Quinn?"

He chuckled. "Yes, Little Dove. I didn't want to risk your car being stolen, so I asked him to stay and keep a watch out."

"That really wasn't necessary. Southborough isn't Boston."

"Bad people are everywhere."

"I'm starting to realize that."

"Where are you going so early?"

"That seems a bit stalkery, don't you think?"

He huffed into the phone. "Can't I be interested in what you're doing?"

"It's all in the way you frame it. Saying, 'So, what are you going to be up to today?' is far more acceptable."

"Isla, what are you going to be up to today before you come in for your shift?"

I couldn't help giggling. Ugh, this man had me giggling of all things. I was a serious scientist, not a vapid co-ed. "I'm going to MIT to meet with my advisor."

"Are you going to tell them that your big brain is driving men wild at the club?"

With a snort, I replied, "Yeah, it's b-words like my boobs and butt, not my brain, that are getting the attention."

"I bet if you started talking about the relationships between plant, animal, and human genetics they might lose their minds."

I sucked in a breath. "You know about molecular biology?"

"I might've done a little research."

Oh my God. This man was going to be the death of me. With a grin, I teasingly asked, "Will you lose your mind if I start talking about the cellular and subcellular level of organisms?"

"Will you be topless and grinding on my cock while you do it?"

"Quinn!" I admonished to which he laughed.

"I'm sorry, Little Dove."

"I thought we were going to try getting to know each other better emotionally than physically."

"I know everything I need to know to confirm how I feel about you."

"Well, I need to catch up."

"I don't mind going slow."

"There's innuendo in there, right?"

"Maybe," he teased.

"Ugh. You're impossible." After a glance at the time on the dashboard, I groaned. "Listen, I have to go, or I'm going to be late."

"Be careful, and I'll see you tonight."

As I started backing down the drive, I caught sight of Niall. "You're not going to start having me followed, are you?"

"No. I'm not that intense."

"Good."

"I might've put a tracking device on your car though." At my screech of horror, Quinn merely laughed. "I'm only teasing, Isla."

"Whatever," I grumbled.

"Have a good day."

"You too."

When I hung up, I couldn't stop smiling. I drove the entire way to MIT with a goofy grin on my face.

After a packed day, I headed into the club. To my surprise, a veritable feast was set up in the main dressing room. Dancers stood around filling their plates with lasagna and ziti and salad. As I headed to get changed, a hand tapped my shoulder.

When I whirled around, Caterina stood smiling at me. "I'm so glad you were on tonight."

As I returned her smile, I replied, "It's good seeing you again."

Motioning around, Caterina said, "What do you think?"

I gasped. "*You* did all this?"

She nodded enthusiastically. "It's my first order of business as a club mom."

"Well, you knocked it out of the park."

"Thanks." Nudging me, she said, "Go get a plate."

"Sure."

As I spooned up the lasagna, Caterina appeared the proud club mom as she talked with some of the other girls. At the first bite, I couldn't help moaning. She was an amazing cook. Before I knew it, I'd devoured the lasagna and salad. Although I was tempted to go back for more, I thought I better wait until I got through my first set. I didn't want to spin upside down and lose my dinner.

When Caterina approached me with a teeming plate, I shook my head wildly. "It was delicious, but I'm positively stuffed."

She grinned. "I thought you might like to take a plate to Quinn."

My gaze spun around us to see if anyone else had heard her. "You're devious."

With a laugh, she replied, "I know."

I threw a glance at the clock over the dressing room door. "I think I have enough time. Just let me throw my costume on."

As Caterina nodded, I rushed into the changing room. I usually came into the club with my hair and makeup done since Brooke always indulged me. Of course, I usually wore a wig to hide my identity. Some nights I wore pink, some nights purple. I had brown and black ones as well. Tonight Brooke had given me a cherry red one.

When I came out, I found Caterina waiting. She winked at me when she handed it over. I playfully rolled my eyes before taking the back stairs up to Quinn's office.

After I knocked on the door, Quinn called, "What?"

I cracked open the door and poked my head inside. He was alone at his desk. "I see the beast is in. When will Quinn be available?" I teased.

"Get in here," he growled.

Heat shot straight between my legs at his command. "Can't you at least say please?"

His hungry gaze swept down my body. "Please, Isla."

"Was that so hard?" I asked as I walked across the marble floor.

"When I'm in a hell of a mood, it is."

"Maybe you just need a good meal." I sat the plate down in front of him. "Caterina wanted me to bring this to you."

"Aye, she started her club mother thing tonight, didn't she?"

"She did."

"How's it going?"

I smiled. "Really well. I think it's going to be a great addition to the club."

"I'm glad to hear it."

Quinn swiveled in his chair before reaching out and grabbing my waist. He then plopped me down on his lap. When he buried his face in my chest, I tried wriggling out of my embrace. "I was only delivering dinner."

He grunted in frustration. "Can't I have some dessert first?"

I laughed. "Not when I'm supposed to go on in about five minutes."

"I could make you come in two."

Cocking my brows at him, I replied, "Is that right?"

"Yes, it is."

"As tempting as that is, I don't want to be slipping and sliding on the pole because I didn't have time to clean up."

Quinn's eyes glittered with lust. "I think I'll purchase a dance from you tonight."

"Oh no you won't."

"Why not?"

"Because I don't want there to be money between us."

"So you'll give me one for free?"

I laughed. "Of course."

"I'll have to take you up on that offer very soon."

"I look forward to it." I then hopped off his lap. Nodding at the plate, I said, "Eat. Maybe you'll be less grumpy."

He snorted. "I'll try."

I wiggled my fingers at him before leaving his office. I had to hurry down the stairs. I'd just gotten into place backstage when my music came on. Since he was eating, I didn't expect to see Quinn. For the first time, he didn't watch my set. I couldn't help missing his eyes on me.

As soon as I came off stage, Angela, Paula's assistant, had a dance set up for me. I hurried down the hallway. I gave a fleeting glance to the bouncer in the doorway before I went inside the room. The middle-aged man seated on the couch gave off an even bigger arrogant vibe than the usual rich guy. Men like him were great for tips, but they made my skin crawl.

My music came on, and I began rolling my hips to the beat. I swished and swayed my ass and breasts in front of him, letting the music flow through me.

"Enough. Lose the top, and get on my lap," he ordered.

Forcing a seductive grin to my lips, I replied, "As you wish."

After untying my top, I tossed the fabric to the floor. At the lick of his lips, I inwardly gagged. I don't know why I was surprised. Men were so predictable, and almost all the clients did that at the sight of my bare breasts.

I dropped down onto his lap, straddling his hips. After placing my hands on each side of his head, my hips ground into his erection. As he groaned with pleasure, I started reciting molecular techniques in my head starting with gel electrophoresis.

I'd moved on to polymerase chain reactions when his hand came around my throat. I froze mid hip thrust. "Um, I'm sorry, but you're not allowed to touch me."

A smirk curved across his lips. "I bet I can change your mind."

I shook my head. "No. It's the club's rules. I could get in trouble."

He released his grip on my neck to slide his hand down my breastbone. "You're such a good little girl to follow the rules."

"Yes, I do. So please remove your hand."

A lecherous smirk curved on his lips. "What if I gave you five thousand dollars to let me put my hands wherever I wanted to?"

"F-Five t-thousand?" I stammered.

He nodded. "I'll make it twenty thousand if you let me put my *dick* wherever I want."

Although momentarily tempted by the large amount of money, revulsion quickly reverberated through me. I could never, ever cross that line and be able to live with myself.

With a shake of my head, I replied, "I'm sorry. But that goes against the club's rules, and I like this job too much to risk it."

While I expected him to be angry, he merely chuckled. "You're a good manipulator."

"That's not what I'm doing."

"Oh yes, it is."

"Remove your hand."

Undeterred he said, "What'll it take to let me fuck you? Fifty thousand?"

I shook my head. "I'm sorry. But there isn't any amount that would make me change my principles."

"Is the innocence all an act, or are you truly so unfucked?"

Warmth flooded my cheeks. "I'm not acting."

"So you're really that innocent?" When I nodded, he shut his eyes in exaggerated bliss. "Fuck me. That's so sexy." His eyes popped open to pin me with an intense stare. "Tell me, Good Girl. Have you ever taken it up the ass?"

Glancing over my shoulder, I tried signaling Dowe. To my horror, the doorway was empty. *Breathe, Isla. Just breathe. He can't be that far away. All you have to do is scream.*

His hand slid back up to grip my throat only this time he added his other hand. "I asked you a question."

"Your question was inappropriate, and I'm not answering it," I wheezed out.

"Mm, that tells me exactly what I want to know about your virgin ass."

As unease continued pricking along my skin, I started sliding off his lap. "Okay. I'm ending the dance."

His eyes darkened to a soulless black. "I didn't come."

As I began backing away from him, I forced a shaky smile to my face. "I know, and I'm sorry. Since it's all my fault, I will tell the house to comp this dance." When his jaw flexed, I quickly added, "I can also offer you a few comp drinks as well."

Like a cobra, he launched forward to grab me by the waist. Before I could fight back, he slung me down on the couch so hard I bounced. It jarred me so badly that for a moment I couldn't move. Dumbstruck, I merely stared up at the ceiling—my heart beating wildly in my ears.

Before I could try to get away, he straddled me. At the feel of his weight on my body, my faculties came back to me, and I began to thrash my arms and legs.

And then both of his hands came around my throat.

"Help! Please help!" I screamed before his grip cut off my oxygen. I dug my nails into the skin on his hands, scratching and clawing until wetness pooled on them and a metallic rush entered my nose.

"You cunt!" he snarled.

As he continued to choke me, panic raged in my mind. Unless someone stopped him, he was going to kill me. I would be snatched away from Brooke and Henry.

No, no, I couldn't leave them! They needed me too much. I had to stay. I had to fight for them.

Please, please, help me!

Then as darkness began to shadow my vision, an image of Quinn flashed before me. Memories of his touch and his lips on mine swirled like foggy wisps through my mind. I didn't want to leave him either.

And just as I slipped under, I thought I heard Quinn's voice. It roared through me, calling me away from the darkness. It pulled me towards it like a magnet.

"Isla, stay with me. Please stay with me!"

Chapter Fifteen: Quinn

As I rubbed my temples, my mind was filled with a mixture of Isla and the latest Bravta attack. This time it came through sabotaging a shipment of guns. Callum and I had spent most of the day trying to smooth things over with those who were expecting deliveries. While Callum worked at reassuring them that their order would be fulfilled, I took the hard ass routine with those whose job it had been to keep the shipments safe.

I rolled my neck, trying to relieve the tension. In the back of my mind, I knew there was only one way I was going to relax. Like the dirty dog I was, I opened my laptop back up.

As I searched the private rooms on the computer for Isla, I worked my already stiff cock over my pants.

But her reflection on the screen caused the world around me to shudder to a stop. She wasn't doing her usual dance. She lay on her back as a man began to straddle her.

Red rage seeped across my vision.

No one was to touch her.

Ever.

Since I didn't know if I could get to her in time, I hit the alarm on the private rooms. Then I sprinted from my desk and out of my office.

I didn't bother with the elevator. I pounded down the stairs and into the main room. The snarling rage emanating from me bled into the room, sending people scattering from my path.

Ignoring Conleth calling my name, I kept running. When I started down the packed hallway, people scurried away like rats on a sinking ship. The blaring alarm had sent them into the area.

When I rushed inside the room, Shane was dragging the man off of Isla. He flung him to the floor, shoving his boot against the man's throat while training his gun on his crotch. I instantly recognized him as Terrance Manning–one of the wealthiest men in the city.

My wild gaze spun to the couch where Isla's crumpled body lay on the leather. Two dancers started towards her before I blared, "Don't touch her!"

They immediately froze. Although I wanted to immediately get my hands on Terrance, I sprinted over to Isla. Without a thought to what was right or wrong, I gathered her into my arms.

"Isla?"

Her limp body flailed in my arms. She didn't appear to be breathing. "No, oh God, no!"

I leaned my cheek over her mouth. At that moment, her body

jolted as she wheezed in a loud breath. "That's right. Breathe, Little Dove," I urged.

Isla's eyelids fluttered as breath began gasping in and out of her. I didn't bother asking if anyone had called 911. We couldn't take the heat. At the very least, we would get Isla to hospital on our own. But I prayed it wouldn't come to that.

With her breathing sufficiently, I drew her to my chest. "Oh, Isla, I'm sorry. I'm so fucking sorry," I crooned.

Instead of giving comfort, my movements only brought her pain because she cried out. It was bittersweet since it meant she was still with us, but at the same time, I didn't want to hurt her.

Slowly, I eased her back to stare into her beautiful face. I swallowed down the tears rising in my throat. "I'm sorry. I shouldn't have moved you."

Her glassy eyes stared into mine. "Like this."

"You want me to hold you like this?" At the slight shake of her head, I asked, "You like being in my arms?"

Since it was obviously too painful to speak, she murmured. "Mm, hmm."

"I like you being in my arms." At her frown of disbelief, I shook my head. "There's no one I want to touch me but you, Isla. Only you."

When a single tear slid from her eye, the monster roared within me. He wanted free to punish those who had hurt Isla. Even though I kept him corralled when I was in the club, I'd been pushed too far not to release him.

Without taking my eyes off Isla, I blared, "Clear the fucking room!"

After everyone had rushed out, I stared at the head bouncer, Gareth. "Who the fuck was assigned to this room?"

"Dowe, sir," Gareth replied.

"Where the hell is he?"

"We're not sure."

"Find him," I bit out.

Gareth nodded before rushing out of the room. I then turned my wrath on Terrance. "Who the fuck do you think you are coming into my club and hurting my dancers?"

At his garbled speech, Shane eased his foot back to allow him to speak. "Let me up right this instant, you mick bastard. Don't you know who I am?"

"I know exactly who you are—you're a piece of shit who assaults innocent women and expects his money and reputation to buy him out of situations." A cruel smile curved on my lips. "Poor men and rich men bleed the very same color."

His eyes bulged. "You lay one fucking finger on me, and I'll take you and your brothers for everything you're worth."

Clenching my jaw, I gritted out, "Not if you're dead."

While a string of curses spilled from his mouth, I jerked my chin at Shane. He once again pressed his foot on his throat, silencing Terrance's bullshit.

At that moment, Gareth reappeared with Dowe. "I'll be right back," I told Isla before I eased her out of my arms as gently as I possibly could. When I shot to my feet, Dowe began backing slowly up.

His cowardly action infuriated me. Grabbing him by the neck, I raised him up off his feet before slamming him up against the wall with one of my hands. "Where the fuck were you?"

"Had. to take.leak."

Tightening my hands, I snarled, "What's the fucking protocol?"

"Find. someone. Cover," he choked.

"Once you took your piss, did you come straight back?" At the shake of his head, I spit in his crimson-splotched face. "You're done."

"Please. No,"

I stared menacingly into his face. "The only reason I won't put you in the ground is because your father has been a loyal clan member all his life." When Dowe started to look relieved, I shook my head. "Trust me when I say that when I'm done with you, you'll wish I'd killed you."

His dark eyes widened in fear. "Please."

"That's right. You'll beg for death, but it's not coming for you. As for this job and your place in this clan, you're fucking done."

Shoving away from him, I jabbed my finger at Gareth. "Get him the hell out of here. Chain him up in the basement until I get there."

"Yes, sir."

Dowe had the audacity to weep as he was dragged from the room. My attention once again reverted to Terrance. "Shane, take this piece of shit as well."

Despite the gun on him, Terrance began thrashing on the floor beneath him. "You can't do this!" he shouted.

I flashed him a shark-like grin. "Looks like I am."

When he continued shouting and fighting against Shane, I pulled the gun from my jacket. As I strode up to him, he continued mouthing off. Turning the gun in my hand, I then smacked the base against his temple, knocking him out.

Before he could crumple to the floor, Shane threw him over his shoulder like he was a sack of potatoes. Once Dowe and Terrance were gone, I went back over to the couch and knelt in front of Isla.

"It's time to get you to the ER to get checked out."

"No hospitals," she whispered.

"You have to have a doctor clear you."

"I'm fine."

"This isn't up for debate, Isla. You were attacked. You were—" I ducked my head as I was unable to say the words. What if we hadn't gotten to her soon enough? What if Terrance ripped her from me? I shuddered at the thought.

Staring up at her, I said, "At the very least your thyroid could be damaged, and at the worst, some of the blood vessels in your neck could've torn and clotted, which could cause a stroke."

Her blue eyes popped wide at the mention of a stroke. "Okay, fine."

"Is there someone we can call to meet you at the ER?"

"You aren't taking me?"

"I can't."

She clutched the front of my shirt. "But I want you."

"I'm sorry, but I can't."

At the trembling of her bottom lip, pain ricocheted through my chest. "Please."

Tenderly, I cupped her cheek. "Little Dove, I would if I could. But I'm not bullshitting you when I say I can't. It's for your safety. If I show up at the hospital with you—even at one of the ones that cater to our clan—word will get out that you belong to me. My enemies could use that information against me by hurting you."

"Oh," she murmured.

"So who can go with you?"

"I don't want to get my sister out this time of night." When I started to protest, an agonized look came over her face. "I'm all she has. I can't worry her."

Reluctantly, I nodded. I knew the best person to handle the situation with Isla was Caterina. Although she would be honored to help, Callum would have my arse for getting his pregnant wife out of bed after midnight.

Then another idea came to me. "Get Mabry in here. Now."

She must've been close by because she quickly appeared in the doorway. I waved her over with a flick of my wrist. As she made her way across the room, she wrung her hands at the sight of Isla.

"Yes, Mr. Kavanaugh?" she questioned.

When I pulled myself off the floor, she cowered back slightly. "I want you to take Ms. Vaughn to the ER. Two of my bodyguards will accompany you."

"I'd be happy to go with her."

"Once she is cleared, is it possible for you to go home with her?"

While Mabry opened her mouth, Isla said, "Not necessary."

"I won't allow you to be alone."

Isla blinked at me. "Allow?"

"It's not up for discussion." Although there was no issue with me being at her house, I had torture to dole out before I could go to her.

Ending Terrance Manning ensured Isla's future safety, and that was the most important thing.

After throwing me a cautious look, Mabry dropped down beside Isla. Taking Isla's hand in hers, she squeezed it tight. "I want to help in any way I can."

Isla swiped the tears from her cheeks. "If my sister sees you, she'll be suspicious."

"You can just tell her I'm your drunk coworker who needed a place to stay for the night," Mabry suggested.

Isla hiccuped a laugh, which caused her to wince. When she recovered, she asked, "Couldn't you have thought of a better excuse?"

With a grin, Mabry replied, "Let me take the fall this time."

"Okay. Just this once."

I jerked my thumb at Mabry. "All right. You can get out of here now."

"Quinn," Isla admonished.

"What?"

"You're being a beast."

Mabry's wide eyes stared between the two of us. I'm sure she was wondering if Isla had a death wish for talking to me like she was, or that I had lost my edge for letting Isla chide me for my behavior.

With a grunt, I said, "My apologies. There's a waiting SUV. Can you please go and get in, Mabry?"

"Um, sure. I mean, yes, sir." She gave Isla a quick smile. "I'll be waiting."

"Thank you."

Once we were alone, I stared down at Isla. "I'm so fucking selfish."

Her brows creased. "Don't say that. You're one of the kindest men I know."

"I'm selfish at the moment because I'm stalling taking you out to the car."

"Why?"

"I don't want you out of my sight."

A shy smile curved on her lips. "I don't want out of your sight either."

At that moment, the realization hit me. Tonight had changed everything between us. There was no going back and no more denying the depth of my feelings for her.

I wanted this woman with every fiber of my being. I wanted to own her mind, body, and soul. I wanted to fill her with my cum and see my child growing within her. I wanted to wake up in the mornings with her wrapped in my arms.

I wanted a future with her that I'd never allowed myself to entertain since the bombing.

I wasn't going to let Isla go.

Chapter Sixteen: Isla

Reaching over, Quinn eased his hands underneath me to gently lift me into his arms. Although I wanted to protest that my legs worked fine, I kept my mouth shut and snuggled against his broad chest.

Although the pain in my throat and neck was agony, a warmth filled me from Quinn's protection and care. He'd told me he hadn't wanted to let me go. More than that, he told me there was no one else he wanted to touch him but me.

When he carried me out the doorway, a hush came over the crowd outside.

"Show's over. Get the fuck out of here!" Quinn commanded.

Dancers, clients, and Quinn's men all scattered. After Quinn nodded at one of his bodyguards, the emergency exit door was opened. At the alarm ringing in my ears, I turned my face into Quinn's neck to escape the noise.

When my lips accidentally brushed against his puckered skin, Quinn froze mid-step. A shudder ran through him. It took a moment before he shook himself out of his stupor.

To my surprise, heat ignited between my thighs at the contact. The intrusive thoughts in my mind wondered what it would be like to lick my way up his scars, planting kisses and tender love bites along the way.

Or to take it even farther by licking down to where they escaped into his shirt's collar. To worship each and every inch of them. To show him they were a part of his beauty and could never disgust me.

At Quinn's clenched jaw, I whispered, "Sorry."

"Don't ever apologize to me," he grunted as he started walking again.

"I must've hurt you."

"Never." When he stared down at me, lust glittered in his eyes. "It's me who should be apologizing since the simple touch of your lips made me want you."

"Why should you apologize for that?"

"Because you've just been assaulted. I'm a bastard for wanting more of your lips on my skin."

"Then I am too because I was thinking the same thing." At the look of shock on his face, I couldn't help giggling.

But when desire charged through his expression, my amusement died, and heat burned within me again. Dipping his head, he whispered into my ear. "Soon."

A shiver shuddered through me at both his words and his proximity to me. After he eased me down on the seat, he reached over to fasten my seatbelt. He flicked his gaze to the bodyguard in the front seat. "You protect her just as you would any member of my family."

My heartbeat accelerated at his words, and I found it hard to breathe. When I stared up into his beautifully imperfect face, there were so many words I wanted to say. In the end, I could only bring my hand to his cheek. Closing his eyes, he leaned into my touch.

And then the moment ended.

He jerked away and slammed the door. As the SUV started moving, I desperately wanted to turn to watch his retreating form, but my neck hurt too much. Instead, I stared ahead–my hand still tingling from the rough satin of his skin.

I fully expected to spend half the night waiting to be seen at the ER. To my surprise, a nurse was waiting on us at the front desk. Instead of filling out paperwork, I was ushered straight back to a room.

After slipping on a gown, I eased onto the bed. When I lay my head on the pillow I winced. Every movement was agony.

Mabry sat in a bedside chair while two men I'd never seen before stood outside the door. When I turned my head to meet her intense gaze, she gave me a knowing look. "You've been keeping secrets."

I furrowed my brows. "I haven't," I whispered.

"You and Mr. Kavanaugh."

Warmth flooded my face. "There's nothing to say."

Mabry snorted. "You're the worst liar."

"Okay, fine, we've kissed." I was too exhausted for the level of conversation that would follow if I told her about coming during my audition. Plus, I didn't want her to think I was some freak.

"From the way he spoke to you and held you, I would've wagered it was far more than that."

"It's not."

"But it will be."

Overwhelmed with the emotions from the evening, I replied, "Yes, it will."

Chapter Seventeen: Quinn

When I exited the torture room shortly before dawn, adrenaline continued pumping through me. Even after I showered and changed, I knew I couldn't sleep. Every inch of my skin buzzed and hummed. So, I made a strong cup of coffee and then took it upstairs to the rooftop terrace.

As I stared out at the city coming awake, I knew somewhere a broken and bloody Dowe was being given over to his family. Like I had foretold, he had begged for death, but I hadn't given it to him. He'd been repentant to the last moment he could speak before he passed out from the pain.

The small sliver of humanity left within me went easier on him in the end. But whatever humanity I showed evaporated when I moved to Terrance. Like the truly black soul he was, he cursed and demeaned me until the very end. I didn't care about his words against me. It was him calling Isla a dirty whore and useless slut that enraged the monster within me.

A noise behind me startled me from my thoughts. I whirled around to see Callum striding towards me wearing nothing but a pair of black briefs.

"Morning," he grumbled.

"What are you doing up?"

He wrinkled his nose. "Caterina spent most of the night puking from the wain."

"I thought that was supposed to happen in the morning?"

Callum's mouth widened in a yawn. "I thought the same thing. But according to the experts in the mountain of fucking prenatal books Caterina's been forcing me to read, it can happen any time of day." With a shudder, he replied, "Sometimes all day."

I snorted. "Has she discovered your weakness yet?"

"I'm working overtime to keep it from her."

No one who had watched Callum maim and torture until he was covered in blood and guts would imagine he had a serious aversion to hearing someone vomit. I couldn't imagine how he was handling poor Caterina throwing up.

Turning away from the sunrise, Callum eyed me curiously. "You spent the night torturing, didn't you?"

"Aye," I murmured around the mouth of my coffee mug.

"I didn't know we had anyone on the block."

"We didn't. It came up last night."

After I drew in a ragged breath, I informed Callum of everything that had happened at the club. When I got to the part about gutting Terrance Manning, he smashed his coffee mug onto the tiled floor. "Fucking hell, Quinn. What were you thinking?"

"He hurt Isla."

"I heard that, and I understand protecting our dancers. But Terrance is connected throughout the city."

"And most of those connections hate his fecking guts."

"True. But that doesn't mean it isn't going to blow back a lot of heat on us. Word is going to get out that he had an altercation in your club shortly before he disappeared."

"Don't act like I didn't think this through."

"You didn't. You thought with your dick."

"Fuck you. It's not like that."

"I know it's not." When I cocked my brows at him, Callum sighed. "Caterina told me about the soup."

"Why am I not surprised," I grumbled.

"But it wasn't the first time I heard it."

Shaking my head, I replied, "Dare is no better than a woman when it comes to gossiping."

Callum chuckled. "Aye, that's true." The amusement slid from his face. "Regardless of your feelings for this dancer, you took your possessiveness too far."

"Excuse me? You killed a man for laying a hand on Caterina at *Bandia*."

"She was my *wife*, and he was a fucking nobody rapist not a rich, connected man." Callum angrily shook his head. "We can't afford this right now."

"Once again, give me some fucking credit, not to mention our IT team."

Callum's brows furrowed. "What do you mean?"

Taking my phone out of my pocket, I opened the internet to the Boston Globe's website. I then handed the phone to Callum.

After his eyes scanned the headline, he jerked his head up. "They're seriously publishing this?"

"Aye. I called in a favor."

Callum's gaze dropped back to the phone. "Millionaire businessman, Terrance Manning, murdered among unearthed secrets of trafficking and drugs," he read aloud. "How the hell did you get them to write this? Terrance's family could sue them for liable."

"Only if it wasn't true."

Callum's jaw unhinged. "This shite is true?"

"Much like us, his empire was built on shady dealings."

"I'll be damned."

My lips curved in a smirk. "When you're ready to apologize, I'm listening."

Callum barked out a laugh. "Bastard."

"What are you guys doing?"

We turned to see Caterina approaching. Dark circles spread under her eyes, but she had a warm smile on her lips. Callum tucked her to his side. "You should be in bed, Kitten."

"I'm starving."

His brows popped wide. "Seriously?"

She grinned. "Yes, seriously. I wanted some pancakes."

"I'll wake Lorna."

"You'll do no such thing. I'm perfectly capable of making some pancakes."

"Fine then. I'll help you," Callum said.

"Fanny-whipped," I teased under my breath to which Callum scowled at me.

"Quinn, would you like some pancakes, too?" Caterina asked.

"No thank you. I need to go check on Isla."

Caterina's brows creased with worry. "What happened?"

After I related last night's events, tears filled Caterina's eyes. "I'm so sorry."

"Thank you. I'll tell her you were thinking of her."

"I'd love to bring her a meal and come for a visit."

I smiled at Caterina. "I'm sure she would like that, too."

After she extricated herself from Callum, Caterina came to hug me. Her touch was one of the few that I welcomed and not just tolerated. Her voice came close to my ear. "She likes you, Quinn."

Warmth spread through my chest. "And I like her. A lot."

She pulled back to stare into my eyes. "I told her you did. Now go and take care of her as well as you have me."

"I promise."

When Caterina bestowed a kiss on my cheek, Callum grunted. A chuckle rumbled through me at his possessiveness. "Easy, mate. She's not putting the moves on me."

Like the ridiculous caveman he was, Callum wrapped his arm around Caterina's waist. "I know that."

"Then ease up before you piss on her leg."

As Caterina giggled, Callum shot me a death glare. "Fuck you."

"I'm off to Southborough."

When I reached the door of the terrace, I remembered not receiving my apology. Turning back, I said, "Over breakfast, maybe Callum can acquaint you with his little aversion to vomit."

As Callum's face turned the shade of an eggplant, I burst out laughing, and I didn't stop until I got into the car.

When I reached Isla's house, I parked behind the security van. Even though I'd neutralized the threat to Isla's immediate safety, there were still measures I wanted to undertake. I'd kept a bodyguard at her house after she returned from the hospital. I'd also called out our clan security company to come put a system in her house.

After I exited my car, Fergus, the bodyguard, strolled up to meet me. "Morning, boss."

"Morning. Everything went okay last night?" I'd received the news when Isla had arrived home from the ER around midnight. Fergus had also texted me when Isla had Mabry sneak out around six am.

"All quiet. The sister left about twenty minutes ago. I put a tracker on her car last night. It appears she's at the gym."

"Good call. And thank you."

"No problem."

"You can head on since I have Shane with me."

Fergus nodded and then headed back to his car. I turned to surmise the modest, but well-kept two-story house that Isla called home. As I made my way up the front walk, I imagined she had a good childhood growing up here. It was a nice neighborhood that appeared safe.

At the sight of the ancient doorbell, I rolled my eyes. "Jaysus," I muttered under my breath. Not even a doorbell camera to make sure Jack the fucking Ripper wasn't at her door. In this day and age, could Isla really be so naïve? As intelligent as she was, it couldn't be an aversion to technology.

"Who is it?" she called from behind the mahogany door.

"It's Quinn."

Silence echoed after my statement. I shifted on my feet. Maybe I should've called first. After everything that transpired last night, maybe her feelings had changed in the light of day. To see me would be a reminder of what had happened.

Finally, I heard the snapping of locks. At least she had the presence of mind to keep things locked up tight.

When the door swung open, my heart dropped into my stomach. While I'd feared extensive bruises on her face and neck, nothing could've prepared me for what I saw.

In Isla's arms she held a dark-haired, dark-eyed baby boy. At the sight of me, his mouth stretched into a gummy grin.

Fuck me.

Isla was a mother?

None of my intel had unearthed a baby. Was his father around? Had she been hiding another man from me? The fragile strands of my sanity snapped at the thought of losing her before she was even truly mine.

After shifting the baby to her hip, Isla smiled warmly at me. "Hi, Quinn."

Without even a hello, I demanded, "Is he yours?"

Isla's cheeks flushed. "No, no. He's my sister's, remember?"

"You never told me about him."

"Yes, I did. At my audition." A sheepish look came over her face. "One of the many times my mouth got away from me."

Relief flooded me. Not that I cared if she had a kid. While they weren't on my top list of priorities, I didn't rule out becoming a father one day.

No, my relief came from the fact there wasn't another man.

Now that she mentioned it, I vaguely remembered something about her sister being a teen mother. I wasn't surprised I had forgotten since that night was such a mind fuck. "Your sister is at the gym," I said.

Isla's brows furrowed. "Wait, how did you know that?"

"I had eyes on the house all night."

"You did?"

With a nod, I replied, "Since I couldn't be here with you, I wanted to make sure you were okay."

"I appreciate it."

As I surveyed the baby in her arms, it unnerved me. I liked the way she looked. I liked the idea of her being a mother. But only if it were my child in her arms. "You look like his mother," I remarked.

Isla's face lit up. "You think so?"

"He looks like you."

"He looks like his mother, and we do favor." When the baby kicked his legs and babbled, Isla eyed him adoringly. "Some days he feels like mine. It's hard imagining that I could love one of my own children more." She wrinkled her nose. "But I know I will. You know, when the time comes. I'm certainly not ready to start a family now. I've got to finish grad school."

Furrowing her brows, she rattled on, "That doesn't mean if it happened, I wouldn't be thrilled since I've always wanted kids." With a laugh, she said, "Considering I got an IUD when Brooke got pregnant, it would have to be a miracle for that to happen. Especially since I'm not having sex at the moment."

As soon as the words left her lips, she clamped her free hand over her mouth. "I can't believe I just said that."

My lips quirked at her rambling. "You're nervous."

"A little," she whispered.

"About me?"

"Yes."

"After everything we've been through, you're still nervous?" When she bobbed her head, I remarked, "You weren't nervous the night you cleaned me up."

"It was the adrenaline coupled with my ridiculous empath side."

"What about last night?"

Her eyes shuttered in pain. "I-I was too scared to feel any other emotion."

A bitter feeling entered my chest. "Is it because of the way I look?" I cleared my throat. "Like my appearance scares you?"

Isla's expression softened. "Of course not." At what must've been my continued disbelief, Isla reached out to touch my arm.

My scarred arm.

Normally, I would've slung away from anyone who dared to touch me. But for whatever reason, I didn't mind when Isla touched me. In fact, I was growing to like it.

Rubbing my arm, Isla said, "Like I said before, you and your scars don't scare me, Quinn. They never have, and they never will."

"Obviously there's something about me that makes you uncomfortable."

Peering up at me, she replied, "I would be lying if I said your behavior last night didn't scare me a little."

"I'd like to tell you I'm sorry for that, but I'm not." When I took a step forward, Isla didn't back away. "I'll make anyone pay who dares to hurt you."

"I know," she whispered.

Tilting my head at her, I asked, "If you know I won't hurt you, then why the fuck do you get nervous around me?"

"Because you're..." She shivered. "Consuming."

"Are you afraid I'm going to consume you?"

Isla's pulse quickened on her neck as her chest heaved. She slowly shook her head. "I'm afraid you won't."

Fucking hell.

Closing the gap between us, my hand cupped her chin. I ran my thumb over her bottom lip. "There's nothing in the whole world I want more than to devour you."

Desire flared in Isla's sapphire eyes. Her tongue darted out to lick her lips, which caused me to groan. "I'm glad," she replied breathlessly.

When I dipped my head to bring my lips to hers, Henry squealed. Isla blinked and then shook her head like she was waking up from a dream. At my frustrated grunt, Henry giggled while Isla's cheeks reddened. "I don't think he wants to share my attention," she mused.

I smiled. "I don't blame him. Look, I don't mean to keep you from caring for him. I just wanted to come by and make sure you're okay."

She blinked at me. "You came all the way here to check on me?"

"Aye. I did."

Eyeing me curiously, Isla asked, "Do you do that for all your dancers?"

With a hard shake of my head, I replied, "Of course I fucking don't." At her surprise, I grunted. "I'm sorry. I just thought after last night you understood the depth of my feelings for you."

A tremble ran through her. "I'm starting to comprehend they run deeper than just the physical side."

"I couldn't sleep until I saw your face."

"You didn't sleep last night?"

"I had matters to take care of."

Although I could see the questions in Isla's eyes, she remained uncharacteristically quiet. "It didn't matter that I'd received your full medical report. I needed to see you for myself."

Her brows popped. "Excuse me? That's against HIPAA."

"Fuck that. I needed to know you were okay."

"You could've called me," she huffed.

"You needed your rest."

She threw up her hands. "You're infuriating, you know that?"

"I've been told that. But it doesn't change me wanting to protect you." After crossing my arms over my chest, I said, "I know how you're doing physically. Now tell me how you're doing emotionally."

Isla shrugged. "Okay, I guess."

"Don't lie to me."

When she nibbled on her bottom lip, I shot her a hard look, which caused her to sigh. "Fine. I didn't sleep very well last night."

"From the pain?"

"Not exactly." She rubbed her arms as she shivered. "Every time I closed my eyes, he was all I could see."

My hand reached out to cup her cheek. "I'm so sorry."

When my gaze dipped to her neck, I realized she was wearing a turtleneck. I'd been so distracted by the baby, I'd forgotten to check on her physically. My hands came to ease the fabric down. At the sight of the purple and blue bruising along her skin, a low growl erupted from my chest.

The noise caused Henry's brows to crease before he burst into tears. "Oh, it's all right, sweet boy," Isla crooned as she rubbed wide circles across his back. Meeting my gaze, she grinned. "Big Bad Mr. Quinn wasn't growling at you."

Sweeping my hands to my hips, I demanded, "Seriously?"

With a giggle, she replied, "Sorry. I couldn't help teasing you."

I blinked at her. The only people in my life who remotely teased me were my brothers. And Caterina. No one else had the balls big enough to do it. "People who dare to tease me usually get punished."

Isla's throat bobbed as she swallowed. "They do?"

"For you, I would find a more pleasurable form of torture."

At her whimper, I inwardly groaned. What the fuck was wrong with me trying to seduce Isla in broad daylight, not to mention while she held her nephew? Deep down, I knew it was because she drove me crazy. Any morality I had in me went out the window when I was with her.

After clearing her throat, Isla said, "Where are my manners? I should've invited you in."

"I'm not a gentleman, so you probably shouldn't."

At the insinuation in my words, heat filled Isla's cheeks. "The least I can do is offer you a cup of coffee." When I continued staring at her, Isla cocked her head at me. "Maybe a glass of water to cool you off?"

A laugh burst from my lips, surprising both of us along with Henry. His tear-stained cheeks widened in a smile. "I think a glass of water would be grand."

Isla held the door open. "Then come in."

When she started to walk down the hallway, I remembered that I hadn't come alone. "Hold on."

She turned with a curious expression. "What's wrong?"

I jerked my thumb to the driveway. "I need to let the men in to work on the security system."

Her brows shot up. "Excuse me?"

"I'm having a security system installed in your house."

Isla's mouth gaped open. "But I—"

I shook my head. "Don't tell me you don't need one. Two women and a baby need one."

"It's not that."

"Then what?"

Her gaze shifted to the floor. "You should understand it's not in the cards right now. You know, financially."

"I don't give a fuck about your finances."

Isla jerked her gaze up to mine. "Quinn, don't curse in front of the baby," she admonished.

With a roll of my eyes, I countered, "Like he knows what I'm saying."

Her blue eyes narrowed at me. "I mean it."

"Fine. I don't *care* about your finances. This is on me."

She shook her head wildly back and forth. "I can't let you do that."

"You don't *let* me do anything—I just do it."

Her perfectly plump lips opened and closed like a fish out of water. "You are a....a...."

"What, Isla?"

"A beast!"

My lips quirked. "Am I?"

"You stomp into my life, bossing me around and not taking no for an answer." She jabbed a finger at me. "I've managed to take care of myself for twenty-three years, not to mention taking care of my sister and Henry all by myself the last two."

"I don't give a shite if you find my behavior overbearing. It was under my watch that you were assaulted. I will not apologize for wanting to ensure your safety, nor will I not do everything within my power to keep you safe."

Her blue eyes stared intently into mine. "You will."

"Aye, I will."

With an exasperated sigh, she said, "Fine. I'm too tired to fight you."

"It's best if you saved your energy since you weren't going to win."

"Beast!" Isla shouted, which caused her to wince and bring her hand to her neck.

One of the security team cleared his throat. "We're about to install the panel by the front door. I thought you might want to clear the personal items in the vicinity."

"Uh, right." Isla glanced from me to Henry and then back to me. "Here. Take him." She then thrust Henry at me.

As I stared into the baby's questioning face, I argued, "Isla, I don't think that's a good idea."

"Don't worry. He's usually good with strangers."

"It's not that," I gritted out.

The corners of Isla's lips quirked. "Don't tell me you've never held a baby before?"

"Of course, I have," I snapped. When she cocked her head at me, I sighed. "Fine. It's been like sixteen years with my kid brother."

"Caterina told me you're going to be an uncle in seven months. You should start practicing for your niece with Henry."

Defeated, I merely rolled my eyes. "Fine."

Isla didn't give me another moment to prepare before shoving Henry into my arms. She then whirled away before I could protest. Henry's wide eyes tracked Isla down the hallway.

Once she was out of sight, he turned his gaze back to me. His chin trembled, causing me to groan. "Come on, kid. Do us both a favor and don't lose it on me." My words only caused his lips to quiver, and his eyes to water. At the rising panic I felt, I tried patting his back as reassuringly as I could. "I promise Auntie Isla will be right back."

With his expression continuing to crumble, I started bouncing him in my arms. I reached into my memory for a lullaby from my childhood. As I envisioned my mam sitting in the antique rocking chair with Eamon in her arms, I began humming *Toora Loora Loora*.

Henry blinked at me in surprise. The intensity of his gaze penetrated my soul. Thankfully, he appeared to enjoy the lullaby because his sniffles dried up. After I shifted him higher on my chest, he stretched his arm out to the intricate tattoos on my neck. His tiny fingers scratched along my skin as he traced the ink. When he reached my scars, I sucked in a breath while waiting for him to jerk away.

But he didn't.

Instead, he babbled something before patting his hand along my gnarled skin. I exhaled a breath of relief. Although I would never voice it, I'd worried about what a child of my own might think of my scars. Would it frighten them? Would they question how I'd gotten them? Worst of all, would my appearance embarrass them around their friends?

At the sound of a gun cocking, I didn't stop to process what was happening or how I should react with a child in my arms. Instead, my free hand went to my jacket pocket and snatched out my gun. When I whirled around, I came face to face with a slightly taller, angrier version of Isla.

"Who the fuck are you, and what are you doing with my baby?" she demanded.

Chapter Eighteen: Isla

Q*uinn* was in *my* house.

His worry and care for me had gone so far that he'd broken HIPAA laws to get my medical records and was forcing a security system on me.

He wanted to consume me physically and emotionally.

The last twenty-four hours had been such a confusing emotional and physical rollercoaster. I'd been released from the ER with no lasting physical issues except for a bruised larynx. The doctor had told me to rest, drink plenty of fluid, and alternate ice packs during the day.

Although he'd prescribed sleeping pills, I hadn't taken any last night. I didn't want to be woozy in front of Brooke. After donning a turtleneck from the back of my closet and claiming my hoarse voice was from coming down with a cold, she hadn't suspected a thing. I'd even offered to keep Henry for her to go to the gym and do our weekly grocery run.

Wincing, I wondered how I was going to explain the new security system to her. More than that, I wondered how I would explain Quinn's presence if he was still here when she got back

After throwing a glance over my shoulder, I watched as he bounced Henry in his arms. The corners of my lips curved at the sight of the scarred, towering man and my tiny nephew.

He looked good with a baby.

"Ma'am?"

I whirled around to face the security man. "I'm so sorry. My head just isn't right today."

He gave me a reassuring smile. "It's okay."

I turned my out-of-control thoughts from Quinn back to the task at hand, which was cleaning off the entrance hall table. I started snatching and grabbing picture frames, loading them into my arms. When I grabbed the last one, I finally allowed myself to focus on the smiling faces staring out at me.

It was Brooke's baptism photo. Her frilly white dress overflowed my mother's arms. The tiny face was so much like Henry's. Next to them, my father, outfitted in his robes, held me. He'd baptized both me and Brooke, but he wouldn't be here to baptize Henry.

The ache in my chest continued to spread as I backed away from the table. When I glanced at the security man, I nodded. "You can take it now."

Before he could respond, Brooke's shout jerked my attention to the kitchen. I didn't bother putting the armload of picture frames down. Instead, I sprinted to the kitchen. To my horror, Brooke and Quinn were pointing guns at each other.

"Brooke!" I shrieked

"Isla, stay back."

"No, no, that's my boss. Quinn."

Brooke didn't take her eyes off Quinn, nor did she lower her gun. "You swear?"

"Yes! Don't you remember him from the club?"

"I don't have my contacts in, and my glasses are in the car."

"Well, it's definitely him, so please put the gun down."

Although she didn't look happy about it, Brooke slid the safety on before lowering her gun. As she put it in her bag, Quinn put his back in his holster.

"How did you plan on shooting me if you couldn't see me?" Quinn smirked.

"I can see enough of your crotch to maim you," Brooke shot back to which Quinn chuckled.

"Since when do you carry a gun?" I demanded.

"Since I had Henry."

"Good point." As I eyed her purse with the gun inside, I said, "Is that one of dad's?"

She snorted. "Yes, it's his–the packing priest."

I laughed at the memory of what my father had jokingly called himself. One might not normally imagine an Episcopal priest carrying a gun, but his work took him into some of the tougher parts of the city where his safety was at risk.

Quinn took a step forward. "Isla asked me to hold him. You can have him back."

Brooke held up a hand. "I'm shaking too hard right now to do that."

I stepped over to the kitchen table and unloaded the picture frames. I pulled out a chair for her. After patting the seat, I said, "Sit."

Brooke was obviously unnerved because she didn't argue with me about bossing her around. Surprisingly, Henry didn't cry or hold his hands out for his mother like he usually did. He seemed completely enraptured with the intricate tattoos on Quinn's neck.

Brooke's loathing gaze slid from Quinn over to me. "What is going on?"

"Quinn came by to oversee the installation of our security system."

Her brows furrowed. "But we really can't afford all that, can we?"

I laughed tightly. "I told him as much." Turning my attention to Quinn, I noted, "He doesn't take no for an answer."

His jaw clenched. "As I told your sister, two single women and a baby shouldn't be without one. Especially after what happened last night."

I pinched my eyes shut at the same time Brooke demanded, "Wait, what happened?"

When I opened my eyes, Brooke stared questioningly at me. "I didn't want to worry you," I began.

Brooke snapped out of her chair like a rubber band. "What the fuck happened, Isla?"

Instead of telling her, I decided to show her. With shaky fingers, I pulled down the fabric of the turtleneck to reveal my throat. Just that much exertion caused me to wince in pain.

Brooke gasped in horror before staggering back to her chair. As she flopped down, she shook her head slowly from side to side. "You promised something like this wouldn't happen. That it wasn't a skeezy club but millionaires and billionaires went there."

I sighed. "I was naive to make that promise. Abusive men aren't just regulated to the lower tax brackets."

"From the look of your neck, it seems he was downright homicidal rather than abusive."

Fiddling with the hem of my shirt, I fought to keep my emotions in check. Despite the anguish churning through me, I couldn't lose it in front of Brooke. I had to be strong for her. "It's over. That's all that matters," I finally replied.

"That's bullshit, and you know it," Brooke replied.

After being silent as a ghost, Quinn stepped forward. "You can rest assured he won't ever hurt your sister again."

With an angry shake of her head, Brooke countered, "You can't possibly promise that."

A cruel smirk curved on Quinn's lips. "Trust me when I say, he has been taken care of."

As the realization hit me, the world around me shuddered to a stop. The only reason Quinn could say what he said with such conviction was if he had murdered my assaulter. He belonged to the Irish mafia, and men in the mafia were killers. At least that's what my limited perspective had been.

My gaze trailed from Quinn's face down to the hands that cradled Henry against him. The very hands on my innocent nephew's skin had committed murder. They'd been stained with blood and God knows what else.

I had to fight the urge to stalk over and snatch Henry away. I wanted to take him upstairs to try to wash the corruption and danger off of him. Even though I knew it was a ridiculous way of thinking, I couldn't stop myself.

While Brooke tilted her head skeptically at Quinn, I croaked, "Please say you didn't."

"He hurt you," Quinn argued.

"But the police–"

He chuckled darkly. "You're being naive again, Isla. Terrance Manning has cops in his pocket. If you had tried prosecuting him, your case would've never seen the light of day."

"But I could've tried."

As Quinn bounced Henry in his arms, you would've thought he was talking about the weather, rather than a man's death. "A man as dark as Terrance would've ensured your silence by horrific means. He would've punished you into silence." Emotion flared in his dark blue eyes. "I couldn't allow that to happen."

Oh God. He truly cared for me. He cared enough to murder the man who had hurt me. He had done it to protect me. To ensure that I would get some warped version of justice, and that I wouldn't be hurt again.

At the same time, revulsion echoed through me. Quinn had killed a man in cold blood. Although it was more than warranted, I didn't want to think of Quinn like that.

As a murderer.

Anguish filled Quinn's expression. "Don't look at me like that."

"Like what?" I whispered.

"Like you fear me now."

"But I do."

Quinn's eyes narrowed. "You've known who I was since that night I was shot."

Brooke gasped. "You witnessed a shooting?"

I shook my head. "No. I just helped him clean up a bullet wound."

Throwing up her hands, Brooke demanded, "What have you gotten yourself into, Isla?"

"Nothing."

"Bullet wounds aren't *nothing*." She stared at Quinn. "Murders aren't *nothing*."

"They are for me when someone hurts someone I care about," he countered.

Once again, Brooke rose out of her chair. This time she strode over to Quinn and snatched Henry out of his arms, causing Henry to cry out. "Shh, it's okay. Mama has you now."

"I'm not the monster here," he growled.

Brooke refused to look at Quinn. She swayed Henry in her arms, running her fingers over his dark hair. She tore her eyes from Henry to stare at me. My chest constricted at the tears welling in her eyes. "We could've lost you last night, Isla."

"I know. And I'm sorry."

"I don't want you going back there."

"I have to, B."

Quinn shook his head. "You're done with private dances."

"What?"

"You're not doing them anymore. I won't allow it."

My mouth dropped open to my chest. "You can't do that."

"I'm the majority owner in the club. What I say goes, and I say no."

"Without the tips from private dances, I won't make any money. The whole point of taking my fucking clothes off is to make money!"

"I'm aware of that."

"And you would still deny me? Is this you being a caveman like Caterina said?"

His lips quirked. "She called me a caveman."

"She said you and your brothers could be possessive cavemen, and now I'm seeing it." I shook my head. "You can't deny me a living just because you can't take me riding some other man's dick."

The amusement swept off his face. "Do you honestly think I would deny you the money you need?"

"If you forbid me from doing private dances, you are."

"Whatever your usual take home was for the night, I'll match it."

This seriously wasn't happening. "Are you insane?"

Quinn's jaw clenched. "Not that I know of," he gritted out.

"Apparently you are if you think I would agree to you paying me like I'm a hooker."

"Oh shit," Brooke muttered under her breath.

Quinn's eyes bulged. "I would never think of you like that."

"What else would I be?"

"Last time I checked, we weren't fucking, and you have to be paid for sex to be a hooker!" Quinn roared.

My cheeks warmed. "I just said it would be *like* I was a prostitute. Who else would I be for money to come between us?"

He threw his hands up in frustration. "The woman I want to take care of."

With a roll of my eyes, I replied, "I'm sure that's what the other girls will think when they get wind that you're paying me not to do lap dances."

"I don't give a fuck what they think."

"Well I do."

"Why are you being so stubborn? This is the best solution for you and your family."

"I'm sorry. But if we're to have any future, I can't feel like I'm indebted to you financially."

Quinn furrowed his brows. "You really don't want me to do this?"

I shook my head furiously back and forth. "No. I don't."

He threw a glance at Brooke before looking intently at me. "You don't want my money?"

"I really don't."

After exhaling a ragged sigh, Quinn dragged his hand through his dark hair. "Then we'll have to find a compromise because I will not allow you into a private room alone again."

"You could always stay in the room with her," Brooke suggested, a wicked gleam in her eyes.

He gritted his teeth at her. "Not happening."

"Then what's your solution, Big Man?" she countered.

As he leaned back against the counter, Quinn appeared to be deep in thought. "No one but you and I would have to know about the money." When I started to protest, he held a hand up. "You could waitress instead of doing lap dances. You're still working for me that way, and it wouldn't be like I was just completely giving you the money."

"But what are the odds you're going to pay me obscenely more than the other waitresses?"

"Pretty fair."

"Quinn," I groaned.

"Oh let him do it," Brooke urged.

"You're seriously taking his side?"

Brooke gave Quinn a contemptuous look. "Only if he can assure me of your safety as a waitress."

"I will personally oversee Isla's shifts."

"You're going to be my stalker?" I demanded.

The corners of his lips quirked. "I would think of it as more of a date."

Brooke snorted. "That's a fucked up date when your girl parades around half-naked for patrons."

Before I could admonish Brooke, Quinn narrowed his eyes on her. "I thought we were on the same side."

"You assume too much."

"Is that right?" Quinn countered.

As she nodded, Brooke took a step towards Quinn. "I never wanted her in your fucking club to begin with, and I sure as hell don't now that she's been assaulted. I begged her to take my inheritance for school. Anything to keep her from doing what she's been doing."

Cutting his eyes to me, Quinn said, "I didn't know she had other choices."

I squared my shoulders to face both my sister and him. "I did, but I didn't. I made the choice that I felt was best. Despite what happened last night, I'd do it again."

"Why?" Quinn demanded.

My heart started beating wildly in my chest. "Because without the club, I never would've met you."

Quinn's blue eyes popped wide at my admission. As he continued standing there in astonishment, I added, "You were worth it."

"Seriously, Isla?" Brooke demanded with a wounded look.

"I'm sorry, B. I never wanted to hurt you with my decisions. But you know as well as I do, you can't help who you fall for."

She narrowed her eyes at me. "I would think that you could try not to fall for the dangerous mafia man," she countered.

"Brooke, please."

With a shake of her head, she started out of the kitchen, but Quinn stepped into her path. "I can understand your aversion to me."

"That's astute of you," she snapped.

Although his jaw clenched, Quinn remained cool and calm. "The moment I first saw your sister, I knew there wasn't another woman in the world I could possibly want. But I fought my feelings. Like you, I didn't want her involved with a man like me. I didn't want to do anything to hurt her physically or emotionally."

He drew in a ragged breath. "Staying away from your sister has been miserable. But I would continue to do it if she didn't want to be with me. I don't know what the future holds. A month or a year from now maybe she'll finally discover she's way too good for me–"

"Quinn," I protested.

"Let me finish."

"Fine."

"If she discovers she's too good for me and leaves, I'll always make sure she's protected from my world. And by extension you and your son. You have my word."

When Quinn extended his hand, Brooke eyed it with disgust. At the same time, Henry lunged in her arms and reached for Quinn. At first, she stared at Henry in horror. And then the longer Henry babbled and stretched out his tiny arms for Quinn, the more her horror faded.

Finally she gave in to Henry and handed him to Quinn. Tears stung my eyes at the sight of Henry patting the scars along Quinn's face, and the sweet expression on Quinn's face as Henry did it.

With a sigh, Brooke shook her head at Quinn. "I still don't like the world you come from and the danger you put Isla in. But I suppose it's only fair for me to give you a chance."

"How diplomatic of you," I mused.

With a shrug, she replied, "It's the truth." A smile tugged at the corners of her lips. "They say children are a good judge of character, and in this case, I'll go with Henry's, rather than my own."

Quinn gave her a genuine smile. "While I appreciate his choice, I would argue that perhaps he's drawn to me more because I have a penis than because I'm a good person."

As my eyes bulged in horror, Brooke laughed. "True. You are an oddity considering we don't have too many men around here."

I rolled my eyes at them. "I'm so glad the two of you could ruin a sweet moment."

Brooke jerked her thumb at the backdoor. "While Henry's occupied, why don't you help me get the groceries in?"

Quinn shook his head. "I'll have Shane do it."

As he reached for his phone, Brooke creased her brows. "Who is Shane?"

"His bodyguard."

She snorted. "Since he's bringing in the groceries, he sounds more like Quinn's bitch."

With a smirk, Quinn countered, "Yeah, go ahead and say that to him when his 6'7", three hundred pound self gets in here."

"We can at least go help him," I replied. When Quinn started to protest, I argued, "The sooner we get the groceries, the sooner I can make us breakfast."

Both Quinn and Brooke yelled, "No, you're not!"

I pinched the bridge above my nose. "Guys, I'm fine."

"You're going to lie down right now," Brooke instructed as Quinn nodded.

"I'll have breakfast delivered from my house. Our cook always makes enough."

Brooke's brows arched into her hairline. "You have a full-time cook?"

"Yes. I do."

A devious little grin broke out on her lips. "Okay, Isla, if you don't marry him maybe I will!"

Chapter Nineteen: Quinn

As I reclined on Isla's sofa with her in my arms, I couldn't remember a time I'd felt happier. It had to have been before the bombing, and the more I thought about it, nothing compared to the feeling of being with her.

Two days had passed since her assault. I'd only left her side long enough to check in at the club. The first night I'd offered to sleep in the guest bedroom, but Isla had refused. Instead, I'd stuffed myself into her Queen sized bed.

After an uncomfortable night, I'd wanted to order a new bedroom suite with a California King to accommodate my large frame, but I knew Isla would lose her mind. She'd already objected to me ordering out for lunch and dinner. So, last night I folded myself into bed once again.

Today she'd talked me into being a couch potato and watching movies. Since I was a huge fan of the cinema, I didn't have any objections. But she'd bypassed the latest action or dramas on Netflix. Instead, she'd gone for some period piece with irritating Brits. I had the feeling I was in for a day of torture. I even debated calling Caterina over to take my place.

Just as the pompous sounding arse of a hero was about to win the equally annoying lass, my phone rang. When I saw Callum's name, I chose to ignore it. I knew he wanted to bring me up to date about the Jersey Bratva. For once, I didn't want to have to deal with the business. I just wanted to be a normal guy and enjoy a day of ease with a girl.

After it continued ringing, Isla raised her brows at me. "Shouldn't you get that?"

"I know it's business, and I don't want anything taking away my time with you."

Her eyes lit up at my remark. "While that's very sweet, I don't want to be the one coming between you and your empire."

I snorted. "My criminal empire?"

"You know what I mean."

"Fine. I'll go ahead and take it since he'll probably just keep blowing up my phone."

Jerking her thumb at the door, Isla asked, "Would you like me to go?"

"No. It's fine."

When I finally picked up my phone, it was now on the third missed call from Callum. He started up again, and I slid my finger across the screen. "Hello?"

"Are you not answering my calls?" Callum demanded.

"I was busy."

"With Isla's pussy?"

"Watch yourself," I growled.

Callum chuckled. "Considering the bullshit you pulled yesterday morning, you owe me."

"Please tell me you didn't just call to give me shit for that?"

"Actually, I need you in a business capacity."

"I don't like the sound of this."

"Caterina isn't feeling well enough to attend the Green and Gold Gala with me tonight."

"I really don't like the sound of this."

"I need you and Isla to attend."

"I *really* fucking don't like the sound of that."

"Before you say no, I'm not talking about sending you on your own. I'll be there as well."

"Why aren't you asking Dare? You know he's a thousand times better in any social situation."

"I need a female face in our party, and Dare has too many females to choose from."

"Why do we need a woman?"

"Because we're trying to sniff out investors for the casino."

"Which is why you want to bring Isla?"

Her gaze shifted from the TV over to me. "What is it?"

"Callum wants us to attend a benefit with him tonight."

Her eyes widened. "I've never been to one of those."

"Would you be willing to go with me?"

"Of course." She frowned. "But I don't think I have anything to wear."

"That's okay. I can handle that."

Her lips quirked up. "You're going to handle a formal dress for me?"

"Trust me. I have connections."

As Isla's hands went to her neck, her amusement faded. "What about my bruises?"

"I'll have a makeup artist cover them."

"Let me guess. You have connections to one of those, too."

"I do," I replied with a smirk.

Isla playfully rolled her eyes. "Of course you do."

"Does that mean you're in?"

She grinned. "I'm in. But if it's all the same to you, I'd rather Brooke do my makeup and hair."

"Whatever you would like." Speaking back to Callum, I said, "Okay, we're in."

"Great. Just come meet me at the house at seven."

"We'll be there."

"Thanks, Quinn."

"Yeah, yeah. You're going to owe me big time for this."

Callum chuckled. "Whatever."

After I hung up, I rose off the couch. "Come on. I'm taking you shopping."

Chapter Twenty: Isla

When Quinn said he was taking me shopping, I imagined we would go to the mall, which for someone like Quinn I had to imagine would be a form of torture. What I didn't imagine was us turning onto Newbury Street with its elite, high-end stores. Growing up when we came into Boston, my family could barely afford to drive down the street least of all shop on it.

With a gaping mouth, I turned to face Quinn. "You can't be serious."

His dark brows furrowed. "What's wrong with shopping here?"

"Maybe because it's about three times outside my budget," I protested.

"Don't worry about that. It's my treat."

"Oh no, it isn't!"

Quinn huffed out a frustrated breath. "Isla, you're attending this gala as my guest, so you're doing me a favor. Therefore, it shouldn't be a big deal for me to buy you a dress."

When I opened my mouth to argue again, he shook his head. "Let me do this." Staring intently into my eyes, he added, "Please."

"Well, you just had to go and use please, didn't you?" At his grin, I sighed. "Fine. And just for you being cheeky about it, I'm going to get the most expensive one I can find."

"Cheeky?"

"I'm picking up all these phrases from this Irish guy I know," I teasingly replied.

"I can assure you I wasn't being cheeky."

"We'll have to agree to disagree."

The driver pulled the SUV in front of a store with a gold and white awning. "Thanks, Mikey. You can circle the block if you need to, and I'll call when we're finished," Quinn instructed.

"Yes, sir."

Before I could open my passenger door, Shane, Quinn's bodyguard, opened it for me. He held out a hand to help me down. "Thank you."

"You're welcome, Ms. Vaughn."

"You don't have to be so formal. You can call me Isla."

"My apologies, but I'll only call you that if Mr. Kavanaugh instructs me to do so."

As I turned around to face Quinn getting out of the car, I said, "Tell him he can call me Isla."

Quinn shook his head. "He will remain formal with you."

"Why?"

"Because that's how it should be."

"Does Caterina still get called Mrs. Kavanaugh by her bodyguard?"

"Yes, she does. And that's even after she held him at gunpoint once."

I widened my eyes. "She did what?"

"It's a story for another time. Come on."

I wanted to protest that there would never be an appropriate time to hear about Caterina wielding a gun on her bodyguard, but I decided to keep my mouth shut instead.

As we started in the door, I froze. "What's wrong?"

"I have a feeling when the salespeople get a look at me, I'm going to have a *Pretty Woman* experience."

"A what?"

My brows popped wide. "Don't tell me you've never seen *Pretty Woman*?" At his continued blank expression, I replied, "Well, we'll have to remedy that right away."

"Let me guess. It's some chick movie with romance and shit."

I laughed. "That pretty much sums it up."

He winced. "I'd rather be tortured."

"Then I look forward to cracking the whip," I teased.

Quinn's blue eyes turned dark. "Don't tell me Miss Sunshine goes in for anything S&M?"

"Maybe a little." Tilting my head up at him, I replied, "Spankings can be nice."

As his jaw flexed, he made a pained noise. "We can't be having this conversation now."

I laughed. "Okay, we'll bench it for another time."

"Yes, we will."

The moment we brushed inside the door, my stomach clenched. Although I wouldn't have pegged him for someone to be at ease in a women's clothing store, Quinn marched determinedly up the waiting saleslady. If she was uneasy with his imposing figure, she hid it well. "Mr. Kavanaugh?" she questioned.

He extended his hand. "You must be Laura."

To my surprise, she gave him a warm smile. "It's very nice to meet you."

"And the same to you."

"Your sister-in-law is one of our best and most beautiful customers."

Quinn returned her smile. "Her transformation since coming to the city is evidence of your talent."

I fought the urge to crane my neck to stare at him and his apparent personality transplant. I'd rarely heard him say so many words at one time to anyone outside of his family, least of all a stranger.

Laura's gaze flicked from Quinn's over to me. Inwardly, I cringed as she apprised me. "This is Isla," Quinn introduced.

"It's nice to meet you," I said, extending my hand.

"Likewise. I hear you're attending a gala tonight, and you need an evening dress."

"Yes, that's—"

Quinn interrupted me by shaking his head. "While we do need an evening dress, Ms. Vaughn will be needing a few things to add to her wardrobe for events. Some cocktail dresses. A few pantsuits." As he turned his attention to me, the corners of his lips quirked. "Some lingerie."

If looks could have killed, Quinn would've been writhing on the floor. Since I didn't want to embarrass myself in front of Laura, I forced a smile to my face. "Now, darling, are you sure *all* of that is necessary?" I bit out with false sweetness.

Quinn had the audacity to chuckle at me. "Don't be shy now, Little Dove. We both know you're only with me for the money, so why shouldn't I spend it?"

At my gasp of horror, Laura smiled. "It's all right, Ms. Vaughn. Your boyfriend informed me on the phone that you would be resistant to spending a lot of money on clothes, but for me to persevere into changing your mind."

I pinched Quinn's arm. "You're in so much trouble."

He merely smiled down at me. "Let me spoil you."

With an indignant huff, I replied, "Fine. But I won't like it."

Quinn chuckled. "I think we can work with that."

She nodded. "Let me show you to the dressing room. While you get undressed, I'll find some things that will be divine on you."

Reluctantly, I followed Laura to the back of the store. Glancing over my shoulder, I watched as Quinn had a seat on an expensive leather sofa. He gave me a smile, which I returned.

After I slipped into the dressing room, I started to get out of my clothes. Laura returned rather quickly with an armload of dresses. The first one she handed me was emerald green. It had intricate beading on the bodice before flowing out in fluffy waves. It was something I would imagine Cinderella wearing, except for the low neckline that showed off all my goodies.

Although it was slightly awkward having Laura inside with me, it did help when the dress needed zipping. "Breathtaking," she said as we stared at my reflection in the mirror.

"Thank you. You have exquisite taste. This is like a princess gown."

"And you look the part." With a playful little nudge, she said, "Go show off to Mr. Kavanaugh."

With a grin, I headed out of the dressing room and made my way down the little runway where Quinn sat. Since his head was buried in his phone, I cleared my throat. When he jerked his gaze to mine, the expression on his face caused my knees to go weak.

Adoration.

I'd never seen it on a man like that before. Especially not directed to me. It caused warmth to tingle from the top of my head down to my feet.

"Well?" I prompted.

"You're a vision."

"Really?"

"Green is one of your colors."

"Usually it's red."

"I like you in green."

"So, I should get this one and forget the rest?" I teased.

He shook his head. "I want to see you in the others."

"You do? I mean, this isn't boring for you?"

"Anytime I get to see you looking so beautiful could never be boring."

My heartbeat broke into a wild gallop at his compliment. "You're very sweet."

"Only to you," Quinn mused. He jerked his chin at me. "Now go and try on more."

"So bossy," I murmured before heading back down the runway. Once I got back into the dressing room, Laura unzipped me and put me in a midnight blue satin dress.

It hugged my curves like a second skin. I feared it might be a little too indecent for a gala raising money for children's charities. But I didn't voice my concerns. Instead, I just went back down the runway.

This time Quinn was ready for me.

His eyes tracked my movements like a hungry lion. He eased forward on the couch. To add fuel to the fire, I did a slow turn, showing off the plunging back. "Well?" I questioned.

"It's indecent."

I laughed. "I thought the same thing."

"Get it."

My eyes bulged. "Quinn, I can't wear this to a charity function."

"We'll find somewhere for you to wear it." He rose off the couch and stalked towards me. "Even if it's just in my bedroom."

A shiver ran down my spine. Since my attack, Quinn had refused to touch me in any way that was remotely sexual. There was nothing more in the world I wanted than for his hands to give me pleasure.

As his breath warmed my earlobe, I replied, "I'll get it only if you promise to tear it off and ravish me."

"I think I can do that."

"Good." Tilting my head at him, I countered, "You'll do it tonight?"

He grimaced. "You're still healing."

I rolled my eyes at him. "I don't think you're going to break me."

"You have no idea what I could do to you."

A shudder ran through me at his words. "At least let me try."

"We have the gala tonight."

"Then after the gala."

"Isla," Quinn groaned.

Shaking my head, I countered, "*Tonight.*"

"Do you know how hard it is for me to say no when you're standing there dressed like sin?"

"Then I'll ask Laura to pick even more sinful dresses."

He chuckled. "You're not letting this go, are you?"

"Nope," I replied, my lips popping on the p.

"Fine. We can try."

"I'm glad you could see it my way."

"Go finish with the dresses."

With a coy smile, I asked, "And then you'll finish me tonight?"

Quinn smacked my behind, causing me to squeal. "If you don't watch your mouth, I'll fuck you against the wall in the dressing room."

My mouth ran dry at his words. "Please?"

With a growl, Quinn shook his head. "You're a *dearg-due*."

"Does that mean tease in Irish?"

With a chuckle, Quinn replied, "It's a female demon who seduces men."

I smacked his arm playfully. "I'm not a demon."

He grinned. "No. You're an angel." With a wink, he added, "A very horny one."

"Is that right?"

"Mm, hmm."

"And what's Irish for asshole?"

"*Gléas.*"

"I'm going to spend more of your money, *gléas.*"

"You do that," he chuckled.

When I turned to flounce back down the runway, he smacked my ass one last time. And it felt so very, very good.

Chapter Twenty-One: Quinn

A fter Isla had been outfitted in formal and casual wear along with shoes and lingerie, we headed back to her house. It took Shane and I three trips to bring in all her bags. Of course, the moment Brooke saw the items she screeched at the top of her lungs. Then she and Isla began gleefully going through all the items while I ended up holding Henry.

Once they were finished, Brooke came over to me. "Nice job, Big Man."

"I'm glad you approve."

"While all this is nice, Isla could probably use a few more shopping trips," she suggested.

"Brooke!" Isla shrieked in admonishment.

With a wink, Brooke replied, "Did I mention we wear the same size?"

When Shane snorted, I shot him a look. But then I couldn't help myself, and I laughed. "If it means keeping me on your good side, I'll be happy to send the two of you shopping."

"You'll do no such thing," Isla protested.

"Ugh, you're such a goody two shoes," Brooke groaned.

As I glanced down at Henry, he grinned up at me. "What about Little Man? Anything he needs?"

"A pony?" Brooke suggested with a grin.

"Absolutely not," Isla remarked before I could answer.

"What about a motorized pony?" I suggested.

"He doesn't need any more spoiling," Isla replied while Brooke gave me a thumbs up.

Leaning over to Brooke, I whispered, "I'll look into one."

"Thanks, Big Guy."

Isla eyed the antique clock above the mantle. "Can you watch Henry while Brooke does my hair and makeup?"

I nodded. "Then we'll need to go to my house, so I can get dressed and we can meet Callum."

"I won't take long," Isla said as she and Brooke started for the stairs.

Brooke grunted. "You act like covering up your neck is nothing at all."

"It only needs touching up from earlier."

They continued bickering up the stairs. Henry grew restless in my arms, so I put him down on his ocean playmat. Shane and I pulled out our phones and checked in on business.

Isla and Brooke hadn't been upstairs very long when a truly foul smell permeated the air. Shane and I exchanged a glance before looking at Henry who was on his playmat. After picking him up, I turned him in my arms.

When I brought his butt to my face, I recoiled. "I think he's had a blow-out."

Shane furrowed his blond brows. "Do you know how to change a nappy?"

I rolled my eyes. "Aye, mate, I do."

He held up his hands. "It was a fair question since I've never seen you around a wain."

Grimacing, I replied, "Truthfully, the last nappy I changed was Eamon's."

Shane's dark eyes bulged. "Jaysus, it's been that long?"

"Aye. Now shut yer trap and get me a nappy." After glancing around the room, I spotted his diaper bag. "Grab that for me."

Once Shane obliged, I got out the wipes and a nappy. After unsnapping his onesie, I fought my gag reflex. Green shit oozed out of the sides of his nappy and down his legs.

When I pulled up the bottom of the onesie, Shane gagged. "That shite is toxic," he muttered.

After undoing the nappy, I slid it off his bum. That's when I noticed shit had seeped all the way up his back and into his dark hair.

"Oh fuck," I muttered.

"Better hose him off," Shane suggested.

"Good point." But then I realized there was only a half bath downstairs. All the bathrooms with tubs were upstairs. I didn't want to risk potentially dribbling shit along the staircase. "Kitchen."

As I started down the hall, Shane hurried ahead of me to turn on the sink. After adjusting the water temperature, he nodded. I eased Henry down into the water. Apparently, he didn't appreciate sink baths because he began to scream bloody murder.

"Shh, it's all right, Little Man."

As Shane and I worked to get the shit out of his hair, Henry continued to howl as big fat tears streaked down his cheeks.

"What the hell are you doing to my kid?" Brooke demanded from the doorway.

Shane and I whirled around to look at her while Henry was still screaming in the sink. "He shit himself," I replied while Shane bobbed his head.

Brooke merely rolled her eyes before coming over to us. Henry reached out his arms to his mother. "Can you grab a towel out of the dryer?" she asked.

Since time was of the essence and Shane had no fucking idea where the laundry room was, I hurried out of the kitchen to grab one. When I returned, Henry was happily smacking at the water in the sink as Brooke finished hosing him off.

When Henry caught my eye, I teasingly murmured, "Traitor."

He grinned before splashing water all over the front of my shirt. "What in God's name have you been feeding him?" I questioned.

With a laugh, Brooke replied, "He just started on some cereal."

"I'm not sure it agrees with him," Shane mused.

As Brooke pulled Henry out of the sink, she grinned at him. "Can you imagine two big bad men being completely taken out by your shitty diaper?"

I swept my hands to my hips. "We were not taken out."

Shane snorted. "Speak for yourself. I was gagging."

At that moment, Isla appeared in the kitchen doorway outfitted in her dress. "What was all the commotion about?" she questioned, as if it were perfectly normal for her to look like a vision in a designer dress. She went with the first one she'd tried on–the emerald green one that made her look like even more of a fairy queen.

For a moment, I couldn't speak. All I could do was stare at her. "*Aingeal álainn,*" I murmured.

"What does that mean?" she asked.

"You're a beautiful angel."

Crimson dotted her cheeks as she crossed the kitchen over to me. She leaned up and bestowed a kiss on my cheeks. "Thanks, Quinn."

"You're welcome."

She then turned to Brooke. "Is Henry okay?"

"Everything is fine," Brooke reassured her. "He just dropped a shit bomb on them, and they tried to clean him up."

"Oh goodness," Isla mused with a smile.

"We better go before it happens again," I teased.

Isla swept through the kitchen and over to her sister. After bestowing a kiss on Henry's cheek, she did the same on Brooke's. "Thanks again for making me beautiful."

"It's hard work, but someone has to do it," Brooke teased. At Isla's playful smack on the arm, Brooke said, "You really are a beautiful angel, sis. Go and have a blast."

Isla smiled and gave Brooke a hug. As we started to open the door, I said, "Don't wait up. Isla will probably sleep over at my house tonight."

Brooke waggled her brows. "Bow chicka wow wow, huh?"

While Isla flushed scarlet, I merely laughed. "Goodnight, Brooke."

"Night, Big Guy."

Chapter Twenty-Two: Isla

Dusk was falling when we arrived at Quinn's house. Of course, I couldn't help staring in awe at the expansive mansion where he lived. "This is really yours?"

"Aye. As well as my brothers."

"It's huge."

"It accommodates the four of us very well."

With wide eyes, I followed him into the backdoor. It certainly wasn't what I had in mind for four Irish mobsters. I don't know why I imagined everything being dark, sleek, and modern. The house had warm colors, expensive art, and other antiques. I wondered how much could be attributed to their mother or Caterina's touch.

Speaking of Caterina, she came down the stairs to greet us. She was terribly pale and had on a silky bathrobe. At the sight of me, her eyes lit up. "Oh, Isla, you are stunning!"

"Aw, thank you. I owe it all to Quinn and my sister."

"You two are going to make quite the gorgeous couple tonight."

"I better go throw on my tux," Quinn said.

Caterina smiled. "I'll entertain her while you get ready."

He kissed her cheek. "I appreciate that."

After Quinn disappeared up the stairs, Caterina ushered me into the living room. I eased down carefully into one of the chairs, making sure not to wrinkle my dress. Caterina plopped down on the couch. "I'm so sorry you're unable to go tonight."

"Thanks. It's been rough the last couple of days."

"My sister never threw up very much when she was pregnant with my nephew, but she could barely eat from the nausea."

"All I've got to say is whoever said pregnancy is beautiful has never simultaneously puked and peed themselves," she joked.

I laughed. "That has to be the worst."

As she rubbed her abdomen, Caterina said, "I just keep telling myself it will all be worth it when she gets here."

"I know we feel that way about Henry. He's the sunshine in my sister's and my world."

"I've heard that he's quite fond of Quinn."

"He is." At my bark of a laugh, Caterina eyed me curiously. "Right before we left, Quinn tried cleaning up a blowout. It didn't go well."

Caterina grinned. "Somehow that doesn't surprise me."

At the sound of footsteps in the hallway, I craned my neck. When Quinn stepped into the doorway, I gasped at how handsome and debonair he looked. I popped out of my chair and went over to him. "You look amazing."

"Sometimes I clean up nicely."

I ran my hand down the front of his tux. "Seriously, you're like James Bond in a tux."

He smiled. "Thank you." He then reached into his jacket pocket to pull out a large velvet box. "I have something for you to wear tonight."

My heartbeat accelerated. "Oh?"

Quinn nodded. "It's been in my mother's family for three generations."

When I gazed down at the box, I shook my head. "Now I really feel like I'm in *Pretty Woman*," I remarked.

Caterina snorted behind me. "I'm pretty sure Quinn doesn't know to snap the lid on your fingers."

He frowned. "Why the hell would I do something like that?"

She and I both laughed. "Trust me. You'll have to see the movie," I replied.

"It sounds like torture," he grunted.

Caterina grinned at him. "Maybe I can organize a movie night."

"That would be wonderful," I replied as Quinn merely rolled his eyes.

Turning my attention back to the box in Quinn's hand, I asked, "Let's see what you have for me."

When he cracked the lid, an emerald and diamond necklace glittered up at me. "That's exquisite."

"I could say the same of you," Quinn remarked.

I flushed under his compliments. "You're too good to me."

"I can never do enough, Little Dove."

He took the necklace from the box and then unfastened it. "Turn around," he instructed.

I did as I was told. I then shifted my waves to the left side so he would have better access to my neck. His breath warmed the bare skin of my shoulders. At his closeness, my heart began to thrum wildly.

Once the necklace was in place, Quinn snapped the clasp. After adjusting my hair, I hurried over to the massive antique mirror on the wall. At the sight of the glittering emeralds and diamonds, I not so eloquently murmured, "Wow."

Quinn came up behind me, and I met his reflection in the mirror. "I think you'd put Cliodna herself to shame tonight."

"I don't think I've ever felt more beautiful."

"You're my beauty. Mine alone." His hands came around my waist, pulling me back against him. He dipped his head to place kisses down my neck. When he reached my collarbone, he slid his tongue along it, causing me to moan.

A throat cleared behind us. When I whirled around, Caterina gave us a sly smile. "Just in case you two forgot you had an audience."

I blushed as I worked to entangle myself from Quinn's embrace. He started to protest, but at that moment, Callum came down the stairs. "Sorry to keep you guys waiting." He then stared pointedly at Quinn. "More bullshit from Mikita."

Quinn tensed next to me. "I don't know what it's going to take for him to get the message."

"Rafe is working on something with Leo and Gianni."

At the mention of those names, Caterina sucked in a harsh breath. Callum went over to her on the couch. "They're not in any danger, Kitten. It's just business."

She frowned as she rubbed her belly. "I hope it stays that way."

At what must've been my questioning look, Caterina said, "Rafe, Leo, and Gianni are my brothers who live in New York."

"It has to be hard worrying about all the men in your life."

She gave me a tight smile. "It is."

Callum kissed her lips and then her tiny belly. "I've asked Dare and Kellan to stay home tonight, so they can watch over my girls."

With a laugh, Caterina replied, "Considering she's only the size of a raspberry, I'm not sure how much watching we'll require."

"Regardless, they'll be here."

She smiled up at him. "I appreciate you looking out for us."

With one last kiss for Caterina, Callum turned to face us. "Let's go."

Apprehension bubbled within me, but I gave Quinn a confident smile as I slipped my hand into his.

Chapter Twenty-Three: Isla

When we pulled up outside The Copley Plaza hotel, my eyes bulged. "The gala is here?"

"Yes," Quinn replied.

I practically bounced in my seat with excitement. "It's famous! I've seen it in so many movies, but I've never actually been inside."

"Tonight's your big chance."

With a grin, I said, "I can't believe I'm going to a gala, least of all one at The Copley Plaza." I grinned at Quinn. "I really feel like Cinderella now."

He winked at me. "We'll have to watch out for your shoes tonight then."

Shane opened the SUV door, and Callum stepped out first. Flashbulbs began to go off all around him. It was at that moment that I realized we were going to have to walk some sort of red carpet. At the thought of all the people staring at me, I froze.

"Isla?" Quinn questioned.

"I don't know if I can do this."

"Yes, you can."

"I'm not someone famous or wealthy. I don't belong."

"You're a smart, beautiful woman who has every right to be at this gala," he murmured into my ear.

Quinn's words gave me the extra jolt I needed to move forward. When I started out of the SUV, Callum held out his hand to help me. "Thank you," I murmured.

"You're welcome."

Quinn quickly exited the SUV and appeared at my side. He reached for my hand and squeezed it. Then he began leading me up the carpet and into the hotel.

Although I initially plastered on a smile, I became more comfortable in my own skin, and as time wore on, my smile became more genuine. Once we reached the lobby, I felt completely at ease. As Quinn introduced me to people, I shook their hands and made small talk.

I don't know how long we spent making the rounds. By the time we sat down for dinner, my feet were aching, and my throat was parched. I reached for my water glass and downed it in several long gulps. Once it was empty, I started on the champagne.

"You were a pro back there," Quinn mused.

"Really?"

He nodded. "After the initial hiccup, I was afraid you might run screaming before we got into the hotel."

"I just needed a minute to get my bearings," I argued.

"You're a star. Everyone wants to know who the beauty is with the beast."

I gasped. "They are not saying that about you, are they?"

He threw back a large gulp of whiskey. "Tonight it's about my personality, not my appearance."

"I don't want them saying it about either," I huffed as I stared daggers down the table at the other guests.

Quinn's fingers came to my chin to pull my attention back to him. "Are you going to fight for my honor, Little Dove?"

"I most certainly am."

Amusement twinkled in his blue eyes. "It's always the little scrappy ones you have to watch out for."

"Damn straight."

The first course was served then, and I parlayed my knowledge learned from *Pretty Woman* to use the appropriate fork. Quinn turned to his neighbor to talk, which was some form of etiquette we were supposed to uphold.

So, I turned to the man beside me. "Good evening," I managed.

He eyed me contemptuously before going back to his salad. Not willing to let him write me off, I asked, "What is it you do?"

"I'm a retired neuroscience professor from Harvard."

My eyes lit up. "How interesting. I'm in graduate school for microbiology at MIT."

The man cut his eyes from his plate back to me. "*You* are a microbiologist?" he questioned.

"I am."

"MIT must be admitting anyone these days."

Gritting my teeth, I replied, "Just those with a 4.0 and a 38 on the ACT. Well, at least that's true in my case."

He snorted contemptuously. "I'm sure your looks had nothing to do with it."

My mouth opened and closed like a fish out of water. Although my parents had ingrained in me the necessity of turning the other cheek in situations like these, I found myself unable to do so. Maybe it was because of feeling helpless after my attack, but I wasn't going to take any man's bullshit.

"You arrogant blowhole!"

Quinn's attention whirled from his conversation to me. "Isla," he warned.

"Do you know what he said?"

"Keep your voice down."

I smacked my napkin on the table. "I don't need to sit between two patronizing jackasses, thank you very much."

After rising out of my chair, I hightailed it out of the dining room. I searched for the bathroom before disappearing inside. I'd started over to the sink when I caught Quinn's reflection behind me. "You can't be in here."

"What the hell was that about back there?"

"Just leave me alone."

"Do you know who that man's family is?"

I narrowed my eyes at him. "I don't care who he is. If he's so important, he should've had better manners than to insult his dinner companion."

Quinn swept his hands to his hips. "What are you talking about?"

"He said that since I attend MIT, they must be admitting anyone. Then he said my looks must've had some bearing on my being admitted.

Quinn's eyes darkened. "He said that?"

"Yeah, he did." I jabbed my finger into his chest. "But you know what? I don't care about that arrogant prick. What I do care about is how you didn't even stop to see what was wrong. You just admonished me like I was a child acting up."

With a repentant look, he jerked a hand through his hair. "I'm so sorry, Isla. I keep fucking up when it comes to you." Shaking his head, he replied, "I don't know how to be soft and tender."

I crossed my arms over my chest. "Well, you're going to have to try harder. I know this is all still new between us, but you need to have my back always, even if I'm in the wrong."

"You're right. And I'm truly sorry." He reached for my hand and brought it to his lips. "Please forgive me, Little Dove."

"Actions speak louder than words."

"Regardless of who he is, I'll go right now and demand that he apologize to you."

"You will?"

"Aye, I will. I'll have words with any man who makes you feel less of the goddess that you are."

"Don't ever do that again."

"I won't." He brushed his lips against mine. "What can I do to make it up to you?"

"Instead of demanding his apology, could you beat his pompous ass?" I suggested.

"Perhaps something less violent?" His hand came to my breast. "Maybe more pleasurable."

"That's how you want to make things right?"

"Can you think of a better way?"

"Here?" I squeaked.

Quinn nodded. "But to punish myself for the way I treated you, only you get to come."

"I'm listening," I replied.

Without answering, Quinn walked over to the bathroom door. To my surprise, it had an inside lock. At the sound of the click, a shiver went through me. It intensified as Quinn stalked over to me. "I need to taste you, Little Dove."

"I'm still mad at you," I claimed, my voice wavering.

"Angry sex is very hot."

"I thought you were going to deny yourself?"

With a smirk, Quinn replied, "I am. I plan to devour your pussy while you angrily moan and pant."

Before I could protest, his massive hands gripped my waist before hoisting me up onto the marble countertop. He then brought his hands to my calves before sliding up my thighs, bunching the fabric of my dress up. Cool air hit the tops of my heated thighs.

All the while the ache between my legs grew. I bit down on my lip when he knelt before me. "I'm on my knees in front of you like the queen that you are."

"You promise not to hurt me again?"

He nodded. "Only pleasure."

I knew it was a ridiculous request, and he couldn't truthfully promise to never hurt me again. But I decided to let it go. Staring down at him, I commanded, "Make me come."

A groan erupted from deep in Quinn's chest. His fingers instantly went to my aching center. He rubbed them over my soaked thong. "Mm," I whimpered.

When he thrust two fingers inside me, I gasped, and my head fell back against the mirror. He swirled them inside me, curling them to rub against my g-spot. "Quinn," I murmured.

"My name on your lips is a fucking siren's song. It drives me crazy."

"You're...driving...me crazy," I panted, as I turned my head to the side against the mirror.

"You're taking my fingers so good. Maybe I should add another."

"Mm, please."

My walls stretched at the addition of a third finger, swirling and plunging within me. To meet the plunges of his fingers, I thrust my hips up as well.

Over and over.

My eyes pinched shut as pleasure enveloped me.

Just as I reached the edge, Quinn's fingers slid out of me. "No! Please don't stop!"

"Easy, Little Dove."

Quinn jerked my thong to the side before dipping his head. His tongue licked up my seam, causing me to cry out. I could barely see him through all the fabric of the dress, but I sure as hell could feel him.

He buried his entire face in my pussy. He sucked and licked my labia, leaving little love bites in his wake. As his nose rubbed against my clit, I thrust my hips up, desperate for more friction. My chest heaved, and I panted like a wanton woman.

"Please, Quinn," I rasped.

His response was to thrust his tongue inside me. It swirled and flicked inside my center. After searching for his head through the fabric, my fingers connected with the strands of his hair. I gripped him for dear life as I pressed him further against me.

It was then his teeth grazed my clit, sending an orgasm charging through me. My thighs shook with the intensity of the pulsing of my walls around Quinn's tongue. My head banged back against the mirror as I rode out wave after wave.

"Quinn!" I shrieked as I clawed at his scalp. I was probably hurting him, but at that moment, I selfishly only cared about my pleasure.

The second orgasm I'd ever been given by a man was life-altering. I'd been amazed by the first, but this put that one to shame. Fuck. What would it be like when his cock was buried inside me, not his tongue?

When my walls finally stopped clenching, my eyes fluttered open. I stared down at Quinn who was still between my legs and was smiling up at me. "Thank you," I rasped.

He chuckled. "You're very welcome."

With a wince, I extricated my fingers from his hair. "Did I hurt you?"

"In the best fucking way."

Quinn then rose to his feet. He reached behind me to grab a handful of paper towels. After wetting one of them, he cleaned my center along with my inner thighs. Then he dried my wet flesh. "You do aftercare well," I remarked.

Quinn snorted. "I can't believe you even know what that is."

"I've read about it in a few books."

"I should've known none of the pussies you fucked would've done it to you."

I laughed. "Very true."

Twisting around, I grabbed a few paper towels of my own. "Bend down," I ordered.

Quinn did as I obliged. With his face inches from mine, I began to clean myself off of his face. Considering he still had people to speak with, I also grabbed some of the scented lotion off the tray with soaps.

His brows creased at the sight of the bottle. "What the feck are you going to do with that?"

"We can't have you going out there smelling like me. It's already going to be suspicious with how long we've been gone."

I rubbed some of the citrus-smelling lotion on Quinn's cheeks. "I'd rather smell like you."

A flush entered my cheeks. "You are such a caveman."

When I finished, Quinn reached for my waist and eased me down onto the ground. After checking my appearance in the mirror, I felt I looked mildly flushed, but not thoroughly fucked. Quinn unlocked the bathroom door and held out his hand to me.

As we started back in the dining room, I expected every face to turn towards us. Thankfully, everyone was too self-absorbed to realize we'd been gone, least of all to speculate what we had been doing. I guess I shouldn't have been surprised since it seemed like typical rich people behavior.

Quinn pulled out my chair. Once I sat down, he turned to the prick. "It's good to see you again, Nathaniel."

Nathaniel had the audacity to smile at Quinn. "Same to you."

As Quinn's expression turned menacing, the smile began to slip from Nathaniel's face. "If you ever dare to condescend to my girlfriend again, I'll knock the self-righteous smirk right off your lips." Tilting his head, Quinn asked, "Understood?"

Nathaniel shrunk down in his seat. "Understood," he replied.

"You'll do good to remember Isla is an intelligent woman who rightfully earned her spot at MIT."

"Of course."

After giving him a tight smile, Quinn leaned over and kissed my cheek. Then he nonchalantly retook his own seat just in time for the last course to be served.

I fought to keep the grin off my lips as I placed my napkin in my lap. To my surprise, Nathaniel said, "So you're in graduate school?"

"I am."

"What is your focus within microbiology?"

Although I could've been a major bitch and ignored him, I continued the conversation. From time to time, I'd feel Quinn's hot gaze on mine. Each time I turned to look at him, he merely nodded his head at me.

Between the orgasm and the words he'd given Nathaniel, he was more than forgiven.

Chapter Twenty-Four: Isla

After dinner was over, we entered the ballroom for dancing. When Quinn didn't ask me to dance after two songs, I couldn't help questioning, "Not a big dancer?"

He shook his head. "I'm sure that won't come as a big surprise."

"It is." With a wink, I added, "Considering your rhythm during our lap dance, I imagined you'd be good at it."

Quinn laughed. "I appreciate the compliment, but I'm not dancing."

Before I could guilt him into taking me for a turn, we were interrupted by Callum appearing before us. "May I have this dance?" he asked.

When I cut my eyes over to Quinn, his jaw clenched. "Um, maybe?" I replied.

Callum chuckled. "Come on, boyo. It's only a dance."

"Fine," Quinn gritted out.

When Callum offered me his hand, I reluctantly slipped mine into his. As he led me onto the dance floor, I couldn't help but throw a glance at Quinn over my shoulder. He gave me a tight smile.

After Callum slid his arm around my waist, he remarked, "You look exquisite tonight."

"Thank you. You and Quinn clean up nice as well. I mean, you always look nice in your suits, but the tuxes are top tier. I bet you didn't even have to rent those, did you?" Before he could answer, I rambled on. "Quinn got this dress for me. I wished he wouldn't have spent so much. But he insisted. He even spent a fortune on lingerie for me." At that admission, I shrieked in horror. "I'm sorry. I shouldn't have said that. When I get nervous, I literally can't stop talking."

He gave me a reassuring smile. "Do I make you nervous?" When I nodded, he asked, "Is it because you don't want to piss off Quinn?"

"A little. I think it's more because of who you are in your organization."

"We call them clans."

"I know. It's just hard for me to say that with the negative connotations here in the states with that word."

"Ah, yes, those eejits who run around in bed sheets have definitely sullied the word," he replied with disgust.

"Exactly."

"You don't need to fear me, Isla."

"Somehow I don't think that's entirely true."

He cocked his brows at me. "What makes you say that?"

"I imagine that you didn't just bring me out here because of your desire to dance."

Callum eyed me shrewdly. "You are smart."

"What is it you wanted to say to me?"

"I don't know you well, Isla, but you could say I'm a pretty good judge of character. It comes with the territory of the work I do. There's also the fact that my wife likes you very much."

I smiled. "I like her, too."

"I trust her assessment of you since she also possesses the ability to judge character."

"Why do I feel there's a but coming?"

"You are very perceptive."

I shrugged. "Once again, why else would you want to get me away from Quinn than to warn me?"

"Quinn isn't just my brother. He's the enforcer in my clan. He's a vital part in the success of our businesses." He drew in a ragged breath. "We almost lost him physically two years ago, and it's still an emotional battle. I can't allow anyone or anything to screw with his head."

A myriad of emotions swirled through me. Part of me was angry that Callum felt the need to threaten me not to hurt Quinn. Another part understood that despite his imposing appearance and menacing attitude, Quinn was truly vulnerable. At the same time, a shiver of fear crept up my spine that my mild-mannered self was having such a conversation with a clan leader.

Callum cocked his head at me. "Do you understand what I'm saying?"

"If I hurt Quinn, I'll sleep with the fishes?"

Callum's blues eyes bulged before a bark of a laugh came from deep in his chest. "I wouldn't use that exact verbiage, but nothing good would come from using or hurting him."

I frowned. "The last thing I would *ever* want to do was hurt Quinn. I care about him."

Callum's eyes searched mine. After what seemed like an eternity, he replied, "I believe you, Isla."

"Good. I'm glad to hear that." Throwing a glance over my shoulder, I surveyed Quinn's almost eggplant-colored face. "I think it's time we end our dance before Quinn has a stroke."

Callum laughed. "I think so, too."

Just as I started to untangle myself from his embrace, he stopped me. "I'm really happy Quinn has found you, Isla. You're really good for him. He hasn't been this happy since the bombing."

"You really mean that?"

"I do. I hope he doesn't fuck things up and keeps you happy."

I laughed. "I hope for the same."

He placed a tender kiss on my cheek. "Thanks for the dance."

"Thank you."

Quinn didn't wait for me to meet him. Instead, he was at my side just as Callum started walking away. "Did you enjoy your dance?" he bit out.

"Not really."

Furrowing his brows, Quinn asked, "Why not?"

"Well, because your brother threatened to hurt me if I mistreated you."

Quinn's blue eyes turned dark. "I'll kill him."

"Easy, now. He was only being the macho clan boss who was looking out for his younger brother."

"I'm still going to kill him."

"Please don't. I want Caterina's baby to have a father," I pleaded.

He exhaled a sigh. "Fine. But only for the wain's sake."

"The what?"

He grinned. "Wain is Irish for baby or child."

"Interesting. I think I'll start calling Henry the wain. It lends a little cultural distinction to our house," I replied with a smile.

"We'll see if Brooke appreciates it."

As we started off the dance floor, Quinn cocked his brows at me. "You're not to dance with Callum or any of my brothers. *Ever.*"

"Quinn, be serious."

He shook his head. "I mean it. I don't ever want to hear of you alone with one of them. Especially Dare."

Sweeping my hands to my hips, I said, "You don't honestly think I would be interested in your brothers?"

Quinn shrugged. "They're handsome men."

I rolled my eyes. "For starters, Callum is married, and I happen to like his wife a lot. Not to mention she's pregnant. I'd have to be a 'see you next Tuesday' to do that to her."

Frowning, Quinn asked, "A what?"

With a giggle, I replied, "A cunt."

His eyes bulged at me using that word. "I can't believe you said that."

"Well, I didn't at first until you made me explain myself." Closing the gap between us, I pressed myself flush against his body. "I want you to listen to me and listen good. There is not a single Kavanaugh I want anything sexual to do with but *you*. There is no one inside or outside of your family that I want but *you*."

"You really mean that, don't you?"

"Yes, I do."

Quinn cupped my face in his hands. "You truly are an angel heaven sent."

"Now will you take me home and ravish me?" When he shook his head, I protested, "You promised."

He flashed me a wicked grin that sent heat straight to my core. "I'm taking you upstairs instead."

Chapter Twenty-Five: Quinn

Isla's blue eyes popped comically wide at my declaration. It hadn't been my intention when the night began. It came to me after seeing her reaction to the hotel. I'd wanted to do everything I could to make our first time together special. What better way to do that than to get one of the finest suites at the hotel. So, I'd dispatched Shane to make the necessary inquiries.

Cocking my brows at her, I asked, "Would you like me to take you upstairs now?"

"Yes, I would like that very much."

I held out my hand to her, and she slipped hers into mine. With my free hand, I texted Callum to tell him we were heading out. I didn't wait for his reply before I slid my phone back into my jacket pocket.

When we reached the elevators, Isla slipped her other hand around mine. I glanced down at her to see her biting her lip. After the elevator doors opened, I asked, "Nervous?"

"Just a little."

After we stepped inside, I pulled her to my side. "There's nothing to be nervous about, Little Dove."

"I don't want to disappoint you."

"How could you possibly do that?"

An anxious laugh bubbled from her lips. "I think we've established my lack of experience."

I took her chin between my fingers. "Just because the men you were with were inept, doesn't mean you're going to be an inept lover."

Her brows creased with worry. "I hope not."

Smiling down at her, I said, "Isla, you made me come in my pants like a teenage boy. None of the other dancers have ever done that."

"Really?"

I nodded. "Besides, you could never disappoint me. I've had a taste, and I know I'm going to be addicted."

The elevator dinged on our floor. I led Isla down the carpeted hallway to our suite. After unlocking the door, I motioned for her to step inside. At the sight of the rose petals littering the carpet, I worked not to laugh at the thought of poor Shane romanticizing the suite. I'd asked him to do the rose petals and light candles.

Considering the amazing job he'd done, I was really going to owe him.

Isla slowly walked into the room, her heels stabbing some of the petals. Her head turned to take in the candles lighting the way. I walked up behind her, bringing my hands to her shoulders. "Do you like it?"

"It's so romantic," she gushed. She glanced at me over her shoulder. "You did all this for me?"

"I did."

Isla whirled around to throw her arms around my neck. She drew my head down to bring her lips to mine. After a tender kiss, she pulled back to stare up at me. "Thank you for this, Quinn. I couldn't imagine a more romantic setting."

I cupped her cheek. "You're welcome, Little Dove." Glancing down at her, I said, "Let's get you undressed."

"It's not like you haven't seen everything I have," she teased.

"I've never seen it in candlelight."

"True," she murmured.

"Regardless, I could never tire of seeing every inch of your beautiful body."

"You flatter me."

"It's the truth. So many men covet what is mine." I cocked my head at her. "But you're mine and only mine."

"I am."

Turning her around, I slid the zipper down on her dress. I pushed the straps down over her arms. Isla pulled them the rest of the way down. Once the bodice fell away, she pushed the dress down over her hips and thighs.

After she stepped out of the dress, she turned around to face me. She stood in only a scrap of a thong and her heels. I exhaled a ragged breath. "I don't deserve such beauty."

Isla closed the gap between us. The expression in her eyes stoked the fire already burning within me. I slid my hands around her waist, drawing her against me. "Kiss me," she demanded.

I happily obliged. As my mouth devoured hers, my hand slid down from her waist to cup her buttocks. I hitched one of her legs over my hip, grinding my need into her. Isla moaned as I moved against her. "I've dreamt of burying myself inside you."

"So have I," she admitted with a shy smile.

"I hope I'll be as good as your dreams."

"I'm sure you will."

As I started leading her to the bed, Isla frowned. "Aren't you taking anything else off?"

"I was waiting for you to undress me."

"Oh," she murmured.

Her trembling fingers came to my neck to undo my tie. Her brows furrowed as she tried to loosen it. I brought my hands up to replace hers. As I worked to undo my tie, Isla reached for the buttons on my shirt. She fumbled with the first one before undoing the rest. She pulled my shirt apart. Starting at my breastbone, she ran her hand down the center of my chest over my abs and then down to my belt buckle.

I sucked in a breath, and my stomach muscles clenched under her fingers. Isla appeared eager to see more of me since she hastily unhooked my buckle and jerked the belt out of the loops. After she tossed it to the ground, she glanced up at me. My heated gaze burned into hers. Warmth flooded her cheeks and spread down her neck. She reached up to push my shirt off my arms.

As her fingers skimmed over my scars, I prepared myself for the usual loathing I felt when a woman touched me there. But like before, I didn't feel them with Isla. Her touch was devoid of judgment and only filled with compassion and care.

Once Isla unbuttoned my fly, her fingers fumbled slightly on the zipper. When she pushed it down, her hand brushed against my erection. I hissed as my dick bucked against my underwear, waiting to be freed to her touch.

She leaned in against me, pressing her body flush to mine as she reached into the back of my waistband to push my pants over my buttocks. Her hands momentarily stopped to cup both of my cheeks before grabbing the material. She slid down my body in the same motion as my pants.

Cupping the backs of my legs, she pushed her way slowly back up. Isla's fingernails raked over my calves and thighs. I couldn't bring myself to take my eyes off of hers.

Once again, Isla cupped my buttocks as she moved her fingers to the waistband of my underwear. Just as she started to free my erection, I jerked her hand away.

When she glanced up at me in surprise, I shook my head. "It's going to be all about you this first time." Then I brought my lips to hers, plunging my tongue into her mouth. She wrapped her arms around my neck as I massaged her tongue with mine.

I kissed a warm trail from her mouth over to her ear as my hand came up to cup her bodice. "You have the most amazing pair of tits I've ever seen."

"Considering all the ones you've seen, that is high praise," she replied with a smile.

"How a tiny wisp of a thing like you could be this stacked is a wonder of genetics."

She laughed. "This isn't the dirty talk I had in mind."

"Would you rather me say how I've jerked off to the thoughts of fucking your tits? That I want to squeeze them together and slide my cock between them. That I can't wait to come all over them, marking them and you as mine?"

She licked her lips. "It's an improvement."

My fingers delved inside the bodice, cupping her warm flesh. When my thumb flicked back and forth across her nipple, Isla gasped. Dipping my head, I licked her nipple. Her head lolled back when my mouth closed over the swollen peak.

I suckled it deeply before flicking and swirling my tongue across it. My hand kept stroking her other breast as my tongue worked the nipple in my mouth into a hardened pebble. Isla couldn't fight the cry of pleasure that escaped her lips. Her fingers automatically went to my hair, tugging and grasping at the strands as the pleasure washed over her.

I licked a wet trail over to the other breast before claiming the nipple. My fingers feathered across her belly teasingly, causing her hips to buck. I hesitated briefly before finally dipping them between her legs. Isla panted against my lips when my fingers worked against her sensitive flesh over the fabric. Her hips arched involuntarily against my hand as she rubbed herself against my fingertips.

I wanted to feel her bare again, so my fingers tugged at the thong's waistband, sliding the underwear down over her buttocks. Just like she had done to me, my body followed the panties to the floor, except I kissed and nibbled a trail down her thighs and legs.

When her knees buckled, I gripped the back of her thighs to keep her steady. I helped Isla step out of her thong. Once again, I knelt before my queen.

"I'm starting to get off on you in that position."

"You like me on my knees?"

She nodded. "I like to feel I own you."

A dark chuckle came from deep within me. "Little Dove, you've owned me since the first night we met. On my knees or upright, you have all of me."

My fingers then traveled between her legs, seeking out her swollen clit. The moment I stroked it, Isla cried out and gripped my shoulders tight. My thumb continued rubbing as my fingers slid into her wet folds. They swirled against Isa's tight walls, working her into a frenzy of desire. Isla bit down on her lip to keep the ecstatic cries buried in her throat from escaping.

"Let me hear you, Little Dove."

Always obedient, Isla's moans echoed through the room becoming music to my ears. I continued my assault on her core and brought her closer and closer to coming. As the wave of her first orgasm crashed over her, she dug her nails into my back and thrust her pelvis hard against my hand.

I rose off the floor. I kept my hands tight on her waist to steady her as she tried to get her bearings. "You're so fucking hot when you come," I murmured into her ear.

She flushed at my words, her breath still coming in uneven pants. Gently, I nudged her toward the bed and then eased her down onto her back. Pushing up on her elbows, she scooted higher on the mattress. I climbed onto the bed, looming over her.

As my body covered hers, I pushed her legs wide apart. I then kissed a path from her neck, down through the valley of her breasts, and over her belly. Although I was desperate to slide inside her, I knew I had to prepare her to take me. She was so tiny, and I didn't want to hurt her.

When my head dipped between her legs, Isla's eyes pinched shut in ecstasy. As my fingers entered her again, my tongue swirled around her clit, sucking it into my mouth. Isla fisted the sheets in both hands. "Oh Quinn!" she screamed.

"That's it, Little Dove. Tell me how good it is for you."

My fingers kept a rapid pace while I went back to licking and sucking at her center.

"Oh yes! Yes, Quinn...please," she murmured, twisting the sheets tighter in her hands. Her hips kept up a manic rhythm as I plunged my fingers and tongue in and out of her. Finally, it sent her over the edge, and she climaxed violently.

When she came back to herself, she gave me a satiated smile. "There's number three for tonight. You know, if we count the bathroom too.."

I laughed. "Are you really keeping an orgasm total?"

"I am."

"Get ready for that number to go off the charts tonight."

"I look forward to it." When I started to rise off the mattress, she questioned, "Where are you going?"

"To get a condom."

She shook her head. "I have an IUD."

I furrowed my brows at her. "You trust me for the rest?"

"You would never hurt me, so I know you won't be with me if there's a chance of any STI's."

"There's not. I've never been with a woman without a condom."

She cupped the scarred side of my face. "Then there can be no barriers between us."

I groaned. "You don't know how fucking amazing that is."

With a cheeky little grin, she countered, "Come show me."

"I will."

When I slid my briefs off, Isla sucked in a breath. "You're even bigger than I thought."

A chuckle rumbled from me. "That's the sweetest thing anyone has ever said to me," I teased.

She gave me a shy grin. "Just don't hurt me with that massive thing."

"Never, Little Dove. Only pleasure, remember?"

Although she nodded, I could tell she was still apprehensive. I bent over her, positioning myself between her thighs. When my cock nudged against her opening, Isla tensed and gripped my shoulders. I bestowed a tender kiss on her forehead. "Don't worry, Little Dove. I'm going to take this nice and slow, okay?"

She nodded and clamped her eyelids shut.

"No, look at me, Isla."

Obeying my command, she peeked up at me. Gently, I started easing myself inside. When Isla gasped, I froze. "Are you all right, Little Dove?"

"Mm, yes," she murmured with a smile.

Taking that as a green light, I slid further inside of her. When I was finally buried so fucking deep, I shuddered. "God, you feel amazing," I whispered into her ear.

"I could say the same about you," she replied.

I remained stock-still for a moment, allowing her to get accustomed to my size. Slowly, I pulled out to thrust back into Isla. "Oh fuck, yes, that's hot," I groaned into her ear.

Once I found a rhythm, Isla began raising her hips to meet me. We moved nearly in unison, our breaths coming in ragged pants. Although I wanted to pound in and out of her, I kept up a languorous pace.

Taking my face in her hands, Isla smiled. "You don't have to hold back on me."

"You're so tight and tiny. I don't want to hurt you," I replied, gritting my teeth from the effort.

"I'm not a virgin, and despite your size, you're not going to tear me in two."

Ignoring her, I continued the slow, almost methodical pace. Isla squeezed my shoulders. "Stop holding back. I want all of you."

"Next time."

"Now, Quinn!" she demanded.

She then shocked the hell out of me by reaching down to send a stinging slap across my ass. "Fuck me hard, Quinn!"

She didn't have to hit me again. "You got it," I growled.

She squealed when I rolled us over to where she was riding me. I lay still, buried deep inside her, waiting for her to take the reins. Tentatively, she rocked against me until she slowly started speeding up the pace. Leaning back, she rested her palms on my thighs.

"That's it, Little Dove. Take your pleasure from me."

Just like the night of our lapdance, Isla popped her hips, sending me almost sliding out of her before bouncing back on me.

She rode me hard and fast, grinding against me until she found just the right spot to send her over the edge again. "Yes. Oh God!" Isla cried.

I rose up into a sitting position. I took one of her swaying breasts in my mouth and sucked deeply while gripping her hips tight. I changed the rhythm to work her against me, pulling her almost off my cock and then slamming her back down on me. I felt myself go deeper and deeper each time. I began grunting in pleasure against her chest.

Just as Isla started building to another orgasm, I pushed her onto her back and brought her legs straight up against my chest so her feet rested at my shoulders. She whimpered when I rammed myself into her.

I smirked down at her with satisfaction. "You said you wanted me to fuck you hard, right?"

"I did," she panted.

"Then get ready."

As I pounded into her, my balls smacked against her ass. I groaned as the position took me deeper again. Her cries of pleasure fueled me as I thrust again and again. I grunted with each pump of my hips. Tension rippled through me as I started to get close.

My hips began pistoning in and out Isla. Her hands gripped my biceps to keep her in place. Our slapping skin and my animalistic noises of pleasure filled the air around us. Sweat broke out on my body as I gave everything I had to fucking Isla.

"Quinn!" Isla cried when her walls clamped my dick in a vise. I couldn't hold on any longer, and I pumped one last time. "Oh fuck, Isla!" I moaned as I let myself go inside her.

When I pulled out, the sight of me sliding out of her sent the caveman in me to beat his chest. I'd marked her inside and out as mine.

After collapsing down beside her, I rolled over onto my back. Staring up at the ceiling, I tried getting my bearings.

"Six," she murmured.

I turned my head on the pillow toward her. "What?"

With a grin, she turned over to prop her head on her hand. "You've given me six orgasms now."

A chuckle rumbled through my chest. "I'm going to give you so many that you'll lose count."

She snuggled up to my side, draping her leg over my thigh. "Mm, I can't wait."

"You're a greedy thing wanting more."

"I can never get enough of you. It's like a whole world of sex has been revealed to me that I never knew existed."

Her words had my caveman roaring with inflated male pride. "I feel the same way."

Isla frowned. "But you've been with so many women. I'm sure ones who knew how to fuck you."

I cupped her cheek. "None of them compare to you, Little Dove."

With a dreamy smile, Isla lay her head down on my chest. Her hand trailed over my abdomen and up my chest in lazy circles. I loved the feel of her hands on me.

As she traced the scars on my left pec with her finger, I sucked in a breath. She immediately snatched her finger away. "I'm sorry."

"You didn't hurt me, Little Dove."

"Maybe not physically."

"It's okay."

Isla stared intently into my eyes. "One day will you tell me about what happened?" she questioned softly.

"I've never talked about that night to anyone."

Her eyes widened. "Never?"

With a shake of my head, I replied, "When I was recovering in the hospital, many psychologists tried to get me to open up, but I refused. There's been times I know my brothers have wanted to ask me questions, but they never have. The only one who has ever come close to getting me to talk was my sister, Maeve."

"What was it about her that made you want to open up?"

Maeve's haunted eyes in the hospital after her rape flashed in my mind. Even though our trauma was very different, our pain bonded us. She'd also refused to talk to anyone about what had happened. We still hadn't heard the story in her words. Kellan and Eamon had said little as well.

"She experienced a horrible incident. I thought we could share our pain, but neither one of us was ready to be that vulnerable," I finally replied.

Isla pressed a tender kiss to my scar. "It's okay. I shouldn't have asked. You don't have to tell me."

I drew in a ragged breath. In my mind, I felt like I was racing towards the edge of a cliff. In the past, I'd always skidded to a stop at the edge, but tonight...tonight I was ready to leap and free fall. "No. I want to tell you."

"You do?"

"Aye."

"Why me?" Isla questioned softly.

I brushed the long strands of hair from her beautiful face. "I just fucked you bare. I should do the same with my emotions. There shouldn't be anything between us."

"But I don't want to cause you pain."

"You won't."

And I knew she wouldn't. It was time to unburden myself of the horrors I'd experienced that night. With Isla, I knew I'd chosen the perfect person. She wouldn't judge me or think less of me as a man. There was only care and concern radiating from her eyes.

After sucking in an anguished breath, the words I'd kept wrapped so tightly within me began to flow. The longer I spoke those tightly woven threads of anguish, grief, and guilt unfurled.

As Isla listened, she remained so still to where she could've been a statue. The only movement in her came with her tears. They started flowing almost as fast as my words. Their salty sorrow dripped onto my chest.

When I finally finished, Isla threw her arms around me. Although I knew she wanted to comfort me, her little body shook so hard I wrapped her in my arms to soothe her.

"I'msorryI'msorryI'msorry," she murmured against the scarred flesh of my neck.

Normally I loathed that word in relation to my scars. I despised any kind of pity. But not from Isla.

"Shh, don't weep, Little Dove."

My words only caused her to sob harder. "Isla, don't waste your tears on me."

She sniffled as she pulled her face from my neck. Staring up at me, she said, "My father used to say that with each tear we shed for someone's suffering, it eases their pain." She cupped my cheek. "I would cry an entire ocean for you."

Her words caused a shudder to ripple through me. After the bombing, I'd never thought I would find a woman I could love, but in the short amount of time I'd come to know Isla, I knew I could love her.

That I already loved her.

But she couldn't know that yet. It was too soon. It made no sense. We hadn't known each other long enough.

"*Tá mo chroí istigh ionat*," I murmured as I stared into her eyes.

She smiled up at me through her tears. "That sounds so beautiful. What does it mean?"

"Your heart is very dear to mine." I rubbed my thumb along her cheekbone. "You have the most beautiful heart I've ever known, Isla. It's so open and caring. It doesn't judge. It only wants to give."

"And receive," she whispered. "From you and you alone."

My hands slid up her back to her neck. Tenderly, I cupped the back of her head. "My heart wants nothing more than to give everything it has to you."

Isla dipped her head to bring her lips to mine. She moaned into my mouth as I flipped us over. As I positioned myself between her thighs, I stroked her tongue with my own. Her hands tangled in the stands of my hair. Since she was still drenched in her arousal and my cum, I thrust back inside her.

With my eyes locked on hers, I made love for the first time in my life to my beautiful fairy goddess.

Chapter Twenty-Six: Isla

After Quinn and I were together for the second time, I found I needed a shower. I was also starving after not eating much at dinner. Quinn placed an order for room service while I got a shower.

The bathroom was just as posh as the rest of the suite. Since I hadn't packed anything, I used the luxurious body wash and shampoo that the hotel provided. To my surprise, Quinn didn't join me in the shower.

When I finished, I dried off and slipped into a plush robe. I came out of the bedroom to find Quinn on the phone, buck naked and pacing around. "I don't care if it was allegedly in my best interest. You are never, *ever* to threaten Isla. Do you hear me?"

Wincing, I hated that he was angry with Callum because of me. Even though it was completely Callum's fault, I didn't want to be the one causing the fight. "Quinn," I said softly.

He whirled around to stare at me. "I told you not to be mad at him."

"He threatened you, Little Dove. No one does that. Not even my fucking brother."

"I just don't want to be the cause of problems between the two of you."

"Don't worry. There's no problem. Isn't that right, Cal?"

After hitting the speaker, Callum's voice rang through the suite. "I'm sorry, Isla. I shouldn't have threatened you. Please accept my apology."

"I do." I crossed my arms over my chest. "Does this mean you guys aren't fighting anymore?"

Both Callum and Quinn chuckled. "We're always fighting, Isla. It's the mad Irish blood in our veins," Callum replied.

"Well, I don't like disharmony in a family, and I especially don't want to be the cause of it."

"You aren't," Quinn assured me.

At the knock at the door, I realized room service had arrived. I motioned to Quinn. "Put some clothes on please."

Callum's chuckle crackled on the line. "Quinn, you randy fucker!"

With a smirk, Quinn replied, "I plan on staying naked as long as I'm in Isla's presence."

I threw up my hands in frustration. "Would you at least go into the bathroom so they can deliver the food?"

"Fine."

Once Quinn was safely in the bathroom, I peeked through the hole to make sure it was actually room service. Considering Quinn's line of work, I could never be too careful. After opening the door, the server pushed the cart inside. I signed the bill and left a ridiculously large tip before hustling the server back outside.

After the door shut, I exhaled a breath. "You can come out now."

Quinn had ended his call with Callum. "Everything good with you guys?" I asked.

"We're fine." He bestowed a quick kiss on my lips.

To my surprise, he'd donned one of the robes. "What happened to staying naked around me?" I teasingly asked.

He flashed me a wicked grin. "The fear of spilling something hot on my junk."

I laughed and followed him over to the cart. Apparently I wasn't the only one who had an appetite. While I devoured my pasta, I also took bites of the steak Quinn had ordered as well as the enormous pile of mashed potatoes and macaroni and cheese.

When I couldn't eat one more bite, I fell over on the bed. "I think I'm going into a carb-induced coma."

"Tired, Little Dove?" Quinn asked as he joined me on the bed.

"Pleasantly."

After grabbing the remote, Quinn turned on the TV. "Let's let our food digest before I ravish you again."

"Again?" I questioned incredulously.

He grinned down at me. "Do you object?"

"No. I'm just afraid I might not be able to walk tomorrow."

"Then I'll carry you," he offered.

I threw my head back with a laugh. "You'd really do that?"

"Of course."

Somehow I knew he was absolutely serious. It was a ridiculous turn on to have a man want to spoil you that intensely. In that moment, I wanted to turn the tables and spoil him.

With Quinn's attention on the TV, I slipped out of the bed. After making a cup of ice from the bucket, I brought it over to the nightstand. I then untied the robe and let it fall to the floor.

The motion caught Quinn's eye, and he flicked his gaze to me. A lazy smile curved on his lips at the sight of me naked. "What are you doing, Little Dove?"

"I'm going to repay you for all the pleasure you've given me."

"Is that right?"

"Mm, hmm."

"How exactly do you plan on doing that?"

"By giving you head."

"Fuck yes." He then stripped comically fast out of his robe.

"You don't need a break?" I asked.

He glanced down at his half-mast cock. "You tell me."

"You're insatiable."

"With you, I am."

Since I couldn't rely solely on my vanilla experience to please Quinn, I had actually done a little research on blow jobs. What I was about to do was one of the tamer suggestions I'd found.

Reaching over, I grabbed a small handful of ice from my glass. I popped a few pieces into my mouth. Bringing one between my teeth, I began teasing a slow trail from the stubble on Quinn's chin, over his bobbing Adam's Apple, down to one of his nipples. I then blew across the moistened skin.

"Oh fuck," he muttered, bucking his hips.

"Patience."

"You're a bleedin' cock tease."

With a giggle, I continued sliding the ice along his skin. Since I wanted him to know there was nothing about his scars that turned me off, I slid the ice down the left side of his chest. The cube circled his left nipple until it was hard and erect. Then I moved on to the right one, slowly circling the nipple until it puckered.

Quinn continued raising his hips, rubbing his enormous erection against my stomach. I pushed myself away so he could no longer get the friction, causing him to groan in frustration. Working my way slowly down, I trailed the remaining cube over his stomach, causing his muscles to clench under my touch.

As I gazed up at him, his chest expanded in harsh pants. Bending over, my hair fell into his lap as I raked my nails up and down the tops of his thighs. I pressed tender kisses along the taut muscles of his abdomen. Then I blew air over the trail of moisture.

"Fuck, Isla."

"Do you want me to take your cock in my mouth now?"

"I've wanted you to since the night we met."

I continued raking my fingernails up and down his thighs. "Have you thought about it when you jerked off?"

"Fuck yes."

"Did it make you come so hard to think of fucking my warm, wet mouth?"

His eyes widened. "I'm going to blow my load just from hearing that come from your lips."

I took his cock into my hand, causing him to hiss. "Do you like your good girl to say such dirty things?"

"I sure as hell do."

"I can be your good, dirty girl," I cooed as I jerked my hand up his shaft. My research had also included things to say that I never thought I possibly could. Somehow with Quinn they flowed from my lips.

"I know you can."

"Open your mouth. Give me your tongue."

Quinn thrust out his tongue, and I sucked it into my mouth just like I would his cock. He groaned into my mouth, which caused wetness to pool between my thighs.

After bobbing on his tongue, I pulled away to murmur against his lips, "Is this what you want me to do to you? Down here." I wrapped my fingers tighter around his shaft.

"Fuck yes."

Since all the ice had already melted, I put another cube into my mouth as I worked my hand over his erection. Once I swallowed the ice, I flattened my tongue against him, sliding from base to shaft.

Quinn shuddered and muttered something in Irish. Circling his cock, I continued licking him like a popsicle, while only letting my tongue give a teasing flick across the tip. Quinn's hips jerked up, trying to wedge himself into my mouth.

After grabbing another piece of ice from the glass, I started licking and nibbling an icy, moist trail up the inside of one of his thighs while my hand rubbed a cube along the other. When I looked up at him again, Quinn's jaw was clenched, and I could see the frustrated lust burning in his eyes.

I took pity on him by sliding only the tip of his cock in my mouth and suctioning it hard. Quinn cried out, his eyes rolling back. Letting him fall free from my mouth, I then blew across the sensitive head glistening with my saliva.

"Please, Isla, you're killing me. Don't stop sucking me off. Please."

Just like Quinn said about me, my undoing came with hearing that word on his lips. With my hand, I stroked him hard and fast for a few minutes before bringing him back to my mouth. As I bobbed up and down at a frenzied pace, his groans and curses echoed through the room.

A sheen of sweat had broken out along his bare chest. "So good...oh Little Dove, I love your mouth."

Changing up the position, I brought my fingers to his base. Twisting my hand back and forth like I was opening a bottle, I alternated between tonguing and hard suctioning the very tip. The saliva that fell from my lips, slid down his length, allowing my fingers to give him an even smoother swirl off my hand, as I pumped up and down.

As I pulled away, I said, "Doing this to you...it's making me so fucking wet."

Quinn's blue eyes gleamed with lust. "Show me."

After sucking him back into my mouth, I slid my hand between my legs. I thrust my fingers inside myself, causing me to moan. Reluctantly, I pulled them out and held up the arousal-coated fingers to him.

"Give me a taste."

"But you just tasted me."

"I'm starving for you."

When I brought my hand to his lips, his tongue darted out to lick my fingers before he sucked them into his mouth. "Just as I thought. You still taste amazing."

"You do, too," I murmured, before I took him back into my mouth, grazing him lightly with my teeth.

Quinn began to lift his hips, thrusting his cock further into my mouth. My eyes watered when he bumped the back of my throat. "Is that okay, Little Dove?"

I hummed my acceptance around his cock. I could tell from the way his hands tensed at his sides that he wanted to bring them to my head. But he was worried about hurting my neck. I knew when I was healed he would fuck my mouth with no restraint.

Until then, I would take what he gave me as long as it meant we could be together. After a few more thrusts, Quinn began tensing up. "Oh fuck...oh yes!"

He arched his hips and tried to pull away from me, but I held his thighs. I wanted all of him tonight. When he came in my mouth, I continued sucking him until I swallowed all of him down.

After I let him fall free from my mouth, Quinn dragged me up to his chest to wrap his arms around him. "That was amazing. You are amazing."

I grinned at him. "I'm glad you liked it."

"I fucking loved it."

As his hand snaked down my stomach, I reached out and stopped him. "I can't take one more orgasm until I get some sleep."

He laughed. "All right, Little Dove. Get some beauty sleep because when I wake up in the morning, I'm planning on fucking your brains out again."

"Sounds like a plan," I drowsily murmured.

Completely spent from the sex and stuffed from the food, it wasn't too long before we fell asleep in each other's arms.

Chapter Twenty-Seven: Quinn

As I sat with Isla at the bar, I couldn't help reflecting what a lucky bastard I was to have such a beautiful and kind woman at my side. Since she was still healing, Isla had yet to return to work. Although Dr. Feany had cleared her for activities a week after the incident, I'd insisted she take another week considering the aerobatics she did on the pole.

The first few nights of not seeing her at the club was torture. That's when I asked her to come stay with me while I was at work. She did her coursework while I took care of club business. We had dinner delivered and pretended as best we could that our arrangement was normal dating.

Tonight we'd come downstairs to find the club empty. I'd gone to pour myself a whiskey for the road when Isla had climbed up on one of the bar stools. With a teasing smile, she said, "Hit me with one those too, bartender."

I snorted. "You hated the taste, remember?"

"I know. But I feel I need to like Irish whiskey if I'm going to date an Irish man."

Reluctantly, I poured her a glass. To my surprise, she downed it in one gulp. "That wasn't meant to be a shot."

After shuddering violently, she croaked, "Delicious."

"You're full of shite."

"I'm always about new experiences." She tilted her head at me. "What about you? Do you ever do anything spontaneous?"

Maura's words came back to me when she broke things off. How I was too staid and too rigid. "In my line of work, I'm not afforded the pleasure of spontaneity."

"I'm not talking about work. I'm talking about right here and right now between us."

"You want me to be spontaneous?"

"Mm, hmm."

I furrowed my brows at her. "By doing what?"

Her face lit up. "I know. Let's dance."

With a groan, I replied, "Like I told you the night of the gala, I'm not much of a dancer."

"You don't say," she teasingly replied.

Grunting, I crossed my arms over my chest. "I'm serious, Isla."

"Please." She batted those damn eyelashes of hers. "For me."

"Fine," I grunted.

At her squeal, I reluctantly grabbed the remote to turn on the stereo system. When music blared around us, Isla pinched her eyes shut and bounced on the balls of her feet. "I love this song. I haven't heard it in forever."

"What is it?"

Her eyes popped open to survey me. "Not much of a music listener either, huh?" At the shake of my head, she replied, "It's *Girls Like You* by Maroon Five."

As she began swaying her hips and waving her arms above her head, she said, "My first concert was Maroon 5." A ghost of a smile played on her lips. "My mom was going to take us, and then she had a terrible RA flare."

"RA?"

"Rheumatoid Arthritis. It's an autoimmune disease. People hear arthritis and think it's a little ache in your joints." Isla shook her head. "I've seen my mom in so much pain she'd be writhing on the bed."

I grimaced. "Jaysus, I'm sorry for her and for you."

"Thanks." Waving her hand as if to dismiss the painful memory, she said, "Anyway, since my mom couldn't go, my dad took Brooke and me."

"Your father the Episcopal priest?"

Isla giggled. "Yes. By the end of the night, he was dancing along with us. He even got a T-shirt." Slowly, the amusement drained from her face. "I found it when we were cleaning out his side of the closet."

Even though I was completely and totally out of my fucking emotional element, I desperately wanted to do something to take away Isla's sadness. Against my better judgment, I followed the beat of the music and started swaying my body.

At the sight of me, Isla's eyes popped wide. "Quinn Kavanaugh, you've been holding out on me."

I froze. "Excuse me?"

"Don't stop! You're good."

"You're taking the piss."

She laughed. "I'm what?"

"It's Irish for mocking me."

"No. I'm serious." She waggled her brows. "You have great rhythm. But I already knew that after seeing you in the bedroom."

"Is that right?"

"Mm, hmm." Apparently the glass of whiskey was fueling her moves because Isla danced in front of me before bending over and twerking her ass against my crotch. I couldn't stop myself from smacking one of the firm globes. At Isla's moan of pleasure, my dick slammed against my zipper.

After she righted herself, she plastered her back against my front. She threw her arm around my neck, drawing my head down. Lifting her chin, she met my lips with hers. Immediately, she thrust her tongue in my mouth.

When she jerked away, breathless and panting, she stared up at me through hooded eyes. "Do something spontaneous now, Quinn."

"Like what?"

"Fuck me on the stage."

I slid my hand over her ribcage to cup her breast. "Is that what you want, Little Dove?"

"I know it's what you want when you watch me dance. I can tell you want to drag me off the pole and fuck me in front of everyone." She swiveled her hips against my erection. "You want to prove to them I'm yours."

I growled into her ear. "You *are* mine." I squeezed her breast. "These tits are mine." My other hand slid to cup her center, causing her to hiss in a breath. "Most of all this pussy is mine."

Isla turned around to face me. She reached for the hem of her sweatshirt before jerking it over her head. She toed out of her boots before stripping her leggings down over her thighs and to the floor.

She stood before me in only a green and gold bra and matching thong. Reaching between us, she took my cock in her hands. "And this? Does it belong to me."

"It's yours and yours alone."

"What are you going to do to me?" she questioned breathlessly.

"Something fucking spontaneous."

I then swept Isla into my arms. I climbed onto the stage and marched her over to the pole. After I set her down on her feet, I jerked my chin at her. "Put your arms up."

Ever obedient, Isla did as I asked. My hands came to my tie. Slowly, I untied it and slid it out of my shirt. I wrapped it around the back of the pole before bringing it around Isla's wrists. After I tied it tight, Isla tried moving her hands, but she couldn't.

"Now you're at my mercy."

Lust flared in her eyes. "What are you going to do to me?" she repeated.

My hand cupped her between her thighs. "Not much foreplay considering how wet you are," I remarked as I worked her over her thong.

Isla gasped and arched her hips against my hand. "Take off your clothes."

I cocked my brows at her. "I think you're confused about who is in charge here. As the one tied up, you'll do as I say."

"Please. I want to feel your skin against mine."

I cupped her mouth. "When you ask so sweetly, I have to oblige you."

Isla kept her eyes glued to mine as I shrugged out of my shirt. I dropped it to the stage floor. Her gaze slid down my chest to my where my fingers undid my belt and pants.

Once I peeled them off, I worked my cock over my briefs. "Do you want this?"

Isla licked her lips. "Very much."

"The only thing I regret about this angle is you can't suck my cock."

"You could untie me."

I shook my head. "Oh no. I like you just as you are. Of course, there is the problem of being over dressed."

Reaching for my discarded pants, I took out my knife. At the sight of the gleaming silver, Isla's eyes widened in fear, not pleasure. "Easy, Little Dove. You know I'll never do anything to hurt you."

"I know," she murmured softly.

I pulled one of the straps of her bra away from her body. With a flick of the knife, I sliced the fabric.

Isla huffed indignantly. "I happened to like this lingerie."

"I'll buy you more."

Considering how hard my cock was growing from cutting her underwear off, it would be worth every penny. I moved to the next strap and cut it. The bra fell from her body, exposing her perfect tits. At the cool air swirling around them, the perfect pink nipples hardened.

Turning the knife in my hand, I slid the handle down Isla's breastbone. I brought it to her nipple, rubbing the aching the bud. Isla sucked in a breath as she tugged on her binds.

"Do you like that?"

"Yes."

Dipping my head, I replaced the handle with my mouth. I sucked the tip deep into my mouth. My mouth twirling around the pebbled flesh. When my teeth grazed her nipple, Isla cried out and bucked her hips.

As I continued sucking her nipple, I slid the knife down her abdomen. I worked it between her legs, the ribbed handle sliding through her slick folds.

"Quinn," Isla panted, her head falling back.

"Do you want to come on my knife?"

"It's so wrong," she murmured.

"But you want it, don't you?"

"Yes," she pleaded.

Abandoning her breast, I pulled the knife back and turned it in my hand. I pulled the corner of her thong from her hip and cut the fabric. After doing it on the other side, the silky fabric fell to the floor.

"Spread your legs," I commanded.

Isla slid her thighs further apart. I brought the ribbed handle back between her legs. As I began to rub it over her clit, I slammed my mouth against Isla's. My tongue thrust against hers just like I was thrusting between her thighs. The harder I rubbed her, the faster her hips moved against the handle.

She tore her lips from mine and cried out. "Please, Quinn!"

I knew she would lose her mind and not in a good way if I was to put it inside her. Instead, I pressed it harder against her clit and furiously rubbed it back it forth.

Isla threw her head back as an orgasm charged through her. She moaned and mewled as her hips continued to rise as she rode out her pleasure.

As she continued coming down, I shoved my briefs down and unleashed my cock. I tossed the knife to the ground. Grabbing her by the ass, I lifted her up to wrap her legs around my waist.

When I plunged into her with a hard thrust, we both moaned. My hips began to relentlessly piston in and out of her. Her ass began to bang back against the pole. I immediately slowed down so I wouldn't hurt her.

"Harder," she pleaded.

"I don't want to hurt you."

She shook her head. "Fuck me hard, Quinn."

There was no way I wouldn't give her what she wanted. With animalistic grunts, I once again began pumping hard in and out of her. Isla's fingers dug into my shoulders, her nails scouring my skin. My mouth once again found hers, and I fucked her mouth with my tongue just like I was her pussy.

It wasn't long before my frantic pace sent Isla over the edge with another orgasm. As her walls clenched around me like a vise, I let myself go, spilling into her.

When I came down from my high, my chest heaved with harsh pants. "Fuck, Isla," I murmured.

A satiated smile curved on her lips. "Bondage and knife play—I'd say that was pretty spontaneous."

I threw back my head with a laugh. "I aim to please."

Chapter Twenty-Eight: Isla

Two Weeks Later

As I twirled on the pole, I couldn't help reflecting that it had been three weeks since my attack, and a week since I'd come back to work. Although the pain subsided quickly, the bruises were trickier. Brooke continued helping me cover them with makeup that was usually used to cover tattoos.

I had been surprised when the other girls were understanding about me not doing lap dances. Of course, I lied and said I was just stopping for a little while. I guess most of them would've been gun-shy themselves. They were equally impressed that our beast of a boss, Quinn, was going to allow me just to waitress.

I couldn't help smiling at the thought of Quinn. The last two weeks had been absolutely magical. We'd spent each and every day of it together. Since he lived with his brothers and Caterina, he stayed with me. After seeing him so uncomfortable in my bed, I'd allowed him to splurge on a new bedroom suite.

In the back of my mind, I told myself it was ridiculous to be doing something so long term when we'd only been together for such a short time. But I shoved the voices of doubt aside. I hadn't been this happy in such a long time, and I didn't want anything to ruin it.

Once the dance was finished, I climbed down the stage steps and started walking through the crowd, stopping occasionally for the cash to slide against my skin into my g-string. Before I could make it to the bar to help deliver drink orders, a hand gripped my forearm.

Hard.

Usually when someone deigned to touch me outside of tips, one of the bouncers stepped in and instructed them to take their hands off. But when no one came to my defense, I quickly turned to see the offender.

My heart dropped at the sight of Quinn's younger brother, Kellan, leering at me.

I couldn't help wondering if he was drunk since it was so out of character for him. I'd seen him a few times since I'd begun dancing. According to Mabry who had serious eyes for him, he only came in on Thursdays for the weekly financials. Whenever she'd corner him to flirt, his face would grow crimson before he quickly excused himself.

The Kellan who stood before me today was not the same shy, mild-mannered man. He stared down at me like a predator surmising his prey, sending anxiety twisting through my stomach.

"I want a private dance," he demanded.

I pulled against his tight grip. "I'm sorry, Mr. Kavanaugh, but I've been instructed not to perform private dances."

He cocked his brows at me. "By who?"

"Um, your brother."

"Bullshit. You're a dancer in this club, aren't you?"

"I-I am."

"Then I want a dance."

When I glanced at Brady, one of the bouncers, for reinforcement, he replied, "Like she said, Quinn's given explicit instructions that no one is to contract Ms. Vaughn for a dance." He crossed his arms over his broad chest. "And I mean, *no one*."

Kellan snorted. "I own a stake in this fucking club. I think that means I can do whatever the fuck I want, don't you?"

Conflict raged in Brady's eyes before he nodded. "Fine."

When I opened my mouth to protest, Brady shot me a look that said to keep my mouth shut. Defeated, I let Kellan pull me down the hall towards the private rooms. Instead of going to the first empty one, Kellan dragged me to the last one.

After he shoved me inside, he jerked his chin at Brady. "Take a walk," Kellan instructed.

Brady glanced past him to me. At what must've been my panic, he shook his head. "As a fucking owner, you should know we don't *ever* leave the girls. Especially after what happened with Isla previously."

"You will this time." Taking a step forward, he jabbed his finger in Brady's chest. "If you know what's good for your job and your health, you'll walk away and mind your own fucking business."

Staring at Brady, tears stung my eyes as I tried to calm my erratic breathing. *Please don't leave me.*

"Whatever," he grumbled.

The tiny thread of hope I clung to plummeted, leaving me shaking in the middle of the room. Without Quinn at the club, I was completely and totally screwed. The only other person I might've been able to plead my case with was Caterina, and she didn't come on Thursdays.

The lock clicking on the door echoed through the room, causing my stomach to lurch. I fought not to hyperventilate as memories of Terrance flooded my mind. My gaze spun around the room trying to find a weapon.

But then I focused back on Kellan. He remained with his back to me. He placed his palms flat against the door before emitting a ragged sigh.

"I'm sorry about that."

His admission took me so off guard that I stumbled back. "W-What?" I questioned.

After what felt like an eternity, he turned around. My breath hitched at the difference in his expression. The Big Bad Wolf ready to devour me was gone. In its place was the Kellan I'd remembered from before.

He held his hands up in front of him. "I'm not going to hurt you, Isla." At what must've been my continued apprehension, he added, "I swear I'm not going to lay a hand on you."

Confusion flooded me. "You're not?"

"I give you my word."

When he took a step forward, I grimaced, which caused him to freeze. "I'm so sorry for my behavior." He nodded to my arm. "I hate myself for manhandling you like that. Are you okay?"

Unable to process the difference in him, I merely bobbed my head.

"I'm sorry for the things I said, too." Motioning to the couch, he said, "Won't you have a seat?"

Considering my knees felt like they were about to give out, I gladly sunk down onto the leather. I licked my lips that had run dry before turning my attention back to Kellan.

He drew in a deep breath and began pacing in front of me. From time to time, he would jerk a hand through his strawberry blonde hair. "Considering you're under Quinn's protection, I imagine you aren't ignorant to what kind of world my brothers and I are in."

I swallowed hard at the reference to the mafia. "No, I'm not."

"In our world, it's difficult to gain respect or to be taken seriously unless you act like—"

"A total bastard?"

The corners of his lips quirked. "Exactly."

It was then that it hit me. "It was all an act," I murmured more for myself than for him.

He nodded. "The bouncers wouldn't listen to me unless I took on the persona of...well, my brothers."

"You were very convincing," I replied.

Kellan laughed. "I guess I could say I've learned from the best."

Furrowing my brows at him, I asked, "But why did you need to do it?"

"I needed to be able to get you alone—" At my sharp intake of breath, he shook his head. "It's not like that, Isla."

"I'm having a hard time believing you considering we're in one of the private rooms"

He dropped to his knees in front of me. "I swear that all I want from you is to talk."

I blinked at him. "*You* want to talk to *me*?" At his emphatic nod, I asked, "But why?"

An agonizing sigh escaped his lips. "I'm trapped by something from my past, and I can't move forward." Ducking his head, he added, "It's messing with me when it comes to..." He glanced back up at me. "Well, with women."

My chest tightened at the pain etched on his face. "I'm so sorry."

"It's crazy because it happened over a year ago. While it was bad then, it's gotten even worse lately."

"Can't you talk to your brothers about it?"

His eyes bulged at the suggestion. "Feck no. That would make me look weak."

"With everything he's been through, Quinn would surely understand."

"As far as I know, Quinn's never spoken to any of us about his accident."

My mind instantly flashed to our first night together and how Quinn described in horrific detail the bombing. "How is that possible?" I questioned more for myself than for Kellan.

Kellan rose to his feet. With his back to me, he replied, "As an outsider, you can never understand. Men are expected to act a certain way in my world. To talk about our feelings—to be depressed—it puts a target on us."

"You're right. I don't understand. My sister and I share everything."

His shoulders drooped in defeat. "You're very lucky."

"I understand men outside your family having those feelings, but it's hard to believe you can't talk to your brothers."

He turned around. "It would be like a nail in my coffin. They already realize I don't have the heart for some of the harsher aspects of the business. I can't bear to become even less of a man—less of a Kavanaugh—in their eyes.

"What about a therapist or a psychologist?"

He shook his head. "Not in our world."

"Tony Soprano did," I protested.

Kellan's eyes widened before a laugh burst from his lips. "That's a TV show, not real life."

"And you're Irish, not Italian," I remarked.

He smiled. "Right."

"But I'm a stranger. How can you possibly trust me?"

His green eyes took on an intense look. "Because like calls to like."

"I don't think I understand."

"If anyone here can understand traumatic events, it's you, Isla."

An icy awareness prickled over me. "The accident?" At his nod, I demanded, "Did Quinn tell you?"

"No. I came across it in your file."

"What file?" I demanded.

"The one we run on all the dancers." At what must've been my continued confusion, Kellan said, "Considering who we are, our background checks are very intense. We have to ensure none of the dancers have ties to our enemies."

I fought to breathe. "What did mine say?"

The empathy in Kellan's eyes sent my stomach churning. "Does it matter?" he questioned softly.

I bolted up from my seat. "Of course it does!"

He exhaled raggedly. "You're the sole survivor from the car accident that took your parents' lives."

The walls began to close in as a swirling storm of anger and hurt rushed through me. Shaking my head, I jabbed a finger at him, "You have *no* right to use my trauma against me."

A horror-stricken look came over Kellan's face. "I swear that's not my intention." When I continued glaring at him, Kellan said, "I'm sorry, Isla. I just thought that besides being different from the other dancers, you were someone who might be able to understand and sympathize with my pain."

At the sincerity of his words and tone, I flopped back down on the couch. "Although I don't like it, I guess I understand."

"Then you'll do it?"

"I didn't say that."

"What are your objections?"

"Besides the glaring fact that I'm not medically qualified to counsel anyone?"

"I'm not asking you to prescribe me happy pills to deal with my shit. I just need you to listen."

"Maybe you should try to talk with someone who isn't burdened with their own baggage?"

"Aren't we all?"

"Good point." When a face popped into my mind, I couldn't help asking, "Why not talk to Mabry? She's really into you."

A flush entered Kellan's cheeks. "The fact that she's into me is the exact reason why I can't talk to her."

Cocking my head, I asked, "Do you like her?"

The red on his cheeks deepened. "I don't have a fucking clue why she's into me."

His self-deprecation was too endearing, and a smile quirked at my lips. "You must not have looked in a mirror lately."

"I don't know about that."

Leaning forward, I placed a hand on his cheek. "You have a lot to offer a woman, Kellan."

"Trust me, I want to believe that more than anything." He leaned his cheek into my hand. "Please say you'll do it, Isla."

As I stared into his handsome face, I sighed. "What is it about you Kavanaugh men that makes me incapable of saying no?"

A playful smirk curved on his lips. "I'd argue it's because we're incredibly handsome, but I think when it comes down to it, the accent clenches it."

"All right. I'll do it."

His eyes lit up. "You will?"

I held up a hand. "I can't promise much, but I'll try."

Kellan took the hand that was against his cheek and kissed it. "Thank you. And to make this worth your trouble, I'll pay you just like I would for a lap dance."

"I can't let you do that."

"I insist."

I gave him a sad smile. "What kind of person would I be to charge you for your trauma?"

"A financially smart one?"

"Kellan—"

"Don't hate me for this, but because of your file, I know why you're working here."

I sucked in a harsh breath. "I see."

With a groan, he replied, "Fuck. I'm making such a mess of this."

"Yes, you are."

"Then let me make it up to you by paying you for your time."

I still didn't like the idea of taking his money, but at the same time, I had to be practical. If I was in a private room with him, then I wasn't serving drinks and making tips. It would be a way to make up the difference. At the same time, it felt greedy considering I was already accepting Quinn's money not to do private dances. Of course, it wasn't like Quinn had given me much of a choice in that.

In the end, I had school and lab fees to worry about. "Okay, fine. You can pay me."

A smirk that was like Quinn's cut across his face. "I'm glad I could finally make you see reason."

I wagged a finger at him. "Don't be getting cocky on me. I can always change my mind."

"Okay, okay." A sincere smile replaced his smirk. "Thank you, Isla. You don't know how much this means to me."

I gave him a sad smile. "I think I do."

"Oh, there's just one more thing."

"Seriously?"

He nodded. "Quinn can't know."

"Kellan," I groaned.

I didn't like the idea of keeping secrets from Quinn. The most important part of a relationship was trust, and I would be lying to him. Well, maybe not lying, but I'd be somehow deceiving him.

"I can't have him knowing."

"But how can you possibly keep this from him or Dare?"

"Dare's focus is on opening a casino, and as for Quinn, I figured we would do it on his off days."

Furrowing my brows, I replied, "But what about the bouncers? Won't they say something?"

"I can bribe a few to keep quiet, and it wouldn't hurt for you to smooth things over with Brady so he thinks that you're fine with doing private dances for me."

"Seriously?"

He gave me a sheepish grin. "Yes."

"You've really thought this out, haven't you?"

"I have."

Heaving a sigh, I suggested, "You think we should have a drink before we do this?"

"What would you like?"

"Well, I'm not really supposed to drink on the job." When Kellan shot me a look, I replied, "Okay, fine. I'll take a margarita on the rocks."

Kellan typed something on his phone. "They'll be here in five minutes."

"Nice." I motioned next to me on the couch. "Why don't you sit down?"

"Okay."

After he eased down beside me, Kellan leaned forward to put his elbows on his knees. He rubbed his hands over his face. Then he shifted back onto the couch.

"Whatever it is, you can tell me."

He jerked a hand through his hair. "It's just now that it's come down to it, it's hard to say it in front of you."

"Why?"

"Because it's personal."

"I imagined as much."

He grimaced. "I mean, it's sexual."

"Oh," I murmured. No wonder he was having a hard time. "Don't be embarrassed. I mean, when it comes down to it, you've seen me practically naked. There's not much left between us, right?"

Kellan's Adam's Apple bobbed. "I tried not to watch you on the pole or when you had your top off. You know, out of respect for Quinn."

"That's kind of you." I patted his leg. "Now tell me what's wrong."

"I can't...be intimate with a woman."

"Like you can't ask them out?"

"No. I can't...well, you know."

At the realization, heat rushed my cheeks. "Don't you think your problem is more suited to a urologist or a reproductive specialist?"

He shook his head. "It isn't a physical issue. I still get morning wood."

Oh God. I felt the urge to crawl under the couch and hide from mortification. But I forced myself to stay seated. "Hmm, it does sound like an emotional block."

"Exactly."

Furrowing my brows, I asked, "What is the trauma it could be stemming from?"

Although I knew he'd prepared himself for my question, a shudder ran through Kellan. He once again began to pace in front of me. "You don't have to do this."

After running his hand over his face, he gave a determined shake of his head. "A year ago, my father forced me and my younger brother at gunpoint to hold my sister down as he allowed her future husband to rape her."

In my mind, I'd worked up many potential scenarios for Kellan's trauma. None of them even remotely touched the horror of what he'd experienced. To be forced to witness your sister's rape had to be the most horrendous torment I'd ever heard. But then to have your own father be your tormentor was unimaginable.

When I could finally speak again, I said, "I think we're going to need more alcohol."

Chapter Twenty-Nine: Quinn

It was a little after two am when a knock came at my office door. "What?" I demanded.

To my surprise, a familiar blonde head poked in. "Aren't you done?"

"Almost." I eyed her curiously. "Why?"

She swept inside the door. Instead of her usual leggings and t-shirts, she wore a form-fitting green dress that hit just at her knees with a mouth-watering pair of green suede knee boots. I remembered seeing her in the dress during our shopping spree, but the boots were definitely new.

Cocking my head at her, I asked, "Why are you all dressed up?"

A mischievous grin lit up her face. "I have a surprise for you."

While I inwardly groaned, I kept my face impassive. "What kind of surprise?"

She swept a hand to her hips. "If I told you, it wouldn't be a surprise, silly."

"Perhaps this is when I tell you I don't like bleedin' surprises," I grumbled.

"No, you don't say," she teasingly replied.

"Isla," I warned.

With a cheeky little grin, she came around the side of my desk. She held out her hand to me. "Come on, Big Guy. You're mine for the rest of the night."

Since the last thing I wanted was to give into her surprise, my hands gripped her tiny waist. "Quinn, what are you–"

She shrieked as I hoisted her up. "Put me down!"

I obliged her by plopping her down on my desk. I then shoved her dress up her thighs. Gripping her knees, I pushed them wide apart. "What are you–"

My head dipped between her thighs. She sucked in a harsh breath when I licked her over the tiny scrap of green lace. Fuck, I could never get enough of her smell or her taste.

"Quinn, no," she panted breathlessly as her hips arched up off the desk.

"Your pussy says yes."

"She's a traitor."

I chuckled against her hot center. "She's loyal to her master."

Isla scowled down at me. "You are not her master."

"Are you sure about that? I command her pleasure."

"So does my rabbit vibrator," she tossed back.

I slid my finger up her wet slit. "You're already soaked for me, Little Dove."

When I glanced up at her, her lips turned down in a pout. "You're ruining my surprise."

"Let me ruin your pussy first, and then I'll let you surprise me."

I then plunged two fingers inside her, causing Isla to gasp. "You don't play fair," she panted.

"Just give yourself to me."

Without another word of protest, Isla widened her thighs, giving me even better access to her glistening pussy. I continued plunging my two fingers in and out of her slick walls. Then I suctioned my mouth against her clit.

Isla cried out and clawed at my hair. She began rocking her hips against my face. "Yes, oh God, yes!" she cried.

When I added a third finger, Isla could barely keep still on the table. Her back arched and her thighs trembled as her arousal coated my fingers to my knuckles. The squelching sound of me finger fucking her pussy was music to my ears.

My cock throbbed painfully against my zipper, signaling as much as I wanted to prolong and torture her with pleasure, I needed to move things along.

When I slid my fingers out of her, Isla mewled, "Don't stop!"

With a teasing smile, I said, "Not until you say it."

"I'll say anything if you'll just make me come."

"Say that I'm the master of your pussy."

"Quinn," she whined.

When I eased back even more, her fingers tightened in my hair. "No, please, okay. I'll say it."

With my index finger teasing her opening, Isla cried, "You're the master of my pussy."

I rewarded her by thrusting all three fingers back inside her and sucking her clit into my mouth. When my teeth grazed her sensitive bud, she tensed, With a scream, her walls clenched against my fingers.

After I lifted my head, I groaned at the glorious sight of her pussy glistening with my saliva and her cum. Standing up, I made quick work of undoing my pants. After sliding them and my underwear down my hips, I gripped Isla's thighs and widened them.

With one harsh thrust, I buried myself deep inside her, causing us both to groan. Isla wrapped her legs around my waist, drawing me closer to her. "Fuck, I love being inside you," I grunted.

"I love you being inside me," she replied with a lazy smile.

"You take me so fucking well, Little Dove."

My fingers then dug into her hips as I began to pound her relentlessly. The sound of our skin slapping together and harsh pants filled the air around us. I reached forward to squeeze one of Isla's bouncing tits. I pinched and tweaked the hardened nipple, causing Isla's eyes to roll back in her head. "Mm, Quinn, I'm so close," she panted.

After I slid my forearms under her knees, I jerked her back onto my harsh thrust. She shrieked with pleasure. My movements were animalistic, but I couldn't seem to bury myself deep enough in her. But Isla didn't protest. She appeared to be as desperate for me as I was for her.

Her orgasm set off, clenching her walls around my cock. The intense grip of her pussy sent me over the edge, and I cried out her name. As my hips bucked, I pumped her full of my cum.

When I was finally spent, I stared down at her satiated face. "That was better than any surprise you have for me."

"We'll have to see about that."

As I started to bend over to kiss her, Isa's foot jabbed against my chest. "Oh no. You don't get any more loving until you clean me up."

I grinned down at her. "But I like the sight of my cum dripping out of you."

Crimson stained her cheeks. "Well, I can't enjoy your surprise if I'm all wet and sticky with your stuff."

"Cum," I corrected.

She wrinkled her nose. "I hate that word."

"Say it," I growled in a command.

Her eyes flashed with a mixture of annoyance and desire. "Fine. I can't enjoy your surprise with your load of cum dripping from me."

A primal growl roared from my chest at her words. "Fuck, Isla.

You can't say shit like that and not expect me to flip you over and fuck your brains out."

"You told me to say it," she protested.

"I know. But it's hearing it on those sinful lips of yours."

When I reached for her again, her eyes widened before she shook her head wildly back and forth. "No, no, no!"

To my amusement, she slid off the desk and then waddled rather comically into the bathroom with her thong around her ankles. After the water turned on, she yelled, "You're impossible!"

When I threw my head back with a laugh, she shouted, "*Gléas!*", which of course only made me laugh harder. I was wiping my eyes when Isla reappeared with her thong back in place, and her dress readjusted.

With all the bravado her pint-sized self could muster, she ordered, "No more funny business, okay?"

I grunted. "Fine."

She grinned and grabbed my hand. I allowed her to drag me down to the elevator. When the doors opened, she practically bounced on the balls of her feet. After our quick descent to the first floor, Isla pulled me off the elevator.

To my surprise, the club was empty. Shadows played around us as the main room was bathed in candlelight. On every table a white votive burned except for the table in the middle that was encircled with votives.

"What is all this?"

"Since we have crazy hours, we really never get to have a date, so I wanted to bring one to us."

"Seriously?"

She nodded. "As a romantic at heart, I wanted to do this to celebrate our anniversary."

I snorted. "We have an anniversary?"

With a playful roll of her eyes, she said, "Yes, Mr. Beasty, we do." With a grin, she added, "It's been a month since we became official the day of my attack."

I sucked in a harsh breath. "Don't remind me of that night."

"I know. I don't like to think of it either, especially now the bruises have all faded." She patted my chest. "That's why it's important to celebrate our anniversary, so we can have happy memories associated with it."

"If you say so."

"I do." She then pulled me over to the center table where it was set for two with an enormous pot in the center. "A little birdy told me what your favorite Irish dinner was."

"You talked to Caterina?"

"Maybe." Reaching over, she pulled the lid off a dish. "Voila. It's Cottage Pie!"

As I stared between her and the dish, I fought to breathe. No woman had ever done something like this for me before. Not even before the bombing. It overwhelmed me. What was left of my dark heart thrummed wildly at Isla's gift.

Once I finally found my voice, I asked, "You really went to all this trouble for me?"

"I sure did."

At the tears pricking my eyes, I dipped my head to hide my face by nuzzling her neck. Pinching my eyes shut, I let my lips travel up her throat. At her satisfied gasp, I said, "I don't deserve you, little dove."

"Aw, you do. More than you could ever know, Quinnie the Pooh."

My eyes popped wide against her neck before I jerked back. "What did you just call me?"

An impish twinkle gleamed in her eyes. "Quinnie the Pooh."

"No one but my sister is allowed to call me that."

"But it's so cute."

"Isla," I growled.

She traced her finger over the rose tattoo on my neck. "Seriously, how precious is it that she couldn't say Quinn and so she said Winn instead?"

I sucked in a breath. Only my extreme inner circle knew about that nickname. "Did Caterina tell you that story?"

"No, Maeve did."

"You talked to my sister?" I questioned incredulously.

Isla nodded. "When Caterina called your mom to get the recipe."

Jesus, Mary, and Joseph. "You talked to my mother?"

Refusing to meet my eye, she replied, "Maybe."

"You didn't tell her you were my girlfriend, did you?"

Hurt radiated in Isla's eyes. "What would you have preferred me to say? That I'm just a dancer in your club who you fuck?"

Shite. I'd gone and done it now. "Isla, I'm sorry. I didn't mean it the way it came out. I just wanted to know what you said, so I could do damage control the next time I talked to them."

"Seriously? I know I'm a stripper and not from one of your precious clans to make a marriage alliance with, but I can't believe you would be so ashamed of me."

I ran my hand over my face. "Jaysus, I'm making such a mess of this."

Isla crossed her arms over her chest. "Maybe it's time you tried cleaning it up and explaining why you would care that I spoke to your mother and sister?"

I exhaled a ragged breath. "There's something you need to understand."

"I'm listening."

"I haven't introduced my mother and sister to a woman since long before the accident."

Isla's brows creased in confusion. "Why not?"

"Because there hasn't been one."

"You haven't dated anyone in two years?"

"No. I haven't. While I might've fucked many women in that amount of time, I certainly didn't feel anything for them or date them." I pushed the hair out of her face. "I swear on all that is holy that I've wanted to tell my mam about you, but I wanted to do it in my own way. Especially not in front of my younger sister who would automatically think she needed to buy a dress to wear to our wedding."

"Oh," Isla murmured.

I smiled at her. "I'm sure the moment they heard we were dating, wedding bells started pealing in their heads."

"I hope you know that the thought of marrying you isn't a bad thing," Isla huffed.

"It isn't?"

She shook her head. "I'm not looking for it anytime soon, but it's not the worst Idea I've ever heard."

"I don't think it is either, Little Dove."

"Good. Now that you've explained yourself, I think we can proceed with celebrating our anniversary, right?"

"Yes, ma'am."

"Sit," she urged.

"Do I look like a dog?" I mused as I plopped down in the chair.

"No. But your behavior lends that way sometimes."

"Ouch. You have the claws out tonight, Little Dove."

To my surprise, Isla eased down on my lap. My hand slid up her back, entangling my fingers in the long waves of her hair. "Are you hungry?"

"Starved," I murmured.

With a gleeful look, Isla dipped a fork in the pie. After scooping out a heaping bite, she brought it to my lips. "This is quite the service," I mused.

"I'm happy to do it."

The moment the pie hit my tongue, I fought my gag reflex. Considering how good it smelled, it was a shock to my system. How she could have made something as delicious as the colcannon soup yet screwed this up was beyond me.

Forcing a smile, I swallowed down the bite. "Delicious."

Isla smacked my shoulder playfully. "How can you be a mafia man and be such a bad liar?"

My eyes popped wide. "I'm not lying."

"Yes, you are."

With a resigned sigh, I replied, "Okay, fine. It's terrible."

Her rosy lips turned down in a pout. "I don't know what I did wrong. I followed the recipe exactly as your mom gave me."

"Maybe some of the measurements were off since they're on the metric system over there," I suggested.

"As a scientist, I should've foreseen that being an issue," she lamented.

I swallowed my laugh. "It's the thought that counts," I remarked.

"You're right." To my dismay, she rose off my lap. But I was quickly rewarded when she bent over the bag next to the table, showing off her ample ass. She pulled up to reveal a pizza box from my favorite pizzeria.

Flashing me a grin, she said, "It's also having a backup prepared."

I threw back my head with a laugh. "Smart, very smart."

She opened the box and then slid it under my nose. At the mouth-watering smell, I closed my eyes. "I'm going to owe you many orgasms for this."

"Somehow I think that's a gift for you as much as it is for me."

"True." As I grabbed a piece, I asked, "How did you know Regina's was my favorite?"

"The same birdy told me as well that you love the sausage and peppers pizza ."

"I'm going to owe Caterina for this," I mused.

"As long as you don't pay her in orgasms like you are me," Isla teased.

"I'm pretty sure Callum would cut off my cock if I even remotely look at Caterina sexually."

"You know, it's kind of sad that we've been together for a month, and I don't even know what kind of pizza you like," Isla pouted.

"You know a lot about me," I scoffed.

"Such as?"

"You know I love eating your pussy and giving you orgasms."

Isla stomped her foot. "I'm serious, Quinn."

I laughed. "You're ridiculously adorable when you're mad."

"I'd like to strangle you right now."

"I'm not sure I'm into erotic asphyxiation."

Just when I thought she was going to explode, I reached over to kiss her. "I'm sorry for teasing you. I'm thinking right now would be a good time to give you my anniversary gift."

Isla gasped. "You remembered?"

With a sheepish smile, I replied, "While I'd like to take credit, it was Caterina who mentioned it to me a few days ago. She thought I should be prepared."

Isla grinned. "Why am I not surprised?"

"You know this beast is a work in progress."

"I appreciate you trying to be a better man for me."

"Would you still feel that way if I hadn't gotten you a gift?" I teasingly asked.

"Yes."

"Liar."

Her eyes popped wide. "I'm not lying. I figured I was the only one who had paid attention to the date."

"Would you like me to get your present now?"

"It's here?" At my nod, she did a giddy clap of her hands. "Yes, get it!"

Until it arrived this morning, I was sweating bullets that it would make it on time. I didn't think flashing her a picture would have the same effect as giving it to her in person. After retrieving the box from the storeroom, I came back out to the main room.

Before I could make it over to Isla, she rushed to my side. You would've thought she was a kid on Christmas morning with her enthusiasm. With much more strength than I imagined her having, she tore open the shipping box. She then pulled the wooden crate out of the box.

At the sight of the name on the box, she gasped. "You got me a microscope?"

"It's an antique one."

"I know."

"You do?"

She smiled. "This particular serial number for an E. Leitz Wetzlar is from before the 1900's."

"You've got a good eye," I mused.

"I know my microscopes."

After setting the wooden box on the table, Isla opened it up to reveal a brass microscope in pristine condition. I'd paid extra to make sure of it. Her fingers ghosted over the equipment.

When she finally turned back to me, there were tears in her eyes. "Fuck. You don't like it."

Without a word, she launched herself at me. As she squeezed me tight, I said, "We can get one you like."

She pulled away to stare into my eyes. "I don't want another one. The one you gave me is absolutely beautiful."

"But you're crying," I protested.

"Because I love it so much." She hopped up into my arms, wrapping her legs around my waist. With her lips against my ear, she whispered, "It's the best present anyone ever gave me."

A jolt shuddered through me at her words. Pulling her back to where I could look into her face, I asked, "It is?"

She nodded. "It was so thoughtful."

"I think cooking for me was pretty thoughtful."

She laughed. "It isn't a competition."

"I know. No woman has ever cooked something I loved before."

Isla's lips turned down in a pout. "But it tasted awful."

"It doesn't matter. It was the thought that counts and all the trouble you went to." I brought my lips to hers. "It was the best present ever."

"But I didn't even buy anything for you."

"You didn't need to. It was perfect."

"Just as yours was."

"I'd thought about a diamond necklace or bracelet," I answered honestly.

Isla shook her head. "Your gift speaks to my heart. It's more beautiful than the most expensive diamond necklace."

I rubbed my thumb along her bottom lip. "I suppose for our second-month anniversary I should find more antique equipment."

With a grin, Isla replied, "I would love that." She tapped her chin. "I'm going to have to talk to Caterina or your brothers to see what I can get you."

"All I want is you."

"And you have me."

"Can I have more of you after we finish the pizza?"

"Yes." Waggling her brows, she replied, "If you make Shane put the partition up, I'll let you have me on the way home."

"Now that's a gift," I mused.

Chapter Thirty: Quinn

A fter fucking Isla in the SUV, we'd stumbled into her house and collapsed in her bed. The sun was up when I'd woken up to her mouth sucking down my morning wood. We'd fallen back asleep before she had to get up at noon to make it to her afternoon classes.

I'd then gone home and gotten ready for the work day. It was almost six when I'd finally made it to *Alainn*. When I opened the door to my office, I momentarily recoiled at the sight of Callum sitting at my desk.

"What are you fecking doing?" I demanded.

Callum barked out a laugh. "Hello to you, too, boyo."

After crossing my arms over my chest, I muttered, "Hello."

Holding up his hands, Callum rose from behind my desk. "I'm sorry for infringing on your turf. I forgot how prickly you can be about your things."

"Bullshit."

As he came around the side of the table to meet me, he clapped my back. "We've got a problem."

"More threats from Mikita's crew?"

Callum grimaced. "No. This conflict is on our home turf."

"I don't like the sound of this."

"Trust me. You aren't going to like this."

After I eased down in my chair, Callum perched on the edge of my desk. "Owen asked for a meeting with me last night. He wanted to bring something to my attention that's been happening here."

"Why didn't he come to me?"

Callum sighed. "He said you were too close to the issue."

I furrowed my brows at him. "What the fuck does that mean?"

"As you know, Owen accompanies Caterina with her mission work here."

"Yes, I've seen him."

"Last night, he noticed Kellan escorting one of the dancers to the private rooms."

My jaw unhinged at the comment. "Fuck me. I didn't think he'd ever partaken in any of the dancers. *Ever*."

"This is the first time."

"Considering he's of age and overdue a little sexual gratification, what's the problem?"

"It seems he only has eyes for one dancer."

I shrugged. "So, he has a preference for a particular pussy."

"This 'particular pussy', as you call it, is raking in three times what normal dancers do."

With a chuckle, I replied, "Who would've thought Mr. Tight Ass would be blowing his wad in more ways than one?"

Callum rolled his eyes. "That's not the point."

"Come on, Cal. It's his money to spend. Considering a percentage of that comes back to the club, I don't see what the problem is with Kellan being generous."

"There's not a percentage coming back."

I sucked in a harsh breath. "Excuse me?"

"Kellan hasn't been taking the house's percentage out on this dancer."

Now I understood Callum's concern. As far as taking care of the club's finances, I'd never given one thought to Kellan ever cooking the books. He'd never exhibited that he possessed a dishonest bone in his body.

But that's the thing about a woman. Or I should say pussy. It warps your mind and ruins even the best of men.

Reaching for my phone, I said, "I'll call him in."

Callum shook his head. "There's more."

"Jaysus," I muttered.

"Owen worries the dancer is taking advantage of Kellan's kindness to milk him dry in more ways than one."

"Fine. We'll call *her* in."

"You may rethink that option."

"Why?"

"Because it's Isla."

At the sound of her name, I froze. Air wheezed from my lungs, and my heart ceased to beat. After a few seconds, a shudder echoed through me as my heart restarted.

Isla was giving private dances after I'd specifically forbidden her. Isla was giving private dances to my brother. Behind my back. In secret.

No, it couldn't be. Isla would never deceive me. She would never step out with anyone, least of all my brother. She'd told me herself she wasn't interested in any of my brothers. She was everything that was good and pure in the world. Surely, Callum was mistaken.

"She doesn't do lap dances," I protested.

"She does for Kellan."

This isn't happening. It can't be fucking true. "Owen saw them with his own eyes?"

Regret flashed in Callum's eyes. "He did."

I swallowed the bile rising in my throat. "He saw her dancing for him?"

With a shake of his head, Callum replied, "He watched them go into a room together." At what must've been my questioning look, he said, "I pulled the tapes from the room."

"And?"

"They've been erased from the time period that the two of them were in the room."

I fought to breathe. For a moment, the pain of Isla cheating on me disappeared. In its place was pure blood betrayal. After everything we had been through, Kellan had deceived me. He'd taken what was mine. "How could he do this?"

Callum snorted. "For fuck's sake, Quinn. You're actually going to blame Kellan and not some outsider piece of ass you've known for two months?"

"Don't talk about her like that," I growled.

Throwing up his hands, Callum countered, "Would you listen to yourself? You're just as blinded by her as Kellan is. You're both completely and totally pussy whipped by her." He began pacing in front of my desk. "I have to admit that she's good. She snowed me as well."

"There still could be another explanation."

Callum stared sadly at me. "I don't believe so, brother."

A fissure line had cut through my chest at Isla's actions. My bruised heart began to thump with a growing rage. Just like Maura, Isla played me. But I wasn't enough. She'd taken advantage of Kellan as well. "Get her in here."

"I've already called her in. She should be here in twenty minutes."

"Good."

Callum's brows creased with worry. "Are you sure you want to be a part of this?"

"I'm a man for fuck's sake. I'm not going to slink out of here with my tail between my legs."

"I wasn't insulting anything about your manhood. I'm just concerned about you."

"I'm not going to kill him or her if that's what you're afraid of."

At the pity flashing in Callum's eyes, I growled. "Fuck you."

"For caring about you? For feeling like my heart is being ripped out for you?"

"I don't want or need your sympathy."

When a knock came at the door, my chest clenched. Callum nodded at Owen who opened the door. Dare came in first wearing a solemn expression. Then with slow, hesitant steps, Isla walked into the room. Her usually peachy complexion appeared white as a ghost. Her blue eyes darted around, nervously taking in the office décor. At the sight of Callum sitting at the desk, she swallowed hard.

Since it was her off day, she wasn't outfitted in her usual sultry attire. Instead, she wore black leggings and an oversized white sweatshirt with the letters MIT emblazoned on it. Her long blonde hair was swept into a messy bun while simple glasses sat atop her perky nose.

At the sight of me, hope bloomed in her expression, and a smile lit up her face. "Hey you," she said. When I stared impassively, her lips turned down. "Quinn?"

I still didn't respond. Instead, Callum replied, "Thank you for coming in so quickly, Ms. Vaughn."

"Quinn, what's going on? Why aren't you speaking to me?"

"I'm the one who called you down, Ms. Vaughn," Callum replied.

Isla gave a jerky nod of her head while her fingers anxiously played with the cuff of her sweatshirt sleeve. Her teeth nibbled anxiously over her bottom lip, and I could tell it was taking everything within her to keep her mouth shut.

Callum motioned to one of the chairs across from the desk. "Please. Have a seat."

After quickly dropping down into the leather chair, Isla placed her hands on her knees that were visibly shaking. The part of me who still loved her desperately wanted to go to her. To wrap her in my arms and tell her everything was okay.

But I didn't.

Heavy silence draped the room. From her shifting in her seat and her trembling hands, Isla was fighting to keep herself in check.

And then the dam broke.

Unable to hold her tongue any longer, Isla blurted, "Please, Quinn, talk to me. Tell me what I've done wrong."

Callum narrowed his eyes at her. "In my club, I ask the questions."

"It's not your bleedin' club," I spat.

Cutting his gaze from Isla to me, Callum cocked his brows. "Aye, you're right, brother. But I am the leader of this family, am I not?"

"Aye," I begrudgingly replied.

"Then I'll be handling the interrogation."

Isla squeaked before clamping a hand over her mouth. When we turned our attention back to her, she stammered, "I-Interrogation?"

"Yes, Ms. Vaughn. It's come to our attention that a rather large sum of money has been passing between our younger brother and yourself." What little color was left in Isla's cheeks drained from her face while her pulse sped up in her neck. At the physical manifestation of her guilt, my heart sank further while my fists clenched at my sides.

After Isla swallowed, Callum leaned forward in his chair. "A sum of money he hasn't been honest with when it comes to the business."

Isla's blue eyes widened. "I don't know anything about the money, I swear."

"But he has been spending cash on your company, correct?"

Isla locked her sorrowful gaze on mine before slowly nodding. "Yes," she murmured.

My heart constricted in my chest like a vise. Although hurt, anger roared through me, causing my fists to clench at my sides. The first woman I'd cared about since the bomb was fucking my brother.

Not only was she fucking my brother, but she was playing me like a fool.

The monster within me snarled to be freed. To inflict physical pain on Isla that mirrored my emotional pain.

At Dare's low growl, Callum leaned forward in his chair. "Normally, I don't give two fucks whose dick you dancers are riding, including my brothers. But you see, Ms. Vaughn, Kellan isn't cut like the rest of us—"

"No, he isn't." At Callum's sharp intake of breath about being interrupted, Isla rushed on. "He is one of the kindest, most generous men I've ever met in my life."

"It's his generosity that has us concerned."

"I don't understand."

With a roll of his eyes, Dare growled, "Quit with the innocent act. You know exactly what you're doing to him, you heartless bitch."

At Isla's horrified gasp, Callum held up his hand. "Keep yer fuckin' trap shut," he ordered Dare. While Dare glowered at Callum's admonishment, he eased back to lean against the desk.

"The next question I ask you better answer with complete and total honesty." His eyes narrowed. "Your life depends on it."

"Y-Yes, S-Sir," she croaked.

"Are you fucking our brother?"

As a shriek escaped Isla's lips, crimson shot across her cheeks and then streaked down her neck. "N-No." After a moment of her chest heaving to catch her breath, she furiously shook her head. "It's not like that with Kellan and me."

"What is it exactly?" Callum demanded.

"We've never been physically intimate in any way. *Ever.*" Isla turned her gaze to mine. "You're the only man I care for, Quinn. I swear."

At the absolute truth reflected in her sapphire eyes, the tightness in my chest receded. She hadn't been playing me for a fool while fucking my brother behind my back.

As much as I wanted to let her off the hook, the issue of her taking Kellan's money remained.

Callum appeared to be weighing her words. After a few moments, he cocked his head. "Then enlighten us, Ms. Vaughn. If the two of you aren't fucking, what is it that you are doing with my brother that ends with a financial transaction?"

"I promised not to tell," she protested.

At Callum's growl, I stepped forward. "Isla, I know you want to be honorable to Kellan, but he's in serious trouble at the moment. The more we know before we have to speak to him the better."

Isla stared intently into my eyes before she finally bobbed her head. "We just talk."

"Like dirty shit?" Dare questioned.

Isla ducked her head. "No, it's not like that. It's very innocent."

"You seriously expect me to believe that my brother buys your time to merely talk?" Callum countered.

"I swear it on the saints," she replied.

I'd fought to keep silent, but I couldn't anymore. "Out of all the dancers, why did he target you when he knows what you mean to me?" I questioned.

"Because I'd experienced trauma like he had."

"Your parents?" I questioned to which Callum and Dare exchanged a look.

She nodded. "Kellan needed someone to talk to, but he felt it was too complicated to reach out to a therapist." After glancing between my brothers and me, she added, "He was also afraid of what you all would think of him if he went to therapy."

Callum grunted. "Silly eejit. Like we would've thought of differently."

"Wouldn't we?"

At my question, both Callum and Dare snapped their attention to me. "It's not like we're mental health advocates, which is unfortunate considering the way we were brought up."

"Good point," Dare mused.

"I'm his leader. There's nothing he can't talk to me about," Callum boasted.

Isla shook her head. "I promise he couldn't."

While Callum grumbled under his breath, I asked Isla, "In all these times together, he's really never touched you?"

"Not entirely."

At the thoughts of Kellan's hands anywhere near Isla's body, my fists tightened at my side. I tried to keep my expression impassive even though I felt murderous.

"After we talk, he likes me to hold him for a little while. Or sometimes he holds me."

"Well, fuck me," Dare muttered under his breath.

"What is it you talk about?" I asked.

Isla's tongue darted out to nervously lick her lips. "That's between Kellan and me."

"Excuse me?" Callum questioned.

"Just like a real therapist, I won't betray his trust."

"Considering your involvement with Quinn, you're well aware of the business we run."

"I know," she whispered.

"Then surely you can see why it is integral to know if that said business has been compromised."

"It hasn't."

At Callum's lethal expression, my muscles tensed. "You will tell us the content of the conversations, Ms. Vaughn," he demanded.

"Please don't ask that of me."

"You mistake my intent." Callum slowly rose to his feet. "It's not a request—it's a demand."

"Leave it," I growled.

Callum cut his eyes to mine. "I will see this through."

Although her body trembled and jerked in fear, Isla shook her head. "I won't betray Kellan."

"Then perhaps I need to acquaint you with a harsher line of questioning."

When Callum started around the desk to Isla, I lunged at him. My body slammed into him with such force I crashed his back against the bookcases. With blood roaring in my ears, my hand gripped his throat. "If you even think about laying one finger on her, I'll fucking end you. Brother or not, *no one* touches her."

Callum's eyes bulged. To my surprise, he didn't try fighting me. He just stared in astonishment as he gasped for air. Within seconds, Dare, Owen, and Fionn flew to us and began extricating me off of Callum.

After bending at the waist, I pinched my eyes shut and tried to curb the monster roaring within me. I'd never raised a hand in malice to any of my brothers. Since we were toddlers, we'd brawled like brothers do, but it was never out of anger that currently coursed through me.

Callum's heavy breathing filled the room as he tried to catch his breath. Once he recovered, he shook his head at me. "Did you actually think I'd hurt her?"

"You were within your rights as the leader of this family to investigate any potential compromise to the organization."

Clenching his jaw, Callum repeated, "Did you actually think I'd hurt her?"

"I was ninety-nine percent sure you wouldn't. But I had to protect her from that one percent."

A smirk curved across his lips. "Never thought I'd see a day the notorious Quinn Kavanaugh was brought to his knees by a woman."

"I must've learned from the best since you're constantly on your knees from Caterina," I spat back.

A chuckle rumbled through his chest. "Touche, mate."

Just as I righted myself, the office door blew open, and Kellan stormed in the room with Caterina on his heels. Pure venom—the likes I'd never seen on him—filled his expression. "What the fuck do you think you're doing?" he blared.

Before any of us could answer, he dropped to his knees in front of Isla's chair. With remorse filling his face, his hand tenderly cupped her cheek. "Are you okay?"

My heart twisted in my chest as regret reverberated through me. Choking envy cut off my oxygen. I'd never envied Kellan.

But at that moment I did.

I envied his trust. His ability to express his emotions. His ability to put everyone's needs above his own. He knew he was walking into a fucking firestorm, but he hadn't cared.

His only worry had been for Isla.

I'd claimed to care for her–to love her even–, yet I'd allowed the travesty of an interrogation to happen. I'd allowed her to be stripped vulnerable to the verbal abuse of my brothers. I'd hurt her because I'd foolishly believed she was cheating on me with Kellan.

I was a fucking bastard.

After tearing his gaze from Isla, Kellan narrowed his eyes at me. Shooting to his feet, he stormed over to me. "How could you do this to her? How could you drag her in here and question her like a fucking criminal?"

"Kellan–" Isla began.

He shook his head at her. "He claims to care for you, yet he allows you to be treated like this."

Kellan's words wounded me the same as if he'd punched me. Anguish and regret raged through me so hard I fought to breathe. Choking on the emotions I needed a release.

"Hit me." At Kellan's wide eyes, I nodded. "Go ahead. Hit me as hard as you fucking can."

"Quinn, no!" Isla protested.

"There's no physical pain that you or anyone else can inflict on me to make me feel any worse than I already do." As Kellan still stared at me in disbelief, my chest rose and fell with harsh breaths. "Fucking hit me, so I can at least bleed for her!" I roared.

Kellan blinked at me in surprise. "I can't."

A mirthless laugh tumbled from my lips. "Come on, boyo. You know you want to have free rein for a piece of me. Hell, I'm giving you my fucking permission."

"You know that's not who I am." He threw his hands up. "Jesus, all this masculine bullshit of guns and fists is why I needed to talk to Isla in the first place. You can't always take your emotions out on someone. You have to talk about it."

"So what can I do?"

That question was both for him and for me. I didn't know what the fuck I could do to stop the agony coursing through me from hurting Isla and losing her.

"Tell me why you didn't put a stop to it?" Kellan demanded.

Instead of replying to Kellan, I glanced past him to stare at Isla. "Because I was a jealous prick. The last woman I cared about played me for a fool, and I thought you were playing, too. My own self-loathing made it impossible not to believe the bullshit Callum was saying." After jerking a hand through my hair, I sighed. "But I was wrong not to believe you, and I was so fucking wrong to ever let Callum question you. There won't be a single day I live that I don't regret every single thing that happened to you in this office."

My gaze flicked back to Kellan. "I wish I could be like you, brother. I wish I could wear my heart on my sleeve and give love so freely. Maybe if I could, I wouldn't have lost the woman I love."

With that, I stalked past the others and out the office door. As I started down the hallway, Isla called to me. "Quinn, don't go!"

When I turned around, I shook my head at her. "Stay away from me, Isla. I'm no good for you. That's very apparent."

Isla slowly walked up to me. "Don't you dare run away from me."

"It's the best thing for both of us."

"No, it isn't. We need to talk."

"What else is there to say? I failed you in every way possible today."

"That isn't true. You were going to fight Callum to protect me."

"It was too little, too late." I clenched my jaw. "How can you say that to me after what I did to you?"

"While I can't say I'm not incredibly hurt and angry, I do understand why you did it."

"It sure as hell doesn't make it right."

Isla shook her head. "I'm to blame as well."

"How can you possibly say that?"

"I should've told you what was happening. When Kellan asked me to keep it a secret, I didn't want to do it. I didn't want to do anything behind your back, especially after you asked me the night of the gala to never be alone with your brothers."

"Your intentions were honorable. You were just trying to help him."

"But in the process, I ended up hurting the man I love."

I sucked in a breath at her words. "You love me?"

A smile played on her lips. "Yes, Quinn Kavanaugh, I love you. One major fuck up isn't enough to drive me away."

With a shake of my head, I argued, "We've only known each other two months."

"Is there a time frame for falling in love?"

I scowled at her. "No, but it's too soon."

She laughed. "It is not."

"You need more time."

"Excuse me?"

"I'm not someone who is easy to love, so you need more time to figure it out."

Isla's blue eyes darkened. "Don't tell me what I need or feel, caveman."

"You can't love me," I countered.

"Too bad. I do."

"No, you can't."

She swept her hands to her hips. "Do you know how infuriating you are right now?"

I jerked my hands desperately through my hair. "You can't love me," I murmured.

Isla placed both her hands on my cheeks. "Listen to me. I do love you."

"But I'm a monster, Isla."

"I know exactly what you are, and I still love you."

"You deserve better."

She shook her head. "I don't deserve a perfect man, and you're certainly not getting a perfect woman in me."

"I sure as hell am."

Isla rolled her eyes. "I love you, Quinn. Get it through your stubborn head that nothing you can say or do is going to change that. Am I going to make you pay for believing something so ludicrous as I was having an affair with Kellan and stealing money? Oh yes. You're going to do a lot of groveling before I let you lay one finger on me again."

"I welcome the punishment."

"Seriously?"

"I do. Even if it kills me, I'll make it up to you."

"Good. I'm glad to hear it." Cocking her head at me, she asked, "Are you all right now?"

"I haven't been alright since the day the first cry of pleasure tore from your lips as you rode my cock."

When heat flared in Isla's eyes at my admission, I continued on. "I'm not alright because a wee faerie goddess stormed into my life and turned everything upside down. I want things—I desire things—I didn't before. The only time I'm alright is when you're in my arms or my cock is buried inside you."

I jerked her to me. "I love you, Isla. I've loved you since the first day I met you."

"You didn't even know me," she protested.

"I still knew that day."

As I started to bring my lips to hers, a throat cleared behind us. When I turned around, Caterina stood behind us. "If you wouldn't mind coming back to the office, my husband would like to apologize for his behavior."

"Let me guess. Callum's in the doghouse as well?" I asked.

Caterina jerked her chin up. "He'll be sleeping on the couch for the foreseeable future."

Isla giggled. "He can always sleep with Quinn because I won't be warming his bed any time soon."

I groaned at their united front. "Come on. Let's get this over with."

"Oh, it's not over by a long shot," Isla replied with a wink.

Chapter Thirty-One: Isla

Two Weeks Later

I made it five days before I let Quinn touch me again. I found his punishment was torture for not just him, but me as well. In those five days, I received daily flowers and letters professing his undying devotion and his utter repentance.

He'd resorted to letters when I refused to reply to any texts or calls. I wanted to prove my point that while I might've forgiven him, I sure as hell had not forgotten. I wanted to instill the fear of God in him to never cross the line again.

As for Caterina, she allowed Callum back in their bedroom after three sleepless nights on the couch. She'd also made him and Quinn babysit Henry while she took me and Brooke for a spa day on Callum's dime. We had an amazing day of relaxation, and Callum and Quinn seemed to enjoy spending the day with Henry. Callum claimed it was good practice for his impending fatherhood.

Tonight after I'd finished my shift, Quinn and I had gone two rounds in his office before ordering Chinese. We ate naked in his office before going for yet another round. It was late when we finally left to head home.

As we got on the elevator, I let out an enormous yawn. "These late nights are killing me."

"Maybe you need to take another night off."

I wrinkled my nose. "I can't afford that."

"You need time to study."

"I know. I'm making it work."

"I don't want you to get run down. You'll end up sick."

With a grin, I countered, "I'm pretty sure you'll change your tune if I start going home after my shift, and you're not getting laid as much."

"I'll just come to your house and climb in bed, so we can have morning sex."

I laughed. "Leave it to you to find a sexual solution."

As Quinn and I started out the backdoor to the waiting SUV, Shane ran to meet us. "What's wrong?" Quinn questioned.

"One of our shipping vessels just exploded as it came into port."

"Fucking Bravta scum!" Quinn shouted.

"Callum has asked you to meet him at the docks."

Quinn nodded before turning to me. "Will you be able to get home okay?"

I gave him a reassuring smile. "I'll be fine. You go on and take care of your business."

"I'll have Niall walk you to your car."

"That isn't necessary."

As usual, Quinn ignored me. He stuck his head back in the door and shouted for Niall. Once he appeared, he informed him of his duty. "Yes, boss," Niall replied.

Quinn drew me into his arms. After placing a tender kiss on my lips, his hand slid over my waist to squeeze my ass. "I'll talk to you in the morning."

I nodded. "Be safe, okay?"

"I will."

After one last kiss, he then hopped into the SUV with Shane and roared away into the night. At what must've been the fear etched across my face, Niall patted my back. "It'll be alright, Ms. Vaughn. The Kavanaughs, with the help of the Neretti's, are closing in on eliminating the threat. Tonight's explosion is just a retaliation because of that."

"I hope so. I don't want anyone getting hurt."

"Come on. Let's get you to your car."

Just as he had been instructed, Niall walked me to my car and insisted on waiting until I was locked inside and cranked up before he walked back inside the building. After checking my phone to see if Brooke had called or texted, I then started to throw the car in reverse.

Gazing in the rearview mirror, I saw a menacing looking man in the backseat. At my scream, he clamped his hand over my mouth. The metal of a gun pressed against my temple. "Don't do anything to draw attention to yourself. If you scream, I'll blow your fucking head off."

At the realization of his Russian accent, a shudder of fear ran through me. I continued trembling so hard I could barely keep my hands on the steering wheel. "Now drive the fucking car."

I shakily nodded my head. When he was satisfied with my answer, he pulled his hand away from my mouth. Unfortunately, the gun stayed pressed against my temple.

Slowly, I eased out of my spot. I then inched the car through the parking lot to the exit. Because of the late hour, the guard shack was closed. There would be no one to see me being held at gunpoint.

After I checked both ways, I eased the car out onto the street. I swallowed the bile rising in my throat. We'd gone barely half a mile when the gun pressed harder into my skin. "Turn into the carwash parking lot."

I did as I was told. When we coasted into an empty space, the man pulled the gun away from me. A shaky breath escaped my lips, and I fought to not start sobbing. "Get out of the car."

Tears stung my eyes as I slid the gear into park. "P-Please don't k-kill me," I sobbed.

He smacked the gun against my skull, causing me to cry out in pain. "Stupid bitch, you're no good to us if you're dead."

And then it hit me. This wasn't some random kidnapping of a dancer. I'd been specifically targeted because I was Quinn's girlfriend. His fear had come true.

I held my hands up. "Okay, I'll get out of the car."

As I opened the door, he kept his gun trained on me. I don't know why. There was nowhere I could've run to that he couldn't have caught me. The four or five businesses were dark and closed for the night.

Once I stood outside the car, he demanded, "Give me your phone."

Reluctantly, I reached back inside the car. I would've given anything in that moment to have had one of my father's guns. Dating Quinn had lured me into a false sense of security.

When I handed it to the man, he slammed it to the ground. I shrieked in horror when his large boot stomped it to pieces. With an evil smile, he replied, "Can't have anyone following us."

I covered my mouth to keep the screams from escaping. I desperately wanted to pinch myself and find this was all just a horrible nightmare. But I knew I would get no respite if I tried.

He motioned to the backseat. "Get in."

Just as I started to bend over, he slammed the butt of the gun against the back of head, causing darkness to envelop me.

Chapter Thirty Two: Quin

After I got down to the docks, Callum walked over to meet me. To my surprise, our uncle Seamus was with him. "Jaysus, look what the cat dragged in," I mused with a smile.

He grinned. "I've not been stateside for more than a day and have to come bail you guys out."

"Bullshit," Callum mused.

Shortly before Caterina's kidnapping, Seamus had gone back to Belfast to work with the Kavanaugh clan there. With only Eamon left in Ireland with Mam and Maeve, there wasn't a real presence to unify the Belfast and Boston clans. He'd also worked on further connections by traveling to Moscow to find us some Russian allies as well as going back to Sicily.

After I exchanged a hug with Seamus, he pulled away to wink at me. "I've got several lasses lined up for potential marital alliances. All tried and true Belfast gals. Although if you'd prefer, there's several Sicilian gals we could work with, too."

His words had the same effect as if he punched me in the stomach or kicked me in the balls. "Surely this explosion is far more important than marrying Quinn off," Callum remarked.

I threw a grateful look his way to which he nodded. Seamus, however, was undaunted. "As precarious as everything is at the moment, it's as good a time as ever to mention it."

Thankfully, the head of the port authority strolled up then. After speaking with him, we reached out to our contacts in the police and media to ensure it was kept as quiet as possible. We alerted the Nerettis of what had gone down. Rafe said he would be down in the morning to meet with us about Mikita.

Once we'd done everything we could at the docks, we headed home. On the way, I opened up the app for Isla's security system. A quick glance showed me she'd arrived home safe and sound.

When we got home, I went upstairs and took a shower. I threw on a t-shirt and a pair of sweatpants. I didn't expect to get much sleep, but I did lie down anyway.

I woke up shortly before eight to the smell of bacon. With my stomach grumbling, I headed downstairs to see what Lorna had prepared. I found Dare already at the table with a heaping plate.

"Why weren't you at the docks last night?" I questioned.

"I was at a business dinner with members from the gaming commission."

"Until two am?"

With a wicked gleam in his eyes, he replied, "One of the commissioners invited me home for a nightcap."

"I hope you rocked her world enough to get the green light for the casino."

"Of course, I did," he replied.

I chuckled as I made my way into the kitchen to fix my plate. Callum was almost finished preparing his while Lorna was toiling over some beige concoction. "What the hell is that?"

"Oatmeal. It's the only thing poor Caterina can keep down in the mornings."

"It looks disgusting."

"It's like some of the porridges back home," Callum remarked.

"Poor thing," I muttered as I began filling my plate.

When I got back to the dining room, Seamus had appeared as well. I sat down next to him. I picked up my fork and dug in.

As a woman's scream pierced the quiet, my fork froze midway to my mouth. Callum's silverware clattered on his plate as he shot out of his chair. It tumbled over in his hot pursuit out of the dining room to check on Caterina. Dare and I hurried to follow him.

Owen appeared in the hallway. "You have to come right now. There's a girl screaming for you."

"Isla?"

He shook his head. "But she looks like her."

"Fuck. It's Brooke."

"What the hell is her sister doing here?" Dare asked.

"I have no idea."

When I opened the door, I recoiled back at the sight of Kellan standing with a wailing Henry in his arms while Brooke sobbed on her knees.

I knelt down beside her. "Brooke, what's happened?"

At the sound of my voice, Brooke jerked her head up. "Is she here?"

"No. Why?"

Her sobs came harsher. "No, oh God, no."

"Where's Isla?"

"I don't know. She didn't come home this morning, and she's not answering her phone."

Icy fear poured over me before twisting in my chest and making it difficult to breathe.

"Come on inside."

When I raised up, Henry stretched his arms out to me. "Come here, Little Man," I said, taking him. Without me asking, Kellan bent down to sweep Brooke into his arms.

Once Kellan eased her onto the couch, Brooke curled into a fetal position, her body wracked with sobs.

Nodding at her, Dare said, "I'll call Dr. Feany to bring a sedative."

"Good thinking."

As I pulled up the security feed to Isla's house, I ran my hand over Henry's back. "It's okay. It's going to be okay," I murmured for him, but at the same time, I needed it myself.

Callum and Caterina appeared in the doorway. After surveying the scene, Callum asked, "What's going on?"

"Isla's missing."

As Caterina gasped, Callum demanded, "For how long?"

"Since her shift ended." I shook my head. "Since the security feed showed someone coming in when she should have, I didn't realize anything had happened."

"It was me," Brooke croaked.

"What?"

"I was the one on the security footage." She pulled herself into a sitting position.

"What the fuck were you doing outside at three am?"

When my words and tone caused Brooke to wince and then start crying again, Caterina went over to the couch to sit beside her. Instead of waiting for her to answer, I sped up the feed. As soon as she appeared, I slowed it down.

At the sight of flame and then curling smoke, I cocked my brows at Brooke. She swiped her eyes. "I needed something to relax."

Glancing down at Henry, I said, "Isn't that bad for him?"

"I stopped breastfeeding when school started."

"What about your scholarship?"

She rolled her eyes. "They don't do random testing."

"Regardless, I think you know how Isla would feel about this."

At the mention of her sister, I expected Brooke to start crying again, but instead, rage burned in her eyes. "Fuck you, Quinn. We both know you're the reason Isla is missing."

"Excuse me?"

She jabbed a finger at me. "Whatever happened to her is because of you and your dirty business!"

"I'm going to do everything within my power to get her back."

She jerked free from Caterina and lunged off the couch. "So help me God if Isla's dead, I'll kill you." She shoved my chest. "Did you hear me? I'll kill you!"

As she broke down into sobs, I handed Henry off to Kellan. I then pulled Brooke into my arms. "I hate you. I hate you. I hate you!" she screamed, beating her fists against my chest.

When Owen took a step forward like he might take her, I growled at him. "No one touches her. Not even if she draws fucking blood. You got me?"

"Yes, sir."

After screaming her throat raw and punching and smacking me until her energy was depleted, Brooke finally collapsed in my arms. Bending down, I swept her off her feet. "I'm taking her to my room."

As Callum nodded, Caterina rose off the couch. "I'll stay with her, so you can find Isla."

"Thank you," I murmured.

Dare jerked his chin at Henry who slept in Kellan's arms. "What about him?"

"Owen, take two soldiers with you and go to Isla's house. Pack up all the baby shit you can find and get Brooke some things. Whatever else they need, we'll order in when Brooke is conscious again. They're staying here with us indefinitely."

"Yes, sir."

When Owen left, I met Callum's gaze. "I suppose you think I should've asked you first if it was okay?"

He shook his head. "I'll do whatever you ask of me to bring Isla home."

Unable to find the right words, I merely nodded. As I started up the stairs with Brooke in my arms, Seamus and Callum fell instep behind me. "It's Mikita, isn't it?" I questioned.

"I'm afraid so. He's our only true threat at the moment—the only one stupid enough to do something so brazen," Seamus replied.

After I slipped into my bedroom, I eased Brooke down on the bed. Caterina came in and went around the other side of the bed. She climbed up on the mattress to sit next to Brooke.

I motioned for the men to leave. When we got out in the hall, I asked, "But isn't kidnapping Isla an odd choice of retaliation? It goes against everything with the explosion and the shipments. Those were specifically targeted to our business. Isla has nothing to do with all of that except she's my girlfriend." When Callum and Seamus exchanged a look, I demanded, "What?"

Seamus sighed. "Do you remember the night you called me about looking into Terrance Manning's past?"

"What the fuck does he have to do with any of this?"

"I told you he had underworld connections. With the time constraints you gave me, I couldn't unearth all of his connections."

I swallowed hard. "Terrance and Mikita were in business together?"

"Aye."

"So this is personal."

"Very."

I staggered back until I banged into the wall. My mind could barely wrap around the type of torture Mikita might inflict on Isla to get back at me. My chest constricted at the thoughts of her being hurt.

Physically
Sexually
"I'll tear him apart," I growled.
Callum brought his hand to my shoulder. "We'll help you, brother."

Chapter Thirty-Three: Isla

I was having a nightmare.

One of the worst of my life.

I'd been kidnapped outside the club.

When I woke up, I felt relieved to be in my bed. Thank God, it had all been just a bad dream. I pulled myself to sit up.

The moment my eyes scanned the room, my chest constricted. I hadn't woken up from the nightmare. I was still in it.

At that moment, the door opened. I screamed at the sight of two men with rifles. "Please, don't hurt me," I begged.

When one of the men started inside, the other stopped him. "The boss said she wasn't to be touched."

The taller of the two merely smirked. "Who says he has to find out? Let me have a turn, and then you can have a go at her."

"He won't like it."

"Fuck him and fuck you."

"Yuri, you're going to get yourself killed."

The taller man named Yuri continued to advance into the room. I scrambled up the mattress until I banged against the headboard. "Please don't do this."

Yuri jerked me by the hair, causing me to scream. As he yanked my hair, he dragged me down the mattress. Then he got on top of me. "Stop! Help! No!" I screamed as I thrashed against him.

We tumbled off the bed and into the floor. His hand jerked the hem of my skirt. Suddenly, the weight lifted off of me, and Yuri flew against the wall. I buried my face in my hands as words were exchanged in Russian before a gun popped twice. I screamed and rolled into a fetal position.

A foot kicked my leg. "Look at me," a voice commanded.

After swiping my eyes, I stared up at the man standing over me. "My apologies, Ms. Vaughn."

He held his hand out to help me up. When I eyed it with disgust, he chuckled. "Not very grateful, are you?"

"You're the man who had me kidnapped."

"I am."

"Why?"

He tsked at me. "Come now, Ms. Vaughn. A woman as smart as you should already know the answer to that."

"Quinn," I whispered.

With a nod, he replied, "Your boyfriend and his family have been making things very hard for me. First, they killed Carmine Lucero which fucked my son's alliance and left him saddled with an Italian bitch for a wife. But that wasn't enough for the Kavanaughs. They, or more importantly Quinn, had to fuck with another lucrative alliance."

"But why take me?"

"Does the name Terrance Manning mean anything to you?"

A shudder ran through me. "He assaulted me at *Alainn*."

"And then Quinn killed him in retaliation."

"Yes," I whispered.

"Guess who my lucrative alliance was?"

"Terrance."

Mikita nodded. "So, you can see why I have very personal beef with Quinn." Mikita tilted his head at me. "Do you know what Bravta calls your boyfriend?" At the shake of my head, he replied, "*Odinokiy volk so shramami*. It means 'scarred lone wolf'. He hasn't had a woman to share his life with." A wicked gleam flickered in his gray eyes. "But he's not so alone anymore, is he?"

I swallowed my fear down. They were going to use me to draw Quinn out. "Are you going to hurt me?"

He ran the back of his hand over my cheek, causing me to shudder. "Not like you fear."

Turning away from me, he surmised Yuri's bleeding corpse. "In Jersey, for a long time the Irish, the Italians, and Bratva believed women shouldn't pay for the sins of the men. But then the pact was broken. A beautiful young Russian woman—a mother of two small sons—was kidnapped. Although she wasn't beaten or wounded, she was raped."

He glanced at me over his shoulder. "Repeatedly by many men."

Fear choked off my ability to speak. Instead, I could only widen my eyes in horror.

"When the dispute between her family and the Italians ended, she was sent back to her family. While there were no physical scars on her body, the emotional ones crippled her. Even though her two sons were so happy to have her back, she was merely a shell of who she was before. A month after she was returned, she jumped off the roof of the family penthouse."

My chest rose and fell. "She was your mother."

"You are very astute."

"I'm sorry. I lost my mother as well."

He cocked a brow at me. "Did she plummet fifteen stories before slamming to the ground and pulverizing into bloody soup?"

My stomach rolled at his description, and I fought not to gag. As he stared expectantly at me, I gave a slight jerk of my head. "Car accident."

"Don't try to empathize with me. We aren't the same."

"I'm sorry," I whispered.

"The reason I told you that story was to explain why I, nor any of my men, would force themselves upon you. It isn't about a weakness in me or them. It's out of respect for her memory."

Since I didn't know what else to say, I merely nodded. "But there are other forms of torture besides rape, Ms. Vaughn."

When he reached out for me, I flinched. He tsked at me. "I'm not so uncivilized that I would resort to beating you."

Although I wanted to ask what he was going to do to me, I feared his answer too much. Anxious tremors already racked my body. Nausea rolled through my stomach that I feared I would vomit at any moment.

As he paced before me, Mikita paused to eye Yuri's body again. "Did you know there are many means of torture that don't require me to lay one finger on that beautiful body of yours?"

When I didn't answer, he continued on. "In Russia, many of the prisons use psychological torture because it breaks men much quicker than physical torture."

He rubbed the stubble on his chin. "Deprivation is a big one. You can starve or dehydrate someone into submission. Or use extreme temperatures on them." He chuckled. "For someone like me who grew up in Russia, it would take a hell of a lot to freeze me into submission."

"But one of the worst is sleep deprivation." He cocked his head at me. "I bet you experienced a little of that when your beautiful sister gave birth to her baby boy."

At the mention of Brooke and Henry, bile rocketed from my

stomach, and I turned my head and retched on the floor. Mikita merely chuckled. "I see I've hit a nerve."

Before I could reach up to swipe my mouth, Mikita produced a handkerchief from his pocket. He slid the silky material across my mouth. "Right now you're experiencing a strong form of psychological torture. Threats."

Tears spilled down my cheeks. "Please don't hurt them."

Mikita returned his handkerchief to his pocket. "Do you know how much money I could get on the human trafficking market for your sister?"

Sobs tore through my chest at the thoughts of Brooke being raped and abused. "Please."

"She would make me millions."

Once again, I croaked, "Please."

He wrinkled his nose. "Of course, she's not pure, and most men don't want pussy that's been through childbirth. She'll probably get beaten a lot when buyers find that out."

Menace flashed in his eyes. "But it's not just about her, is it? There's that sweet, innocent baby boy."

A violent shudder rocketed through me. Pinching my eyes shut, I shook my head. "Enough."

"Although I don't condone kiddie fuckers in my organization, there is a lucrative market of them. Can you imagine that for your nephew? Being passed from buyer to buyer, his innocence stripped from him."

My eyes snapped open. "Shut your fucking mouth!" I screamed.

"I'm afraid that most of the babies on the market don't live very long. Someone always ends up taking things too far, and they're very fragile."

Unable to stand it any longer, I lunged out of my chair. I leapt at Mikita, punching and slapping him. Instead of deflecting me, he merely laughed. I stepped back from him, my fist clenched at my sides. "Take me instead."

Mikita eyed me curiously. When he continued staring at me, I smacked my chest. "I said take me instead."

He remained impassively staring at me. Grabbing the lapels of his suit, I shouted, "Kill *me*. Fuck *me*. Beat *me*. I don't care what you do to me. Just don't touch them."

To my utter shock, Mikita began clapping. "I'm truly in awe of how quickly you broke. Your love for your sister and nephew is truly admirable."

Unable to control my anger, I spat, "Fuck you."

Mikita chuckled. "Such fire for a little thing."

"Are you going to hurt them?"

"That depends on you, Ms. Vaughn."

"What do you want me to do?"

"I'm sure you think I kidnapped you to try to draw Quinn out to have some epic showdown. But that wasn't my intention."

When a malicious thought entered my mind, I stumbled back over to the chair and sat down. "You're going to make me kill him," I choked out.

Mikita's eyes widened. "While it's an intriguing idea and one I wish I'd thought of, that is not my intention."

A relieved breath whooshed out of me. I thanked God for small mercies that I wouldn't be expected to choose my family over Quinn.

"I don't want Quinn dead."

I furrowed my brows. "You don't?"

"No. I want him alive, so he can suffer."

Fear once again twisted in my chest. "What do you plan to do to him?"

"Actually, it's what *you're* going to do to him."

"I don't understand."

"You're going to leave him."

"What?"

Mikita grinned. "The lone wolf has a mate. To make him suffer, I need to remove the mate. I'll be honest that I did think of killing you at first. But then I realized that was too easy. While you worried I would make you physically kill Quinn, you're going to emotionally kill him."

"No, no, no," I moaned.

"Yes, Ms. Vaughn, you're going to leave him. You're going to tell him you can't be with someone who endangers the ones you love, yourself included. I don't really care what you say as long as you deliver the blow."

"Please, don't make me do this!"

"You'll do good to remember I'm sparing your life, Ms. Vaughn. If I kill you now, nothing will stop me from taking your sister and nephew."

His words had the same effect as if he was slapping me across the face. In some ways, I wished he would've just beat me. At least the pain would have an outlet then. I could bleed and break. It was now all contained in my mind.

My chest was constricted in a vise so tight I couldn't breathe. I wanted so much to weep to get rid of the agony, but I couldn't. I just jerked and shook all over. The last time I'd felt this way was when I came back into consciousness in the ER and a nurse with tears in her eyes told me my parents were dead.

I don't know how long I sat in torment, staring ahead and trembling uncontrollably. A voice broke through the torture. "Do we have a deal, Ms. Vaughn?"

"If I promise this, you won't hurt me or my family."

"You have my word."

"This will be the only revenge you seek against the Kavanaughs or Caterina's brothers?"

"I'm afraid this deal relates only to Quinn and me. Whatever retaliation they seek, I'll have to deal with." He pursed his lips. "Unless you can convince Quinn not to."

"If it means you won't hurt any of them, I will. I swear it."

"You're a remarkable woman, Ms. Vaughn. I hate that we had to meet under these circumstances."

I didn't respond. Instead I kept staring at the wall in front of me.

The next thing I knew Mikita jerked my arm. "What are you doing?" I demanded.

"Just giving you a nice sedative, so you'll sleep through the drop off."

"You're letting me go?"

"Since you're willing to cooperate, there's no need for you to stay any longer." He tilted his head at me. "Unless you would like to join me for dinner?"

I furiously shook my head back and forth. "No," I gritted out.

He smiled maniacally at me. "Pity. You'd make an intriguing mistress for me."

I bit down on my lip to keep from spitting in his face. "Just take me home, please."

At the prick on my arm, I winced. Then the world around me grew as dark as my emotions.

Chapter Thirty-Four: Quinn

In the hours after finding out about Isla's kidnapping, I spent the majority of the time pacing around our home office with my phone in my hand. Stationed at other places in the office, my brothers and Seamus did the same. We'd reached out to all of our allies for information about where Mikita could be harboring Isla. With each minute that passed with no answers, my hope began to wane.

Dr. Feeny arrived to check on Brooke. He gave her a sedative to keep her calm. Caterina remained at her side, having her meals brought to the bedroom.

When Henry woke up from his nap, he was inconsolable in Kellan's arms. Since Seamus was the only one of us who had any experience as a father, he went to fix his bottle. When I took him from Kellan, he still screamed.

When Seamus returned with the bottle, he eyed Henry with sadness. "Wains are very perceptive about traumatic events. He knows something is wrong."

"I know, Little Man. I want your auntie back, too," I said, as I rubbed wide circles on his back.

Seamus's phone rang, and he handed me the bottle before stepping out of the office to answer it. Before I could pop the bottle in Henry's waiting mouth, my phone rang.

Since Dare was closest to me and Henry had wailed with Kellan, I handed Henry off to Dare. His eyes bulged in horror. "Wait, no, I don't–"

"Just take him," I commanded.

To my utter surprise, Henry stared wide-eyed at Dare. His cries waned into snubs. Turning away from them, I answered the call. "Hey Gianni, do you have anything for me?"

At his ragged sigh, my chest clenched. "I'm sorry, Quinn. I'm doing everything I can to hack into his system, but the fucker is locked up tight."

"Thanks for trying."

"I'm not giving up. I will break this."

"I appreciate it, G."

"I'll call you back when I have something. Not if, but *when*."

"Thanks," I choked off.

When I hung up, I turned around to see Dare feeding Henry. At the way he held him like a bomb about to go off, I barked out a laugh. "He's not an incendiary device," I mused.

"Bullshit. He has the ability to explode at any moment."

But Henry seemed content with Dare just as he had been with Kellan before. I leaned down and kissed his head, my eyes closing at the intoxicatingly sweet smell of his baby shampoo.

"I never thought I'd see the day you'd love a wain who didn't belong to you," Dare mused. He shook his head. "Frankly, I'd be just as surprised to see the love in your eyes if he was yours."

"I'm not an anti-wain bastard like you are." I brushed my finger over Henry's forehead. "Besides, he does belong to me. He's part of Isla, and in turn, he's part of me."

Dare eyed me in disbelief. But then his expression softened. "You'll be a good father someday, Quinn."

"I don't know about that."

"Somehow I think you'll be even more whipped than Callum."

"Is that right?"

"Aye. The harder the person, the harder the fall."

"Then God help us all when you become a father."

"Not happening."

"As much as you fuck, the statistics are pretty high."

Dare frowned. "I use protection."

"Unless you're abstaining, it isn't 100% effective."

For the first time I could remember, fear rippled through Dare's face. He then shoved Henry at me, causing him to grunt in protest. "He's happy with you. Go sit down and burp him."

"Like I know how to fucking do that."

"Just pat his back, mate. It's not that hard."

Seamus and Callum came back into the office then. Callum had slipped out on the pretense of checking on Brooke, but I knew he really wanted to make sure Caterina was okay.

Waving his phone, Seamus said, "The security cameras at the club are fucked. They freeze in intervals that must've been when the kidnapper arrived and then when Isla's car left the parking lot."

"Fuck. It's obvious Mikita is tech savvy. Gianni isn't having any luck hacking them."

"If anybody can, it's Gianni," Seamus replied.

"Quinn."

Whirling around, my heart dropped into my chest at the sight of Shane in the doorway with an ashen expression. It was the first time he'd ever called me by my first name and not boss. Without a word, Dare and Callum came to flank my left and right side.

"What's happened?"

"Isla was just found at the back of *Alainn*–"

"Is she dead?" I demanded.

"She's alive."

My knees gave out, and I sank to the floor. I sucked in a ragged breath as I processed that Isla was found. "Was she harmed?"

"Mikey and Niall are enroute to Mass General with her."

"Was she harmed?" I repeated.

Shane rubbed the back of his neck. "They said there was no apparent physical wounds. As for anything–" his voice choked off.

I winced at the thought of the sexual assault she might've faced. "They won't be able to tell until she's examined at the hospital," I murmured.

He nodded. "I don't know if it will make you feel any better, but they said she still wore the dress she had on when she disappeared. It wasn't torn or anything like that."

It did little to dispel my fears.

"Get me to the hospital."

"Yes, sir," he replied.

Without another word to the others, I barrelled out of the office and broke into a jog down the hallway. I beat Shane out to the garage, but he hustled to hop into the driver's seat. He cranked up and threw the SUV into reverse.

We careened out of the driveway and started tearing down Beacon Street. Even though I knew Isla was alive and back with us, the fear constricting my lungs hadn't waned. Horrible scenarios filled my mind of what they had done to her.

I don't know how Shane managed to get us through traffic so quickly. I was going to owe him a raise for his quick thinking and maneuvering. He wheeled us up to the entrance of the ER.

Before the SUV had come to a stop, I opened the door and flung myself out. I sprinted through the mechanical doors and up to the front desk. The nurse behind it shrank down in her chair at the sight of me. "Can I help you?" she squeaked.

"I want to know what room Isla Vaughn is in. She was just brought in."

Her trembling fingers flew across the keyboard. "She's in room 3."

"Thank you."

I knew she should've asked me if we were related or asked to see my ID. But instead, she buzzed open the door for me. While I appreciated it at this moment, I sure as hell wouldn't under any other circumstances. No one should have such easy access to Isla.

Mikey and Niall stood on either side of Isla's room. When I stormed up to them, they held up their hands. "We wouldn't have left her, but they insisted we did to complete the physical exam."

Although I didn't like it, I nodded. "Is she talking?"

"She's awake. A little woozy because they gave her something."

"Has she been asking for me? Did you tell her I was on the way?"

Mikey and Niall exchanged a look. "No, sir. But she's really not been talking," Mikey replied.

I started up pacing again. My phone buzzed alerting me that my brothers and Seamus were in the waiting room, and Owen stayed at the house with Brooke and Caterina. It seemed like an eternity passed before a nurse and doctor emerged from the room.

At the sight of me, recognition flooded the doctor's face. His ID read Dr. Jason McElroy. "You're Mr. Kavanaugh?"

"Aye, I am."

"Although you aren't Ms. Vaughn's next of kin, I find it would be in my best interest to inform you of her condition."

"That would be correct," I replied menacingly.

"I'm happy to tell you there was no physical trauma to Ms. Vaughn's body."

"What about..." I couldn't bring myself to say the words.

He shook his head. "While she insisted she wasn't assaulted, I did do a brief examination, and there was no vaginal trauma."

A relieved breath whooshed from me. "Thank God."

Dr. McElroy's expression grew grave. "While there is no physical trauma, the level of emotional trauma that Ms. Vaughn has experienced is very serious. She has all the indications of being in shock."

"I can assure you she will receive the best psychological care."

"Good. She's going to need it."

My heart ached at the thought of Isla in pain. "Can I see her?"

"Yes. But I would ask that you limit your visit to only yourself. She's been through a harrowing experience."

In a hushed voice, I asked, "She told you about the abduction."

"She did. Knowing her involvement with you and your family, I'm sure it would be futile to file a police report."

"It would. You can rest assured I will handle it."

Dr McElroy nodded. "I'm glad to hear it."

He started to walk away, but I stopped him. "For your care of Isla and your discretion, I am in your debt. I will not forget you should you need me someday."

His dark eyes widened. "Thank you," he mumbled before he hurried away.

Although I wanted to burst into Isla's room and drag her into my arms, I carefully eased the door open. When I stepped inside, Isla was staring ahead.

"Little Dove?" I questioned.

Her attention snapped to me. While I expected tears or even anger, I wasn't prepared for the emotionless way she regarded me. Slowly, I made my way to her side. I knelt down beside the bed. "I'm so very, very sorry."

"He didn't rape me if that's what you're worried about."

"I know. The doctor told me."

"He didn't even threaten to rape me."

"He didn't?"

She shook her head. "He killed one of the men who tried to."

A low growl came from within me at the thought of any man attempting that. "I never imagined Mikita had a heart."

"His mother committed suicide after she was gang raped during an abduction."

Jaysus. I knew Mikita's father had been a widower, but I'd always heard he'd lost his wife to illness, which it was in a way.

My eyes shuttered in pain. "I would give anything in the world if I could turn back the clock twenty-four hours. I would never let you out of my sight."

"I know you think you can always protect me, Quinn, but it's very evident that you can't."

"That's not true."

She shook her head. "Deep down, you know it is. Your enemies will always find a chink in your armour, and I'll be the one to pay for it. But I can't let it happen again."

An icy fear prickled its way up my spine. "What are you saying?"

"I can't see you anymore."

"No, Isla. Please don't say that."

"I'm sorry, but it's how I feel. It's been made very evident how unsafe your world is for me."

"Don't do this," I pleaded.

Tears shimmered in her eyes. "You know I have no choice."

"Yes, you do. You can fucking choose to stay with me and us make a life together." A shaky smile formed on my lips. "You can be a mad scientist just like you planned. We'll get a house of our own, or I'll get one big enough for Brooke and Henry. It's whatever you want." I squeezed her hand. "Just please don't leave me."

A sob tore through her chest. When I reached to take her into my arms, she smacked me away. "No, no, no!"

"Isla–"

"You—your life, your world—broke me. I've got nothing left." She swiped her eyes with her sleeve.

"I'll take whatever you can give me. I'll work night and day to earn your trust back. I'll move mountains to ensure you feel safe and protected."

"What little I have isn't for you. Brooke and Henry are my world. They rely on me—"

"They can rely on me just as you can. They're at my house right now being watched over by Owen."

"Why isn't Brooke here with you?"

I sucked in a ragged breath. "She wasn't in any shape to come."

"What do you mean?"

"She was so upset she had to be sedated."

A rueful smile curved on her lips. "And this is what comes when we rely on you."

"Isla, I'm sorry. Caterina hasn't left her side. I promise she's in good hands."

"My sister was hurt because of me. But what happens when Brooke and Henry become pawns in your world because of me? Brooke could be trafficked to the highest bidder by your enemies, or Henry's decapitated head could be sent to our house in a box over something as trivial as a territory dispute." Her head shook violently back and forth. "As much as you profess you can protect us, you can't."

Agony spread through my chest. As much as I wanted to argue with her, I knew it was pointless because she was right. I couldn't protect her. Regardless of how hard I tried, there would always be the potential she could be hurt or Brooke or Henry.

"Please, don't do this. Don't leave me."

"If I stay with you, I could die. Even worse than that, my child could be tortured and killed all because of who their father is."

"I know I can't promise you nothing will happen, but I love you, and I can't bear the thought of living without you. You're my soulmate, Isla."

"Stop it. Just get out! Get out! Get out!" she screamed. Her body then collapsed into sobs.

A nurse came running into the room. She gave me a disapproving look. "I think it's best that you leave."

I didn't argue with her. When I turned to go, I realized my feet wouldn't move. It was like my body was so drawn to Isla it couldn't bring itself to abandon her.

Like a zombie, I ambled through the mechanized doors back into the ER's waiting room. Callum appeared before me, his expression ashen. "How is she?"

"Emotionally shattered."

His eyes closed in pain. "Fuck, Quinn. I'm so sorry." His hand squeezed my shoulder. "Whatever she needs, I'll take care of it. You just take care of her."

I slid my hand over my face. "She doesn't want me."

"What?"

"She threw me out of her room."

Callum's eyes bulged, but then he shook his head. "She doesn't mean it."

"I'm pretty sure she does."

"Quinn, she's been through hell. She needs time to recover."

"She doesn't want me because of the danger I pose to her family." I exhaled raggedly. "So, she told me to leave."

"Jaysus," Callum muttered.

I stared down at the tiled floor. Although I couldn't believe I was going to say it, the words flowed easily off my tongue. "I'm out."

"What?"

I jerked my head up to glare at him. "You're not fucking deaf—you heard me."

"Maybe I needed you to repeat it."

"I said I'm out."

As the color drained from his face, Callum held up a finger. "Not fucking here." Turning around, he jerked his head at Dare, Kellan, and Seamus. Without a word, they rose out of their chairs to join him in the hallway. "Chapel," Callum said.

They fell into step behind us as we made our way down the hall. After an elevator trip two floors up, we passed the ICU cubicles to a small room. We'd spent a ridiculous amount of time there after Caterina's attack. Now we reconvened there after yet another woman had suffered on our watch.

After holding open the door to the interfaith chapel, Callum ushered us inside. Only one man sat on one of the benches. At the sight of us, he quickly got up and left.

Once we were alone, Callum locked the door. When he turned back to me, he said, "Tell them what you said to me in the hallway."

I stared into their expectant faces. "I'm done."

Dare's eyes popped wide. "You want out?"

"It's not about fucking wanting it. I'm out.

"But you can't do that," Seamus countered.

"I don't care about the fucking oath. I'm *done*."

Seamus shook his head. "This is your birthright and your family."

"What more can this fucking family take from me?"

"Quinn—"

I threw my hands up in desperation. "I've given my blood. I've been disfigured. Now it's taking the only woman I've ever truly loved." I shook my head. "I'm fucking done."

"You're in pain. You're not thinking clearly," Callum argued.

"There's nothing left for me. Without Isla, there's nothing for me in our world or in this fucking miserable life."

Seamus stepped up to place his hands on my cheeks. "Oh son, I know just how you feel. After Rian and then Elena, I didn't want to live."

"Why didn't you just check out?"

"I came close once or twice. But then something always stopped me. Some tiny flicker within me that grew as time went on. Most days, it's a muted flame, but it's still hope. There's hope for me, and there's hope for you. You've endured so much physically and emotionally that I understand why you feel as you do." He shook his head. "You have to keep fighting, Quinn."

"I don't know if I want to."

Kellan cleared his throat. "I felt like you did for a long time after

Maeve's rape. I didn't want to be part of such a world that bred men like our father. I feared I would somehow give over to the dark side."

He swallowed hard. "Even though I didn't talk about it with you guys then, you got me through–even though you didn't know it." He placed a hand on my shoulder. "We'll get you through this, Quinn. Just don't fucking give up on us or yourself."

Although I wanted to turn and flee, Isla had brought me too far to do that. Instead, I didn't shy away from letting my brothers see my tears. "I feel like I'm on fire again, but there's nothing that will ever douse these flames."

"We'll figure it out. We'll find a way," Callum said.

Dare nodded. "We'll see you through."

I wanted to feed off their strength. I wanted to believe with that tiny flicker that Seamus spoke of. But it all seemed too desperate.

"Come on. Let's get you home. You need to shower and sleep," Seamus said.

"So it can all look better in the morning?" I bit out.

Seamus shook his head. "No, that's utter bullshit. You're still going to feel like hell, but you will be a little better physically."

At the thought of going home and seeing Brooke and Henry, I shuttered my eyes in pain. "I can't go home."

"You need to be with the people who love you," Seamus protested.

"I can't see Brooke and Henry."

"Then you can get a hotel room."

I opened my eyes to take in the concerned faces of my brothers and Seamus. "As much as I appreciate what you're offering, I need to get out of the city to process all this shit." I exhaled a ragged sigh. "I need to go home."

Callum's brows shot wide. "You want to go to Belfast? But you haven't–"

"Been there since the accident. I'm aware of that."

Seamus frowned. "I don't think that's a good idea."

"If I promise to see a shrink while I'm there will it make you feel better?"

"Slightly."

"Then come with me and babysit," I suggested.

"I just got back," he protested.

"So let me go alone in peace."

"Are you sure? I really don't mind going."

"You know I'd rather be by myself."

"If you're sure."

"I am."

Callum eyed me warily. "What about your things? Should I call Lorna and have her pack your bag?"

With a shake of my head, I replied, "I'll buy new shit when I get there."

"You're determined to do this," Callum remarked.

"Aye. I am."

"I guess there's no point arguing then."

I smiled. "We both know we're too stubborn to change."

"So you're off to the airport?"

"Yes, I'll get them to gas up the jet."

Callum nodded. "I'll call one of the soldiers to bring your passport to you."

"I appreciate it." When I started to open the chapel door, Dare stopped me.

"Don't you hink you should stay and fight for her?"

Surprise filled me that the words had come out of my womanizing brother. "As much as I want to, I know when I'm licked."

"But she could change her mind. She's been through such a horrible ordeal. I mean, look at Caterina. After we kidnapped her, I never imagined she could fall in love with Callum, but she did," Dare protested.

"Caterina came from our world. She grew up with the dangers. Isla can't resign herself to what could happen to her and to her family. I have to respect her feelings. And I can't change the world I come from. Even when I wanted to leave, I knew I could never escape the danger."

Dare's forlorn expression truly touched me. "We'll make sure to keep someone on the house while you're gone. We'll protect her just as you would have."

"Thank you, brother," I choked out.

After hugging each of my brothers and Seamus, I then started out of the door. They fell in step behind me, a silent brotherhood united not just by our blood but by the oath we'd taken.

An oath that I would continue to uphold despite the agony it caused.

Chapter Thirty-Five: Isla

One Month Later

As I stared up at the sign for Club Marquis, I swallowed down the bile rising in my throat. If *Alainn* had been a Five Star club, this one would have hit somewhere between three and a half stars. It was certainly a last resort.

It had been a hellish month. What energy I had, I'd thrown into my studies. As for my job, I'd never gone back to *Alainn* after the night I was kidnapped. Caterina had been kind to bring me my things. It had been agony seeing her. She promised to stay in touch as a friend, but I knew I couldn't and not just because of the pain her presence caused.

I knew Mikita wouldn't take kindly to us remaining friends. I remained in a state of paranoia that he had the house and my phone bugged. Probably even my car. If I made one misstep, I imagined he would swoop in to retaliate against me.

With the money I'd stashed away dwindling, I'd spent the day driving around to clubs looking for a job. None of them moved me past filling out an application. It was like the universe was trying to tell me to get the hell away from stripping, but my stubborn self wasn't taking the message.

"You've got to be joking," Brooke sniped from the passenger seat.

"I wish I was."

She shook her head vehemently back and forth. "You're not dancing in this dump, Isla."

"Trust me. I don't want to."

"Then don't. Let's get the hell out of here, and you can use my inheritance."

"No," I gritted out.

"Would you stop being so damn stubborn? I told you you could pay me back. Hell, if you're going to be such a stupid Girl Scout about it, you can sell me your half of the house. I sure as hell don't want you to do that, but if it would mean getting it through your thick skull you don't have to strip, then I would do it."

I reached over to squeeze her hand. "I'll think about it, okay?"

"So we can get the hell out of here?"

"I need to see this through, Brooke."

She snatched her hand from mine. "Unfuckingbelievable."

"On that note, I'll be right back."

Turning her head from me, Brooke stared out the window. With a resigned sigh, I grabbed my purse and hopped out of the SUV. Deep down, I knew I should take her up on her offer. But I felt like I had to exhaust all options before I did that. Even if it meant dancing in a skeezy club.

When I entered the door, it was a lot smokier and darker than

Alainn. Peering through the haze, I searched for someone in charge. A hulking bouncer approached me. "Can I help you?"

"Yes, I was wanting to inquire about a position."

"Follow me."

"Um, okay, thanks."

As I fell in step behind him, I tried keeping my eyes down. I figured it was better to see less of what was in store for me. Yes, I was that deluded about my current situation.

When we got to a door labeled "Employees Only", the bouncer rapped his knuckles against the wood. "Yeah?" came a voice within.

"Got a girl for you."

"Bring her in."

After the bouncer opened the door, my feet seemed rooted to the spot. For the life of me I couldn't seem to make my feet get with the program. Finally, I pitched forward and walked through the doorway.

The stereotypical sleazy looking strip club owner sat behind an enormous black desk. If he'd only been puffing on a cigar, I would've felt like I'd stumbled into a bad Lifetime movie. "So you're interested in a position here?"

"Yes, sir," I reluctantly replied.

"Waitress or dancer."

"Either. Although I have more experience with dancing."

His gaze trailed down my body. "I'd say you're exactly what we're looking for."

Although his leer made my skin crawl, I forced a smile to my face. "Great. When could I audition?"

"First, I need you to fill out our application." He swiveled in his chair to grab a stapled packet. Motioning to the seat in front of his desk, he said, "Sit down."

Reluctantly, I eased down in the uncomfortable chair. He then handed me the packet and a pen.

"While you're filling out most of the info, can I get your name and social security number to start the background check?"

"Sure. It's Isla Vaugh, and my social is–"

He held up a hand to me. "I'm sorry. Did you say Isla Vaughn?"

"Yes. Why?"

His over-tanned face paled. "I'm sorry, but I can't have you working in my club."

"I don't understand."

"I'm going to have to ask you to leave."

"You're joking."

"I'm very serious."

"Just because of my name?" I sputtered incredulously.

He glanced left and right before leaning forward in his chair. "Don't act like you don't know."

"I can assure you that I'm not acting. I'm completely clueless as to why you're advertising for dancers, yet won't audition me."

He studied me curiously for a moment. "You really don't know, do you?" When I shook my head, he exhaled noisily. "Look, I don't know what you did to piss off Quinn Kavanaugh, but whatever it was, he's not taking it lightly."

At the sound of Quinn's name, a shudder ran through me. "What does this have to do with him?"

"That's between the two of you. All I know is I received a hand delivered note telling me under no certain circumstances was I to hire a dancer named Isla Vaughn."

I gasped. "Seriously?"

He nodded. "I would imagine that if I got a letter, your name is shit in all the clubs all over the city."

That's when it hit me. All the time I'd spent beating the pavement today and being turned down wasn't about my looks or my dancing ability. It was all because of Quinn and the power he held.

Unable to speak, I merely nodded. Then I whirled around and sprinted out of the office. I didn't stop running until I got to the car. After I tried opening the door, I had to wait for Brooke to unlock it. She'd gotten in the driver's seat while I was gone.

At the sight of me, her eyes popped wide. "Isla, what happened?"

It took a few moments for me to catch my breath. As I paced around the open door, my mind whirled with out of control thoughts. When I could finally breathe again, I shook my head. "I never would've believed Quinn would sink so low as to sabotage me having a job." At Brooke's confused look, I said, "He sent a note to all the club owners threatening them if they hired me."

She gasped. "You're joking."

"No. The owner of this club just admitted it to me."

"So that's why you couldn't get an audition anywhere?"

"Exactly."

Brooke let out a low whistle. "That's harsh."

"I know."

"I guess that answers how he's dealing with the break up."

In a way, I couldn't blame him for lashing out. I'd broken his heart. If the tables were turned and I had the chance, I would've probably done the same. With a sigh, I jerked my hands through my hair, wrapping it into a messy bun.

"You're ruining your hair!"

"Thanks to Quinn there's no need for it to look good for any more auditions since I won't be getting a job."

"Home or the liquor store?" Brooke suggested.

"Liquor store," I grumbled.

"Good choice. I'll drive us home in case you want to get a head start."

I snorted. "With my luck, we'd get pulled over by the police, and I'd have another mark against me."

As we pulled out of the club parking lot, my phone rang. When I grabbed it out of my purse, our local bank's name flashed on the screen. "Jesus, could this day get any worse," I grumbled.

"Don't tell me it's Quinn?"

"No, the bank." I swiped to answer it. "Hello?"

"Yes, may I speak to Isla Vaughn?"

"This is her."

"Hello, Ms. Vaughn, I was calling on behalf of Regions. We had flagged your account for some suspicious activity."

Great. What little money I had someone must've tried to steal. "Has there been fraudulent charges?"

"No. It's more about a pending wire payment."

I furrowed my brows. "I don't know anything about any payments."

"Normally, we don't alert customers about funds being deposited into their account, but because of the size of this deposit, we just wanted to confirm everything was normal."

"I'm sorry. Are you trying to say someone is depositing a large amount of money into my checking account?"

"That's correct?"

"How much?"

"A million dollars."

At my wheeze, Brooke jerked her eyes off the road. "What's wrong?"

Unable to speak, I just clutched the phone to my ear. "Someone has deposited a million dollars into my account," I choked out.

Now it was Brooke's turn to shriek. "Holy fucking shit!"

Turning my attention back to the call, I asked, "What is the name or the business associated with the transfer?"

"It's sort of an odd name. Let me look at it again." I heard the click clack of a keyboard in the background. "Cliodna Enterprises."

My heart did a dizzying flip-flop at the name Cliodna. It was from Quinn.

I cleared my throat. "Yes, I know that business. It belongs to my ex."

"So you were expecting this payment?"

How in my right mind could I be expecting a million dollars? I hadn't expected any money from him, least of all that much. I'd never wanted any of his money–only him.

"Yes, well, I mean, I knew a deposit was coming. Just not that much."

"Oh, good. Have a nice day then."

"You, too." I ended the call and turned to Brooke.

She stared wide-eyed at me. "Quinn sent you a *million* dollars?"

"Yes."

"Holy shit!"

"My sentiments exactly."

"So much for him being an asshole," she mused.

"Just because he sent me a lot of money doesn't take away from what he did about my job." At Brooke's gasp, I questioned, "What?"

"He wasn't being an asshole with the job thing."

"Excuse me?" I demanded.

"Don't you get it? He didn't want you to risk getting hurt again. That's why he sent the letters for no one to hire you."

"But he knew I'd still need the money," I murmured.

"Exactly. So he made sure you would be taken care of without having to take your clothes off."

My heart clenched in my chest. At that moment, I wished his motives had been vindictive to me. I couldn't take the thoughts of him still looking out for me. But there was also the matter of the money. How could he honestly think I would accept a million dollars? "Why does he have to be so damn infuriating?"

"I don't see a problem with this situation at all."

Turning to her, I asked, "How can I accept it?"

"How can you not?" Brooke countered back.

With a groan, I placed my head in my hands. "I'd be morally and ethically bankrupt if I did."

"Says the chick who just tried to be a stripper. *Again.*"

I jerked my head up to stare incredulous at Brooke. "Now is not a time for jokes."

She grinned. "If there was ever a time for jokes, it's now."

"Come on now. This is serious."

"Only because your stubborn ass is making it."

"You know how I felt when he was going to pay me for not doing lap dances. This is the same thing."

"It is not." When I opened my mouth to protest, Brooke squeezed my hand. "Because of Quinn, you were kidnapped and emotionally abused. Consider it like severance pay or parting gift."

"He doesn't owe me money for my kidnapping."

"He will for your future therapy bills."

At that moment, all the stress of keeping Mikita's secret finally snapped within me. I knew I had to tell someone, or it was going to drive me crazy. "Pull over!" I demanded.

"Excuse me?"

My frantic glance took in the businesses around us. "I want Taco Bell."

"Ew, seriously?"

"Yes. Pull over. *Now!*"

After flicking a quick look in the rearview mirror, Brooke then whipped the car across the lane and careened into the parking lot of Taco Bell. Once the car came to a stop, I reached over to Brooke and grabbed her phone. After I tossed it in the backseat, I put my finger over my lips.

"Isla, what are you—"

I shook my head wildly back and forth. Finally, Brooke nodded her head. Then I jerked my thumb for us to get out of the car. I left my phone as well.

Brooke willingly followed me. I pulled her inside the building and over to a secluded booth. There was no way in hell Mikita could've possibly bugged a random Taco Bell.

She grabbed my hands in hers. "Isla, you're scaring me. What's going on? Are our phones and the car bugged or something?"

"I don't know."

"Does this have something to do with the money Quinn sent?"

"No. It's nothing like that."

"Then tell me what the fuck is going on!"

"You can't breathe a word of what I'm about to tell you."

"I promise."

"I didn't leave Quinn because I wanted to."

She frowned. "What do you mean?"

"It was Mikita's plan. He wanted to punish Quinn, and he felt making me leave Quinn would hurt him worse than killing me."

"Jesus," Brooke muttered.

"I know."

"But why didn't you just lie to him and tell him you'd break up."

"Because he threatened that he would retaliate against you and Henry."

Brooke gasped in horror. "He did?"

"Yes. It was his form of fucked up psychological torture."

"How did he threaten me?"

Bile rose in my throat as Mikita's twisted threat flashed before my eyes. "It's not important."

"Obviously it is if it made you leave the man you love."

Pinching my eyes shut, I shook my head. "Don't ask me to tell you. I won't do it." A sob tore from my throat. "I *can't* do it."

"Jesus, Isla," Brooke murmured before she drew me into her arms. "You're always doing too much to protect me. You should've told me this from the start."

"I was too afraid." I swiped my eyes. "I'm *still* afraid, but I knew if I didn't tell you, it was going to mentally break me."

She shook her head. "You can't let him get away with ruining your life, Isla."

"But there is some truth to the lies I've told about leaving Quinn. As much as he tries, he cannot guarantee my safety and in turn, yours and Henry's. How can I possibly live a life where I'm in constant fear of being kidnapped or having you or Henry kidnapped?"

"You know how I've always felt about Quinn's world."

"I do."

"But what kind of life will you be living if you deny yourself the man you love?"

"A safe one."

Brooke shook her head. "A life lived in fear isn't a life worth living—"

"Exactly. I couldn't spend all my time in fear."

"But you are now, and you don't have Quinn."

I opened my mouth to argue with Brooke but then shut it. She was right. I was constantly looking over my shoulder for Mikita. I would be living in fear of him until he died or I died.

At the same time, I was doing it all alone, and I was miserable.

Brooke grabbed my hands in hers. "You don't have to do this, Isla. We can go to Quinn and tell him the truth. They can take out this bastard Mikita. You can have the happiness you deserve."

I wanted to believe it was that simple. That I could just run back into Quinn's waiting arms without any repercussions. Or that it would be easy to take out a Bratva mastermind. Men would die in the conflict. Quinn could die. Or Kellan. Caterina could lose Callum before her daughter was born.

In the end, I just shook my head. "I can't think about it right now."

"Always so fucking stubborn."

I gave her a sad smile. "That I am."

"Come on. I think we both could use a drink."

"Liquour store?"

She shook her head. "Let's use my fake ID and go out."

Although it was the worst idea possible, I nodded. "Let's go."

Chapter Thirty-Six: Isla

For the fifth night in a row, I couldn't sleep. Although I was exhausted, I tossed and turned, tangling myself in the sheets. Finally, I huffed in frustration and conceded I wasn't going to fall asleep anytime soon. Since there was no point in staying in bed, I got up.

After peeking in on Henry, who thankfully was sleeping like an angel, I headed downstairs. Normally, I would've taken something, but since I was babysitting Henry, I couldn't be completely knocked out. I'd pressured Brooke to go out with friends because I was tired of hearing her yell at me to get out of the house. If she was gone, I could wallow in peace.

I headed downstairs to the kitchen. After I prepared the cliched warm milk and downed half a glass, I then curled up on the couch. With the *The Golden Girls* for background noise, I snuggled into a blanket.

I was floating in that area between wakefulness and sleep when I heard a noise. Straining my ears, I held my breath. I'd forgotten to bring the baby monitor with me, and I hoped it wasn't Henry waking up early.

When I didn't hear it again, I started slipping back asleep. But then a bang came from the kitchen, and I bolted upright on the couch.

With my heart beating like a brass band in my chest, I peered around the room dimly lit by the television.

"Fuck," a man's voice whispered.

My hand flew to my mouth. Oh God, there was a man in the house. Fear momentarily choked off my breathing, and I shuddered. Was it one of Mikita's men who'd come back to settle the score despite the fact Quinn and I were no longer together?

I was too far away from the security panel to set off the silent alarm. Instead, I would have to rely on myself. Inching up the couch, I leaned over the arm to open the end table drawer. After grabbing my gun, I eased off the safety.

Slowly, I pulled myself to my feet. I tiptoed across the rug, hoping and praying for the floorboards not to creak out a tune. I continued my snail's pace down to the kitchen.

Peeking around the corner, I bit down on my lip to keep my shriek from echoing through the kitchen. Not only was there a man in my kitchen, but he was *naked*. His bare ass glowed in the moonlight as he was bent over inside the fridge.

With the revelation, I realized I could mark Bratva off the list of suspects. If they'd come to kill or kidnap me, I doubted they would've stopped to get undressed and have a snack.

Great. Some tweaker had broken into my house and was now raiding my fridge. Once again, I couldn't help feeling like Quinn had failed me since the security system hadn't stopped him. It was me and only me left to handle it.

"Put your hands on your head and slowly turn around!" I growled in my best badass voice.

The man froze. "I'm happy to turn around, but I think it's in both of our best interests if my hands keep me covered."

Disbelief ricocheted through me as I recognized the voice. "Kellan?" I shrieked.

"Yeah, it's me."

I jerked the gun down to my side. "What the hell are you doing in my kitchen naked?"

Slowly, he turned around, his hands cupping his crotch. From the way he barely covered himself, I could see being well endowed ran in the Kavanaugh family.

With a sheepish grin, he replied, "Uh, I was looking for something to drink."

With shock still radiating through me, I repeated, "Why are you *naked* in my kitchen?"

Even in the dim light, I could see his crimson colored cheeks. "Well, you see, I, uh–"

Immediately I feared Kellan had experienced some psychotic break. What else could explain why he was naked in my kitchen and rifling through my fridge? I desperately needed my phone from the living room, so I could call 911. While I didn't think he would ever hurt me, it was clear he'd completely lost his mind.

At a noise behind me, I whirled around. To my utter horror, Brooke appeared in the doorway with wild bed hair and outfitted in only a man's white dress shirt with the buttons haphazardly done. In her hands, she held a towel.

When the realization hit me of what had transpired, my hand flew to my mouth. "Oh my God."

Kellan momentarily held up a hand before realizing his junk wasn't adequately covered. "Isla, it's not what you think."

"What else could it possibly be?" I screeched.

"Shh, you'll wake up Henry," Brooke admonished.

"Oh, *now*, you're thinking of Henry? Not when you just fucked some random guy in our house."

Brooke snorted as she bypassed me to stand beside Kellan. She handed him the towel, which he quickly draped around his waist. Smiling up at him, Brooke argued, "Kellan isn't a random guy. He's practically family."

Feeling lightheaded, I leaned back against the table. "I can't believe this." Shaking my head at Kellan, I said, "After everything we went through, you repay me by taking advantage of my sister?"

"I swear, I didn't!" Kellan protested.

With a roll of her eyes, Brooke replied, "As much time as you spent with him, can you honestly stand there and believe he would do that?"

Although I hated to admit it, Brooke was right. After what had transpired with Maeve, Kellan would never take advantage of a woman.

I turned my wrath from Kellan back to Brooke. "With what I told you today, how could you involve yourself with him? What if it brought you know who back around?"

Kellan glanced between the two of us. "Who are you guys talking about?"

"No one," Brooke and I echoed at the same time.

Brooke held her hands up. "I get what you're saying. At the same time, I didn't know anything about that when I first started talking to Kellan."

"You still brought a Kavanaugh into our house after everything I sacrificed to keep you and Henry safe!"

Giving me a knowing look, Brooke countered, "I'm sorry. I truly didn't think it was an issue considering the deal was about Quinn. Nothing was mentioned about any other Kavanaugh, right?"

As much as I hated to admit it, she was right. Mikita wanted his revenge on Quinn specifically, and he hadn't mentioned any of the other Kavanaugh's. I sighed. "Fine. Forgetting everything else, help me understand the two of you sleeping together."

With a hesitant smile, Kellan turned to stare at Brooke. "Your kind, beautiful sister helped me overcome my...problem."

My anger momentarily faded. "That's what this was about?"

He bobbed his head. "During your abduction, we were thrown together. I found I could talk to her as easily as I could to you. After telling her about how I'd been talking to you about my problem, she wanted to help me. Physically. And she did." He once again smiled at Brooke. "I can never thank you enough."

She grinned at him. "I'm the one who should be thanking you. I mean, you're amazing. Like a complete and total sex god."

"Brooke!" I admonished.

At the same time Kellan's cheeks reddened, a cocky little smirk curved on his lips. "Thank you. If I'm a god, then you're a goddess."

"Enough!" I blared. Turning to Brooke, I asked, "Was this just about you scratching a postpartum itch?"

"In a way. I mean, I kinda lost myself in the last six months being Henry's mom. I just wanted to be young and carefree for a minute. With Kellan, I knew I would be safe."

My heart softened. Sometimes I forgot how much adulthood had been thrown at her at such a young age. "I get it." At her look of surprise, I added, "I can get it, but that doesn't mean I like it."

She laughed. "There was also a part of me that was kinda obsessed with my post-Henry body, and I wanted to make sure everything worked like it once had before I got into a relationship down the road."

Although I shouldn't have, I couldn't help asking, "And I assume everything is fine?"

She shot a coy grin at Kellan. "I think even better than before."

While he ducked his head, I rolled my eyes. "I'm glad to hear that. So, what now? Are the two of you dating?"

"No," Kellan and Brooke said in unison.

I swept my hands to my hips. "Why not?"

"Because it's not like that between us," Brooke argued as Kellan nodded.

"Then you're like friends with benefits or something?"

While Brooke shrugged, a sheepish look came over Kellan's face. "Actually, now that my problem is gone, I was thinking about seeing if Mabry was still interested."

To my utter shock, Brooke nodded enthusiastically. "Oh my God! Yes, you have to talk to her."

I glanced between the two of them. "You know about Mabry?" I asked Brooke.

She rolled her eyes. "Seriously, Isla, we told you we were friends, and don't friends talk about everything?"

"I suppose so."

"Well, I know. I think Kellan knows as much about our parents and Henry's dad as you do."

At the mention of Henry, a thought popped in my head. "Please tell me the two of you were safe."

"Double safe with my IUD and condoms."

"Uh, good. I'm glad to hear it."

Kellan smiled at Brooke. "As amazing as Henry is, I wouldn't ever put Brooke in a situation where she has to be a single mom again."

I wanted to argue that nothing was one hundred percent effective except abstinence, but I decided to let them continue in their happy little fantasy world. The same world I'd once traipsed blindly around in with Quinn.

At the thought of my former happiness I'd experienced with him, my chest constricted. It pulled even tighter when Kellan took Brooke's hand in his. "We better get back to sleep, or we won't have the energy to take Henry to the zoo tomorrow."

"Oh, you're going together?" I asked.

Brooke nodded. "I think Henry's old enough now to really enjoy it."

"He is." After we stood there for a moment, I said, "Right, well, I better get back to bed myself. Now that I know you can get Henry if he wakes, I think I'll take a sleeping pill. I haven't been sleeping well lately."

Kellan's brows furrowed. "Isla—"

I waved my hand dismissively. "But that's nothing you need to concern yourself with. You just need to be young and carefree and..." I swallowed hard. "Happy."

Even though I felt the heat of Kellan and Brooke's gazes, I refused to look at them. "Well, anyway, I'm really happy for the both of you." Before I could choke down the sob, it erupted from my lips. The next thing I knew I was sinking to my knees on the hardwood floor as my chest shuddered in harsh sobs.

Both Kellan and Brooke rushed to my side. "Oh Isla, I'm so sorry," Brooke murmured as she wrapped her arms around me.

I tried to push her away. "Just leave me. I don't want to bring you down."

"You could never do that, silly."

My cries must've subconsciously woken Henry because his wails could be heard above me. Brooke pulled away from me to rise to her feet. "I'll go get him."

Kellan shook his head. "Let me, and you can stay with Isla."

"No, no. It's fine. He's not used to a male voice in the middle of the night."

After Brooke rushed out of the kitchen and started pounding up the stairs, I gave Kellan a sad smile. "I'm sorry," I said.

Kellan's hand came to cup my cheek. "Don't apologize, especially to me. You've seen me at my worst. Let me be here for you."

Although I knew I shouldn't, there was one question I had to ask. "How is he?" I whispered.

"Not good."

With a mirthless laugh, I replied, "I know the feeling."

"He left for Belfast two weeks ago."

My mouth dropped open in surprise. "Did he have business to attend to there?"

Kellan shook his head. "He said he couldn't bear to be in the city anymore."

"I know the feeling," I murmured.

"He loves you," Kellan said earnestly.

"And I love him."

"He loves you so much he wants out of the life."

I gasped. "But he can't leave you guys."

"No. He can't. Once you take the oath, you only leave in a box."

My heartbeat accelerated at his words. "He won't do *that*, will he?" I couldn't bear the thought of Quinn leaving the life and forcing Callum's hand. Or worse for him to do something reckless to have someone else take his life.

With a shake of his head, Kellan replied, "Quinn isn't a quitter. Regardless of the hell he's been through and currently finds himself."

Tears pooled in my eyes at the thought that I was the cause of so much of his pain. At the same time, rage filled me that Mikita was forcing me to hurt Quinn. His revenge was affecting my life as well as Quinn's.

I thought about my conversation with Brooke earlier. Was it possible to find a way out of this mess and still keep everyone safe? My paranoia fueled me to rise off the floor and go over to one of the kitchen drawers.

"Isla?" Kellan questioned.

"I'm fine."

After pulling out a piece of paper, I turned on the kitchen light. I then began to scribble down everything that had happened with Mikita. When I finished, I handed it to Kellan. Then like I had with Brooke, I put my finger over my lips.

His brows creased in confusion before his gaze dipped down to the sheet of paper. When he was done, he jerked his head up to stare at me in shock. "We can fix this."

To keep the conversation as generic as possible in case someone was listening in, I replied, "Are you sure we can fix this without anyone getting hurt?"

"We'll find a way."

Kellan then went over to the counter to grab my pen. He scribbled something down before handing it back to me.

> *I'm going to go get dressed and tell Brooke goodbye. I need to speak to Callum and Dare as well as Caterina's brothers. Mikita will not fuck up Quinn's life and yours. I promise you that."*

When I glanced up at him, I nodded. Then I leaned up and kissed his cheek. With my lips next to his ear, I whispered, "Thank you."

"I owe you more than you can ever know, Isla. I intend to pay you back by fixing this."

Without another word, he started back upstairs. For the first time in weeks, I felt hope.

Chapter Thirty-Seven: Quinn

After spending a couple of weeks in Belfast with Mam and Eamon, I grew anxious to get out of the city. Or I suppose I should say Northern Ireland since Mam had insisted we go to our beach house for a few days. She desperately clung to the idea that a little sun and sea air might clear the dark melancholy I found myself in.

There was one person I was anxious to see. So, for the first time in a decade, I took a commercial flight. After Mam gave me Maeve's schedule, I arrived just as she was set to get out of class. One phone call to her bodyguard later and I found myself outside of Trinity college.

As I leaned against the car I'd rented, I watched men and women scurrying around the campus, arms laden with books or a coffee in their hands. I wondered for a moment what my life might've been like had I not been born into the clan. Sure, I'd graduated from Queen's College in Belfast with the traditional business degree that the men in my family earned. But my experience hadn't been like other carefree college students. In between classes, I'd interrogated and tortured men.

At the sight of Maeve striding across the green, I rose off the car's hood. She chatted animatedly to someone on the phone. I couldn't remember when I'd seen her so happy.

When she glanced at the car, she caught sight of me. Her face lit up even brighter. After saying something to the person on the phone, she ended the call. Sprinting towards me, she cried, "Quinnie the Pooh!"

Normally the nickname she'd called me when she was a child mortified me to no end. But today, it was the purest music to my soul.

She dove into my waiting arms. "Oh my God, it's so good to see you," she said, as she squeezed me tight.

Not shying from her touch, I squeezed her back. "I feel the same way."

When she pinched my back, I jumped. "What the feck was that for?"

She giggled. "I was just trying to see if you were real."

With a chuckle, I replied, "Aren't you supposed to do that to yourself?"

"Maybe," she replied with a wink. "So, what are you doing here?"

"Do I have to have a reason to see my baby sister?"

She grinned up at me. "I meant, what are you doing in Dublin?"

"As I'm sure Mam has told you, I've been visiting with her and Eamon."

"Aye, she did."

"So, I decided to take a little trip to see you while I'm across the pond."

Her emerald eyes stared intently into mine. "What's wrong?"

I forced a smile to my lips. "What's with all the suspicion?"

"For starters, you might love Belfast, but you hate Dublin."

"That's because I'm a Northern man through and through."

She rolled her eyes. "I'm serious, Quinn."

With a shrug, I replied, "I just wanted to check on you."

"Bullshite!" she countered.

"Listen to your mouth. Mam would have your hide if she heard you."

She laughed. "It's the hazard of having five brothers."

A genuine smile curved on my lips. "Aye, you never stood a chance, did you?"

"Never."

"You have my apologies for corrupting you."

"I'd rather you buy me a drink."

"Cursing *and* drinking now, eh? Where did my innocent little sister go?"

Maeve's bright eyes darkened. "She died a long time ago."

I winced at her words. "I'm sorry I said that, Mae."

"It's okay. We've both had our traumas."

"Regardless, the last thing I would ever do is hurt you."

"I know that, Quinnie."

With a mirthless laugh, I replied, "But you know what? Maybe you shouldn't trust me. I mean, I say I would never, ever hurt people, and then I do."

Her auburn brows furrowed. "What's really happened?"

"I'll tell you over a pint."

She nodded. "There's a decent pub just up the street. Fancy a walk?"

"Yes, the air would be nice."

After a quick word with Maeve's bodyguard, we started walking to the pub. Silence hung heavy around us. "Did something happen with Isla?"

Since I wasn't ready to talk out in the open, I countered, "Who were you all smiles with on the phone?"

Maeve's porcelain cheeks flushed. "None of your business."

"So it was a man?"

She jerked her chin defiantly at me. "I asked you a question first."

"Does this man know who you are?"

"We're not talking about me. It's you who mysteriously appeared, saying you hurt people when you don't mean to." Lowering her voice, she added, "Since we both know hurting people is part of your job, I'm to assume that it means you've hurt a certain woman you care about very much."

"You're too smart for your own good, Mae." With a grin, I held open the pub's door. After we swept inside, we took a seat at a booth in a far corner. After a waitress came and took our order, Maeve crossed her arms over her chest.

"Out with it."

"I'm in love with Isla."

Maeve's face lit up. "Oh Quinnie, that's wonderful."

"She left me."

"No!" Maeve exclaimed.

I nodded. "But she had a very good reason."

"There could never be a good reason to hurt you."

"No one can fault the lass considering she was kidnapped and psychologically tortured because of me and my world."

Maeve gasped. The waitress returned with our drinks. After sucking down half of my pint, I began to tell Maeve what had happened with Isla and Mikita. When I finished, tears glittered in her green eyes.

She reached out to grab my hand in hers. "There aren't enough words to express how sorry I am. For you and for Isla."

"I want to leave the clan."

Maeve's green eyes shot wide. "But you can't. You took an oath."

"Aye, but oaths can be broken."

"Not without bloodshed." She shuddered. "Not without death."

"I don't have anything left, Mae. I loved Rian like a brother, and this world took him from me. Then I truly gave my heart to a woman for the first time, and this world takes her as well." I slowly shook my head. "I don't know if I can take all this pain, Mae."

She squeezed my hand. "Our family needs you. *I* need you."

I exhaled a ragged breath. "How do you do it?"

"Do what?"

"Find the will to get up in the morning. Resist the urge to just end it all."

Maeve's expression grew grave. "Because then they would win. In my case, it doesn't matter that Father and Oisinn are dead. By giving up, they've won, and I will never, ever allow that as long as I have a breath within me." Jerking her chin up, she added, "I'll survive and I'll thrive out of pure spite."

"That's talking like a true Kavanaugh."

"Thank you, brother."

"Gah, you're so fucking strong, Mae."

"Most days, I don't feel that way. I wonder if I'll ever not wake up screaming because of that night. If I'll truly ever be able to give myself to a man without seeing Oisinn's face or feeling his hands on me."

I momentarily shuttered my eyes at the thought of what she endured. When I opened them, I had to ask the question that had been on my mind for such a long time. "Were we wrong to never ask you about that night? I know it's a delicate matter, but did you need us at least to ask? Did you need to tell us what happened?"

Maeve gave me a shadow of a smile. "As much as you all have sheltered and protected me, there's some horrors I need to keep to myself."

"Kellan had to talk to Isla about what happened."

"I'm glad he did. It's liberating when you free yourself of the pain."

"You aren't angry he shared what happened?"

She shook her head. "I want him to be able to be in my presence without crying. I want him to be everything he can be in our family without being riddled with guilt and remorse."

"I think he's well on his way to doing that."

"Good. Now we can just focus on you."

"I might be a lost cause."

"Never."

"I want to believe you."

She gave me an encouraging smile. "We will find a way to get her back."

"I think that's as much a lost cause as I am."

"Trust me."

"I'll try."

Maeve rose out of the booth. "Got to nip to the loo. I'll be right back."

"Do I need to come with you?"

She rolled her eyes. "Seriously, Quinn? I think I can go to a random restaurant's loo alone without you or my bodyguard.

"Fine."

Maeve had just gone down the hallway to the bathrooms when her phone rang. I couldn't help glancing down at it. When the name *Rúnsearc* flashed on the screen, I almost came out of the booth. *Rúnsearc* meant my secret love.

Who the fuck was Maeve calling that?"

Without a second thought, I grabbed the phone and answered it. "Who the fuck is this?"

A pause came on the line. "I suppose I could ask you the same thing."

My brows furrowed. I knew that voice. "Rafe?"

Another pause. "Quinn?"

The world spun around me. Raphael Neretti was Maeve's secret love? Oh hell no. This wasn't happening. "What the fuck are you doing calling my sister?" I growled.

"I don't think that's any of your business."

A dark chuckle came from my chest. "Oh, I bet Callum would love to weigh in on why my sister has you saved into her phone as 'secret lover'."

"Maeve's a grown woman, Quinn. I think she's allowed to make her own decisions without her brothers' consent."

"You cheeky bastard. You'd be losing your mind if the tables were turned, and Caterina had someone saved as a secret lover."

"Considering she was in a religious order when you and your brothers *kidnapped* her, that would have been very surprising indeed."

Of all times for my phone to start ringing, now wasn't the time. Since it was Callum, I knew I needed to answer it. At that moment, Maeve appeared. The sight of me holding her phone to my ear caused crimson to flood her cheeks.

I shoved the phone at her. "I have to take this call from Calum. But when I'm finished, we're going to have a little chat about Raphael Neretti."

Before she could protest, I then spun around and grabbed my phone out of my pocket. "Yeah?"

"I need you to step outside the pub."

Furrowing my brows, I asked, "How the fuck do you know where I am?"

"Your tracker."

"Was it necessary to stalk me down? I told Mam I was going to Dublin to see Maeve."

"Just go outside."

I flung open the door and stepped out into the street. "What am I to do now? A little dance?"

"Look up the street to your right."

"Jaysus Christ, Callum, I'm not in the mood for your fucking games. I flew thousands of miles to get away from your bullshit"

"Just do it."

When I whirled around, I stared up the street. The phone

dropped to my side at the sight of a tiny blonde standing just a few yards away. "Little Dove," I murmured.

She was so close yet so far away.

We stood there for a moment, staring at each other like we feared the other might disappear before our eyes. And then I took one step forward.

That was all it took for Isla to start running to me. My heart leapt into my throat at the sight. She'd come for me. She still loved me.

Hope wasn't lost.

And just before we could reach out to touch each other, a dark figure swept from the alley, grabbing Isla off her feet and jerking her back against his front. My heart dropped to my feet at the sight of Mikita holding a gun to Isla's head. He dragged her further away from me.

When I reached for my gun, a pop went off. Anguished horror rocketed through me that Mikita had shot Isla. When I saw her unharmed still struggling against him, relief filled me. It was short lived at the sight of Maeve's bodyguard sinking to the ground, blood and brain matter spraying from a wound in his head.

Screams and shouting rang out all around me as people began to drop to the ground or scramble to try to find safety behind cars or bins in the street. After a few seconds, nothing stood between me and Mikita.

"Throw down your gun and any other weapons you have, or this will all end sooner than later."

I stared into Isla's frightened eyes. Slowly, I reached inside for my gun. I tossed it to the ground and then added my knife next to it–the same one I'd used to give Isla pleasure.

"That's it?"

"Yes."

"I hope for her sake it is." Tilting his head, he mused, "Bet you never thought you'd see me here."

"Look, this is between the two of us. It has nothing to do with Isla."

"That's where you're wrong. You see, your girlfriend and I had a deal. She would leave and break you, which perfectly enacted my revenge. In turn, I wouldn't hurt her sister and nephew."

"What?" I questioned Isla more than Mikita.

Mikita laughed. "She was pretty convincing, wasn't she? Considering how you've left home and tried to leave your clan, revenge was looking really sweet. But then, she just had to go to your brothers and spill her guts about what had gone down between us." He tsked at Isla. "That was supposed to be our secret. I'm going to have to punish you for that."

Bringing his hand up from Isla's waist, he sent a stinging slap across her cheek, causing me to lunge forward. "Don't fucking take another step."

I froze. Desperation pricked along my spine. I didn't know how the fuck I was going to get Isla out of this.

"After tattling to your brothers, the next thing I knew she and her sister were packing up and coming here to hide from me." Turning his attention to Isla, he maniacally laughed. "I bet you never imagined when I gave you that sedative, I also put a tracking device in you."

"Obviously not," she bit out.

With a shake of my head, I said, "You left me because of him?"

Tears streaked down Isla's face. "I had to. He threatened Brooke and Henry." A sob tore through her chest. "I didn't want to leave you, Quinn. I love you. I always have."

Agony rocketed through my chest. I had to fix this. I couldn't lose her. Not now when I was getting her back. "What do you want, Mikita? Territory? Money? Drug routes? Whatever it is, I'll ensure you get it. I'll work with the Neretti brothers. We can uphold the alliance you would've had with Carmine if he and Alessio hadn't been killed."

Mikita narrowed his eyes at me. "Do you honestly think I would *ever* trust you?"

"Stranger deals have been struck by men in our world. Trust is always built on quicksand when it comes to alliances. But we don't have to sink beneath the surface. We can rise."

"There's nothing that you can give me but your suffering." He cocked his gun–the noise ricocheting through me. "I thought I could achieve it by keeping her alive, but she double crossed me. You and I both know what happens to traitors in our world."

"NO!" I screamed as I charged forward.

At the crack of a gun, the world slowed to a crawl around me. Mikita and Isla's bodies jolted back before collapsing to the ground. I sprinted to close the distance between us. After falling to the ground, I drew Isla into my arms. With shaking hands, I searched her head for a bullet wound. When I didn't see one, I felt along her chest.

"Now's not the time for that," a soft voice said.

I jerked my gaze to her face. "You're not hit."

A shaky smile curved on her lips. "No."

A sob tore from my throat. "But how–"

Isla jerked her chin over my shoulder. Glancing behind me, I sucked in a harsh breath at the sight of Maeve with a gun in her hand–a satisfied expression on her face. "You?" I demanded.

"Even with a bodyguard, I'm never without a gun."

Turning back to Mikita, I surveyed the gaping wound between his eyes. "Fuck me, Maeve. Most men couldn't make that shot."

"I'm not most men." The corners of her lips quirked. "I'm a Kavanaugh."

"Damn straight."

As I pulled myself to my feet, I swept Isla in my arms. "Are you okay?" I asked.

"Considering I just survived being almost killed, I'm more than okay."

"I'm sorry, Little Dove. In light of what just happened, I won't blame you if you want to leave me again."

She shook her head. "I can't say that I'm not fearful of something bad happening again. But I know it's not worth forsaking the love and happiness I have with you."

"I'm so glad to hear you say that. I didn't think I could do life without you."

Just before I could bring my lips to hers, the Garda Síochána appeared. "What the hell happened here?" a tall officer asked.

I glanced between Maeve and Isla, giving them a look that said let me do the talking. "Well officer, that man over there was stalking this woman. He had a gun to her head. I was walking down the street when I saw it. I drew my weapon and shot him before he could kill her."

The officer narrowed his eyes on Isla. "Is that what happened?"

"Yes, sir. He tracked me in from the states."

"What's your name?"

"Um, Isla Vaughn."

The officer scribbled it down in his notebook. His gaze fell on mine. "And your name?"

"Quinn Kavanaugh."

"Kavanaugh?" He blinked. "As in the Belfast Kavanaughs?"

"Aye. I came up to Dublin to visit my sister," I replied, motioning to Maeve.

"Right. Well, um, thanks for the information."

When he started walking off, his partner stopped him. "What the feck are you doing?"

"Keeping myself alive."

As they hurried away, I glanced down at Isla. "Let's get out of here."

"We have suites at the Shelborne," she said.

"Whose we?"

"Dare, Kellan, Brooke and Henry."

Her eyes popped wide. "Brooke and Henry are here?

"We were planning to hide them away here while we took care of Mikita."

"And he took care of himself."

A shudder ran through Isla. "That's true."

"I have a rental car up the street."

"You don't need to carry me. I can walk," Isla protested.

I grinned down at her. "I'm not letting you out of my sight or out of my arms anytime soon. In fact, Maeve can drive, and we'll take the backseat."

Maeve snorted. "As long as there's no shenanigans."

At Isla's blush, I laughed. "I can't make any promises."

Isla rolled her eyes. "You're a caveman."

"Aye. And a beast."

Isla smiled. "I love you just as you are."

"And I love you."

I then started up the street feeling lighter than I had in weeks.

Chapter Thirty-Eight: Isla

While the others went back home to Boston, Quinn took me to Belfast to meet his mother and to see where he'd grown up. Since it was my first time out of the country, I'd wanted to drag him to all the tourist sites, but with my classes, I only had a long weekend to be away. Quinn promised to bring me back in the summer.

When we'd arrived at his house, or I should say mansion since it was bigger than the one in Boston, I'd been a rambling, nervous wreck. Although she'd been as friendly as she could be during our one phone call, I'd worried the staunchly Catholic woman would change her tune and look down on me for being a dancer in Quinn's club.

While Quinn got our luggage, he nudged me forward to go on to the front door. Before I could make it up the path, Orla Kavanaugh came to greet me. "Hi, it's good to see you again. Or I should say in person," I began before she threw her arms around me and swept me into a warm embrace.

Tears pricked the back of my eyelids at the intensity of the emotions swirling through me. Hugging her was like receiving one of my own mother's hugs. I'd missed them so very much in the last two years.

When she pulled away, there were tears in her eyes. "Don't you look like Cliodna herself," she mused.

I smiled. "That's what Quinn calls me."

She cupped my face with her hands. "I can't tell you how happy you've made me to see my son so happy."

"But he came to you so broken-hearted."

"Aye, he did. But that's in the past. The look on his face just now as he stepped out of the car warmed me from head to toe." She winked at me. "It was pure bliss etched on his face."

"I hate that I hurt him. I want nothing more than to make him happy for the rest of my life."

"Aye, you have and you will continue to, sweet girl." She wagged a finger at me. "Just don't let him walk all over you."

I laughed. "Don't worry. I won't."

"Good. I'm glad to see you're going to be as strong as Caterina when it comes to my sons."

At that moment, Quinn appeared with our suitcases. "Let me guess. You're talking absolute shite about me already."

"We're doing no such thing," Orla huffed.

"You haven't told her to keep a firm hand on me?" he mused.

"Perhaps," she replied while winking at me.

"I don't mind admitting Isla has me wrapped around her little finger and leads me around by the balls."

My eyes widened in horror. "Quinn!" I admonished.

He merely chuckled before bestowing a kiss on my cheek. "Come on. Let's get inside."

"Are you hungry?" Orla asked.

"Yes, ma'am."

"Starved," Quinn replied.

"I made your favorite, Quinn."

His eyes rolled back in his head. "I can't wait."

She smiled before turning to me. "I forgot to check in to see how yours turned out."

Quinn snorted while I frowned. "It was terrible."

"Oh no," she replied while elbowing Quinn.

"You're going to have to teach me how. I made such a mess of your recipe."

"Don't worry. You'll learn."

"I hope so."

Orla slid her arm around my waist as we started in the house. "I hear you're a scientist."

"Yes, ma'am. A microbiologist. I'm currently in graduate school."

"My, that sounds like an important career."

I smiled. "I like to think so."

"I hope you can focus more on your studies now that you're not dancing anymore."

I froze. "You knew about me...dancing?"

"Quinn told me."

I cut my eyes over to his. "He didn't tell me that."

"I think he was afraid I would make some scene. Like grabbing my rosary and praying for your immortal soul," she teased.

"You can if you want. My late father was an Episcopal priest, so I'm sure he would've done the same."

Orla laughed. "Oh honey, I don't care about your past. You were doing it to take care of your family and put yourself through school. That's truly noble."

Tears once again filled my eyes. "That means a lot, and I thank you."

She wagged a finger at Quinn. "With that said, don't think that the two of you are going to be sharing a bed under my roof."

"Mam," Quinn groaned with a roll of his eyes.

"Not until you're married."

"We've just been reunited after a month apart."

"Not under my roof." She then made the sign of the cross before heading down the hallway.

Quinn exhaled a ragged breath. "Maybe we should stay in a hotel?" he suggested.

"I wouldn't dream of insulting your mother like that."

"Don't act like you're not horny for me."

With a laugh, I countered, "I can abstain to please your mother."

Quinn crossed his arms over his chest. "I didn't think the lack of sex would start until *after* we were married."

"If that's a proposal, it needs work," I mused before I started down the hallway to the kitchen.

I didn't get far before Quinn grabbed my arm and spun me to him. The intensity of his stare caused my heartbeat to accelerate. "Say the word, and we'll go down to the church after lunch."

"You're just saying that so you can fuck me in your mother's house."

He shook his head. "I've wanted to marry you since the first day I saw you."

My eyes bulged. "You didn't even know me."

"I knew you were beautiful and kind. That was enough for me."

"You're serious about us getting married today?"

"Aye, I am."

As I stared into his eyes, there was nothing more in the world that I wanted than to become his wife. "Yes, I'll marry you, Quinn." When his eyes lit up, I shook my head. "But not today."

"Why not?" he demanded.

"Because I'm a girly girl who wants a big church wedding. I want to spend hours toiling bridesmaids dresses and which calligraphy to put on the invitations. I want to see you standing at the altar in your form-fitted tux. I want to dance with you under sparkling lights as man and wife."

His lips curved in amusement. "You don't want much, do you?"

"Oh, I also want a big, poofy designer dress and a rented antique tiara."

"Jaysus, woman. You drive a hard bargain," he teased.

"Do you think you can deliver all that?"

"Aye, I can and then some."

"Oh my," I murmured as he sank to one knee.

"Isla Grace Vaughn, will you overlook the fact that your beast of a boyfriend didn't pull out all the stops to give you the over-the-top proposal you deserve and instead went with his heart?"

Tears overflowed my cheeks. "I will."

"Will you do me the biggest honor of becoming my wife?"

"Yes, yes, a million times yes!" I cried before I threw my arms around him.

Quinn grabbed me by the nape of my neck and pulled my head to his. He slammed his lips against mine, causing me to moan. When he released my mouth, tears shone in his own eyes. "I love you, Little Dove. You've made me the happiest man in all of Ireland and the world."

"I love you, too."

"Tomorrow we'll go to the jewelers, and you can pick the biggest diamond you can find."

"Don't tempt me," I teased.

"We could still nip round to the church to be married and then have a big ceremony later in America."

"Quinn," I warned.

He groaned. "There's two women in the world I fear: you and my mother. As much as I want to sneak into your room tonight, I know she'd kill me. But if I don't have you, I'm going to explode."

I giggled at the thought of Quinn fearing me and his mother. Then I thought about how close I came to losing him. How much pain I was in when we were apart. "All right. We can get married today on the condition that only your mother knows. Everyone else will believe our massive, over-the-top wedding is our first. Agreed?"

"Agreed."

"I think you're going to owe me live doves at the reception now as well as a live band"

He threw back his head with a laugh. "I agree with the doves, especially if they're little like you." He held out his hand to me. "Come on. Let's go tell Mam the good news."

"I hope she won't think we're doing this just to sleep with each other."

"I think she'll see it exactly as it is: two people so very madly in love they can't wait another moment to be man and wife."

"Even though they've only known each other barely four months," I countered.

"Callum and Caterina knew each other for three days before they were married, and they were in love by six weeks. In the end, time isn't a true measure."

"It will be when we get to fifty years," I said.

Quinn smiled down at me. "I can't wait to spend the next fifty years with you, Little Dove. I can't wait for you to become Dr. Kavanaugh. And when the time is right and we're ready, I can't wait for you to be the mother of my children."

I took his hand and mine. "Let's go and get married."

"Married?" Orla shrieked from the kitchen doorway.

"Yes, married," Quinn replied.

"Oh no. Not until we take care of a few things."

"Such as?" Quinn questioned.

"Isla needs something old, something new, something borrowed, and something blue."

"My dress is new." I smiled at Quinn. "Well, it's the first time I've worn it since you took me shopping."

"That should work," Orla remarked. She then took off the pearls around her neck. "These can be your borrowed and your old."

Waggling his brows, Quinn replied, "You could wear some blue knickers."

Both Orla and I huffed an indignant breath at him. "Give me one minute to go grab a pair of sapphire earrings. They'll look lovely with your dress."

As Orla started up the stairs, Quinn drew me into his arms. "Instead of blue knickers, will you wear some green ones tonight?"

With a roll of my eyes, I said, "I didn't come prepared with any lingerie when I was racing to get to you."

"Then we'll make a pit stop after the ceremony."

"You're a beast."

"Aye, my beauty. That I am."

As he brought his lips to mine, I sighed with pleasure. In that moment, I wasn't silly enough to think we would live happily ever after. But I knew we would come pretty close.

Chapter Thirty-Nine: Quinn

Two Hours Later

I'd never imagined what my wedding would look like. Before the bombing, I'd never been one for monogamy, not to mention I was expecting my marriage to be arranged.

After the bombing, I never imagined a woman wanting to marry me. Even if it was forced on her for an alliance.

As I stood at the altar of the church, I couldn't help feeling like the luckiest bastard in the world. I had a beautiful, kind, sexy, and smart woman who loved me with all her heart.

With a bouquet of lilies tucked in her hands, Isla made her way up the aisle. In her delicate green dress and with her hair flowing down to her waist, she was my fairy goddess.

When she reached the altar, I took her hand. After bringing it to my lips, I placed a tender kiss on it before turning my attention to the priest.

As he began to go through the ceremony, I turned my attention back to Isla. I couldn't believe she was really consenting to marry me. When she glanced up at me, she gave me a beaming smile.

At a sniffle behind me, I glanced past Isla to see Mam dabbing her eyes with a handkerchief. "Happy tears," she murmured when she caught my eyes.

Isla grinned. The priest continued on when we heard another sniffle. I glanced over my shoulder to see Eamon dabbing his eyes with the backs of his hands. "What?" he demanded, which caused Isla to giggle.

Although we would've liked to have kept the news from him a secret out of fear of him blabbing to the others, he came in from school just in time to attend. It was nice since he could be my best man, and Mam could be Isla's matron of honor.

"And now we come to the giving and receiving of rings," the priest said.

Mam had produced her parents' first set of wedding bands. At their fiftieth wedding anniversary they'd gotten new ones. Although their marriage had been arranged, my grandparents did have a good marriage, unlike my parents.

"Repeat after me: With this ring, I thee wed."

I slid the ring on Isla's left hand. Then in turn, she did for me.

The priest then pronounced us man and wife, and it was time to kiss the bride. I cupped Isla's face in my hands. Since we were in church and I knew Mam would have a coronary if I was disrespectful, I bestowed a tender kiss on her lips. "I love you," I pronounced.

"I love you, too."

"Let's go to our happily ever after, Mrs. Kavanaugh."

She grinned. "I agree, Mr. Kavanaugh."

Our wedding feast consisted of the cottage pie Mam had made along with a cake she had delivered. Isla and I managed not to smash it in each other's faces. When we finished eating, we toasted each other with glasses of a vintage champagne from the wine cellar.

Although it was only seven, Isla couldn't stop yawning. "It must be the jet lag," I remarked.

She flushed. "It's been a stressful couple of days."

Stretching my hands over my head, I said, "I should probably get my wife to bed so she can rest."

Eamon snorted. "Yeah, right."

I smacked him playfully on the back of the head. Isla rose out of her chair. When I started to follow, she shook her head. "Stay and visit with your family. I'm just going to go up and take a nice relaxing bath."

Inwardly, I groaned. This woman would be the death of me.

When she started out of the dining room, she threw a teasing smile at me. To keep my mind off Isla being wet and naked, I turned to Mam. "Has Maeve mentioned seeing anyone?"

Her brows popped. "Like a man?"

"Yes."

She shook her head. "She hasn't said a thing. Why do you ask?"

I shrugged. "She was talking to someone when I met up with her. She looked giddy like women do when they're in love." For the moment, I thought it best to leave out the part about Rafe being her "secret lover".

"Would it be such a bad thing if she's in love?"

If it was with Caterina's brother whose impending engagement was soon to be announced, then yes, it was. Sure, it was an arranged marriage, so it wasn't like he was cheating. From what Callum had said, he hadn't even met the girl, and she studying abroad in Italy.

Regardless, I would not sit back and let my sister be used. Not after everything she'd been through.

"I just don't want her to get hurt."

"She's stronger than you think."

I chuckled at the thought of Maeve taking Mikita out between the eyes. "Aye, she is."

Mam rose from her chair. "Eamon, with Quinn and Isla staying with us, I need to get more groceries. Be a dear and drive me."

"Why can't you just get your bodyguard to take you or order in?"

She gave him a knowing look. "Because I want my son to take me, and you know I like to do my own shopping."

He rolled his eyes. "You just want us to get out of the house, so Quinn and Isla can consummate their marriage in peace."

I threw my head back with a laugh. "Considering how vast this house is, I'm not worried about our privacy."

Mam waved at Eamon. "Come on. Let's go."

As the two of them started out of the dining room, Mam turned back to me and winked. "Have at it then."

Chapter Forty: Isla

I was lounging in a billowing bubble bath when the bathroom door jerked open. Quinn appeared in nothing but his boxers.

"Not wasting any time, are you?" I mused.

"Mam and Eamon just went grocery shopping, so we have the house to ourselves."

"Were you planning on consummating our marriage throughout the house?" I teased.

Quinn shook his head. "No. Just right here and right now."

Glancing around the bathroom, I asked, "Here?"

"I gave you your second orgasm in a hotel bathroom."

With a grin, I replied, "I remember."

He tore off his briefs before stepping over to the tub. "Let me in."

"I think you forget you're massive. This tub isn't built for a lumbering man like yourself."

"We'll make it work."

After I squeezed to one side of the tub, Quinn stepped inside. After he sat down, he then pulled me onto his lap. My center rubbed against his erection, causing us both to moan.

"This is nice," I murmured as I stared into his eyes.

"This time last week I never would've imagined being about to fuck you in the bath."

"You're so romantic."

He laughed. As he stared intently into my eyes, his expression sobered. He brushed the soapy strands of hair out of my face. "Thank you for loving me. I know it hasn't been easy. You've been to hell and back because of me. I won't ever forget that, Isla."

I brought my forehead against his. "I would do it all again to be with you."

Quinn brought his lips to mine. His kiss was tender and sweet and tasted like cake and champagne. But then it turned hungry. His hand grasped the back of my neck, tilting my head so he could thrust his tongue harder and faster against my own.

His other hand came to cup my breast. He kneaded the slick flesh before pinching my nipple. I moaned into his mouth. His hand came from my neck to my other breast. He cupped and squeezed them in his hands.

Reaching between us, I took his cock in my hands. I rose up on my knees to bring him to my center. Slowly, I slid down his length, taking him inch by inch. Our eyes stayed locked on each other.

Once I was fully seated, I smiled at him. "Now we're officially man and wife."

He grinned back at me before flexing his hips, sending his cock deeper inside of me. His hands came to my waist to push me on and off of him. As he sped up the pace, water began sloshing around us.

His breath warmed against my breasts. "It's been too long, and you feel too good. I'm not going to last."

"I'll take whatever you have to give me."

Quinn reached between us to bring his fingers to massage my clit. "I'd be a shitty husband if I didn't make sure my wife came."

I gasped as he added pressure to my clit. His thumb worked frantically against me as his hips pumped his cock furiously in and out of me.

As I gripped his shoulders, I rolled my hips against his hand. Within seconds, I started to come. My head fell forward onto his shoulder as I wrapped my arms tightly around him.

My orgasm kicked off Quinn's, and he cried out my name as he pumped into me. I held him as he rode out his pleasure. When he came back to himself, he gave me a satisfied smile. "Thanks for that, my beautiful wife."

"You're welcome."

Quinn turned me around to where I lay back against his chest. "I like it just like this. Nothing between us, just skin on skin."

"So do I. After everything we've been through, I don't want anything between us again."

"No walls, no barriers. We've burned them all to ashes and dust to dust."

"And we'll build a new life together," I said.

"Just the two of us."

Epilogue: Isla

"You're married?!!"

I winced at the furious expression on Brooke's face. With her hands on her hips, she looked just like our mother when we were in deep trouble.

"And hello to you, too," I mused as I sat my purse down on the table in the foyer of the Kavanaugh mansion.

"I cannot believe you didn't tell me!"

If Quinn and I thought keeping our marriage a secret was going to be easy, we were thoroughly and completely wrong. Our first mistake came in having witnesses from Quinn's family. I don't know who broke first, Orla or Eamon. By the time we touched down this morning in Boston, a whopping three days after our wedding, Quinn's entire family knew. And because Kellan and Brooke were friends, he had apparently spread the news to her, which led to her current interrogation.

"It was all very spontaneous. Quinn didn't even have an engagement ring for me."

"I call bullshit since Quinn doesn't do spontaneous," she argued.

I laughed. "He did this time."

"Jesus, Isla, you just got back together. Don't you think you needed a little time before taking the plunge?"

"After we both faced down death at Mikita's hands, why would we wait?"

Although I had kept my wedding secret, I had filled Brooke in on what had happened with Mikita. At first, I hadn't wanted to tell her since it once again highlighted the danger of Quinn's world. But I knew she needed the finality of knowing he was dead and no longer a threat.

Her lips turned down in a pout. "Couldn't you have done it before we all went back to Boston?"

"No. Because that's where being spontaneous comes in," I teased.

"But I always thought I would be your Maid of Honor and take you on a wild bachelorette party where some oily stripper in a banana hammock would dry hump you."

"I'm still down for all of that except dudes with banana hammocks."

Brooke eyed me curiously. "What do you mean?"

"One stipulation of marrying Quinn was I got to have the wedding of my dreams."

Her face lit up. "Really? I can still be your Maid of Honor?"

"There's no one I'd rather have in the world."

Brooke threw her arms around me. After squeezing me tight, she said, "I'm so happy for you."

When I pulled back to stare into her face, I asked, "Do you really mean that?"

She nodded. "I still have my worries about Quinn's world, but more than anything, I want you to be happy."

"Thank you, B. That means so much."

"So, when is this dream wedding taking place?"

"I'm not sure. I'd love to have it right away, but the thoughts of wedding planning during this semester is overwhelming."

"I can help."

"Oh, that's a given. You're going to endure every cake testing and dress fitting with me." I kissed her cheek. "I can't do this without you."

"I'm down for it." She jerked her chin at Henry in his bouncer. "Before we conquer your big day, we have his."

Even though he was seven months old, we had yet to have Henry baptized. Brooke's main struggle was in finding a godfather for Henry. I was a shoe-in for the godmother, but Brooke hadn't felt the call to any of the men in our family or of our acquaintance.

And then it hit me.

I gasped. "Kellan would be an amazing godfather."

Brooke smiled. "Yes, he would. Henry adores him."

"Have you thought about asking him?"

She shook her head. "Actually, I had someone else in mind."

"Who?"

With a shy smile, she replied, "Quinn."

My brows shot wide. "Really?"

"Henry has always been crazy about him. Despite his line of work, Quinn has always shown he would sacrifice himself for Henry." With a smile, she said, "What more could you want in a godfather?"

Tears pooled in my eyes. "I think he would be honored."

"I would be honored to do what?" Quinn questioned behind us.

Both Brooke and I whirled around to face him. I clasped my hand over my heart. "Way to sneak up on us like a creeper."

He chuckled. "You know I'm stealthy." He glanced between Brooke and me. "What is it you wanted me to do?"

Brooke nervously licked her lips. "Well, I was just thinking that you might want to be Henry's godfather."

Quinn blinked at Brooke. Time seemed to crawl by as he stood there frozen like a statue. I placed my hand on his arm. "Quinn?"

He cleared his throat. "You want me to be your son's godfather?"

Brooke bobbed her head enthusiastically. "I do."

"But Kellan—"

"Is a wonderful man. While our lives will be tied together through the two of you, we might not always be as close as we are now." Brooke's voice began to tremble. "You're my brother-in-law, and if we become as close as me and Isla, you'll be my brother."

"Jaysus, Brooke, you know how to cut a man in two," Quinn croaked.

She laughed as she swiped a tear away. "Is that a yes?"

"Aye, it is." When he drew her into his arms for a hug, I couldn't hold back my own tears.

At Henry's happy screech, I went over and picked him up. "What do you think about that, Henny Poo? Do you want Quinn to be your godfather?"

He grinned, showing off the new top teeth he'd just cut. "I think he approves," I mused to Brooke and Quinn.

Quinn came over to us and held out his arms to Henry. "Come here, Little Man."

Henry happily dove from my arms over to Quinn's. And then something happened that none of us could have expected.

After patting the scars on Quinn's neck, he pronounced, "Da-da."

We all froze. "Did he just—" Brooke began just as Henry said, "Da-da, da-da."

"Oh shit," Quinn muttered with a panicked expression.

I held up my hand. "Babies often say da-da even to their mothers because it's easier to say."

"How would he even know to say it?" Brooke asked.

"Maybe he heard it at daycare or watching Baby Einstein?"

Quinn shook his head. "Don't look at me. I sure as hell wasn't saying it to him."

"Maybe he's just confused." Brooke glanced between us. "Henry, who am I?" she questioned.

Henry eyed her before blowing a spit bubble. Brooke persisted by patting herself and saying, "Da-da."

His little brows furrowed. He peered into Quinn's horrified face and said, "Da-da."

At that moment, I couldn't help the laugh that burst from my lips. "Isla, this isn't funny," Quinn argued.

"If you could see your face, you would think so."

Brooke rolled her eyes. "Would you get a grip? My kid is calling your *husband* daddy."

"Da-da!" Henry exclaimed again, which caused me to laugh harder. At my laughter, Henry began giggling.

"Isla, do something," Quinn muttered.

"We can correct him when he gets older. What's the harm in letting him say it right now?"

"Oh, sure, it's fine now. Just wait until he goes to preschool and says his uncle is his daddy," Brooke protested.

And once again, I dissolved into giggles. Quinn and Brooke shared an exasperated look at me. At that moment, Caterina and Callum came into the living room. Caterina's bump was much more pronounced now that she was almost six months along.

"What's so funny?" she asked.

"Henry just called Quinn da-da."

Both Callum and Caterina's eyes bulged comically wide causing Quinn to say, "See, I told you it was bad."

Caterina shook her head. "I didn't think that. I was just surprised."

"I tried to tell them he's too young to understand, and when he's old enough, we can explain that Quinn is a father figure, but not his father," I replied.

"Exactly," Caterina replied.

With a little pout, Callum said, "I thought I was going to be the first Kavanaugh to be called da-da."

Quinn snorted. "Way to make this about you."

Callum elbowed him. "We came in to tell you guys that Lorna is making a special wedding feast. Dare and Kellan will be here soon, so we can all celebrate."

Before I could say anything, Quinn cleared his throat. "While that is lovely, Isla and I will be having a stateside wedding that includes a big poofy dress, an antique tiara, live doves, and a live band."

I laughed at him remembering my must-haves. "We just have to get it planned."

Clapping Quinn on the back, Callum asked, "It would be my honor to be your best man."

Quinn smiled at him. "As much as I would love that, I don't want to choose between any of my brothers. You're all my best men."

"I mean, you could get around it because I'm the oldest," Callum pressed.

Quinn shook his head. "Nope. Not doing it."

"Then who will it be?"

"I want to ask Seamus. In a way, it can honor Rian as well."

Callum's jaw clenched, and I could tell he was holding back his emotions. "I think that would be grand, brother."

I turned to Caterina. "Would you be a bridesmaid?"

Her face lit up. "I would love to. As long as you don't mind me waddling down the aisle."

With a laugh, I replied, "I would love that. We'll hurry and do it before you give birth."

"That works for me," she replied.

Dare and Kellan appeared then, and we filled them in on all the details. As we started into the dining room to eat, I couldn't help the tears that pooled in my eyes. Always in tune with my emotions, Quinn appeared at my side.

"Are you okay?" he questioned in a low voice.

I nodded. "I was just thinking how incredibly blessed I am. After we lost my parents, I felt like Brooke and I were so alone. Now we're part of a big, loving family. I'm so thankful Henry can grow up with you and your brothers."

Quinn smiled. "We'll certainly make a man out of him."

"Just not a clan man."

"We'll see. He could follow in his father's footsteps."

When he winked at me, I playfully smacked his arm. Quinn brought his lips to mine, and I welcomed the kiss from my husband, my protector, and my lover.

My forever beast.

Coming in November: Fix You

R afe & Maeve's story

Poison and Wine: Book One in the Irish Rogues Series

Caterina

As the only daughter of a formidable capo, my existence unfolded within the confines of a gilded cage. At eighteen, I would become a pawn in the intricate game of power, destined to be wed to a high-ranking member of my father's regime. My fate oscillated between my father's grasp and that of my future husband. Fleeing was not an option; they would track me down relentlessly. In an act of both self-preservation and rebellion, I sought refuge in a local convent—the sole sanctuary untouched by the shadows of the mafia. Yet, before I could take my final vows, the devil himself knocked at my door — a devastatingly handsome dark-haired, blue-eyed rogue. With an Irish accent that sent shivers down my spine, he declared me his future wife. No one had touched me; no one would. But despite my aversion to a forced marriage, an irresistible attraction brewed between us—for he was both poison and wine.

Katie Ashley

. . .

Callum

When I abducted a nun, my expectations were simple—she'd be submissive, pliable, the ideal mafia wife. Little did I imagine that the fiery brunette would wield a mouth and body I craved, both in and out of the bedroom. She was a means to an end—a marriage forged out of convenience, a strategic alliance with an enemy family to solidify our standing in the underworld. Tradition dictated that I claim her, yet the last thing I'd do is coerce her. She won't be forced. I promised she would beg me to take her, and anyone who dared to touch her would die. For she was mine and mine alone.

In the unforgiving realm of the underworld, brace yourself for an electrifying romance pulsating with danger and desire.

Also By Katie Ashley

The Proposition Series: She hates her manwhore coworker, but he's the only one willing to offer his DNA to help her dreams of motherhood come true. Of course, he's only willing to conceive the baby naturally by hitting the sheets...or the desk....or the wall.

The Proposition
The Proposal
The Pairing
The Pursuit
The Predicament: A Proposition series novella
The Plan: A Proposition series novella

Runaway Train Rock Star Series:
Music of the Heart: Forced Proximity, Alphahole, Virgin FMC
Beat of the Heart: Secret Baby, Who Hurt You, Second Chance
Music of the Soul: a wedding novella for Music of the Heart
Strings of the Heart: Best Friend's Little Sister, Second Chance, Age-Gap

Melody of the Heart: Second Chance Romance, Small Town Romance

Runaway Train Companion Series: Jacob's Ladder
Jacob's Ladder: Gabe: Single Mom, Small Town, Enemies to Lovers
Jacob's Ladder: Eli: Best Friends to Lovers, Widow, Forced Proximity

The White House Billionaires Series:
Running Mate: Fake fiance, Alphahole, Forced Proximity
Office Mate: Bosshole, Office Romance, Enemies to Lovers
Roommate: Bodyguard Romance, Forced Proximity, Office Romance

Hells Raiders Motorcycle Series
Vicious Cycle
Amazon, B&N, Apple, Kobo, Google Play, B.A.M
Redemption Road
Amazon, B&N, iBooks, Kobo, Google Play, B.A.M
Last Mile: Amazon, B&N, iBooks, Kobo, Google Play, B.A.M

Sports Romance
The Hard Way: College Football Player, Second Chance, Small Town,
The Right Way: College Football Player, Secret Baby, Brother's Baby Mama
Don't Hate the Player: Young Adult, Loss of a Best Friend, Best Friend's Ex

. . .

Dust to Dust: Book Two of The Irish Rogues

Stand-alones

Reining Her In: Single Dad Small Town, Second Chance

The Actress and the Aristocrat: Grumpy/Sunshine, British Hero, Fake Relationship

Bound to Me: Small town, BDSM, Boss Romance

Drop Dead Sexy: Small Town, UnCozy Mystery with Smut

Search Me: New Adult, Small Town, Second Chance

Young Adult

Jules, The Bounty Hunter
Nets and Lies
The Guardians

Printed in Great Britain
by Amazon